Praise ιᴏɪ
*Unearthing the Dawn
and the Era of Shadows Series*

Terrific. Epic.

— Wᴇɴᴅʏ

Leaves you wanting more. Excellent read! Completely grabbed my attention
from the first chapter until the last. Character development was perfect ...
three dimensional ... with a perfect blend of humility, bravery, and persistence
with a dash of humor. [Y]ou become enveloped in the intrigue and mystery
of Egyptian history.

— Sᴇʀᴇɴᴀ

Amazing Story.

— Mᴀᴛᴛ

Enjoyed every word!

— Vɪᴄᴛᴏʀɪᴀ Tʀᴀᴠɪsᴀɴᴏ

[T]here are characters you love and those you love to hate! I have put R.M. Schultz
on my favorite author list, for sure!

— Jᴀɴɪᴄᴇ Mᴀɴɴ

A page turner that takes you to the wildest areas

— Aᴍᴀᴢᴏɴ ʀᴇᴠɪᴇᴡ

This ... book is ... amazing ...

— Jᴀsᴏɴ

[W]anting more. If you like Tolkien-style writing then you will like this book.
Every line has a purpose, and each story matters. I laughed, I ... cried, and my
chest tightened from suspense. Well worth ... it.

— Nᴇɪsʜᴀ

Croc is the coolest cat ever. He has the kind of relationship with his owner that most cat parents are jealous of.

— Danielle Rowen

I highly recommend giving this author a read.

— Timarie Simmons

Another page turner!

— Virginia Ingham

This book grabs your attention right from the start. It starts action-packed and suspenseful and does not stop.

— Danielle Rowen

Could not put it down!! A page turner for sure! A great story line and the characters present and past feed off each other and keep you wanting more.

— Amazon review

The characters were so well written …

— Amazon review

R.M. SCHULTZ

UNEARTHING THE DAWN

Era *of* Shadows Series

BOOK THREE

For information about this title or to order other books and/or electronic media, contact the publisher:
R.M. Schultz
email: rschultz.imaging@gmail.com
website: http://www.rmschultzauthor.com/

ISBN: 978-0-9988918-5-9 (print)
       978-0-9988918-6-6 (eBook)

Printed in the United States of America

Cover and Interior design: 1106 Design

For all those who have made the journey and returned home.
To Matt and my family and our childhood home, and to
Creslin and Jocelyn: wherever you are is now home.

Acknowledgements

Thank you to the following people for their insight and assistance with the story:

Laura Veals, Timarie Simmons, Jason Weersma, Serena Craft, Danielle Contreras, and Laura Robertson.

Also, thank you to my editors Phil Athans and Laura Josephsen, and to 1106 Design.

This story is based on numerous written records
referencing historical events and people of ancient Egypt.
The discovered monuments, temples, and architecture are factual.

Ancient thread character list:

Akhenaten: Pharaoh, the god-king

Aten: The sun and god, also what Akhenaten believed he would become

Ay: Nefertiti and Mutnedjmet's father, brother of Tiye the former queen

Beketaten: Akhenaten's sister, Nefertiti and Mutnedjmet's cousin, Pharaoh Amenhotep's daughter

Chisisi: The freeman leader who worked and escaped with the slave group

Croc: Heb's pet cat

Dark Ones or The Shadows: Mysterious monsters from children's tales

Devouring Monster: Creature that is a mixture of a crocodile, lion, and hippopotamus—from the underworld and devours the hearts and souls of men

Harkhuf: The muscular dancing dwarf brother from Nubia

Heb: Main character of the ancient thread, also goes by the name 'Rem' to hide from his enemies

Kiya: One of Akhenaten's significant foreign wives

Mahu: Akhenaten's Chief of Police

Maya: The royal scribe

Mutnedjmet: Nefertiti's younger sister

Nefertiti: The queen of Egypt as well as Pharaoh Akhenaten's cousin, daughter of Ay, sister of Mutnedjmet

Paramessu: Egyptian military captain, now one of the companions

Pentju: Akhenaten's chief physician

Seneb: The boyish dancing dwarf brother from Nubia

The son of Hapu: The royal magician

Suty: Akhenaten's bodyguard

Thutmose: Akhenaten's older brother who was to become pharaoh before his mysterious death, son of Amenhotep

Tia: Lover of Paramessu, former slave woman

Wahankh: Muscular Egyptian companion, used to be the slave bully

Chapter 1

Journal Translation

ICE-COLD FINGERS DRAGGED ALONG my neck before shoving me forward into the fire-lit chamber of judgment. My eyes adjusted to the dim light, and the ghostly forms around me faded into the fog, leaving the smell of sickeningly sweet incense. Gold and red carpets that had stretched onward now ended. Fear wracked my trembling body.

I had entered the *Duat*—the Egyptian underworld.

I wore silky white robes that caressed my skin as I stood before Anubis, the towering god with the head of a jackal. My own heart sat in my open palms. The squishy flesh of the organ beat faster and louder, its contracting muscles vibrating my hands and carrying up my arms and into my chest. Its pounding radiated into my ears, and sticky blood streamed between my fingers.

Anubis reached out with a human hand three times the size of mine, and his fingers wrapped around my heart, squeezing. My chest burned, as if filled with fire. I nearly collapsed in pain. Golden eyes bored into mine, searching my soul. Saliva strung from his curled lips. The fog of my breath billowed from my mouth like smoke into the darkness. Anubis snarled and set my beating heart upon one of the massive scales.

The feather on the opposite scale fluttered in a breeze that I could not feel. Squawking, a baboon ran back and forth atop the scales, testing the wood and twine.

Shrouded in shadow at the far end of the room, the face of a man rested atop another giant being. His skin was deep green, and he sat atop a golden throne. Osiris himself. My hands shook. Small creatures with gangly limbs scuttled around his throne, squeaking and pointing at my waiting heart.

Then deathly silence.

Something squawked. I jumped in surprise. A falcon perched atop a stone pillar beside me, but its face was human, and young ... familiar.

It was my face. My *ba*—part of my soul—awaited our fate. I shivered in terror.

The scales tipped, and my heart descended, foretelling that my very existence was going to end right here and now. Seated in the audience surrounding the hall, robed humanoids with animal heads shouted and jeered, their voices pounding into my brain.

"You have not lived a balanced life," a figure with the head of a falcon yelled through a parting beak as it stood, its voice screeching and ringing my ears. Its purple robe waved open to reveal a human chest, shaven and toned with thick muscle. "You have not listened to the god within you, and you have not cared deeply enough for your friends and family. Nor have you helped those who are less fortunate."

"I have," I screamed, attempting to deny all the accusations. The taste of salt filled my mouth. My *ba* shrieked as it took flight to escape. This would be the end, when everything, even a piece of my soul abandoned me ...

I quaked with fear, but something sparked in my mind. A memory.

Anubis glanced to the Devouring Monster's platform. The creature would be waiting to consume any hearts tossed his way. I imagined that I could see the crocodile jaws gaping from the darkness, awaiting their next meal, though such a feast would never end its eternal hunger.

"Hail to you, gods in this Hall of Judgment," I shouted, unable to control my words. My voice was soft at first, but it grew louder and echoed through the chamber. Spinning and facing Anubis and Osiris, I recalled the spell from the Book of the Dead—the one upon the walls of the tomb at Crocodilopolis. "I know you, and I know your names on this day of great reckoning. I was born in Rosetjau. I have given bread to the hungry and water to the thirsty. And your power was given to me."

The contingent of humanoids in the audience didn't budge. Their shining scepters sat frozen against colorful robes as they stared in silence.

I held my breath.

The scales wavered, and Anubis howled like a wild beast.

My legs tensed, telling me to run away and—

Then, the scales righted—my heart and the feather an even weight. Air rushed from my lungs in a burst of relief as I collapsed to my knees. My chest spasmed as I gasped for breath.

Anubis paced around the scales and scooped up my still-beating heart. He glanced back for the Devouring Monster, but it was gone. Akhenaten had somehow summoned the Devourer to the world of the living to consume souls of men there. Only a pile of dead hearts sat waiting beside the monster's platform.

Anubis sighed, as if he missed his horrid pet.

The scratch of a pen on papyrus made the roots of my teeth twinge with discomfort. Another bird-headed figure behind the scales wrote and nodded, the long, hooked beak of an ibis parting to speak.

The dark ceiling opened up and blinding light poured down, engulfing me. My ears rang.

Chapter 2

Journal Translation

WIND BLEW THROUGH MY short hair and whistled in my ears as I flapped mighty feather-covered wings at my side. Now I was a falcon with the head of a man, a *ba,* soaring through the sky. I was flying. Each flap of my wings came as naturally as taking a step. Land and river blurred by beneath me, the shining Aten descending for the western horizon.

A torrent of joy overcame me as the familiar comforting beat of my heart pounded inside my feathered chest, the organ back where it should be. Throwing my human head back into the gale, I smiled as I spread wings like sails. My body felt light, drifting on the air currents—a real bird. I'd passed judgment. Me, the cursed servant boy of Akhenaten …

But how did a common man ever pass all of the tests before the *Duat* and cast all of the spells needed from the Book of the Dead? There'd been so many spells, and I only knew them by studying the book inside that tomb in Crocodilopolis. Were common men and women doomed to achieve the afterlife without the assistance of royalty? Everyone knew more about the next life than me—Akhenaten had purposely shielded me from any sacred knowledge for some reason I did not yet understand—but did others have to wait until someone else came through, someone who knew the secrets, or were they cursed to wander the darkness, like a Dark One, searching for the Hall of Judgment for eternity?

"Father, where are you?" I said into the gusting wind of the upper reaches of the sky. I should be able to find him now. And the son of Hapu … was he also here, in the land of the dead? My heart froze. No, Father might not have a *ba* to find and speak with—his body and heart had been consumed by fire, the work of my vile former master, Akhenaten, and his monstrous bodyguard, Suty.

Wind snagged my feathers and twisted my limbs—similar to when Suty had wrenched my arms. I plummeted. The black and red margins of the fertile and barren desert around the Nile raced up to me.

Whipping my arms, I fought the gust, as if swimming and fighting against the current of the Nile. It was no use. I couldn't overpower such force.

The ground neared.

Then, instead of fighting, I turned with the wind, reversing and giving in to the pressure. The feathers around my wings billowed like sails and I shot skyward, into the clouds, my stomach catching in my throat. I flapped my wings and steadied myself within the currents, my body feeling as if it had no weight at all. Angling myself, I flew on, racing over the kingdom of Egypt.

I was unsure what I was supposed to do now, since I'd been unsure that I'd even end up as a *ba*. All I'd known was that only someone who'd known death and the beauty of the dead—whatever that meant—could confront an immortal god-king and ever hope to defeat him. And because the magician was dead, I was hoping to find his soul so that he could teach me whatever it was that I needed to know.

People wandered below, toiling under the Aten. They appeared to be living humans. I shouted to them, diving lower by sucking my wings, which felt like my hands and arms, into my sides and buzzing so closely over one man's head that his stubbly hair brushed my taloned feet. I flapped my wings before I hit the ground and rose back up into the air. The wind ruffled the feathers on my tail as I angled them and my body to steer myself and turn around.

The man didn't even look up, and no others responded to my cries. I screamed like my soul, and Nefertiti's and Father's, depended on it. Nothing. I gazed into the horizon, riding the gale.

Where were the deceased souls? Perhaps living people could not see the dead, but hopefully that meant that I now could.

A dark cloud took shape in the skies ahead, as if rain and thunder gathered together in one focus of anger. Black dots sailed into the cloud, building its size and blotting out the Aten. My wings stopped flapping, but the gale carried me closer. I stuck my taloned feet into the air, as if to dig into something and stop. It did nothing to slow my momentum. Then I attempted to fly backward, but my feathers folded. No use. Wings didn't work that way.

A whispering chorus hummed over the wind. The cloud advanced, the whispers growing quickly and amplifying to shouts. My ears rattled and my head rang. Tucking my wings, I attempted to dive back for the earth. But it was too late.

Dark shapes assaulted the sky around me, diving against the wind with dark feathers. Their howling screams deafened me. The silhouette of an eagle, a heron, a duck … Human heads sat atop many of these birds, but the heads of other animals, beasts of all types, intermixed with them—in afterlives of their own. There must've been tens of thousands of them … One knocked into me as they flew past, sending pain—even in this life—across my chest. I tumbled and twirled into the fray, and something snapped. More pain.

The sky and earth spun. More fowl of all sorts shot past me for what felt like ten minutes.

Several of my broken feathers flapped against the wind as I righted myself, the horizon still tilting. I faced the gale that these creatures were flying into.

The cloud made up of these tightly gathered *ba* rose like smoke, funneled into a long tube, and raced up for the setting Aten. They paused. Fanning out, the *ba* and cloud dispersed. Black dots dived back to the earth but split up—each traveling their own separate way. The Aten was about to set, and *ba* could travel the world only by day or risk losing their soul to the chaos all around us.

I flapped my wings and chased after them. How would I find whom I was looking for—the magician, or Father, or my beloved cat, Croc—unless Croc was the beast that I'd seen before I'd drowned and still wandered the world of the living?

Tucking my wings, I dived and careened toward at the closest fleeing fowl. The bird flew for the western hills and landed upon a jutting cliff.

Turning, this *ba* walked into the face of the mountain and disappeared. I flapped again, trying to slow my momentum as I sailed at the cliff face. Where had *the ba* gone?

My talons collided with hard dirt and scraped against rock, but my bird body tumbled forward and smacked into the cliff face with a thud. Pain pounded my skull and exploded in my back. I tasted metal. Shaking my head, I fought to stand, using my wings like arms and the tips of my feathers like fingers. The hot rock beneath my feet was hard, but it also felt shaky. Shadows descended all around me.

The lower half of the disc of the Aten set behind the mountains. Soon, I would need to get inside.

I examined the cliff face, looking for an opening. Nothing. I stuck out the two broken feathers at the end of my wing and prodded the rock. Stabbing pain arose in what should have been my hands. The rock was solid. How had that *ba* disappeared? There must be a way inside—one I couldn't see.

Closing my eyes, I sucked in a breath and stepped into the cliff. Everything went dark. I was inside. Feeling along the inner walls, I followed a narrow passage. It spiraled downward, into the roots of the mountain.

I crept—

A deep voice boomed, shaking the air around me, "Who enters my home?"

I froze.

"This is *my* sanctuary," the voice yelled. "Find your own curse."

I swallowed in fear. What was a *ba* supposed to do? Find its mummified human body and its tomb to rest during the night? I didn't have one …

"Come no closer." Feathers flapped in the darkness, swirling stagnant air. The smell of death and rot blew across my face as dust tickled my throat. I coughed, and the sound echoed into the depths of the mountain.

Two lights appeared—no, two eyes, green eyes reflecting whatever light reached into these depths.

"I am looking for someone," I whispered. "I need help."

"Do you know how many times I've heard that over the millennia?" The green lights flickered as the *ba* blinked. "How many recently deceased have tried to enter my home?"

"I need to find someone so that I may return to the world of the living."

Silence.

The eyes narrowed as the creature approached with stomping feet. Green light surrounded me, casting an eerie glow across the tunnel. Feathers from the *ba*'s wings extended like fingers, making shadows like claws appear on the walls. "No one returns to the world of the living after arriving here. You shouldn't even want to go back there; the pain ..."

"I have left too much unfinished to—"

"You all say that in your first days." The *ba* stepped into the light—a white shore bird with long legs carrying the head of an elderly man with wrinkles so deep they appeared like trenches. Spider veins ran under his skin. "Within a week you'll forget, and then you'll live free here."

I gritted my teeth. "I will still seek freedom for myself and my loved ones in the world of the living. And I will for eternity."

The old man's lips parted slowly, as if they'd been mummified. "Find where your body was buried and be off." His upper lip rose into a snarl and revealed teeth like a predator's, which flashed green.

I stumbled back and fell, crashing into the dirt as I heaved for breath. Thick grit caked my bloody feathers like mud as they folded beneath me. I grunted and pushed myself to my taloned feet and faced the dead man. "I'm looking for the son of Hapu, the reincarnation of Imhotep."

The snarling face retracted back into the shadows. "You will not find him here; I am merely someone forgotten, erased from history. But I know of whom you speak. For which pharaoh are you seeking his assistance?"

Images of Akhenaten's elongated face and sunken cheeks formed in my mind, his black-painted eyes growing like sockets of a skull as they closed, his animosity directed at me. Rage ignited in my heart. My former master—the one who had taken Nefertiti from me and harmed her beyond my understanding, murdered my father, and thrown me into slavery. But this *ba* shouldn't know what I'd want to do to Akhenaten—if I was ever able to face him again.

"I am searching for answers that only the magician could know," I said. But what could even the magician do? I was already dead. "The son of Hapu was training me ... to help Egypt recover from its current leadership. Only he knew how to accomplish what needs to be done in the world of the living, and I was told that only someone who knew the dead could ever have a chance of achieving it."

Echoing laughter erupted, and the white feathers of the *ba*'s wings retracted back into darkness. "Perhaps you found me for a reason. Or perhaps you are a fool. To die because someone told you to." More laughter. "I once thought as you did." His face appeared in the green light again, his eyes wandering over memories inside his head. "Have you ever heard of the intermediate periods?"

My lips pursed against my rising agitation. I tapped my talons against the rock wall, the scaly skin of my falcon's feet scraping against the ground. "No."

"Of course not," the old man replied. "Because men like me have been erased. Men who overthrew the notion of pharaoh as the one god."

"I've learned there are many gods."

"But have you considered the possibility that Pharaoh is not immortal—only a man himself?" He fell into a brief silence. "I did, as did several others during my time. We tried but could not overthrow him. However, once his line ended, we brought about a time of shared leadership … between ordinary men."

"This 'intermediate period'?" I asked. "It must've been a time filled with chaos and wars for power and dominion."

He shook his shadowed head. "That is what the following pharaohs told their people—and history—but we and our children experienced a time of self-expression, knowledge, freedom, and economic advancement rarely seen during the rule of the god-king. Common man could achieve the afterlife, not only the privileged few."

My forehead pulled back in surprise. This old man had at one time altered Egypt's fate? As I was attempting to do? Images of el-Amarna—Pharaoh's new capital city—ran through my mind. The artists had portrayed his chosen land upon walls and monuments as flourishing with life and abundance: gardens, birds, butterflies, happy citizens. But in reality, there was hunger, back-breaking work, and death—even for the free laborers.

"You must be a mighty king in the land of the deceased," I said.

"It didn't last." His glowing green eyes closed. "Those who control power only desire more. In time, the tale of the legendary King Menes receiving the throne from the god Horus returned. And so did Pharaoh and his right for complete power. To know the past is to know the future … Man's desire to rise to power will always return. But now—here—we are all equals." He spread his wings, as if to indicate the world of the dead all around us.

"But you were punished for your actions?" I asked. "To live here in this mountain alone, even though you passed Anubis's judgment?"

"The reasons for my solitude are none of your business." He raked his shore bird's nails at the end of his three long toes along stone. The resulting screech made the roots of my teeth tingle and ache. "Everyone in the underworld could be an equal to anyone else, if they believed they deserved it. Still they toil, serving others who command such an illusion ..."

"Complacency is not my forte," I whispered. "It is the reason I am here. Perhaps more could become equals in our world as well." I pictured my companions; Nefertiti, my lost love; and Mutnedjmet, Nefertiti's curious sister who'd befriended me before my banishment to slavery for defying my former master. *Father ... could I still save your soul if I return to the world of the living?*

"Complacency will help you if you return to the world of the living." The slapping steps of his long bird toes faded as he strode deeper into the darkness. "The other path is one of great suffering. You've already seen much, but not as much as you will if you return. A memory for you: He who commands the sphinx rules Egypt, and no one has done so in millennia."

The bridge of my nose furrowed in confusion. I'd heard that somewhere before, several times ... but what did it even mean?

"Be off; you will find no more answers here. The magician is dead, supposedly a product of his own hand. Dead, like the Dark Ones and your father ... and a power does not allow the magician to fly about the underworld."

I gasped, air sucking through my open lips and into my bird lungs. "Do you know my father?"

"No more answers."

Images of the curses I could face if I took the treasure from within the hidden tomb of Amenhotep—as the magician had suggested I do—popped into my head. "Tell me one last thing: Do the dead really need material possessions, ones from the world of the living?"

The footsteps of the *ba* paused. Then they pounded the soft ground, growing louder. The *ba* appeared from the darkness in a flash, rushing straight at me. He barreled into my face and neck with a smack that slammed me down to the hard ground. He grabbed my broken feathers between his wings and dragged me—my back digging a line through the gritty dirt—to the entrance and tossed me outside. Sliding out of the mountain's cliff face, I teetered on a ledge, the darkness of twilight all around me. I stepped again into the rock cliff but hit the hard surface with my nose. Dull pain spread across my face. The opening the other *ba* and I had passed through was gone, as if the darkness sealed the entrance.

I had no knowledge of the magic at work in this new world and didn't have time to ponder my circumstances. As a *ba,* I needed to find shelter or suffer unknown consequences, possibly similar to the Dark Ones, whose souls had been consumed.

The wind gusted, catching my feathers. Flapping my wings, I leapt into the air, and the wind lifted me as if I were made of papyrus. I soared into the dusk, and something tugged at my heart, directing me northwest—as if I'd grown in instinct for migration. I flapped against the raging air currents with all my might, racing for the remaining Aten—the orange sliver of its crest, barely peeking over the mountains.

Screeching arose behind me.

I glanced back over the feathers of my back. Dark forms flooded the sky, glowing eyes of green darting about, hunting. They flew in packs, scouring the land below.

Were these dead birds searching for *ba* who remained out at night? Would they hunt down the lost souls? My chest felt like ice as it constricted, my breathing straining against my hollow ribs.

A pair of green eyes settled on me and a feathered form dived in my direction.

I flapped my wings as fast as I could, but wind shoved against me in pounding gusts. Screams from the dead birds with green eyes called out to me, sending shudders along my spine. Dark Ones or Hunters? Coming for me?

But soft whispers also called out to me under the fading light of the Aten, though I couldn't see where they originated from. I followed the direction my heart was guiding me, and the whispers amplified.

Soaring over the Nile, I followed a lone branch to the west. Memories sprang into my mind. Crocodilopolis … the dancing dwarf brothers from Nubia, collected as slaves for Egyptian royalty; Tia, the slave woman; my companions …

The cries of my pursuers grew louder as they closed in. Beaks tore into the feathers on my tail, plucking and pecking. Pain jolted across my backside as my tail feathers were ripped out in clumps. Of all the sensations that I wished would have disappeared in the afterlife, pain might be it. I flapped harder, straining for breath.

Another beak sank into my flesh, and warm liquid rolled through rows of my feathers. I cried out for help, my heart racing.

Twinkling appeared below. The soft ripples of water—a lake stretched across the desert. I dived downward. A group of people stood along the shore.

The tip of the Aten sank below the western hills.

I drew closer to the earth, and the group of people below became clearer. One man lay alone, sprawled out across the sand beside the lake, his skin blue. Something receded into the water with waving ripples, as if it'd just flung the body onto the shore away from the others. The group ran over to him.

A red-headed man ran faster than the rest. His face was familiar—he was the former captain of the Egyptian army, Paramessu. A demure woman sprinted behind him, along with two dark-skinned dwarves. Tia, Harkhuf, and Seneb.

But Wahankh was not here … Was the body his? Was he dead?

I flew closer, but the group of people reached the body and stopped, their heads hovering over the dead person's face.

The pursuing *ba,* these dead birds—or were they Dark Ones?—surrounded me, squawking. One veered and rammed against my right wing with a crunch. My wing collapsed against my body, and I spiraled downward.

Something emerged from the rippling water—a pale woman with skin like milk. Dragging herself along with her arms, she inched for the dead man on shore. Her lower half appeared between breaking waves. A fish-like lower body.

A gap in the hovering group opened up and I could see the body—a man, fit, as if he'd been conditioning himself for some time. He might be in his mid-thirties, with a wide face and short, stubbly hair—not much facial definition, resembling any average person …

Recognition burst into my mind, as if waking from a long dream. The Extinct Ones who had dragged me under, who'd drowned me, were coming out of the lake. That was me. My body ... dead.

The whispers and pull inside my heart grew stronger, summoning me to the dead man. I flapped with my one good wing, angling myself for him.

Spiraling out of control, I barreled into the group at full speed. A clap sounded, and everything went dark.

Chapter 3

Journal Translation

LIPS PRESSED AGAINST MINE—soft, tender. Nefertiti? Air was blown, forced into my lungs, which expanded my chest. My eyes fluttered. Flashes of the pale woman in the lake appeared between blinking darkness ... Her face lifted from mine and her hand slipped away, my callused palm rubbing against hers, which felt as smooth as sea grass. Only our middle fingertips remained touching, hers lingering as she smiled. Then she winked and lowered her body, receding into the rolling waves of the lake outside Crocodilopolis.

I coughed and sputtered, my body spasming out of control. People surrounded me. Rolling over, I gagged as water spewed from my mouth. My body heaved again and again.

Minutes passed before I stopped coughing and sat up. My hands grasped my body. There were no feathers but skin across my chest, arms, and legs; the drenched kilt around my waist; and, as always, Father's bronze bracelet on my wrist.

I rolled onto my back and stared blankly into the distance.

Waning purple light outlined the summit of the hills on the horizon. A shadowy tree sat in the distance. A tamarisk tree, the kind Father and I used to sit and relax under when I was a small child, watching the soaring clouds dance in the wind and play with the sunlight. But this one sucked in the light like a bottomless hole, like Akhenaten's eyes. Petals covered its limbs—flowers of sheer blackness. I gasped and coughed, jerking onto my side.

The people around me spoke in whispers. Inhaling, I glanced up at my companions and reached out for them. They all shouted and patted my head and arms.

I fell to my back as my mind raced with images of *ba*. What'd happened? It seemed like I'd just awoken from some foggy dream. I recalled a humanoid woman with the lower half of a fish pulling me down into the lake. Then, a ferry had sailed across the night sky and I'd faced many trials before flying, being chased, talking to someone or something with green eyes and knowledge of the past. Had any of it been real, or only another nightmare? My eyes closed as I shut out the voices of my companions, and time slowed as if the time bender's magic was cast upon me again.

It seemed as though I'd been gone for weeks, but the twilight fading over the hills was the same as when I'd been pulled under the water, and my friends were still here. It must still be the same day ... I couldn't recall much detail of what had occurred in the underworld, but I didn't remember speaking to the magician or Father—the entire reason I'd subjected myself to the drowning.

My heart sank and my stomach cramped.

A vacillating hum sounded in my head, like overtones of far-off singing backset with soft music. Voices of the deceased? Could I hear them now that I had died?

"Stand him up," a deep voice shouted, "before he gives up."

Strong hands gripped my elbows and hoisted me to my feet. I wobbled, but someone's arms supported me. Tia's demure features narrowed, but a thin eyebrow pulled back onto her forehead. Her black hair floated in a gentle breeze.

"Your soul must've felt the need to hang on," a gruff voice with a thick Nubian accent said as his hardened palm smacked my lower back—one of the dancing dwarf brothers, Harkhuf, who'd once been enslaved by Egyptians for their entertainment. His dark-skinned face looked me over as he tugged at his black beard. "What in all the gods' names were you trying to do?" he asked, his triceps contracting into a horseshoe of striated muscle. "They take you under water and drown you just to bring you back out and revive you?"

"I don't get it," Seneb, the kind brother with the smooth, boyish face replied in a slighter Nubian accent, staring at the fading ripples on the lake lit with orange twilight. "She was beautiful but gave me the creeps ... like my ex-lover."

"He needs to rest," Paramessu, the former captain, said, his strong jaw clenching under his hooked nose and red hair. He eased me back onto the earth. "I almost died after being bitten by that cloaked beast with the crocodile jaws, and I don't remember wanting to be forced to stand."

Gritty sand dug into my back as I sprawled out. "I dreamt of things I could never explain." Darkness crept around my vision, surrounding everything but a small tunnel of light in the center. The tree with the black petals lay at the center of the tunnel of light. My companions spoke to each other, but I could no longer make out their voices, only sounds. The tunnel of light started to fade into the darkness. But something soft brushed against my ankle. I glanced down. Orange and white fur. A cat—Croc, he was still alive! The encompassing darkness slowly withdrew, and my vision cleared. I scooped Croc up and clutched him to my chest, hugging the air from his lungs. Soft fur caressed my skin, and his deep purr vibrated through my muscles. Tears burned my eyes. I'd thought the Devouring Monster might have killed him—the only living thing I considered a sibling—before we'd sailed to Nubia, planning to return the dwarf brothers home.

But several of Croc's toes on his rear left leg were missing. A twisting scar ran up over his ankle and leg, like the one I'd received from the hippopotamus. Gobs of thick pus drained from his wound. And he was emaciated, as if he hadn't been able to take care of himself with the injury. My pet whom I'd saved as a kitten, who often disappeared for days or months at a time, but who also reappeared several times now in moments of crises to turn into a ferocious beast. Gray hair had grown in thick around his eyes and cheeks, and his face was sunken with age.

Tia knelt over me. "I thought we'd lost you for a second time."

"You looked dead," Paramessu said, peering over her shoulder.

I gazed deep into Croc's stripes as I stroked along his bony back, my vision blurring. "I was."

"What happened to you?" Harkhuf folded his arms across his chest.

"I—I saw the land of the dead," I whispered as the rumble of Croc's purr vibrated against my skin. "But I was unable to accomplish anything that I was supposed to. I couldn't find and speak to the magician or Father."

Tia laid a gentle hand across my forehead. "Well, we're glad to have you back."

Harkhuf sighed, as if disappointed.

Was I glad to be back? My head fell back into the coarse sand that gritted against the back of my scalp. What could we do from here ... what was I supposed to do now? Everything seemed lost. I'd failed even at death. My eyes clamped shut.

"Take him back to our accommodations," Paramessu said. "He needs rest."

Chapter 4

Present Day

FLICKERING CANDLELIGHT DANCED across a wooden table between Maddie and me, also shimmering against her long dark hair. The restaurant table was small, only meant for two, but it seemed as if she sat on the other end of one of those tables old English royalty used for dinner parties. The pungent aroma of freshly fired pita bread hung thick, making my stomach growl with hunger, although the echoing chatter of patrons muted the sound. Couples and small parties filled the tables inside this small building with green walls. I shifted in the hard wood of my chair, the desert heat still weighing on me.

The light of the flame reflected off the lenses of Maddie's fashionably sheer glasses, veiling her eyes. She hadn't spoken to me in nearly five minutes and wasn't eating either. This was a mistake, trying to take her out on a date and get her mind off of things. What was she thinking about? Her recent abduction; the final clues that had been destroyed, those we couldn't solve together; or, hopefully, me as a hero saving her?

I bit into a crumbly ball of falafel caked with hummus. Pungent garlic permeated my sinuses as thick spice bit into my tongue.

The sound of a horn blared from my pocket, and my phone vibrated against my thigh with an incoming text.

I swallowed the bite of food and took a long drink of off-tasting water that the waiter had claimed came from a bottle, the recommendation when drinking in Egypt. "Maddie, are you doing okay?"

Maddie nodded. "I'm fine. I just need to use the restroom." Her chair rumbled across the floor as she scooted it back, stood, and walked to the back of the crowded restaurant. I watched her short and thin but shapely frame as she went.

Maybe she needed to be alone for a while, or to stay in and rest, although I thought that was the problem, her drowning in bad thoughts because she couldn't take her mind off the recent past. I'd tried to get her to fly home and see her family after the abduction, but she adamantly refused, saying that she needed to go over the clues to the Hall of Records and also finish up the fieldwork portion of her PhD research before returning home.

My phone buzzed again.

I pulled it out. There were a couple of texts from Aiden, Kaylin's teenage brother who tagged along on this trip because their dad funded the expedition and had probably forced him out of the house for a bit. The texts read: 'What you up to? Is Maddie okay?'

'She's distant still,' I replied. 'Where are you guys?'

The horns sounded. 'Out at some random ancient site following what Kaylin or Mr. Scalone thought the last clue might suggest. We've been here all day and haven't found anything. I told them about Maddie, but they either didn't hear me or don't care.'

I shook my head. Kaylin, Maddie's and my old mutual friend since our first year of college, sure didn't seem too concerned about Maddie at all lately. Kaylin only seemed to be interested in still discovering the Hall and had also tried to seduce and manipulate me to her end. And even after her and Aiden's bodyguard had been shot and killed, Kaylin and Aiden still weren't going home. Was Mr. Scalone—the man who'd pretended to be our guide through Egypt but turned out to be a treasure hunter hired by Kaylin's dad—driving her, or was it her dad who was telling them to stick it out and find the treasure? Or was it Kaylin's own inner drive for riches and fame?

'Which ancient site?' I texted back.

'The Rameseum, I think???'

The Rameseum? That was one of Rameses II's, also known as Rameses the Great's, most famous temples. But why him? He didn't have much to do with the story; his life came some time after Akhenaten's. What would've brought Kaylin or Mr. Scalone there?

Maddie returned and slumped back into her chair with a quiet thud, then scooted back up to the table, her face drawn.

Her expression appeared so much different from when I'd rescued her. After I'd stabilized her wound, a look of sheer happiness had come over her, a sparkle radiated from her eyes, and her lips had felt so soft and tender when she'd kissed me. All of my anxiety had let loose when I'd realized that she was going to be okay after fearing the worst about her safety for so long. Now I wasn't sure ... the sparkle was gone. The abduction had taken a toll on her, and I was still trying to be her hero, to help her get her mind off of things, but it didn't seem to be working.

Her gaze briefly rose and met mine before shifting away. "Where do you think the Hall could be hidden after all this time? You must've considered this quite a bit by now."

I huffed with uncertainty. That couldn't be all that what was plaguing her thoughts. "I'd thought of Deir el-Bahari, the final resting place of the female pharaoh Hatshepsut. They mentioned her in the journal at one point, and it rests against the base of a mountain. No one has found any passages leading into the cliffs, but there might be something in there."

She shuddered. "It's intriguing, but I always think of the sixty-some tourists who were cornered in there and butchered by terrorists a few years back."

"But the locals condemned the terrorists after that, since tourism fell off the map in the area for a while. And that was over twenty years ago. I think it would be fine to visit now."

Her eyes grew distant. "Yeah, as long as no more mysterious men show up and try to stop us."

I winced. *Touché.* She probably didn't need to be reminded of them. She fell silent again and absently played with something in her lap. I should keep her talking. "What would be your choice for a location for the Hall?" I asked.

"I thought that it'd be hidden inside Tut's tomb," she said as she rolled up her long hair and wound it into a bun on top of her head. "Just recently, researchers with sonar have detected empty spaces beyond its known boundaries, and there's evidence to suggest that Tut was buried in a small outer chamber of a much larger tomb—because of his early and unexpected death. The much larger and deeper tomb could be Nefertiti's final resting place, and that would fit with the ancient story."

My forehead wrinkled as I pondered the possibility. It was a great thought. I'd heard the same new theories about Tut's tomb and Nefertiti and the recent discoveries. So why did explorations always take so long to even commence when something that exciting was found or suspected? Was it the funding or the acquisition of rights to the claim or that the overseeing government didn't believe such theories and didn't want people destroying ancient sites? Or did certain people in power actually want specific things to remain hidden from the public?

I rubbed my scratchy eyes. "There're also supposed to be miles of empty shafts that have been detected with sonar beneath the Sphinx, which lead toward the Giza Pyramids. I always wondered what those tunnels were for. Supposedly, no one's been allowed to dig them up for fear of collapsing the Sphinx or damaging the foundations of the pyramids. And the pyramids are only glorified burial mounds after all, marking a location."

"Yeah, the location of a dead pharaoh," Maddie said. "Originally, anyway, before their mummies were moved years later."

"I'm just saying maybe there's more under the Sphinx and the pyramids."

Maddie picked up her fork and rolled over a stuffed grape leaf, eyeing it. "Well, the Sphinx and the Great Pyramid are where conspiracy theorists and old-time Egyptologists believed the Hall may've been hidden—if the Hall is even real. I was asking for possibilities other than there. Can you summarize the location of our last clues again? Since the time that I was abducted."

I shut my eyes, picturing the scenes as I rubbed at my forehead. We'd been over this many times in great detail after her rescue. We'd looked over everything from the Faiyum oasis, and after Maddie recovered from her injury, we'd spent the last two weeks revisiting the location and the giant crocodile skeleton that rested beneath ancient cliff paintings. All that hunting and we still couldn't find a clue showing us where to dig for the Hall of Records or where to look next. We'd tried everything.

Finally I said, "The oasis at the Faiyum."

"And the clue before that?" she asked, although she already knew. "The oasis might've been incorrect."

"No." I repeatedly jabbed my fingertip into the scarred wood of the tabletop to help solidify my statement. "Those men were there waiting for us to continue along the path, and they held you near there in case we found the clue. So the Faiyum oasis had to be right. But the clue before that was the *serdab* at the step pyramid. And the hieroglyphs that would've been illuminated by starlight had recently been scratched away, so I had to use the story in the journal as a guide and make an educated guess to find you in time. The clue before that was el-Amarna, with the outline of the sun rays creating the step pyramid, and before that the Colossi of Amenhotep, with the cryptic use of a hieroglyphic image leading us to el-Amarna."

Maddie dropped her fork onto her plate with a rattle and looked away, staring blankly at the wall. "But we've already spent days searching the entire crocodile skeleton and the cliff paintings. There's nothing else there, not even a remnant of something that was destroyed. I'm not sure about anything now, and I suspect that Kaylin and Mr. Scalone are out looking for something without us." She pushed her full plate of food farther away. "Nothing makes sense anymore."

A Middle Eastern waiter in a pressed shirt stepped up to the side of our table with a bottle of water in hand, on the opposite side of where Maddie was looking. He reached for Maddie's glass and bumped it. The glass skittered across the table as he leaned farther over for it.

Maddie whirled around to face to the man. Her eyes gaped as she screamed and smacked the man's arm with both of hers. "Get away from me!"

The waiter jerked his hand back and jumped in surprise.

Maddie raised her hands to her open mouth, her face flushing with embarrassment. "I-I'm so, so sorry."

The waiter grimaced, spun about, and marched away.

My chair flew back as I leapt up and reached out for her. "Maddie …"

She was far more traumatized by her abduction and abductors than she ever wanted to let me know.

She pushed my hand away and leapt up. "Don't touch me, Gavin." Sobbing, she covered her face and ran out of the restaurant.

Chapter 5

Present Day

DURING THE COUPLE OF DAYS following our failed dinner date, Maddie had refused to talk about the incident, claiming only that she'd been really tired that day. But she'd grown even more distant.

Now Maddie stood by herself as she stared off into shadows that crawled toward the reflecting Nile, upon which a mirror image of the city and its lights wavered. The ancient river stretched wide beyond the walkway she stood upon, and layers of pink, purple, and orange twilight vanished from its rippling surface, replaced by darkness. The distant honking of cars and the rumble of the city faded to background noise, and the heat clinging to my skin started to subside.

I paced along the walkway, striding up to her.

She turned away from me, her chin on her fist as she leaned against the stone banister.

My forehead tensed as anxiety rose like the morning sun inside me. I braced myself against the same unforgiving banister separating us from the Nile. What was she thinking we should do now?

"Gavin," she whispered, "did you end up sleeping with Kaylin?"

What? Was she more concerned about our friend, whom she'd brought along on this trip, and if we'd done anything together, rather than her abduction or the lost trail?

"After I'd been abducted and you guys were in the hotel," Maddie said, leaning over the banister and peering down into the dark water, her eyes unblinking. "A few days ago, you said she came on to you after you'd figured out the clue with the Colossi of Amenhotep and essentially demoted Mr. Scalone as the leader of our group."

"Sh-she did," I stuttered, the pit of my stomach feeling hollow. "I wasn't prepared. I didn't think anything like that would happen. But no, she was just using me to help her find the Hall."

"So you didn't sleep with her?" Maddie asked.

I stood straight and folded my arms. "No, I was too worried about you." Would she believe me? It was the truth.

Her eyes remained vacant as she stared into the distance. "What did you do?" she asked.

"She touched me and climbed on me, trying to seduce me," I said, "but I didn't do anything. She might've kissed me."

"But you put yourself in that situation, let her on top of you, and let her kiss you," Maddie replied. "Kaylin, our friend from school, but not the type of girl I'd picture you with."

I stumbled backward in defense. "I was trying to find you by following the path to the Hall. That was the only time those men showed themselves, like they were following us, or the path."

"Hmm." Maddie pursed her lips and tightened the irregular bun on top of her head. "It worked and I really appreciate it; I just thought you were different from most guys. I thought you were into me, not just some hot blonde because she came on to you when you were feeling discouraged."

My jaw dropped. "I am. I've always been into you."

"But when I was abducted and being held in some old temple out in the desert, you and Kaylin were messing around with each other?" She stood straight, still facing the river running through Cairo.

I sighed and bit my lip. "I turned her down long before—"

"After you let it go for a bit."

My head drooped. Had I messed up my chances with Maddie because of Kaylin? I'd saved Maddie. But before that, I'd been discussing the clues with Kaylin, and I'd let her touch me. I didn't even know why—maybe because that kind of attention from a glamorous woman like Kaylin made me feel like I wasn't so ordinary. And these two had a falling out in a heated argument right before Maddie's abduction but had been good friends before that, going back to college. This was ridiculous, but I could understand her frustration and resentment—if one of my friends had done the same with

Maddie, I'd be furious with both of them. Maybe if I could find the clues to the Hall, she'd forget about it for a while.

She ran her fingers along the decorative linear carvings along stone banister. "Maybe you should go home for now and beg your medical school to let you back in so you can finish. Explain that you didn't make it back because of all this, not because of the surgeon's and your mistake with that old woman. I'll wrap up the fieldwork research for my PhD and keep looking over everything with the Hall while I'm here."

My eyes closed with regret, and sadness settled around me like rain falling from the sky, adding weight and thickness to the air as the heat left the desert for the night. Maybe Maddie just needed some time to get over it all, without me around. She probably did have post-traumatic stress disorder, or something like that, after her abduction. And so much for being her hero and saving her; that didn't even seem to matter now. "I can try to help you find someone to talk to about everything that happened."

Her body froze, and her muscles locked up. "I can deal with that on my own. Just go, Gavin. Finish being a doctor. That can still be something you can achieve, something that will make you more than ordinary, if that's why you're always turning every which way. Maybe I'll see you back home sometime." She strode away along the walk, fading into the shadows of the scattered streetlights.

My stomach twisted but thankfully only in remorse—the flaring and painful bouts of Crohn's disease had subsided after we'd rescued Maddie. Still, I'd need an infusion soon or it could flare up at any time.

Was this really it … time to go home? After everything I'd been through and fought against, finally I'd run out of options. There were no more leads. My fingers squeezed the bronze bracelet on my forearm—my deceased dad's gift. I tore the bracelet off in anger and frustration. *Yes, Dad, you brought me here to live both of our dreams, but it didn't change my life; it only ended up causing more intense anguish after having been so close to the Hall.* Because I hadn't been able to uncover any more clues, even with Maddie's assistance—she was much better at this than me—we were probably out of options. The love and the high she'd probably felt when I'd found and rescued her must've faded to jealousy and disappointment.

Two children ran from the shadows beyond the streetlight that Maddie was headed for. Laughing, they dodged Maddie's dark silhouette and kept running.

"Sorry about that, bro," a teenage male's voice said from the opposite side of the walkway as the running children. Kaylin's younger brother's beanpole frame stepped from the shadows, and he nodded at me. He removed his flat-billed cap, and his red dreadlocks spilled over the buzzed sides of his head. "I was headed out to see what you guys were up to but heard you arguing. Women … I stopped just back there. Didn't want to interrupt but didn't mean to eavesdrop."

I groaned and shook my head. "Doesn't matter."

"Honestly, bro," Aiden tugged on a leash and his tiny desert fox trotted into view, sniffing, "you should just stop trying so hard. You're trying to discover some lost secret or become a doctor like someone's running after you with a hot poker. When I feel like you, I just chill out for a few weeks, maybe have a smoke or two."

The slapping footfalls of the running children neared. I turned to them and held out an open hand, the cold metal of my bracelet sitting in my palm.

The two boys stopped, their eyes wide as they eyed the bronze. But they wouldn't come any closer.

"Take it," I said, tossing it at them.

They jumped back, and the bracelet hit the stone walk with a ping before it rolled into the shadows with a soft rumble. One of boys lunged and grabbed it, his eyes sparkling as he studied its reflective surface.

"It's only brought me pain." I walked back for our hotel with scuffing footfalls. "I'm going back, Aiden."

Maddie had stopped at the edge of a sphere of light, beneath a streetlight in the distance. She stared at me.

Was I really going to give it up—my search for the Hall? But with the way things stood now, I had no other leads, and Maddie didn't want me around. I couldn't bear becoming like my dad with her anyway, letting her down like he had my mom. I didn't want Maddie to despise me for good. Maybe I should go home, at least until the pain softened, and become a doctor, something she and others would respect. I'd still have a great story about my one big adventure for my future children someday.

And I'd keep the journal that I'd found with the corpse of Dr. Shelsher's student inside the lost tomb of Amenhotep. That journal held the translation of the ancient Egyptian tale, although the tale was incomplete and ended abruptly.

Aiden's running footsteps sounded behind me. "Wait up, bro. I can come with you and go have a drink or something."

Lowering my head, I marched away. I'd fly back home and finish school, or I'd also end up like Aiden.

The engines roared as the airplane lifted off Egyptian ground and threw me back into my lumpy seat. My fingers dug into my knees, the adjustable air above whistling and blowing into my face as I sat in the middle of two husky men whose arms lay over the armrests. The smell of sweat hung in the air. Glancing out the window, I tried to think of something besides Maddie and the Hall. I unlatched my seatbelt, but the tightness inside of me didn't recede. There was no escape.

My mind wandered as I looked at the blue fabric on the back of the seat in front of me. Maybe there'd be a terrorist attack on this plane, and maybe I could actually help people …

I imagined that two men suddenly stood up and drew guns, screaming at the passengers. One's back would be to me. Without hesitation, I'd leap up as he'd swing his gun wildly about, but I'd grab and twist the magazine and his gun back into him, utilizing the leverage of the metal extension. With his hand inside the metal finger grip, the man would scream in pain as his joints locked up and his finger twisted. And I'd continue to tear his gun away from him while kicking him to the ground. Taking up the handle, I'd raise the barrel of the weapon and aim at the other terrorist, who'd stare back at me in complete shock. I'd fire, and the second terrorist's gun would fall harmlessly to the ground. Turning back to the first terrorist, I'd use the stock of the gun to smash his forehead and knock him unconscious before—

"Sir," a flight attendant said, glaring at me. "Fasten your seatbelt."

I sighed and clicked the ends of my seatbelt together. Through the side window, the view of Cairo grew smaller and smaller before clouds floated along beside us—obscuring everything below.

I should look for a new beginning back home. Maybe I'd finally be able to put all of my past mistakes behind me and face the only future this life would bring. I could be a doctor and help people. That would be more than enough. Another great woman would eventually come into my life, we'd end up together, and someday after I found a cure for Crohn's disease, we could explore every inch of ancient Egypt together.

I closed my eyes, the hum of the engines drowning out the conversations around me as well as the other voices inside my head telling me that I should not have left. But after this long flight, a layover, and another long flight, I'd be back home.

My fingers ran over the cracked leather cover of the journal inside my messenger bag—the cover peeling like scales of a reptile and digging into my palm—the journal with the ancient story.

Chapter 6

Journal Translation

Croc's warm body was nestled into my armpit that night as I lay upon my coarse blanket inside our accommodations at Crocodilopolis. His toes kneaded the fabric, his claws tearing into it with quiet pops as his purr hummed in my ears. I stared at his claws—such weapons that could be used for defense or violence. My vision blurred, and my eyes closed.

Vivid dreams of the past raged in my head as I fell asleep. I dreamt of human-headed birds and of figures cloaked in black with glowing green eyes and white, linen-wrapped faces—the Dark Ones. I shuddered in a cold sweat. I'd learned that the Dark Ones were the Devoured Souls of the dead, and they haunted me everywhere I went. I could not escape them.

But then my dream faded into something else, a dream I'd never had before, something I'd suppressed from such a young age—an event that would have been so horrifyingly simple to change or to never do in the first place. Something that had altered the very core of my existence, but I never would've foreseen the outcome back then. My recent death and rebirth into the world of the living must have unlocked it—like the music again humming inside my head …

I was young when I was ordered to fill in for one of the royal family's servants who'd recently turned mad. I ended up meeting that servant years later in the solitary cave prison … but I'd still never discovered why Akhenaten had gotten rid of him and if the servant had really turned mad before his confinement or if Akhenaten had caused his insanity.

Images shifted in my dream. At that time, Amenhotep had ruled Egypt and the people lived in peace. Great wealth flowed through the country, more than its inhabitants had ever seen. Stores of grain were stocked away—large enough to last many seasons. And I was supposed to serve Pharaoh's second son, Akhenaten, for a short time, before a replacement was found.

I trailed Akhenaten, a youth at the time, into the palace's kitchen. His gangly frame swung beneath his elongated skull and face as his flat feet slapped the tile of the floor. A young beauty walked beside us—Nefertiti, his cousin. My eyes were drawn to her, wanting to take in her heart-shaped face and green-painted eyes. Something inside me lit up when I studied the perfect symmetry of her sculpted features.

"Nothing will satisfy my hunger like the sour and sweet seeds of the pomegranate mashed into the pulp of a watermelon," Akhenaten muttered, the dark lids of his eyes growing like sockets of a skull as they closed. He nudged me. "I will douse them in honey. You will learn what I like, and you will serve me well."

Saliva wetted the inside of my mouth as I imagined the sour sensation and a distaste for the bizarre mixture. Who was this strange young man? But I shouldn't need to worry or remember his wishes; I'd only be serving him for a week or so before being trained as a scribe. Father had worked hard to get me into school so that I could have a better life than him.

"I think we're supposed to be in the dining hall," Nefertiti said, glancing back. "Not in the kitchen."

Akhenaten screamed, kicking baskets of woven papyrus reeds into the air. They fell back to the ground, landing with a sharp crinkling.

My eyes bulged, and my muscles tensed. I'd never witnessed such rash—

"They are all gone!" He grabbed a jar of honey and threw it against a pristine white wall.

Clay shattered with a crack that jolted my ears. Thick yellow paste smeared and clung to the bright red and blue floral paintings upon the wall.

I swallowed and my toes curled, fear taking over my previous surprise.

Nefertiti cringed and cowered into the far corner.

Akhenaten continued smashing jugs of beer and stomping on intact watermelons. Red pulp sprayed up his shins. I should get away from this crazy boy.

Stepping back, I exited the kitchen. Nefertiti crouched and followed, and we snuck away.

Men feasted in the audience hall just ahead. The Aten shone through the open-air chamber, its morning heat and rays soft and orange.

Should I run to Father and let him know about Akhenaten's behavior? Father would be inside the audience hall serving Pharaoh his breakfast. I crept over and peeked around the doorway. There he was. Father's broad face—without the loving smile I was used to seeing him wear with me. But Father was removing and offering plates of sweet bread to the rest of the royal family.

Father was the only reason I was to become a scribe and not a servant like him—the latter something I now believed I would not enjoy. Typically, being taught to read and write was reserved for those boys born to elite families, but Father had relinquished his life to Pharaoh. Over time, he bargained and offered the god-king undying servitude in this life and next, giving up all of his days and nights of freedom. He'd become Pharaoh's most devoted servant so that my life could be better. As a high-ranking member of society, I'd have a much better life—thanks to his sacrifice. Father would do anything for me.

Nefertiti pointed. "There, just go and take it. You don't want to see what Akhenaten will do otherwise."

I saw it: the red and pink rind of a pomegranate. It sat on the plate of an elderly man to my right. His back was turned. A white sash ran across his chest, and a white cat perched on his shoulder. Rolls of fat from the feline's belly dangled around its hind feet.

Sneaking closer, I reached out. The wrinkled face of the man was engulfed with spider veins, and he chatted with another man beside him. The crystal-blue eyes of the cat on his shoulder locked on mine, unblinking. I froze. What would it do?

The cat meowed. My skin crawled, my fingers hovering over the fruit. The old man's attention shifted, but his gaze froze just off to the other side of his plate—as if he didn't want to see me.

After snatching the hard shell of the fruit, I darted out of the chamber and hid by pressing my back against the stone on the far side of the doorway. But in this dream, I could somehow see a smile creeping over the old man's lips, lines of black running across his face like a spider's web. Haunting gray eyes …

"You stole a pomegranate." Akhenaten ripped the fruit from my palm and sank his teeth into the rind. Red juice flowed around his lips, dribbling off of his chin and splattering onto his sagging chest. Although overall he was a thin young man, his stomach and pectorals carried oddly distributed fat. His eyes closed in sheer pleasure, his mouth hanging open but not issuing a sound for a moment. "Have a taste."

I shook my head.

"Take a bite." He shoved the fruit into my hands.

My fingers shook as I bit into an inner pocket of seeds. Sour, yet sweet. Juice ran down my chin.

After picking up a cracked-open watermelon, Akhenaten took the pomegranate from me and scooped its seeds into the watermelon, as if the melon rind were a bowl. He turned to the honey that was smeared and dripping down the wall of the kitchen. As he rubbed the watermelon over the wall, he laughed. The sticky sweet paste of honey coated the fruit, but the fruit also left streaks of red across the white-painted wall. "Now, if only I could mix in the flesh of His animals," Akhenaten said. "But Pharaoh would never allow for it, not meat."

Strong hands grabbed me beneath my armpits, hauling me backward and dragging me away.

"He stole it?" a voice said from behind me.

Akhenaten threw pomegranate seeds across my chest. "Yes."

I twisted and squirmed, fighting to see what was happening as my sandaled feet skittered backward over hard tile.

The orange light of the Aten greeted me—blinding me—as I was thrown onto the floor of the audience hall with a thud.

I winced in pain. The silhouettes of men emerged, seated before the throne.

"This boy just stole from the plate of the son of Hapu," the man behind me said in an uneducated dialect. He was a young soldier with a shaven head and scar running sideways over its length, down over a deformed ear that jutted outward like a pig's—Suty.

A man rose before me, his form hunched, but most of his skin reflected gold across my vision, as if he were a god.

Pharaoh Amenhotep smacked a flail made of multiple whips down onto the table. The crack of leather followed. "To steal from this family or our guests is to be cast from the palace. This includes stealing from the magician."

Violent trembling shook my small body, sheer terror consuming me.

"Did you steal it because you wished to savor the delicacy of the seeded fruit?" Pharaoh asked. "Is the bread and beer I pay you with not enough for you, little boy?"

"N-no," I said. "I took it for Ak—"

"He ate it," the oddly deep voice of Akhenaten echoed as he stepped up beside me, his chin wiped clean.

Pharaoh motioned with a golden scepter. "Drag him away. He can live in the slums."

"No!" a voice screamed—a man's but so high-pitched that I'd heard nothing like it. Father fell to his knees, his palms stretched out to Pharaoh in adoration. "This is my boy. The one who is to become a scribe."

Pharaoh studied Father and then me, and the dark outline of the god-king's form straightened. "We cannot keep anyone who steals. Nor can a scribe lie. It would negatively affect the records of the kingdom. If he recorded extra bushels of grain that weren't there ..."

Father wailed.

The man whom I'd taken the pomegranate from—the magician—stood at a table. Lines like a spider's web ran across his face. "Please offer this boy a second chance to become a scribe. Egypt may need it some—"

"He can continue to serve me," Akhenaten said, the rind of the watermelon still in his hands.

Pharaoh paced about with his head down. "This is unfortunate, but as your father is my greatest servant, I will grant you another choice. As you now serve my second son," his voice changed, underlying emotion breaking through, "you can leave for the slums, or you can stay here and serve Akhenaten ... forever. But you will never steal or lie a second time, or you will be banished or put to death."

I couldn't even nod or utter a response. The god-king was talking to me, and I'd disgraced myself and Father.

"Stand up, boy," Pharaoh said. "Answer me."

Suty grabbed me by my sidelock—a braid of hair on the side of my head, one that all young men wore—and yanked me to my feet. Blinding pain ran across and into my scalp, as if it might tear off.

"What will it be?" Pharaoh asked.

Father's face rose in front of me, stricken with horror, his skin white like his kilt. He stared at me.

With one fateful decision, I'd ruined everything Father had done for me—everything he had tried to accomplish in his life.

Suty dragged me out of the audience hall and flung me against the far wall. I hit with a crack, pain shooting up my elbow and into my shoulder and spine. I grimaced.

Nefertiti's eyes gaped, her hand over her mouth. She'd stood just outside the doorway, having witnessed my shame. She ran off, sobbing.

Akhenaten appeared, sucking on the fluid inside his watermelon rind with loud slurps. The red pulp and juice across his cheeks lifted with his grin …

Something at my waist felt hot, almost burning my skin through my kilt and waking me. The darkness of the night lay thick with only the faint light of the moon slipping through a high, open window. I grabbed for the hot object at my waist—the soft fronds of a deep-blue ostrich feather grazing my hand—the Feather of Truth, the Feather of Ma'at. My former master, Akhenaten, had given it to me after he'd beaten me, taken Nefertiti, and sent me into slavery—to remember the truth and the wrongs I'd done to him. He'd wanted me to suffer for a lifetime, toiling as a slave and building his monuments only to have my heart consumed by the Devouring Monster when I finally passed, which would erase my soul, as if I'd never even existed. There was no greater punishment in all the world.

I recalled saving Akhenaten from drowning in the river after a hippopotamus attack that almost left me crippled. Mahu, the captain of his personal guard, had revived him. And at another point, I'd spied on Akhenaten inside his room in the palace, before he was ever pharaoh—back when his older brother, Thutmose, was the crown prince. He'd been discussing the visions he'd seen when he was temporarily dead. He'd spoken of seeing people and about flying, but he had seen the Aten as well. At one point he'd been terrified … when he believed people in the next world were all equals and part of some intricate web of the universe, too complex to understand. He'd alluded to there being no person at the pinnacle leading the others. Was that why he'd said to live for today and that the world of the living was the world of the gods? Did he only wish to live forever, here, where his power was not questioned, not limited?

My stomach burned with rage. No, I wouldn't let Akhenaten get away with everything—all of his heinous acts—not now, not even after all these years. Even the love of Nefertiti could not extinguish my need for vengeance. I would take the power from Akhenaten for everything he'd done. I'd already let him get away with the murder of my father and others, and usurping Egypt's throne, for far too long. The years of his reign, power, and vicious leadership had already given him far too much pleasure while driving the people of Egypt into despair. I should've faced him again years ago. I would not allow myself to become complacent in this life, not like the *ba* in the underworld, hoping that in the next life Akhenaten would receive appropriate punishment. My fingernails dug into my palms, bringing slicing pain and drawing blood.

With my plain face, I'd be difficult to recognize after all the years that'd passed, but should I grow my hair out—that on my head? Facial or body hair would not work, as that would stand out in civilized Egypt like water on the open desert. I'd need a mask of some kind …

Chapter 7

Journal Translation

THE NEXT MORNING, I woke to voices and the smell of sweet smoke mixed with the earthy aroma of honey. My companions talked as they spooned lumpy grains between their lips and crunched on their breakfasts. Orange rays from the morning Aten streamed through the window into the small house that we were staying at in Crocodilopolis—Tia's hometown. She'd faced the demons of her past and was stronger for it, like Harkhuf and Seneb, the dwarf brothers from Nubia, and Wahankh, the former bully whom we'd allowed to come with us as we'd escaped from slavery. Only Paramessu hadn't yet returned to face his father—an officer of the Egyptian military. And I hadn't returned for Nefertiti and to confront my former master …

Croc shivered against my armpit, shaking my arm. But it wasn't cold inside the chamber. The wound around his left ankle and foot, so similar to mine, grabbed my attention. I'd also shivered when my wound had become infected, feeling as cold as the white snow on the island mountain of Keftiu. But Croc's skin was dark and twisted. How had he lived with this injury for so long? Or was his fever because of a curse bestowed by the Devouring Monster—the creature from the underworld who was part lion, part crocodile, and part hippopotamus? And why did Croc appear so old now?

I pressed on the wound. Croc hissed and snaked his head out to bite my fingers, but his teeth rested on my skin—a warning.

"I'm trying to help you," I whispered.

Green pus oozed from a hole in the scar tissue near his missing toes. A lump protruded under his skin, just above the draining hole. How could it still be swollen?

I probed the area with my fingertips. Firm, like bone. Croc's teeth sank into the skin of my hand with biting pain. I jerked away and shouted. He darted away, leapt up to the high window, and disappeared outside. My companions stopped talking and stared at me. Blood trickled from the puncture marks on my hand, and a stabbing sensation persisted.

Croc's injury must really still hurt him. But how could I ever look at it, clean it up, and try to help heal it if he wouldn't even allow me to touch it? And if Croc was sick enough that he couldn't fight, we wouldn't stand a chance if monsters were sent against us again. He was our only defense against the might of the Devourer—the Devouring Monster—that Akhenaten had sent to kill off all of the remaining magicians of Egypt and anyone with intangible power.

"Can we leave soon?" Harkhuf asked. "These people still stare at me as they pass by. And I am no hero. I tried to help … only for my family." His teeth grated together, as if he were in pain.

Seneb patted his brother's broad back, issuing the slap of skin on skin.

"We will leave," I said, recalling the dead magician's secret note—the one he'd told me not to read unless he died. But I hadn't waited that long, opening it the night I saw it. Inside was a map to a buried tomb with riches beyond comprehension, which also mentioned some weapon the magician thought I'd need to pursue my desires. I'd avoided searching for the tomb, as I once believed I'd return my former slave companions to their homes and continue on myself. But it turned out that once my companions faced their demons, we all felt more and more like family and everyone wanted to stay together. Everyone but Chisisi—the freeman who'd wanted to lead our group at any cost, even with manipulation and lies. Thankfully, he'd left a short time ago, after almost leading Seneb to his death against the giant crocodile in the lake we'd—

"Good." Harkhuf started shoving his gear into a sack. "You said something about el-Amarna before. And when we visited Thebes, we were looking for supplies to find something out in the desert, before those strange people wearing ram masks abducted us."

"Yes," I said, nodding. "It's time to unearth a lost tomb."

I led my companions outside as the young Aten cast its searing heat across the desert city. Two horses stood nearby, attached to carts with stacks of food and tools for an excavation piled inside.

Tia motioned at the city behind us. "Since we rid my people of their curse—the beast in the lake—I asked them to supply the equipment we'd been trying to acquire at Thebes. And my people keep their promises. They were very grateful."

Seneb reached up to stroke the long neck of a chestnut horse, breathed into its nostrils, and whispered. The equine flicked its ears at buzzing flies and stomped its hoof, its muscles rippling up to its shoulder. Taking up the horse's lead rope, Seneb moved to hand the beast off to his brother but paused. Harkhuf shook his head as he eyed the horse towering over him. Smirking, Seneb gave the rope to Paramessu.

"This one is built to run, like Harkhuf fleeing a crocodile, only with much more grace and speed," Seneb said to the former captain as he nodded at the magnificent creature. "Perhaps you will be a chariot warrior again someday."

Paramessu's pale eyes closed, and the muscles around his jaw bulged. "In which direction is this secret of yours hidden?" Seneb asked me.

I pointed into the distance, south, toward the origin of the Nile.

Seneb folded his arms, and his eyes narrowed. "You know, we could all leave our pasts behind and start a nice farm along the river. You'd never have to think about returning to that awful city we were building … ever again."

My stomach clenched with knee-buckling pain. I grimaced until the pain receded, then shook my head.

Seneb shrugged and led the other horse and cart south.

Long days passed before we found the massive boat of the Sea People—the one we'd hidden, covered with brush, just beyond a lonely bank of the Nile.

"I'm surprised no one took our boat," Wahankh said, shoving at the boat's hull. His stubble-covered head appeared small against his towering frame and bulging muscles.

I shoved against the oiled wood, and together we all drove the bottom of the hull through the hard-baked dirt of the desert like a plow. The grating sensation sent jarring vibrations into my hands and arms.

As we approached the Nile, I reached out with my index and little fingers extended in the crocodile ward that I'd learned long ago. The water bubbled as if my small amount of inner magic pushed some kind of energy through the water, repelling the unwanted beasts.

The bow of our boat dipped into the river with a splash, and hull and stern followed. We loaded the horses and carts on board and disembarked. Croc meowed from the shore and leapt across a few feet of water, landing inside the hull with a quiet thud. He skittered away on stiff joints and hid amongst the crates at the stern.

The boat glided into the gentle waves, the bow turning north with the current. I unrolled the sail. Dusty cloth the color of a storm cloud billowed open. The ever-present wind along the river gusted and caught the sail, overpowering the current and driving us south. I ran back to the stern, near the horses and carts, for the long oar at the rear—the rudder. My fingers wrapped around the cracked wood of the handle as the howling of the wind rang in my ears.

Hours drifted by.

Tia leaned back into the hull and closed her eyes, a smile creeping across her lips as she clung to Paramessu's arm. She was finally happy. She'd confronted her demons and found love in another man—something she'd once believed she could never do again after the death of her father and being raised by her abusive uncle.

But Paramessu's demeanor was not as joyous. His jaw muscles protruded over and over again, as if he chewed on something as hard as a rock. Images of what would happen to him if he returned and faced his father must be running through his mind now.

The dwarf brothers sat beside each other, surveying the horizon all around us. Neither regret nor fear weighed on them. They'd both returned to their home in Nubia, cleansed the land of poison, and now appeared to spend each day in the moment as if it could be their last. Except a lingering shadow remained in the corner of Harkhuf's eyes, reminding me that he would never be free of his guilt, not in this life.

Wahankh's broad shoulders obscured a portion of the river in front of the bow. He had recently confronted some of men's greatest fears. And although he was large and strong, this previous bully used to be afraid of anyone besides the meekest of men—stealing food only from them.

Croc lay flopped over on his side in the shade beside a crate, his eyes closed. What went through my best friend's mind, especially now that he appeared so old? Did it matter? His presence alone lifted a piece of my heart.

Should I just sail away with these people and begin a new life with friends, working on a farm? I'd be free, something I'd longed for since I'd become indentured to Akhenaten ... so much easier a life. But my animosity would rot my insides and eventually pour out and contaminate everyone and everything around me. My head throbbed. I released a stale breath. No, I couldn't let my past go.

* * *

I maintained my physical exercises and conditioned my mind with books and reading every night into the early hours as the magician had convinced me I must do if I were to fulfill my revenge.

Days and nights faded away, the roaring of the wind constantly in my ears. The world slipped by.

A massive city appeared on the east bank—Thebes—its stone monuments towering over the land. We sailed past the populated area before docking on the western bank of the Nile, attached the horses to the packed carts, unloaded, and hid our boat.

I found the magician's secret map inside the sack of supplies he'd left me before we'd fled from slavery. The others, besides Croc, followed and led the horses. Heat pounded down upon my back and shoulders, and I felt as hot as a mud brick baking under the Aten. The moisture in my mouth vanished, leaving a dry but sticky sensation across my tongue.

After unrolling the crinkling papyrus with the wax seal that I'd broken long ago, I scanned the message. Written directions and markings showed a location upon a hillside in an area called the Valley of the Gates of the Kings. Writing on the back of the papyrus read:

> *My final secret. I would have told you when it was time, but if you are reading this, I have not succeeded. I've shared this with no one, but it could be the reason they came for me. The map will guide you to the resting place of Amenhotep, his unfathomable gold and treasure, and the weapon you must acquire. Utilize the rain. Locate the eye of Horus!*

At the bottom corner: *The Mask: The touch of the underworld.* And several arcane symbols were scrawled beneath it. I'd seen this before, though I hadn't thought twice about it at the time. But now that I'd used several spells, this looked similar ...

A shudder of excitement shook my core, and the strumming of chords on a stringed instrument sounded in my head, but the music was quiet, as if far away, as if coming from the underworld or the invisible *ba* all around me. Was this treasure even real, or had the old trickster planned on toying with me again? He'd done so many times in the past. His pale, haunting eyes and his face, ravaged by deep wrinkles traced with black paint to appear as a tangled web of lines, appeared in my mind. *Where are you, magician, with your fat white cat? And why would you take your own life? Did you completely lose hope? And why would you banish a group of lepers from el-Amarna, believing they were not fit to live with the other workers? That was all you ever accomplished in spite of your master plan of ridding the world of Akhenaten?*

The girl-priest of Sobek, from Crocodilopolis, had suggested that the magician committed suicide because he couldn't bear the guilt of exiling the lepers. Maybe in the end, Akhenaten had grown so powerful that the only escape the magician could foresee was killing himself. I'd never understood the son of Hapu, but hating others was not his way ... It didn't make sense.

I scanned the desert and mountains for the first marker upon the magician's map: *The oldest pyramid of all.* It appeared to be a mountain in the valley ... A natural pyramid for the god-kings of old?

Taking swigs of warm water, I trudged up the hills and motioned for my companions to follow. Their heaving breaths and grumbling carried over the wind and strumming music in my head.

A summit of pointed rock eventually loomed against the horizon. There was no question there was a pyramidion—the capstone of a pyramid—atop that peak.

We approached the base of the mountain as the Aten sank toward the horizon.

The next note on the magician's map said: *Locate the base of the stone pyramidion.*

We staggered up the steep slopes of the mountain-pyramid, having left the horses and carts at the bottom. Shadows stretched across the ground, creating areas of orange and black. We wouldn't have long until the light was gone.

My breathing turned raspy, my parched throat feeling like the cracking bed of a dried-up creek. But I finally reached the rocky summit and searched along its base by prodding with the tip of a pickax. No markings or writing was visible in the rock, nothing to indicate any type of entrance. Tapping along the stone with the bronze head of the tool, I listened for a hollow echo. Nothing but sharp clanks.

Night fell across the land like a curtain.

"You're sure there's a tomb way up here?" Seneb asked, lighting an oil lamp. Shadows danced across his boyish features.

I nodded.

No one else said a word.

"Confused, like a young boy attempting his first intimate kiss," Seneb said. "I'm going down to feed and water the horses. You should camp down in the valley with us; it's probably safer." He turned and picked his way down the slopes between craggy rock, his flame outlining the silhouette of his body and the others, who followed after him.

None of my companions were crazy enough to sleep on the side of a mountain. And I'd probably freeze up here at night.

I lit my own lamp and followed the margin between desert mountain and rocky summit for what felt like hours. There was no sign that anything could've been dug into this peak. How could someone even do it?

Groaning, I finally descended, my legs wobbling with each downward footfall.

Was this another trick or a lesson from the son of Hapu? He'd once given me papyrus scrolls to try to read. The learning process had probably taken nearly a year, and once I'd read his messages, I'd found out they were complete nonsense and that he only wrote them as incentive for me to learn to read and write.

But how could locating a tomb fit with his lessons? Did he only wish to teach me how to follow directions?

I stumbled toward a small fire at the base of the mountain and collapsed onto my blankets. The others already snored. My scratchy eyes closed, rubbing dusty grit across the surface, and my mind drifted off.

Hours later, something cold tapped my cheeks, then my nose. My eyes fluttered, and my dreams vanished. More tapping. Was it morning already? I sat up. The fire had faded to red embers, but stars still scattered the night sky, which appeared as a dark ocean holding millions of torches in its depths.

The others still slept. There it was again, the patter of water upon my face. Rain?

Directly overhead, the night was devoid of starlight. A giant cloud?

Droplets sprinkled my face.

"We should find shelter," Tia said, rising to her elbows as she kicked at Harkhuf, who snored like a donkey. "Wake up."

Harkhuf grumbled and shook his head as he yawned. "It's not morning yet."

Paramessu rubbed his eyes as he sat up. "The rains are coming. It is the time of year when even the desert feels the cool caress of moisture."

Something in my head lit up, a memory—one from the magician.

"But we should not stay at the base of such a large mountain," Paramessu said. "Flash floods are common with rain on parched dirt."

That was it: *Utilize the rain. Locate the eye of Horus!*

I snatched my sack of supplies, lit an oil torch, and stepped onto the incline of the mountain. The torch's flame hissed and sputtered as droplets of water assaulted it.

"Not up." Paramessu shook his head as he lit another lamp. "Not in this."

"We must follow the rain," I said, pointing to the peak.

Chapter 8

Journal Translation

I MOTIONED FOR MY companions to follow me up the slopes of the mountain-pyramid through the drizzle of warm rain.

"He's gone mad," Seneb said, referring to me as he stared, "like a monkey with a head injury."

I turned to hike upward. "You don't have to come."

"Rain flows downward," Paramessu said, pointing to water trickling down the mountain's slope to the desert floor. "We are closer to following its path down here."

"But we need to be near the stone summit," I said as the patter of rain grew louder and surrounded us.

"Can't we wait until morning light?" Wahankh asked. "This seems unnecessarily more difficult in the dark."

"We must use the rain while it lasts," I said. "Before long, it will be absorbed by the thirsty desert."

Wahankh grunted but followed me. The others did as well.

Dirt softened and turned to sloppy mud, causing my sandaled feet to slide beneath me. I used my free hand to assist in the ascension as I gasped for breath, the others somewhere behind me in the hum of increasing rain. Streams formed and started gushing around me as I approached the summit.

A pool of water expanded across a small plateau below the rocky slopes. Small rivers raged along crevasses in the stone overhead, spilling onto the dirt at its base with irregular splashes and gurgles.

Holding a hand well above the flame of my torch to protect it from moisture, I stomped through the mud, studying the spraying liquid. *What were you trying to tell me, magician?*

The pool of water wasn't growing, but it wasn't pouring over the plateau either. Where was it draining?

I sloshed over to the base of the plateau, away from the waterfalls cascading down the peak. Whatever clue I was looking for, it should be revealed by the accumulated rainwater. Dropping to my knees, I plunged my free hand into the pool. Mud. I crept along the edge of the cliff, prodding and searching.

Could this entire plateau give way and slide down the mountain? I froze, holding my breath. I'd plunge to my death, and all this earth would crush my companions as—

"Where's the rain up here leading you?" Paramessu's voice came from behind the flickering flame of a lamp at the edge of the pool.

I inched along, and my fingers fell into deeper water. There was nothing beneath. "Down into the mountain." The water tugged at my arm, threatening to pull me downward as it swirled and drained. An opening. I wedged my torch against the mountain, braced myself by burying my feet into the cold muck, and plunged my head into the water.

Solid stone lay beneath, but water drained around its edges. My heart leapt with excitement. I shoved downward, and the engravings upon the stone's surface embedded themselves into my palms. My fingers then traced the inside margin of the hieroglyphs. The floating eye of Horus …

I pushed again, and the stone gave way, not down but inward—into the rocky cliff face. Water rushed around me, sucking me downward. I fought against the current and popped my head above the shallow pool, gasping for breath.

I shoved again. Stone grated on stone as the block slid in another inch and the water around me rushed faster, whipping at my legs as it whooshed by. The pool around me drained and turned to sloppy mud. I heaved again. My feet popped free of the muck, and I nearly face-planted as I toppled over with a splat. Mud clung to my legs and torso. "Help," I said.

Strong arms from the dwarf brothers, Paramessu, and Wahankh joined me, along with the flickering flame of lamps. We shoved, and the block grated and slid before disappearing into the darkness inside the mountain. Water sloshed down below, and diminishing echoes from a falling stone resonated—as if a long shaft awaited us. My chest rose and fell with rapid breaths.

Orange light from our lamps flickered across Paramessu's bulging eyes. He stared into the abyss. "What is down there? A tomb? We could be cursed—or worse—if we disturb the dead's eternal rest."

It was Amenhotep's tomb … But I had better keep the name of the deceased to myself, or no one would enter. "The magician led us here so that we could benefit from the riches inside. He believed it would help our cause."

"You mean that it would help your cause, not ours," Harkhuf growled, his bulging arms folding across his chest. "I never spoke with this magician. And it may not be as frightening as a poisonous beast, but I'm not going down there."

I snatched my sputtering torch and stepped into the opening. "Then you will miss the excitement of the discovery."

"Or the excitement of death," Harkhuf replied. "As a slave, my former master often told a story of some acquaintance who'd found a tomb and robbed from the dead. The man took all of the gold and hid it under his house in a basement. But that very night, just as he fell asleep, strange noises woke him and kept him up until dawn. Similar nights followed, and the man started to see strange figures. He'd described them as men cloaked in black with linen-wrapped heads, but whenever he'd try to point one out, no one else could see it. The man started to believe everyone was lying, to trick him into believing he'd gone mad so that they could steal his treasure. One night, the man's servants awoke to screaming and found the man covered in blood, standing over the bodies of his dead family with a knife in his hand. After that incident, my former master didn't hear from this man for months and traveled to his farm. There he found all of the farmhands slain and the grave robber also dead, his skin flayed open and his body drained of all blood and liquid, mummified."

I froze. Was any of that true? From what the *ba* in the *Duat* had told me, such tales were only stories to fulfill the illusion of power in this world. Either way, I'd gone too far to turn around now. I stepped downward.

Tia slipped past the stocky brother and grabbed my shoulder. "I will come with you." But her hand trembled. Wahankh trailed behind her.

Harkhuf groaned. "I have no choice when I've vowed to accompany the woman who will name her children after mine and make me their protector."

Paramessu and the brothers followed as their eyes darted about.

I crept forward, clutching my bracelet as I held my torch aloft. Stone stairs spiraled downward. What riches or terrors would we find inside this mountain?

Chapter 9

Journal Translation

I HELD MY BREATH AND STEPPED onto the stairway leading down into the mountain. A block—the one we'd shoved inside—the size of a hippopotamus hung from ropes, dangling over the stairs. But something else made of stone had tumbled downward when we'd pushed the entrance block inside … I glanced around. Perhaps it was only a piece of the now dangling block that had broken off, or an appropriately placed stone that'd been set just inside the entrance to create echoes and frighten people away … or to awaken something within the tomb.

The flame of my torch flickered as if rain or water still assaulted it, but the air was still, musky. My lungs heaved and sucked in stale air. Burning carried along my throat and into my chest, as if I breathed smoke. I gasped. What was this?

But the feeling passed. I slowly exhaled.

My skin tingled. Something more than air not breathed in decades or longer had entered my body. Something was down here. "Be wary," I whispered over my shoulder as I inched down the steps, my firelight dancing across the dark walls.

A stream of water ran off into the shadows beside the stairs and disappeared, draining into some chamber far below.

I stifled my breathing, afraid that something down below would hear me. But rock had already crashed inward. If there was some monster lurking down there, it would be ready for us. I descended, the plummeting temperature prickling my skin and raising the stubble of my shaven body hair.

I stepped onto the lower landing. A sealed door of well-fitted bricks of limestone barred the way.

"No one is supposed to go in there," Paramessu whispered, his voice croaking like a frog's.

Harkhuf back-paddled.

"We didn't find this place just to stop now," Tia said, rummaging around in her pack. She pulled out a pickax, nudged me aside, and swung. The tool's tip buried into the wall with a ringing sound.

She withdrew the pickax and swung again. Seneb joined her, then Wahankh and I, taking turns in the narrow confines.

The handle of the pickax vibrated through my hands and arms as it thudded into stone and chipped away chunks.

Paramessu watched with wide eyes, his face pale and drawn.

Hours passed. One by one, the stones crumbled and broke away. The doorway opened into utter blackness. I lifted my torch inside. The light of the flame fought for distance but was swallowed by the shadows just beyond. Something shimmered from the darkness. I gasped and stepped back.

Paramessu approached. "The chamber inside is filled with mirrors." He eased Tia back, his hand on his shield as he stepped in front of me. "Heb, you've already saved my life. It is time that I return the favor."

He held a lamp aloft and stepped across the threshold.

His flame faded into the darkness. I gave Tia my torch and pulled my swords from my waist, sneaking after him.

Paramessu screamed.

I jerked upright in fear, then crouched and ran after him.

I bumped into his back, which was only a shadow, as his flame was hidden in front of him. He turned, and the room lit up like a thousand lamps had sprung to life. I shielded my eyes, my swords rising in front of me.

Reflective metal … everywhere. Gold.

Stacks of gold necklaces, earrings, chairs, and other furniture surrounded us, stockpiled for the dead pharaoh and his next life. Red and blue stones dotted the panorama of gold, images of men and gods littering the walls like stars across the night sky. My knees wobbled, and my swords dropped to my sides.

"Only a god-king could command such wealth," Paramessu whispered, and his jaw hung open. "The skin of the gods lies all around us."

The others entered, and everyone's eyes lit up with the reflective sparkle of gold. No one blinked.

"In all the mines of Kush," Seneb said, "there could not be this much gold."

Paramessu squeezed the back of my neck with trembling fingers. "My friend, you could be the richest mortal to have walked the earth. But we should not disturb this treasure."

I shrugged him off. If everyone was equal in the next life, why would one person need all of this? My fingertips brushed the engraved surface of a necklace that was nearly the size of my chest—the breastplate of a god. "I was assured by the dead that no deceased person needs such things."

We stared for probably an hour, studying the inner chamber and its contents. Treasure beyond imagination. *Thank you, magician.*

"I have no choice but to take this treasure," I said. "Paramessu, you can take Tia and leave if you wish."

Tia shook her head. "We've been over this many times. We stick together, and we trust you. Not until you decide that it is safe for us all to settle down will we rest. And we all already lead cursed lives anyway. You've saved us in more ways than one. Where else would we go? We're wanted by the Egyptian military and the living Pharaoh himself, remember?"

Paramessu's eyes grew distant under our dwindling flames. He knew he could never return and face the military, as he'd killed one of his own to save Tia. But he probably couldn't live with himself until he faced his father again and explained his side of our story.

"Let's start loading it up," I said, scooping up armfuls of gold jewelry that clunked together. The cold metal weighed me down much more than I would've guessed, given its size. "We will bring this all down to the horses and carts and haul it somewhere far away."

Harkhuf nodded as he picked up one end of a golden bed and Seneb picked up the other. Above wide eyes, beads of sweat glistened on their foreheads.

We emptied the chamber, bringing everything to the surface, and broke through additional walls that revealed more chambers full of gold, food, mummified animals, and statuettes. Images of men and beasts and spells from the Book of the Dead watched over us making my skin crawl and my stomach burn with worry.

I stepped inside another inner chamber. A granite sarcophagus waited—still, eternal, like the mummy inside. The singing that often rose inside my head since my recovery from the drowning suddenly silenced.

My breathing quickened and my heart raced as I stood frozen in fear and awe. "We do not touch the sarcophagus." Sculpted stone rested atop the granite—an ovoid ball not attached to the sarcophagus. A wooden handle stuck out of the stone ball. I exhaled and crept forward. Upon this stone sphere were images of a man towering over his enemies, smiting them with this very object—a mace head or club. Images of scorpions surrounded the conqueror, as well as a message: *The Scorpion King—the legendary King Menes, who was granted the first pharaoh's throne from the god Horus.*

My toes curled into my sandals. Scorpions, like with Akhenaten's false plague and—

"I do not think that the deceased pharaoh will forgive us for only leaving his remains alone," Paramessu said. The breath coming from his lips turned cloudy, as if the air around us were freezing.

Perhaps this mace was the weapon that the magician had said I'd need …

I snatched the wooden handle of the engraved mace. The skin of my palm grew cold, as if the wood were encased in snow—like the mountain peak on the island of the Sea People. I shoved the weapon into the sack the magician had given me and searched the remaining chambers, including another chamber just beyond Pharaoh's burial chamber—the treasure room. The entire space inside was packed with gold.

Working for weeks, we loaded up treasure and hauled it away on our carts, packing it onto our boat and covering it with cloth. Harkhuf remained at our vessel to guard it as the rest of us continued emptying the tomb. At night or in the early mornings, I continued my conditioning and reading, although with each passing day, my mind filled with more and more images of facing Akhenaten and Nefertiti—so close now.

✳ ✳ ✳

After our ship of the Sea People hung low in the water, as if it would sink if we loaded any more gold, we sailed north upon the Nile.

I steered our vessel, my lengthening hair blowing in the wind, brushing my cheeks and bringing a hint of moisture to my skin. Only the occasional cacophony of ducks protesting our passage interrupted the howling of the wind.

The midday Aten's heat rained upon us as the first farm and houses appeared off in the distance, beyond the fertile banks of the western shore. I settled our vessel against the bank, and Seneb unloaded a horse and cart. He and Harkhuf marched with the horse for the largest house in the distance. I trailed behind.

We hiked through cracking fields—the time of the desert rains did not coincide with the annual inundation, the yearly flooding of the Nile. And I never understood how the Aten made water work in such a way.

Dust drifted into the air around me in clouds sent up from the wheels of the cart, bringing grit into my eyes and nostrils. Farmhands stopped in the middle of tilling fields or carrying buckets of water from the river and stared. The skin of their shoulders and back were so darkened by the Aten, I could not tell if they were Egyptian or Nubian, and their faces were as wrinkled as untended leather.

Shouting arose from the largest house in the distance. A middle-aged man with streaks of gray running through his black hair rushed out, shouting at the workers in the field and waving his arms. Two younger men followed at his heels.

"If the grains do not grow, you do not eat," the older man bellowed, raising a flail as he approached a worker.

The worker crouched down and dug into the earth again with a bronze tool.

"This is my farm," the man with the flail said, approaching us, his bodyguards or sons flanking him. "Who are you and why are you distracting my workers?" He looked over the dwarves at me as he stepped closer.

Harkhuf stopped him by holding up a hand.

"You are that man's entertainment, nothing more than an acrobatic jester," the farm owner said to Harkhuf as he pointed at me and waved his hand, indicating for Harkhuf to step aside. Harkhuf didn't budge. "I demand to know why your master is on my farm. I cannot offer any free meals at this time. The land has grown selfish."

"My master"—Harkhuf folded his arms across his massive chest—"wishes to purchase your farm from you."

I stopped and waited in the distance, hiding my smirk.

The farm owner laughed. "This land is not worth it. Too much work for too little reward, and much of what I grow is taken from me, shipped directly to el-Amarna. The earth here used to give us so much when I was a child, but still my property is vast, and no man who desires to live way out here could compensate me for it. This is where most of the food of the region comes from, and what would I—?"

Harkhuf held up his hand and silenced the farm owner. "As well as purchasing all of your workers."

The young men at the farm owner's back scowled and approached the dwarf, towering over him. One grabbed the flail from his father.

The son raised the flail over his head. "I will teach this Nubian midget some respect."

My body tensed. If he struck Harkhuf, Harkhuf might retaliate—which could be lethal. I jogged up to them.

Harkhuf's triceps contracted into horseshoes of striated muscle as he reached back.

"No—" I shouted.

Harkhuf instead yanked something from the cart, from beneath the cloth that covered the inner contents. The object now in his hands glowed like flames, glittering in the rays of the Aten—a scepter of solid gold.

The son with the flail froze, and his weapon fell to the ground with a quiet thud as he stared into the cart. The farm owner fell to his knees, his face as white as the woman's with the fish tail—the one who resided in the lake and who had drowned me.

Chapter 10

Journal Translation

THE FARM OWNER, HIS WIFE, daughters, and sons rode several skiffs down the Nile, their vessels loaded up with payment for the farm. They would live in luxury, somewhere far away.

I walked to one of the farm's giant storehouses. The double doors hung at an angle, fitting poorly against the mud bricks, as if they hadn't been repaired in many seasons. I yanked open the doors, which wobbled on their hinges, nearly falling off in my hands, and creaked like an old man's bones.

Empty. No grain at all, only dirt and scattered pieces of chaff. Dust particles floated into the air, and my nose itched. My body jerked and I sneezed, the sound echoing around the inside of the mud-brick chamber.

I investigated another storehouse, and another—either empty or minimally filled with ankle-deep levels of grain.

My companions and I secretly transferred all of the gold that our boat had carried in covered carts to the empty storage buildings. Then we hid the treasure by pouring what grain the farm still had on top of it, the sprinkling of grain on metal pinging in my ears before the gold was buried. If one of the farmhands looked inside a storehouse, they wouldn't suspect anything out of the ordinary, perhaps only that we'd transferred our grain stores from a previous farm to this one.

The following day, and over the next several weeks, we returned to the tomb of Amenhotep several more times, emptying all of the treasure except for the sarcophagus. We stashed nearly all of the boatloads of gold at the farm but kept a few pieces onboard in preparation for our return to el-Amarna.

The night after we'd finally finished stowing away the treasure, my companions sat around a crackling bonfire at the edge of the fields. A bouquet of smoke, robust drink, and baked bread wafted across the desert. They consumed food as if they'd been starved for months and guzzled wine from the farm's cellar. I sat against the side of the main house, alone, and twirled my deep blue ostrich feather between my fingers, its surfaces glowing and fading in the light of the flames. Even Croc was here, but he lay like a loaf of bread beside the fire, his eyes closed, content. His tongue lolled out, and he turned to lick at his rear leg, the one with the scar and draining wound. One day soon he'd have to let me look at it, but I didn't know how I could; he'd just bite me and run off again.

Wahankh bellowed, stumbling to the edge of the fire. He danced and shimmied around the flames, looking at the stars, his arms spread wide, a bottle in each hand.

I'd never seen him act in such a way. He was always quiet and reserved, holding back. Was he … happy? Did he finally feel safe, part of a family, like he belonged somewhere? My stomach cramped. I did not, not here.

"Come, we have plenty to eat and drink," Tia shouted into the night. In the distance, farmhands gathered in the shadows around their own fires beside a cluster of small huts.

Heads turned in our direction, curious eyes standing out as reflections in the darkness.

Tia motioned for them to come to the bonfire. "Join us."

One woman stood and led two children by the hand. Together, they slowly walked across the distance, their eyes wide, as if afraid this was a trick. Other families stood and trailed behind them. The light of our bonfire lit up their taut faces as they shuffled closer and closer.

Harkhuf held two loaves in outstretched arms. "Have some bread."

The children, two young girls, hid behind their mother.

"What is that wide, dark child with a beard, Mother?" one girl asked, clutching her mother's dirty dress as she peeked around her waist.

Harkhuf straightened, his teeth grinding together with a sound similar to stone grating on stone. His nostrils flared as he heaved for breath, but his arms fell to his sides.

Was he insulted, like when his tribe would not accept him as a warrior because of his height?

Then Harkhuf fell to his knees and held the food out before him—an offering.

The mother, a woman with tangled hair and a fraying dress, took the bread and gave it to her daughters. The one who'd spoken shouted and jumped up and down. "Thank you, dark boy," she said.

Harkhuf huffed and bowed his head.

About twenty men cautiously approached, leading their families.

How many people lived on this farm in these tiny huts?

"Come and sit by the fire," Tia said, waving them closer.

Families circled around our crackling blaze as Tia, Harkhuf, Seneb, and Paramessu handed out food and drink. Sun-wrinkled faces broke into smiles as they chomped on crusty bread. Seneb started dancing, stomping, and clapping to a rhythmic beat. Laughter erupted from the children. Seneb slid over to his brother's side and pointed to Harkhuf.

"Oh, no," Harkhuf grumbled. "I disposed of our former master so that we wouldn't ever have to dance again."

"Angry, like a daddy lion with nine cubs trying to suckle him," Seneb said. He smiled a boyish grin, ran, and back-flipped four times across the desert before leaping into the air and spinning. He landed firmly on his feet with a thud and threw his hands up into the air.

Men, women, and children burst into applause, and their laughter stretched across the farm. Then they too danced and sang.

The corner of my lips almost lifted into a grin, but my forehead furrowed. I was delaying everything I'd meant to do. My musings of Akhenaten and Nefertiti returned, their faces filling my mind. But after my companions and I departed, would these farmhands find the gold and take it all for themselves? Perhaps I should leave someone here when I sailed for—

"Why aren't you joining in the celebrations?" Paramessu asked, dropping down into the dirt beside me.

I stared blankly off into the night sky, studying the moon and its face—haunting, like that of Akhenaten's, with the black paint surrounding his eyes.

"I see them all around us," I whispered under my breath, trying to ignore images of linen-wrapped heads with glowing green eyes floating in the darkness. "The Dark Ones, the devoured souls of the dead."

"You should be the happiest of anyone," he replied, as if he didn't understand. "We all know that the gold is rightfully yours. The brothers and I, Tia and Wahankh, we are all indebted to you. Your treasure is safe here. And the farmhands wouldn't dare take any. Please, enjoy yourself. This is the time; there is much to celebrate."

I recalled some of the magician's words from long ago—when he realized how much my need for vengeance consumed me. And the emotion had not receded over the years. "My insides rot like decay is festering within my heart and spreading through my bones." More haunting images formed in my mind—the tangled spider web of lines crossing the magician's face. "The fetid disease that I wish upon my enemies lives within me. Perhaps I shouldn't have let the world alter the morality I carried as a child. But soon the decay will burst through and consume my flesh. Then it will spread to the rest of you."

Paramessu stopped breathing and scooted away, studying me. After all these years, he had finally glimpsed the ugly beast that I really was.

"I have lived with this and masked my insides for longer than I've known you, my friend," I said. "And its toll has ravaged my body and soul. I will never recover."

"By the Aten," Paramessu swore. "I have never heard of such poison. Surely, you have all that you could ever need now. Look around you. Family, friends, more wealth than anyone but the god-king himself. You could live in happiness the rest of your days and be surrounded by those who … love you."

My stomach spasmed and released acid that burned and twisted my insides.

"How can we help you?" he asked.

"You cannot help. Confronting my demons will not cure me," I replied, "it will only lead to my death. No material possessions, friends, or family—not even the undying love of Nefertiti—can save me now. This has gone on for too long, taken hold in my soul, and become part of me."

Shocked silence followed. "H-how did all of this begin?"

"You are more than welcome to stay here with Tia and build a life," I said. "If you come with me tomorrow, you will see … but you might not return. Tomorrow I travel back to el-Amarna."

Chapter 11

Journal Translation

I BATHED IN HEATED RIVER water the following morning, the warm
liquid soaking through the dirt and grime smeared into my skin.
After dressing in the finest white kilt the farm owner possessed, I also
discarded the worn sandals I'd had since before I was a slave and slipped
my feet into new, barely worn leather replacements.

The others followed my lead, bathing and dressing, and stepped outside of the main house. Wahankh held his forehead and leaned against the
mud-brick wall, as if in pain from his celebrating. He groaned.

I glanced around the surrounding farmland, studying the morning
Aten and its yellow light. After inhaling a deep breath of clean air, I slowly
let it out. I must leave, for Father, for Nefertiti, and for all of Egypt.

Reaching up to an open windowsill of the house, I scooped up Croc,
who slept in the warm sunlight. He felt lighter than normal, his joints knob-
bier, and he didn't even open his eyes. I led my companions to the river and
boarded our Sea People's boat. Seneb loaded the two horses and carts into
the hull near the stern.

The howling wind assaulted my ears as I stared into the vast ribbon of
blue water without a beginning or end. Birds chirped and sang along the
shoreline, flittering about in the brush. The other companions dawdled,
gathering their gear so slowly that it became obvious a part of them would
rather stay behind.

I waved at the farmhands and their families in the distance. They
smiled and waved back. Would they be happier alone, working without
oversight? Tightness rose in my throat—the feeling I'd lived with when I was
constantly under Akhenaten's supervision. Would ridding someone of that

feeling make life less taxing and grant them added energy to help save the farm and feed all of its workers? Perhaps I would find out when we returned.

The current grabbed our boat with a swift tug, and I angled the rudder to steer us into the river's belly. I pointed us north.

We sailed for days and nights amidst the gentle rocking of the Nile. I'd grown so accustomed to sailing during the dark, with Akhenaten's inexplicable commands and when fleeing the Egyptian military, that I didn't see a need to stop—especially since Tia knew how to steer and we could trade off sleeping and navigating.

Desert spread out in the twilight all around us, interrupted only by the hills to the east and west. A whisper of music played in my head—a *sistra* rattle, a drum, and stringed instruments. Where did this noise come from, and why did it keep occurring? Was it only my imagination, or was I still connected to the underworld, a piece of me still there hearing the music or voices of the dead? Slow beats registered over the gusting wind that my brain tuned out.

Tia took the rudder from me and nudged my shoulder. "Why do we to return to el-Amarna?"

My eyes popped open, having shut on their own. A book tumbled from my lap and hit the hull with a smack. Croc meowed in surprise, his body curled up at my feet. Moonlight shimmered against the waves around us as exhaustion crept through my body like locusts through a field.

"Go lie down." Tia pushed me away. "But eventually we will need to know what we're trying to accomplish by returning to that city we helped build. I realize that after all these years, no one may recognize us, but we are all still taking on a great risk. You cannot expect the others to throw their lives away now without an explanation, an estimate of how long we will be staying, and what we need to accomplish before you will find peace. Not letting us know these things was how Chisisi tried to lead us, remember?"

I lay down on the hull, and my eyelids dropped closed. "You should just drop me off and be on your way with the others. We all may be traveling to our deaths."

Tia kicked my leg with the leather toe of her sandal. "You can't push us away; you've already tried too many times. I will see you overcome whatever demon you have waiting from your past life as you did for each of us. And I will see Paramessu vanquish his so that I can stop watching him lie awake at night staring into the nothingness of the dark."

I pictured Akhenaten and his hulking bodyguard, Suty, murdering everyone who stood against them. Then Chisisi's thin features appeared in my mind, framed by long hair. His decisions with the crocodile in the lake could have cost Seneb, if not all of us, our lives—all because he wanted to gain a group of faithful followers. Where in Egypt had he wandered off to? "I will not lead through intimidation and fear, nor manipulation or lies. I go to el-Amarna to rescue the queen of Egypt, my one love, Nefertiti, from the god-king himself."

Tia gasped, her inhaling breath sharper than the wind. "How do you hope to ever accomplish this?"

I rolled over, faced away from her, and squeezed my eyes shut. Should I dare tell her or the companions about my other need—the need for revenge against my former master and his minions? No, at least not yet.

Tia rustled around by the rudder and muttered, as if she wanted to ask or say more but couldn't.

Dreams eventually took me and raged along with the rising music inside my head, which became an orchestra.

Light tore through my eyelids, rousing me. I groaned and sat up, looking to the desert. Emptiness surrounded us. We were far from any of the old cities, nearing the midway point between the capitals of Memphis in the north and Thebes in the south. That meant that el-Amarna would soon emerge along the banks of the Nile.

"Why?" Wahankh shouted over the wind.

The others had gathered at the stern with Tia, whispering to each other. I clenched my jaw. They would be discussing my intentions for our return and weighing the risks. Did they all doubt my abilities as a leader? Maybe they should; I had never been good at it. I had only wanted to travel my own path, free to choose my own life.

I turned and faced north, allowing my companions to converse and make their own decisions. A mountain range clawed at the horizon with jagged peaks. Two of the tallest lay beside each other, unmistakable. This was the enclosure for the forbidden city of the rising Aten, the cradle where the Aten rose every morning to bring life-giving rays to our world.

The deep drumming that rang inside my head grew louder, the tempo quickening. Wind instruments whistled in beautiful harmony, amplifying. The banks of the city approached too quickly, as if the time bender's magic were speeding up the rate of time's passage all around me.

My fingers dug into my white kilt, wrinkling the silky fabric and gouging into my tense thighs.

Our bow veered and pointed at the shore. I swallowed. Drums deafened me.

We settled onto the bank. My head spun, lights and images swirling in a haze. But I stumbled out of the boat before falling to my knees, my skin and bones sinking into the mud. My hands clawed and shuffled for dry land. The horizon teetered and dipped to my left. My head pounded, as if the worst headache I'd ever experienced raged battle with my brain. What was happening? I clung to Father's bracelet as an aid.

"This is our last chance to turn back," Wahankh said, reaching out for me. "Take us somewhere else, please."

I scrambled on all fours until I felt the dry dust of the desert. My fingers sank into the scalding sand, the pain bringing clarity.

The drums beat one last time, so loudly that I thought my head might explode. My eyes clamped shut. Then silence.

I pulled out a crinkling papyrus but instead spoke the spell of the Mask on the magician's treasure note from memory, tracing those arcane symbols in the air as I muttered. Energy carried up my fingers, through my arms and body, and settled into the left side of my face with a burning sensation. The air around me vibrated and turned warm. I grimaced in pain.

Chords started in, the sweet hum of strings and the harp, followed by a crescendo of whistling notes from flutes.

I stood, rising slowly, as if I could collapse from my madness at any second. I cracked my eyelids.

The horizon settled and the city emerged. Expansive, mud-brick buildings crawled across the land like a disease. Towers and pillars reached for the clouded sky, attempting to celebrate the Aten—now the only god of Egypt. And Akhenaten had become one with the Aten.

I slowly lifted my head, my eyes fully opening as I scanned the area. Standing straight and proud, I inhaled, breathing in the nostalgia and memories, both horrendous and good. My jaw clenched, along with my fists.

I had returned.

Home.

Chapter 12

Present Day

I YAWNED AND STRETCHED OUT against my sagging mattress inside my mom's house in the Pacific Northwest. A kink in my lower back shot a twinge of pain up my spine. I grimaced and rolled over. The mattress squeaked and rattled. Muted light crept through the closed blinds of the single window. The clock on the stand beside my bed glowed with faint green numbers—eleven thirty-eight in the morning ... and I was just waking up.

It'd been about two months or so since I'd originally left this place to fly to Egypt and start a short rotation with Doctors Without Borders, a rotation I'd completed prior to meeting up with Maddie and enticing her into searching for the Hall with me.

Almost another week had passed since I'd arrived home and moved back in with my mom. I'd had plenty of free time, but my reading of the journal translation had slowed down—I didn't care as much about Heb's life and outcome now. It didn't seem like it would affect mine in any lasting way, and I'd never know the real ending, as the journal was incomplete, the story fading in the middle of its last ancient sentence. But a memory flashed through my mind: dark twisting stairs leading me into the roots of the pyramid mountain, the lost tomb of Amenhotep that had kicked off our journey in Egypt. I could hear my feet slapping the hard rock of the stairs, Maddie beside me, and we descended. Our flashlight beams pierced the blackness but only found empty rooms, devoid of any ancient artifacts. A vision of Heb and his friends removing the loot followed. Shock and awe settled over me like a splash of icy water. Our dreams of grandeur vanished because of them. I couldn't imagine a better use for the treasure than to help rid the world of Akhenaten, but Heb was bound to lose, as his name and memory hadn't survived from the time of ancient Egypt.

The only thing I'd accomplished since I'd returned home was applying to be reaccepted into my fourth year of medical school or to start my clinical rotations with the following year's class, but I'd had to face up for my past mistakes at school. And I'd decided it would best for my future career and conscience to tell the administration of Dr. Banks's and my mistake of amputating the incorrect foot of the elderly diabetic woman's and then altering the medical records to cover it up. And I'd told them of Dr. Banks and his nurse threatening me that if I didn't help, they'd accuse me of stealing opioids from the hospital. Unfortunately, that forced me to attend some kind of half-day-long deposition in front of several administrator types at the medical school. The last thing a woman in a suit who sat on the other side of a long table said was, "This conversation doesn't leave this room. Don't speak of this to anyone, not the press, not your girlfriend, and not even your mother. Reaccepting you will depend on what our investigation uncovers and how you handle the situation."

But I hadn't heard anything from them about reinstatement, and I hadn't heard from Maddie. I didn't want to get up and go downstairs, or my mom would pester me with all the same questions about if I'd heard anything from the med school.

My vision blurred as I yawned again and stared at the ceiling, my mind forming images in the irregularities of the texture.

I imagined myself finishing med school, marching up the stairs to the main stage in a crowded auditorium. Some old man in a graduation gown and weird cap would shove a wooden frame into my open palm, say my full name for the first time in his life into a microphone that would echo around the massive chamber, and shake my other hand with a strong grip. Applause would erupt from the audience, reverberating inside the room, and I'd smile and beam for all the photographs my mom would want to take. I'd glance down at the frame in my hand and see the diploma and M.D. initials after my name. A sense of accomplishment would fill my chest for a moment but not one of pride or happiness. I'd march off the stage on my heeled shoes to make way for the next one of my hundred-plus classmates, and one my guy friends would come up and slap me on the back and shout, "Gavin, you're a doctor."

I'd nod and reply, "You too, Dr. Thompson." We'd laugh and head out for drinks with our entire class—one last hurrah before never seeing most of them again. But while I was sipping crisp wine with a light fruit bouquet and mingling but mostly listening to stories and words of advice from family and peers without much to say myself, I'd see something on the label of a wine bottle, something old, ancient, an image … A hieroglyph trying to relate something in its name to ancient Egypt.

An epiphany would strike my brain like a bolt of lightning. I'd recall how the last clue on the path to the Hall had led us to the Faiyum. We'd taken a detour when we discovered that Maddie was held nearby, but still, afterward, we'd searched the entire area and the skeleton of the enormous crocodile buried beneath the ancient cliff painting of the same animal. But right then, something would unlock in my mind. I'd race out of the reception, fling open a pair of double doors that would smack into brick walls, and leap down stairs to the walk outside. Darkness would surround me as I called Maddie. She'd answer, "Gavin?" I'd reply, "Maddie, I figured it out. I don't know why after all this time, but it finally sank in. We need to go back to Egypt, back to the Faiyum." Then she'd say, "I'm in town; let's meet up and talk about it."

She'd be waiting for me at a corner table in a small coffee shop. The little bell would ring as I'd swing the door of the café open and step inside, stopping as I saw her. She'd hurry over and wrap me up in a giant hug—buried emotion and love resurfacing. We'd sit, and I'd play the video footage that I'd taken at the oasis on my phone. Something would stand out in the red light of sunset, and I'd point to it and explain the obscure clue and its meaning. Maddie would jump up and down and plant a tender kiss on my cheek. We'd race out of the café, headed back to Egypt to uncover the secret location of the legendary Hall of Records …

I stared at my phone lying on the dark wood of my bedside table and returned to the present and my mom's house. How many times in the last week had I started to write a text or stared at Maddie's phone number but couldn't bring myself to push the call button. I'd type out a long text asking about how she was doing, that I wished she was feeling okay, and that I hoped to see her again soon. Then I'd edit the message for fifteen minutes and end up with something as simple as 'I hope you are doing well.' But I still wouldn't send it. Partly because she wanted me to leave her alone, and partly because I was afraid of her response.

I'd also texted a college friend of mine the other day—a guy who'd recently become a paramedic and rode around in an ambulance—and asked if I could ride along with him for some medical experience. That would look good for the school.

A new text message waited, from Aiden: 'Hey, haven't heard from you in a fat minute. Kaylin said Maddie's boyfriend flew out here and is going to surprise her I guess. What a douche. I think we're going out for drinks tonight if you're around, unless you're still working on cracking that last clue.'

My stomach churned, Maddie's *boyfriend*? Since when? Since before our entire ordeal had begun? She'd never mentioned him while I was there. Maybe that was why she'd wanted me to leave, so she could be alone with him. There wasn't anything I could do now anyway. And I guess I hadn't even told Aiden that I'd left Egypt and flown home—too disappointed after my last discussion with Maddie.

I sighed as I sat up, and the mattress under me creaked. My stomach cramped, but the tightness receded a moment later. I'd had an infusion a few days ago, so hopefully the pain from my Crohn's disease would be under control soon and this cramping would stop … unless too much inflammation had built up from skipping out on treatments while in Egypt.

My fingers reached out for my bracelet, seeking the comfort it brought me, but they only found the bare skin of my forearm and wrist. Oh, yeah, I'd given my dad's gift to some random Egyptian kid. Regret burned in my heart as I pictured my deceased dad and our final times together. I didn't want to end up like him, crippled from his disease—the disease we both carried—unable to even care for himself.

The blaring horns on my phone announced another incoming message from Aiden. They must already be going out, as Cairo was nine hours ahead of my current time zone. I could see Aiden texting me as Kaylin would fling her blond hair back over her shoulders and march on, clapping high heels down the lighted sidewalk beside Mr. Scalone, the treasure hunter. Both

Kaylin's dad and Mr. Scalone were probably trying to locate the Hall of Records for themselves. I could see Mr. Scalone's myriad of tattoos covering his muscled arms, his shirt only buttoned at the bottom so that his rippling abs were exposed. Kaylin would be texting on her phone and smoothing out her dress as Mr. Scalone would be trying to impress her with some tale of his bravery on some past adventure of his, saying in his thick Italian accent something like, "Reminds me of the time I single-handedly had to save two naked women from a pouncing lion in Tanzania by tackling it just before it sprang." They'd wait outside some bar for Maddie and her boyfriend before—

I shook my head and looked at the new message. It was from Kaylin this time. 'If you've gone back to finish med school, congrats. I think you'll make a good doctor.'

What did that mean? That I wouldn't be a good Egyptologist, or that I hadn't helped find enough answers to the clues and let her down?

I could picture Mr. Scalone laughing as Kaylin sent the message. He'd jerk his head to toss his gelled locks back over his shoulders and rub at the thick stubble ravaging his face. He'd say, "That kid needs to give up. He won't ever amount to anything."

'I flew back home,' I texted back.

My phone blared again; it was Aiden. 'Whoa, dude. Kaylin said you flew home and didn't even tell me, what's with that?'

I dropped my phone and stumbled out of my bed, my bare feet pressing against the cold wood of the floorboards. The boards creaked. Shaking my head cleared some of the fog suffocating my brain. I wandered for my doorway, rubbing my forehead. My toes jammed into something hard, which scooted across the floor with a whoosh, and a throbbing pain radiated up from my little toe. I winced, grabbed my toe, and hopped up and down.

A brown cardboard box about the size of a backpack sat on the hardwood floor—all of the clues we'd worked on, papers, pictures, and memories of my trip to Egypt were trapped inside. I should just get rid of it all so that I could stop thinking about everything: Maddie and now her boyfriend, the Hall of Records, our time together in Egypt. Move on. Maddie had made her choice, and it had never been me. I had to accept that and stop fooling myself. That would be the healthiest thing to do. I picked up the box, tromped down the stairs, and threw open the sliding glass back door with a rolling sound of metal wheels.

"Gavin?" my mom's tense voice carried from another room. "Are you going into school today?"

I shook my head but didn't respond.

The damp chill of a Pacific Northwest autumn stung the exposed skin of my face and arms as I trudged to the nearby metal garbage can. Ripping off the lid of the garbage can created a hollow ring within the empty inner barrel.

I reached out and held the box over the opening as if I were about to feed the heart of my past life to the Devouring Monster itself. Images of Dad's face floated through my mind. My hands trembled, and I tried to let go of my box, but I couldn't. I shouldn't get rid of Dr. Shelsher's letter and all the notes I'd taken from actually visiting the ancient sites, ones I once had thought I might never see in real life.

I slammed the metal lid of the garbage can back down. Maybe I could just hide everything up in the attic so that I wouldn't be reminded of it all until time had long dulled my emotions. Then I could relive the memories in my later years. My entire future was a blank slate now, completely empty. A shudder of fear and uncertainty rolled up my spine.

As I shuffled back inside the house, Mom—now a frighteningly thin middle-aged woman—appeared at the open doorway between the kitchen and living room. "Gavin?"

"Not now, Mom," I said as I ran back for the creaking stairs. I stepped onto the second floor of the house, and something brushed the short hair on top of my head.

The rope to pull down the sliding ladder leading up to the attic hung just above my head. I stared for a minute. Grabbing the rope, I tugged, and the panel and ladder swung down and unfolded, revealing a dark entrance into the ceiling.

I clung to the dry wood of the cracking rungs and scaled up the steps that bowed beneath my feet. Darkness engulfed my head. Something brushed against my face, and I jerked away as I threw one hand up in defense. A string swung back against my palm. I tugged on it, and a single bulb illuminated the slanting walls inside the roof of the house with pale light. Pink fluff insulation and angling shadows surrounded a small walkway, and a few boxes sat at the far end near a slatted vent in the outer wall.

With my box in hand, I inched across creaking slats of wood that made up the narrow walk, headed for the stack of boxes. I held my breath, the air heavy up here and thick with stagnant dust, also a musty smell. I grunted as I plopped my stuff down on top of another box and brushed off my hands, wiping my thoughts and memories away with—

A single word was scribbled across the outside of the box beneath mine: Russ, my dad's nickname. Was that dad's stuff, the things that mom couldn't force herself to part with?

I moved my box onto the top of the stack next to it and opened the interfolded four flaps of the box marked with Dad's name. The stiff cardboard rubbed together and released a high-pitched grating sound that made me cringe. But I peeked inside … piles of envelopes and pictures that my dad had sent to my mom many years before. I grabbed a stack and shuffled through them.

Faded pictures of foreign cities: attractions, my dad sporting his famous moustache and standing in front of buildings, groups of people with him—those whom he was helping by selling them low-cost used medical equipment that would've been destroyed in the States.

I dug through a few other objects: a rough Turkish blanket, an African mask that looked like a scared monster, a bowl and reed pen—these were Egyptian and ancient. Stuck inside the bowl, a Post-it simply read: *My love, write to me if I pass before you.*

I froze. The reed pen and bowl that ancient Egyptians used to write letters to the dead, how Heb had written to his deceased father when he was in slavery in el-Amarna. My dad left this for my mom. And she probably never understood it, never looked at it, or she thought it was some cute joke from when she used to love him.

Writing a letter to my dad on the surface of a bowl and filling it with the earthly items he liked to consume—to feed his soul for a quick visit—had to be utter nonsense … But I wanted to talk to him so badly, to ask for forgiveness and tell him that I'd loved him all along and that I'd tried everything I could think of to find the Hall.

I located a small flask of ink inside the box, removed the stopper, and dipped the reed pen inside. The ink seemed to suck the pen deeper, attempting to swallow it—thick ink like oil, but white, and it crawled up the pen as if it knew its purpose.

After yanking the pen out, I wrote words onto the outer surface of the bowl in hieroglyphs. I'd pen a final letter to Dad about how I shouldn't have turned away from him just to spite him, the dark turns in my life and where I was, and that I needed his help and advice.

How alike Dad and I were to Heb and his father. If only I could share the discovery and the entire story with my dad. And, Heb, how I wished to talk to you, to consult on your hardships and resilience and encourage you with all your being to continue to fight Akhenaten and not leave to find an easier life, or worse, accept his madness.

I worked feverishly, recalling so many hieroglyphs from the translation of the tale that I barely even registered what I wrote. The reed pen scratched along the outer surface of the bowl until every writable surface was full. I clambered down the ladder and raced off to find his favorite beer—the one that always coated his moustache in bubbly film.

I ran downstairs to the cramped kitchen with spotless tile counters, not knowing if my mom would keep any kind of beer on hand. My trembling fingers grasped the cold handle of the white refrigerator door and yanked it open with a squeak ... Leafy green vegetables and red strawberries in plastic bins, a carton of eggs, three open cans of cat food ...

"Gavin, what are you doing?" My mom stood at the doorway again and folded her arms as she glared at me. "Shouldn't you give the school a call and just see what's happening?"

I sighed as I scooted aside a carton of almond milk. One brown bottle sat at the back corner, as if in hiding or in shame, as if my mom couldn't force herself to throw it out even after all these years, like the box in the attic. I hoped she wouldn't mind me taking the beer, but there would probably never be a better use for it than to have my dad's soul drink it—if that were remotely possible. I snatched the chill glass of the bottle and hid it from her view behind the crinkling wrappings of a leftover sub sandwich.

I'd return to the attic and fill that bowl up to its brim.

My phone blared with the sound of a horn—an incoming text from my paramedic friend: 'Sure. I asked my boss and she said since you're a med student you can ride along and help where you can. I have a shift tonight. It's probably not going to be as exciting as you're thinking though.'

Chapter 13

Present Day

I SAT SEAT BELTED INTO the back seat—placed against the front partition—of an ambulance cabin, facing the rear doors. Our red emergency lights intermittently flashed through the darkness outside our windows, accompanied by the muted splatter of pounding rain. The metal floor jostled and vibrated under my feet, and the rattle of emergency equipment and the stretcher in front of me rang in my ears. My paramedic friend, Sam, a short Asian-American guy with black hair and small glasses, sat up front in the passenger seat, his driver at the wheel. We bounded along a city street as yellow headlights and red brake lights from cars pulling over in front of us shone through the windshield and reflected off the rear windows.

My limbs were tense as I tried to look out and see what was going on. I'd only recently met up with Sam outside his station, and we'd been immediately sent out on a call.

"It might not be boring tonight," Sam shouted back to me. "Good night to tag along."

I twisted my head around to see him. "This isn't typical?"

Sam listened to an emergency radio of some sort, the voices muffled by the rattles around me.

Sam glanced over his shoulder. "We always get accidents, but most are just fender benders. This one sounds bad. A semi-truck jackknifed on the freeway and slid across several lanes. It took out a few cars." He flicked something, and a muffled scream from our siren rang overhead.

I attempted to see out the windshield, but only blurred lights showed through, rain droplets splattering across the glass as fast as the wipers swept them away. This was the life I was choosing now, and I had to make the best of it.

"Too much traffic, and they're not gettin' outta the way," the driver, a stout African American woman named Makayla, said. She honked repeatedly.

"There's nowhere for them to go," Sam replied. "Every lane's jammed up."

My upper body was yanked to the left as our ambulance swerved and crawled along on the shoulder between lines of stopped headlights and brake lights and the median.

"There," Sam shouted.

The night outside seemed to light up as a flood of yellow washed over the windows.

Sam squeezed my shoulder. "We're going to stop in just a second. You can follow me with a backboard. I'm not sure what we'll be doing yet and if we'll need the stretcher. There're a lot of trucks already here."

I studied the metal frame of the stretcher in front of me. Would I be riding back with someone in here with me, administering fluids, medications?

The ambulance jerked to a halt, flinging me against the seat, and our siren fell silent.

Sam popped the handle on his door and leapt outside.

I released my seatbelt, jumped up, and threw open the back doors.

Flashing red, blue, and yellow lights blinded me as I stumbled down the step on the bumper and fell onto my left knee with a smack and a shot of pain. I grimaced and stood up, hobbling around the side of the ambulance to the outer compartment where Sam had showed me the backboards were stored. Police cars, fire trucks, and another ambulance or two pulled in or already surrounded us. Shouting voices carried from every direction.

I pulled the metal handle of the side compartment door and yanked it open. Several backboards were stacked inside—green, yellow, orange.

"Gavin," Sam said. "Grab one and get over here."

I grabbed the green one and spun around. Sam was already marching for a semi-truck trailer parked lengthwise across three lanes of the freeway. Cars had smashed into each other in a pile-up, with crushed hoods and bumpers. Officers were opening doors, and Sam continued past them, knocking on a window and looking in before jogging to the truck trailer. I ran after him.

He stopped. A silver car and a blue SUV were smashed into the wheels of the trailer. A firefighter turned on a screaming saw and another lifted metal bars, trying to get the door off of the SUV.

I froze. Another car was impaled at an angle beneath the rear of the semi-truck trailer, the driver's side of the vehicle shorn off at the level of the windshield through the area of the front seat. The hood of the car was buried beneath the trailer. No one was looking in there …

I ran around to the uncrushed passenger side.

The passenger door was wide open, calling me onward. Sweat caked my palms, making my grip on the backboard slick. The uneasy tingle of dread filled my core as I approached. A woman with long brown hair sat still buckled into the passenger seat, her head and arms hanging limp. Blood was splattered across her face and neck, her eyes closed. Her head dangled at a lifeless angle. My heart sank into my stomach, and my throat clamped shut as I gasped for air.

Somehow, I managed to inch closer and knelt so that I could try to see her face and check for a pulse. A vision flashed through my mind, a recent memory in a similar situation: Bloodied surgical instruments had littered a green-tiled room and the stench of formaldehyde had funneled into my nose and turned my stomach. Bodies lay beneath sheets on metal tables … An Egyptian detective stopped beside a body, pivoted around to face me, and crossed his arms. He reached for the sheet, the one I thought Maddie's body had lain under. The detective flung the sheet aside to reveal the face …

Maddie … But Maddie was still in Egypt and could be in danger if she continued to look for the Hall by herself. And it didn't seem like she had completely given up. She could be hurt, like this woman in the car, and I'd just left her there alone.

My stomach cramped, as if in a vice, and vomit poured out of my lips, splattering onto the street.

I leaned against the smashed car to steady myself and shook my head to clear the memory. Glasses with black frames lay on the street below the car wreck victim, glasses like Maddie's, those I'd returned to her after I'd rescued her from the abduction. I'd placed those around her ears as the sun had risen and shone through the doorway of the ancient temple, and she'd smiled and kissed—

Some muffled sound called out from inside the car. My body tensed as I forced myself to look back inside.

The driver's area was a mess of metal, and I couldn't make myself look at it in detail. But something was in the rear seat, on the driver's side—a child seat. A redheaded kid hung against his shoulder belts with his head down, sobbing uncontrollably.

I leaned into the vehicle, across the woman. "You're going to be—"

The woman lurched forward and hit my side, coughing. Blood sprayed from her mouth across my face in a red mist. I jerked and stumbled backward, reeling as I fell onto the street and smacked my head. My vision lit up with white light but was then swallowed by darkness.

Chapter 14

Present Day

THE NIGHT OF MY FIRST ambulance ride, I awoke as Sam and another man I didn't recognize helped lift me out of the back of their ambulance with the rattle of metal and then the rumble of wheels on concrete. My head throbbed, and a radiating pain spread along the back of my skull. A metallic taste coated my mouth. I attempted to sit up, but I was strapped down on a stretcher, the tie across my waist biting into my skin. Bright lights glowed ahead, above sliding double doors: the emergency entrance to a hospital. I groaned.

"Gavin," Sam said, placing a comforting hand on my chest as he rolled me to the entrance. The doors slid open with a whoosh and they rushed me inside, through a lobby teeming with people hovering around the front desk and asking questions about family members. "You scared me for a bit there. You passed out from the shock of that scene, but there's a knot on the back of your head from a fall. I requested you stay the night at the hospital for monitoring for a concussion or intracranial hemorrhage. They might get you a CT scan."

The flash of overhead fluorescent lights passed by as we rolled down a long hallway, making my head hurt worse.

I grunted and tried to sit up. "I'm fine. I just ... What happened to them, the people in that car?"

Sam adjusted his glasses and wiped his forehead as he continued looking straight ahead. "The child is fine and the woman will be, thanks in part to you for getting someone else over there right away, although I wished you hadn't also gotten hurt. The woman wasn't dead, only unconscious with internal hemorrhage, and she was stabilized. The man is ..."

They rolled me into a room and transferred me with strong arms to a sagging hospital bed, the limp mattress groaning as my weight settled down. Sam slipped an SpO$_2$ monitor over my finger and hooked up EKG leads on my chest before turning on the overhead monitor, which beeped to the rhythm of my heart, much faster than normal.

Sam adjusted the straps on the stretcher and folded a side up. "I'd love to stay and make sure everything is okay with you, but we have to get back out there. A nurse will be in with you soon. Just rest."

Heat rose in my cheeks with embarrassment. "Go, I'm fine." I'd tried to help out and get experience but had turned the situation into a disaster for others who were trying to help real victims.

Sam waved. "I'm not saying you still can't be a good doctor, even a surgeon, but you might do better in a controlled environment like an OR, or you could be a family practice doctor or a dermatologist." He grinned. "Text me tomorrow."

I scoffed as they left and flicked off the lights, the rumble of their stretcher fading down the hallway.

My eyes closed. The family in the car accident had reminded me of myself, Maddie, and Aiden. I had to get back to Egypt as soon as possible, right after I was cleared to leave.

I stared at the darkened ceiling and at shadows that appeared to creep across it, forming an image like an amorphous spider's web. Only faint, clouded moonlight slipped around my blinds. I lay awake for hours as nurses probably attended to many more urgent patients, my eyes turning dry and scratchy.

I'd seen horror this night that I'd never stopped to imagine and never wanted to. If after I made sure that Maddie was okay and was able to bring her back home, would the med school have contacted me for readmittance? Sam wouldn't tell them about my blunder, and they'd probably have decided something either way by the time I returned.

My eyelids eventually grew heavy, and I drifted off.

I strode through a green mist in my dream—a glowing haze surrounded by darkness. Cold. Wisps of fog trailed away through the air, as if revealing a path in which I should walk—city streets, but they were devoid of people and sound. Clusters of off-white, high-rise buildings loomed on either side of me like guardians waiting for me to make the wrong move and to crush me. The surrounding structures were strange but familiar, and a belt of placid water lay ahead at the end of the dark street, just beyond a row of blacked-out street lamps—Modern Cairo. Wind whispered in my ears. Dark forms emerged, hovering just beyond the green light that didn't appear to have a point of origin. A stark-white face wrapped in linen appeared, peeking around the hood of a parked car ... and green eyes glowed from beneath the thin wrappings. But its gaze wasn't focused on me. I exhaled in relief as I shuddered in fear. Was this a Dark One—like from Heb's tale, a soul of the devoured dead? Hopefully it wouldn't notice me.

I inched onward, but the hairs on the back of my neck stood on end as if something was watching me. A sickeningly sweet scent wafted through the air. I glanced around.

More glowing green eyes appeared in the darkness overhead, looking through the windows of the surrounding high-rise buildings. At first there were only a few, but more linen-bound faces appeared in the windows of the stories above or below. The glowing eyes of these beings jostled about before they all settled on me at once.

My throat constricted with terror.

Then the dream faded into black.

My feet sank into sand and dirt ... I was wearing sandals, sandals made with flat leather straps—ancient in style. The white kilt at my waist stood out against the darkness. My skin was different too, darker, my limbs more toned. Veins rose on my forearms. Something also reflected the green light, something on my wrist. I tapped at it with my fingernail. Metal clanged and vibrated my wrist—bronze metal. My dad's bracelet? I studied it: simple in style with facets along its length and rounded edges at the top and bottom. It looked like the gift that my dad had given me.

A pale light emerged somewhere in the distance through a green mist hovering along the ground. The walls of a beige corridor appeared, surrounded me, and pressed in. Double doors leading to an operating room in the medical school I'd attended sat just ahead.

"Hold up," someone said from the darkness.

A muscular man in a barely buttoned white shirt with long, gelled locks ran out of the OR and held a tattoo-covered arm and hand up in front of me—Mr. Scalone.

What was he doing? It didn't seem like he even saw me but was talking to someone else.

A tall, thin blonde—Kaylin—approached from behind me and knocked Mr. Scalone's upturned hand away with a slap.

Her younger brother, Aiden, followed her, carrying the tiny fox he'd purchased as a pet while in Egypt. His red dreadlocks dangled around the buzzed sides of his head from beneath his flat-billed cap and wobbled as he nodded at his sister.

Were they all still in Egypt, or were they in my school? Or were they trying to find the Hall without Maddie so that they could stake the claim for themselves?

Mr. Scalone, Aiden, and Kaylin yelled at each other as they waved their hands wildly, but I couldn't hear exactly what it was they were shouting about.

I stepped through the swirling green fog.

Another man marched past. He was dressed in a fine white suit—the Minister of Antiquities we'd spoken with and who originally denied us our request to search closed sites for the Hall. But then later, after Maddie's abduction, he'd helped us by granting us access to any site in Egypt in order to help us find her. He'd claimed that her abduction would mar Egypt's reputation again and would scare away more of their already depressed tourism. So he vowed to do everything he could to help.

Two hefty bodyguards in gray suits, who stood with their arms folded over their massive chests, flanked the Minister of Antiquities. The minister removed his sunglasses with a flick of his wrist, his face freshly shaven, and he patted down his wavy gray hair as he stepped up to Kaylin and Mr. Scalone and spoke with only a slight Egyptian accent—although I still couldn't make out the words.

My stomach twisted with anxiety.

I stepped from the swirling mist, my body not under my control. The group's attention shifted as they gazed upon me, and their faces contorted with fright.

"It's him," Mr. Scalone said, pointing at me.

The others screamed.

My arm extended, although I didn't wish or command it to.

The shimmering metal bracelet tugged on my forearm, pulling me closer to them … but I was still wearing ancient Egyptian garb.

My other hand grasped the bracelet and pried it off my left wrist.

They all turned and fled, as if I'd been haunting their lives for years.

Chasing after them, I yelled for them to stop, but my voice was muffled and weak. They vanished in the darkness.

A crystal mirror spread out across the wall, partially veiled by the green haze. Darkness surrounded me, except for twinkling lights buried within the depths of the mirror's reflection.

I stepped closer to the mirror and leaned over. Stars and the moon reflected in its still surface as if it were a placid pond in an open field. But this wasn't a pond or a mirror … blue siding for a window appeared around it—a small window of my mom's house, the one for my bedroom. I blinked and peeked inside, searching for my sleeping body and my—

A face emerged in the reflection, the features not mine. I was old and young at the same time, a boy and a man, but I was Egyptian.

Gasping, I grasped at my face, poking, prodding, and feeling around.

The shrill screech of birds erupted above me, as if they were circling me, waiting for their meal of carrion.

Then I started to speak, but I didn't know what I was going to say. The voice was not my own.

"I crawled through a tunnel of time."

I could hear the whispered words in my head, my lips moving in my window reflection, although I couldn't feel my mouth moving or hear the words aloud.

"You have shouted with the voice of the suffering. Has the time come when the secrets must be revealed?"

I stared into the window.

My reflection turned and stretched its arms out to the side. Images of a winding trail of rock and dirt arose in the glass, but the ground of the path lit up with green fire.

The words in my head said, "Even those with the desire to find the desecrated path above any other desire have still lost."

I fell, plummeting into thick liquid with a plop rather than a splash. I stroked with my arms, but I couldn't swim through this water. It was as thick as oil. My air disappeared as I continued to thrash, my muscles burning with fatigue.

But the window was still in front me, as was my altered reflection. A shimmer of gold carried across the window as the man, or I, extended his hand and arm out of the glass. I blinked as light reflected back into my eyes and momentarily blinded me.

I gasped for air, and burning liquid rolled down my throat and into my chest like molten metal.

This protruding hand grabbed my wrist and yanked me from the oil. I clasped his forearm to strengthen our grip as I coughed, but I only felt warm metal. He pulled me onto a dark shore where waves lapped at my feet, his arm still the only part of him that was protruding from the window. I studied his hand and the metal upon it. It wasn't gold as the reflection had first appeared; it was bronze, a simple bracelet. The man smiled and pointed to the reflection of silent green flames still raging along an empty trail as I sputtered and heaved oil—

My mattress groaned as I jolted upright and screamed. A nurse who was taking my vitals jerked. I vaguely recalled others also coming in and monitoring me during the night.

"You okay?" the stout woman in green scrubs asked as she studied my face, hers pale.

I nodded. "I'm fine. You just scared me."

No sunlight streamed around the closed blinds of the hospital. Six fourteen glowed in green numbers on the clock near the far wall—the earliest morning I'd had in the last week. The rumble of a car engine turning over and firing to life came from outside my window, and chatter still sounded out in the hall, along with hurrying footsteps. I was drowning here, like in my dream …

I rubbed my forehead to ease a throbbing pain that radiated across my temples as I recalled bits and pieces of a vivid dream. What'd all that meant—strange people, green mist and fire, Dark Ones? My body tensed with realization as I sucked in a hissing breath. Had I talked to the dead, to Dad? *Magic,* like in the journal's story when Heb spoke to his deceased father in a dream after penning a letter to the dead? No, I wasn't inside an ancient tomb where my mind often wandered and started to believe in crazy things like magic; I'd just had a concussion. And I hadn't seen Dad's face in my dream. But the more the journal showed things, the more I started to question …

"Okay, be back in an hour." The nurse's clogs clomped the floor as she exited.

I grabbed my bare wrist.

An image flashed through my mind—the sparkling bracelet in the reflection of the man in my dream, who also could've been me. Was that bracelet supposed to represent the one I'd had?

My heart lurched into my chest. The same bracelet that I'd worn—the one that Dad had given me when I was young—and my dad had told me to keep the bracelet forever, for it held great secrets from the past.

Could my bracelet have held some clue? Could it have been an artifact from a real man of ancient Egypt? There'd been some weird markings on the inside that I'd studied when I'd first received it and when I found it again when moving out to start college several years ago, but the markings seemed random and didn't make any sense at all.

Maybe if I could see it again …

My dad had brought that bracelet home many years ago and told me he'd purchased it from an Egyptian man on the black market. The seller claimed the artifact originated from a tomb he'd uncovered and the bracelet would've belonged to a simple man in ancient Egypt over three thousand years ago. My dad had never brought the bracelet to an expert, either because he'd wanted to believe it was genuine or feared the artifact might be confiscated.

Snatching my phone, I found Maddie's name at the top of my favorites list. My finger hovered over the call button. I'd left Egypt per her request, although before all she'd wanted me to do was stay and commit to that life—a life both of us had desired. She was upset about Kaylin touching me, but there wasn't much I could do about it, as Kaylin's actions had been a surprise to me as well. And Kaylin and I hadn't done anything even though Maddie and I weren't together—technically *Maddie* even had a boyfriend, although that guy never flew out to look for her when she was missing. Maddie's recent change in demeanor must've in part been due to her trauma from her abduction. Maybe she needed help but didn't know how to ask for it.

I sucked in a deep breath and tapped the button.

Her phone rang and rang before going to voicemail.

"Sorry, I can't take your call," Maddie's voice recording said. "I'm taking a few days off. Erik flew out to see me, and I'm not answering my phone or working while he's here."

My stomach twisted and cramped with jealousy, and my eyes closed. Her boyfriend—the same on-again, off-again guy from her hometown—had flown out to see her in Egypt, now that she'd been rescued and was okay. He'd be there to talk her through her trauma after the abduction. She'd probably find comfort and feel safe in his arms even though he'd never showed up after we'd called Maddie's family and let them know about the situation. I squeezed the phone.

Beep.

"I need to find my bracelet," I whispered into the phone as it slipped from my relaxing grip and landed on the floor with a clatter.

Was I the type of guy who'd just let it all go? Yes. Yes, I was. I never resisted or argued when someone told me to go, as I didn't want to annoy them and make them dislike me more. But this was way too much. And I wouldn't let Maddie's boyfriend swoop in now, not after everything Maddie and I had been through back there.

I threw the coarse sheets of the hospital's bed off of me and stood in my gown, searching for my clothes.

I'd probably never find my bracelet, but I could find Maddie.

Chapter 15

Journal Translation

E L-AMARNA WAS AS MUCH of a home as I'd ever known, since everyone I grew up with now lived here. I exhaled. My mind cleared of foggy memories as buzzing insects swarmed around my head. The prick of a small bite stung the back of my neck. I swatted my skin and shooed the pests a few more inches away.

I shaded my eyes, searching for the palace where Akhenaten resided with Nefertiti.

Much of the fertile bank that used to be farmland had been converted to buildings. People wandered in hordes to or away from the river—more people packed into one area than in the slums of Memphis.

Akhenaten and his city must feed on all the farms of the kingdom in order to sustain the vast population here when there was minimal land in the region reserved for growing crops. So many people, including the majority of Egypt's extensive military, were stationed at this city in the middle of the country rather than at its borders.

Soldiers in rawhide caps, with leather shields and glistening spears, marched for us and surrounded our docked boat.

"You have arrived at el-Amarna," someone said from among of the ranks of similar-appearing soldiers. "We do not offer admittance or refuge to any of the Sea People. You shouldn't even be trading in Egypt now. Be off."

"I am Egyptian," I shouted as I stood straighter. "I have been traveling for many years and have returned home to find that the city of the rising Aten is now the city of the god-king. And I yearn to live beside our god."

Harkhuf and Seneb stepped up beside me.

"You have one of two choices," the voice replied, and I spotted the speaking soldier by his moving lips. His beady eyes and flat nose were his only distinguishing features. "You can sail away from the holy city now, or you can accompany us to the police building. Pharaoh also does not allow any random Egyptian such as yourself to take up residence here if you were not brought for a needed skill or for labor. Our population is expanding rapidly, and construction lags behind."

"I will accompany you and make whatever offerings are necessary," I said. "This is what I desire."

The soldier groaned, and his men parted like stubborn donkeys, creating a path for me to travel between them.

Tia climbed out of the boat and brushed her long hair across her demure features to partially obstruct the view of her face. Paramessu followed, his head and eyebrows completely shaven, no doubt to help hide his identity and rare red hair. He glanced over at me before his chin jerked back and he blinked several times, noticing my magically disfigured face.

Wahankh slowly rose from within the hull and peeked over the railing.

I pointed at Wahankh. "Stay and watch over the boat and care for the horses. We will leave our spears and larger weapons here, or these soldiers will … worry."

"I am still afraid," Wahankh whispered, his eyes wild as he glanced around and rubbed at the stubble on his head. "Someone could recognize me."

Harkhuf planted his hands at his hips. "It has been too many years." Harkhuf's beard was gone, his face recently shaven and as smooth as his brother's—save for the bulging muscles at his jaw. He was also worried. "Maybe ten years, maybe more. Too long for someone to recognize a slave. And if they did, they'd recognize a small, dark man from Nubia long before they'd recognized you in your fancy white kilt, Egyptian. You all look the same."

"You two Nubians look the same as every other dancing dwarf I've ever seen," Wahankh whispered, watching the soldiers closely. "And every single elite man who can so much as link a distant cousin to someone working near Pharaoh has a couple of you already."

Seneb tossed his spear over the boat's railing, back into the hull with a clatter of wood and metal. Harkhuf's fingers slowly parted, as if breaking free from ice. His spear fell from his hand, and its shaft planted into the dirt beside the boat, but his bow remained at his back. Paramessu and Tia left their spears as well.

I placed my bow inside the boat but kept my swords at my waist as I glanced at my reflection in the rippling water. Snaking blue veins bulged all across the left side of my face, distorting my features and casting a tinge of blue across the overlying skin. I gingerly prodded the squishy vessels and shuddered at the sight of the monster I'd become before turning and following the path between the soldiers.

The soldiers surrounded us as we marched through their ranks and led us along the great road—a throughway so wide that an army could march its breadth. Buildings towered on either side, almost like a tunnel through the desert. The Window of Appearances—a massive covered bridge spanning the length of the great road—emerged in the distance, as I'd seen in my vision through the desert fox's eyes.

Images sprang into my mind—Akhenaten parading himself and my love up and down the great road in a chariot of gold, driven by white horses with plumes of giant feathers on their heads; the people all falling to their knees in fear, reaching out with palms up in adoration of the divine. My stomach knotted, and I doubled over in pain as I swallowed a rising wave of acid.

The soldier's marching feet wafted dust into the air, and it hovered around us like a brown cloud. Hordes of men and women walked the length of the great road, not casting us a second look. Other inhabitants of el-Amarna labored on buildings and in shops or sold items outside. Much of the product was shiny blue glass fashioned into tile.

A boy wiped at his sweating brow and bartered with an old shopkeeper for a translucent brown jug and pitcher. The shopkeeper waved him off, but the boy stayed.

"My family needs your glass," the boy said as we walked by. "The clay vessels we bought are seeping something into our water and food. We can all taste it, something acidic or sour—a flavor that's not supposed to be there. My little brother and sister have grown sick."

"You can't afford my glass, boy," the shopkeeper said, his hunched form tucked into the shade just inside the lower level of a two-story building that doubled as a house and store.

The boy snatched the brown-glass jug and ran. Shouting, the old man hobbled to his feet and pointed. The boy tripped and stumbled, and the jug sailed into the air. I froze, wanting to catch the object, but I was too far away. And I wished to give the impression of current Egyptian nobility—who would not care for the less fortunate.

The jug smashed into the ground with a crack, shattering into a thousand pieces.

One of the soldiers marched over and offered his hand to help the boy to his feet. The boy reluctantly reached out. Yanking the boy to his feet, the soldier spun him around and twisted his arm behind his back. The boy screamed in pain as the soldier shoved him back to the shop and made him kneel before the shopkeeper.

The shopkeeper smacked the boy across the face.

"He will work for you until he has paid for his crime," the soldier said, jerking the boy up to his feet and pushing him into the shop.

The boy fell down in the shadows inside.

"You will not see your mother for some time," the old shopkeeper said, smirking as he stepped up behind the boy and kicked him farther inside.

I swallowed to hide my rising anger.

Chapter 16

Journal Translation

WE FOLLOWED TWO OF THE soldiers into a massive rectangular building with a wide entryway. Torch flames wavered against the walls, helping to light an expansive inner room where scattered men wearing padded caps held spears and shields and shouted at disheveled men in dirt-stained kilts.

"See if the chief is available," the beady-eyed soldier whispered to the one who'd led us inside, probably thinking I couldn't hear them. "These are strange men with a boat of the Sea People's."

My companions and I stood amongst the echoing of men's shouting voices and waited for some time.

A middle-aged man stepped through the disarray of armed men. "I am the Chief of Police at el-Amarna. What business do you bring to Pharaoh's city, Egyptian, sailing in a boat of the Sea People's?" The man was tall and lean, his voice clear and familiar. Streaks of gray ran along the sides of his head, and a twisting scar carried from his knee down past his ankle. The outer half of his foot was missing, which left a portion of his sandal exposed.

I remembered a story I'd heard long ago—one about a boy defying his father's wishes and playing at the river's edge. A crocodile had lunged from the water and nearly cost the boy his life.

This was Mahu, Akhenaten's previous captain. He had been my friend but chose loyalty to Pharaoh over my well-being every time except once. That one time, he hadn't turned me in for sneaking out of my room when I'd been confined for suspicion of carrying the plague. This man was not my true enemy.

I dangled my long hair over my forehead and around my cheeks, hoping to go unrecognized. My hair had strands of gray, I had a plain face, and it'd been a decade or even two since I'd been the scrawny boy who'd sailed alongside Mahu. I'd grown taller and thicker, thanks to the torture of exercise from the magician's teachings, and now I prayed that this magical mask hid my true face. I felt along the stinging left side of my face. Bulging veins popped from the skin of my forehead and cheek, as if I had some kind of large vascular deformity. An image of the snaking blue vessels I'd seen in my reflection popped into my head—like half of me had been touched by death, by the kiss of the underworld.

"Answer me," Mahu said, his voice deep, commanding respect. Veins also popped from Mahu's forearm as he clenched the shaft of a spear and studied me. "Who are you and why have you come to the holy city, the capital of the known world?"

My lips parted, attempting to speak, but my mouth quivered and my tongue turned flaccid, like a worm.

Paramessu stepped forward and stood proudly beside me. "Our master, the mighty Rem, devoted of Akhenaten, born of Egypt, has traveled to the corners of the world in the name of Pharaoh. He brings gifts for the god-king and, after years of exploration and labor, wishes to make his home alongside Egypt's chosen ones, to assist Pharaoh and the Aten in any way he can. I am his guard and council. His woman." Paramessu grimaced as he pointed at Tia, his hand trembling a bit.

Tia's demure features pulled back in surprise.

Mahu relaxed his spear hand as he studied us. "You are welcome here, as long as you worship the one god of everything, the Aten and Akhenaten."

Paramessu nodded, which for him was not a lie.

"You didn't bring anything for the disgusting worship of other false deities or devils, did you?" Mahu asked. "Anything on your foreign boat?"

I shook my head, studying his wrinkled face and the streaks of gray hair at his temples. How life had passed by for everyone ... I would've lived such a different life if I'd stayed content as Akhenaten's servant.

"You did not bring beasts?" Mahu asked. "At least not those representing the gods of old?"

I kept my hair draped around my face. "Only steeds for towing our carts, and a pet cat. Animals are not our gods; they are simply commodities for human gain." I glanced around—hopefully Croc hadn't followed us.

"If any of you cause trouble," Mahu said, tapping Paramessu with the butt of his spear, "there are barracks and cells on the backside of this building. You don't ever want to find yourself in there, unless you work for me or are my guest. And don't try to visit the palace up north. Pharaoh distances himself from his crazed human worshippers to find a little peace. Traveling up there without permission is the fastest way for you to come back and see me and my men."

My eyes shot northward. *He* was here, and Nefertiti would be here too. I cast Mahu a beaming smile. He studied me, his eyes narrowing as if confused.

I tapped my chin as I glanced around. "Where can I find a suitable house to take up residence? One for the likes of Egyptian nobility."

"Housing is an issue for any newcomer," Mahu replied. "You will probably be sleeping on your boat for a while, unless you'd like to give the slums a try."

I made a display of grimacing. "Who do I contact to purchase a house?"

Mahu's brows pulled together in skepticism. "If you truly have wealth in grain or other goods and will make large offerings to Pharaoh, I can have one of my men send word for a palace scribe. Pharaoh's vizier, Ay, sets the prices and will charge a steep fee, but if you are able, they might be interested. Those men are swamped with duties, however, and if they allow you an audience, it will still be weeks, if the luck of the Aten shines upon you."

I folded my arms across my chest. "Please tell them to hurry. One poor family of the el-Amarna nobility is going to lose their house."

Mahu's face relaxed—his training would teach him not to show surprise, but the emotion crept into his expression for a moment. Right now, he probably thought that I was an arrogant fool or, just as I would need him to believe, someone very important. The more unlike my former self I became, in everyone's eyes, the more unlikely it would be for anyone to recognize me.

I flashed Mahu an overconfident smile, spun about, and strode away. "I shall pick out the house that I believe my wife and I would most enjoy living in," I shouted back as I exited the police building into the blinding light of the Aten and headed north.

My companions hurried after me.

"If you want the police of el-Amarna to despise us," Seneb said, jogging to my side, "like a rooster that crows before the sun even rises, then I think you said the right things. But I advise caution. We were slaves the last time we lived here, and if we are arrested, it will increase the chance that someone will remember us."

"Precisely," I said. "I know this land. No one who saw that display could even imagine the possibility that we used to be slaves of el-Amarna, not now."

We hiked the royal road, walking past the magnificent temple of the Aten. I'd not seen a temple inside Memphis or Thebes that was covered with as much shimmering gold. The reflective metal coated the walls and emblazoned flags that whipped in the wind overhead, temporarily blinding me with their brilliance.

Akhenaten had succeeded in every regard. My blood turned hot, my face burning.

After marching with my head down for what felt like an hour, we approached the northern outskirts of the city, where large mansions were clustered together. But the road continued on to massive walls in the distance, walls that surrounded a structure even bigger than the Great Aten Temple—Akhenaten's palace. Nefertiti would be inside. My eyes lingered over the structure, the towering stories, the ramparts, the guards. The magical *benben* stone would also be in there somewhere—the original piece of earth that arose from the waters of chaos all around us and allowed for the dawn of life. This yellowish pyramid would grant even the mighty Akhenaten far more power, power beyond what I'd ever witnessed him evoke upon others.

Forcing a deep breath, I wandered amongst the grand houses along the northern periphery of the city, my hands clasped behind my back, my posture rigid. My companions followed at my heels, probably in shock, not knowing what to think or how to act. I scrutinized each structure and its location for hours, searching for something I could use to my advantage. I'd been plotting my return for decades, but now that I stood so close to my objective, it still seemed like once again I was a servant boy without many options. How could I quickly work my way into that palace without drawing too much negative attention to myself and my companions?

Twilight eventually settled in around us as I strolled down the great road, my mind filled with nostalgic memories of my childhood, slavery, and who my companions and I had once been.

An emaciated girl leaned against a building at the edge of the road. Her gaze met mine and she jogged over, dropping to her knees at my feet. "Bread? Beer? Please." She brushed tangled dark hair from her face.

Other faces watched from the shadows around us—children of all ages, as thin as her, lurking in the alleyways between shops along the great road.

"Why are there so many homeless children in the wealthiest city of the most powerful kingdom in the world?" Harkhuf said as he reached out for the emaciated girl's hand. "I have nothing on me, girl, but I promise I will get you a full loaf of bread, and more." His newly exposed chin and cheeks wrinkled, as if he were in pain.

"That's a lie." The girl stood and hobbled away to another group of kilt-wearing men who walked the road north.

"Get away, scum," a man in the group yelled at the girl as she approached. "If you believed in the Aten, truly believed and sacrificed, you wouldn't be in such a situation. You might even be rich. Your circumstances are your own fault." He laughed and kicked dirt at the girl, who covered her face and dashed off.

My heart melted with sympathy. This was what the mightiest of kingdoms, Egypt, had become? *My* home.

Chapter 17

Journal Translation

WE RETURNED TO OUR BOAT, still docked at the banks of el-Amarna. Our weapons sat at our sides, ready—just in case. The Aten set, and darkness crawled across the land.

My companions' teeth tore into hunks of crusty bread with ripping and chomping, everyone but Harkhuf's. They ate as if seeing other people starving increased their appetites. But Harkhuf rummaged around in our store crates, grunting and mumbling to himself.

Wahankh downed a jug of beer with loud gulps and a prolonged "Ah."

Harkhuf turned and climbed out of the boat, marching away with a sack of food.

"Where are you going?" I asked. "It'll be completely dark soon."

Harkhuf grumbled, then said, "Keeping a promise."

I watched him disappear into the twilight. My stomach rolled. He shouldn't go alone, not a Nubian dwarf. The people of this city would think that he was a slave whose only purpose was to entertain his master. Egyptians might harass him, and if they pushed too far, Harkhuf might harm or even kill them.

"I'll accompany you," Paramessu said, leaping out of the boat. He pointed at Tia, who frowned. "Stay here. We'll be right back."

I wanted to follow the men, but I needed to brood and ponder what else I could do to make my way into the company of the elite of el-Amarna, into the palace …

Night fell, and I drifted off. My dreams raged with images of assassins coming for my heart and soul.

Light rained across our boat's hull, waking me. Blinking, I glanced around, my body shivering beneath my blankets. No Harkhuf or Paramessu. A sinking feeling pulled at my stomach.

My hands found the cold bronze of my sword hilts, the exposed blades shimmering in the sunlight. I climbed to my feet, my weapons at the ready. Tia and Seneb were also gone. Only Wahankh slept in the boat with me, and Croc lay on the railing with his eyes closed.

"Wake up," I shouted, searching the crates and our supplies. No one else had rummaged through or taken anything.

Wahankh grumbled, rising to his elbows.

I nudged him with my foot. "We need to go. Harkhuf and Paramessu haven't returned, and the others are also gone."

"They're fine," Wahankh said, flopping back down against the wood with a thud.

My jaw clenched with anger. "Get up. I don't care how afraid you are of returning to el-Amarna; our friends need our help."

He buried his head under a blanket. "No, they don't. If they did, I'd go with you. They came back last night and mentioned a starving girl they'd given food to. This girl lived in a house of some kind and offered them warm shelter in return. Paramessu brought Tia back with him, and Harkhuf took Seneb."

My lips pursed. Their behavior would risk our entire act—portraying myself as their master.

"You were asleep and haven't been sleeping well for months," Wahankh said, nestling back into his blankets. "They wanted to leave you be. And I'd rather stay out of the city."

I sat beside Croc, and my chin fell into my hand as I contemplated how to keep my companions from jeopardizing my plans. My fingers found Croc's back leg, the scar and the draining wound. Yellow fluid still seeped from the opening. I prodded hardened tissue that felt thick, like the callused soles of a slave's—

Hissing, Croc leapt to his feet, swatted my hand with his claws, and dashed from the boat. He hobbled off along the bank and disappeared into the brush. My hand burned, the flesh flayed open in four distinct lines.

Four silhouettes appeared on the bank, outlined by the rising Aten—my companions. They approached the boat.

"Do you think it wise to separate at night?" I asked as they came closer and their footsteps crunched through the sand. "If someone found that you had abandoned your master, they might grow suspicious and question who we are and what we're doing." My arms folded across my chest, my chin jutting out.

Paramessu's head drooped. "We were careful."

Harkhuf grumbled, climbed aboard the boat, and dug through our crates. "You can come with us, back to the abandoned house where the girl and other children sleep, or not. But I'm bringing them breakfast."

Seneb shrugged and mouthed the word, "Sorry," as his brother loaded up another sack of food.

"We need to be careful, or we'll be dead," I said. "No, not just dead: Our souls will be devoured."

Harkhuf waved me off. "I'm always careful. Don't forget who you're talking to."

"I know, but you become nearsighted when trying to help a female," I said. "Especially one that may remind you of your daughter."

He shot upright, his eyelids pulling back as his jaw muscles bulged. Fire ignited behind his irises—the rage I'd seen inside of him when we were slaves.

Tension strangled the air between us. I swallowed.

Snatching his sack, Harkhuf climbed over the boat and marched away.

I sheathed my swords at my kilt and followed the dwarf at a distance. More footsteps followed me. I glanced back … everyone but Wahankh.

We hiked along the great road, through dawn's chill, but turned and headed east, angling down small roads and between houses and shops. Harkhuf led us beyond a large building with bars across all of the windows to a barracks at its rear.

The mud-brick walls of this structure crumbled and leaned to the west, and the doorway was bare—open.

I followed Harkhuf inside. My eyes adjusted to the dim lighting of a single torch on the far wall and the small amount of sunlight sneaking through the doorway. Blankets littered the room, piled in heaps, but in rows … no, they covered bodies. My hands squeezed my sword hilts.

Harkhuf clapped as he stomped around. "I've got breakfast."

High-pitched voices groaned, and blankets shuffled around. Heads appeared from beneath the blankets, curious eyes scouting about before settling on us.

"Bread, real bread," a small boy said as he stood and ran for Harkhuf.

Harkhuf emptied his sack, exposing white teeth—a beaming smile I'd never seen upon those lips. His smile lit the room more so than his clean kilt or the burning torch. He watched the dirty children run to him on bare feet that slapped the dirt floor, scoop up the food, and laugh and dance around. Girls shrieked with glee.

Something pulled at my heart with a longing ache. It was as if Harkhuf were a father watching his children experience utter happiness, and seeing that emotion in those he loved brought him profound joy. The very essence of life ... Seeing Harkhuf and these children at this moment made nothing else I'd ever witnessed feel so bittersweet. If only they could stay that way forever and hide themselves from all the pain of the world.

Had my father felt the same way during my childhood?

Father, I will avenge you.

Children stuffed their faces with bread. The emaciated girl hugged another taller girl and patted her friend on the back as she tried to say something through a mouthful of food. Skipping over, she and her friend both wrapped themselves around Harkhuf's thick waist in a crushing hug.

Moisture brimmed in the dwarf's eyes as he patted the girls on their backs, their dirty dresses unable to hide the protruding bones of their shoulder blades.

I choked back emotion, clearing my throat. I needed to remain focused on the goal at hand, or I'd slip and someone would discover us.

Seneb stepped up beside me. "Now you see why we wouldn't help you stop my brother from coming back here. I'd gladly starve to death myself to witness this. In this moment, Harkhuf is forgiving himself as much as he will ever be able to."

I nodded and cleared my throat again. A furry creature rustled in the blankets, standing and shaking itself off—a tiny fox that could not have weighed more than a couple of pounds—a desert fox, but slow moving, with gray hair around its face. Its golden eyes locked on mine. Something familiar ... The creature walked up to me, sniffing. It licked my hand.

Those eyes appeared in my mind as if they were part of my own. I'd seen through them before … several times.

"That's our pet," the emaciated girl I'd seen on the street the other day said, pointing. "He's lived here longer than any of us. Been here since before this chamber was abandoned, or so that's what the older kids say. He acts like a domesticated greyhound, just tinier, and likes being around kids."

The fox's tail wagged back and forth as she hopped up and placed the cracking pads of her front feet on my bare shin, her tongue lolling out in a quiet pant. Scooping up the tiny creature, I embraced her with a warm hug and stroked her wiry fur—the small fox we'd found after nearly dying from the elements in the desert when fleeing slavery at el-Amarna. She'd led me to water and then assisted me with visions, keeping me current on the happenings ever since. I was bound to this creature, like with Croc. There were not many humans I was that close to. "I may still have a need for your services, my friend." I scratched at her ears. "If you can still get around without too much pain in those stiff joints of yours."

The children shouted and pointed behind me.

A soldier with a spear stepped through the doorway behind us. His scarred leg and the gray hair at his temples were familiar—Mahu, my former friend, now the Chief of Police of el-Amarna.

Chapter 18

Journal Translation

MAHU'S EYES NARROWED as he studied us in the dim lighting of the crumbling building. "So, you've already found the orphaned children? Rem, was it? One of my men sent word that your servants and you had come to visit the old barracks. I had to see why."

Thirty children rushed around me with stomping feet and flailing elbows, jumping and clinging to Mahu's waist and legs.

My forehead tightened, my grip releasing my bracelet. These children loved Mahu? I set the tiny fox on the ground, and she crawled onto the children's blankets near the entrance and curled up.

Mahu opened a sack upon his shoulder and produced a bowl of grain. Only a few children dug their hands in, raking their fingers through the food before chomping on hard kernels.

"Looks like you've already fed them," Mahu said, studying the chunks of bread in their hands. "Why?"

I froze, hesitating as I tried—

Harkhuf straightened. "My master, Rem, has always had a soft spot for needy children."

My eyes closed as I nodded to the brother in thanks.

"You have?" Mahu looked me up and down, perplexed. "I do what I can, but even in my position I don't get extra rations beyond what my family needs. Too many jubilees lately. I keep this old barracks around for the children so they have a warm place to sleep at night. And everyone stays away. The people of el-Amarna believe this was an old prison where evil men lived and died. Truthfully, this chamber is where the slaves used to sleep at night during the initial construction of the city, many years ago."

My throat constricted, my mind wandering as I glanced around. I didn't even recognize the city since it had been built up and sprawled out so much. But was this the barracks where I'd slept all those nights so long ago? When the magician lit the green candle to summon me outside when it was safe to learn and train? My lower lip quivered. I bit into its soft flesh to steady myself. Is that why the fox chose to live here—because it was still bound to me, awaiting my return?

"I'm sure these children will be very thankful to have you in el-Amarna," Mahu said. "I have to admit, I did not suspect you for the caring type after we talked yesterday."

I shrugged. "I knew a boy once, one who grew up in Memphis and Thebes but was sent into slavery and lived around these parts." Should I tempt his memory of me? My muscles tensed. I might be recognized and put to death.

Mahu straightened from ruffling the black hair of a child and stared into my eyes and the distorted side of my face, waiting for more.

I dismissed the conversation with a wave. "You probably didn't know him."

"I've known many boys from here," he said. "I would probably have a difficult time recalling one, but try me. Was he related to you?"

"In a way," I replied. "I met him many years ago when we were both young. His father called him Heb, an abbreviated version of his real name, like my father did with me. But that boy grew up as Akhenaten's servant."

Mahu's eyes grew distant as they moved side to side, searching his memories. "I remember him. A scrawny boy with a huge heart and terrible luck."

"What happened to him?" I asked. "I don't know much beyond his servitude, whereafter he disappeared from my life. Did his luck ever change?"

Mahu's eyes closed. "No. This boy endured the tragedy of five lifetimes: a near-death experience with a hippopotamus, a plague brought to Egypt by his father—one that killed his only family—falling in love with the wrong woman, being sent into slavery, disrespecting the future pharaoh, and his mother even turned against Egypt."

"My god." My heart raced. My mother turned against Egypt? "No, this boy's mother died during his birth."

Mahu's forehead tugged at his graying temples, as if confused or concerned. "They did say that for a time afterward, to hide what she'd done."

"No," I said. "I would've known the truth. He and I were close at one point. He would've told me."

"He didn't know," Mahu replied. "They told him only the lie."

My jaw dropped. "Why?" I nearly screamed.

Mahu was silent for a moment. "It has to do with the forbidden words and false gods."

What? I nearly drew my swords, wishing to shove the blades against the tender skin of his throat and demand answers.

"The boy eventually became an outcast but still tried to stay and serve Pharaoh, only because he was in love with the queen of Egypt."

I forced a slow breath. "A servant was in love with the queen?"

"She was not the queen at the time." Mahu folded his arms as if defending my former self. "And he didn't mean anything by it—dumb, young love. And she is the most beautiful woman in all the world, and they were friends. I could understand why the boy was confused, infatuated with her, and why he believed he might even have a chance."

"Why's that?" I asked.

Mahu was silent for another moment. "But the boy propositioned her when she was already Pharaoh's. That's when he was sent into slavery—probably worked here in el-Amarna at some point, although I don't think I ever saw or talked to him again. Rumors said that he may've even escaped, that he fled and died in the desert or drowned at sea. I used to hear women whisper a tale that the boy's heart only carried true love but was so broken and shattered that it wouldn't let go. They said that his *ba* still roams the desert and sea at night, threatening men and terrifying women as he searches for his lost true love."

My eyes were as big as gold-hoop earrings. By the gods …

"Just a legend." Mahu chuckled, a forced sound, as if he wanted to believe it or hated remembering the story.

"That's a shame he met such a fate," I said. "I knew him well and believed he could have transformed himself, like a monarch butterfly." I pulled my long hair back away from my face and stared Mahu directly in the eye. When I'd been imprisoned in solitary confinement, in a cave,

Mahu had come and told me that I could still become the monarch butterfly and transform myself from a grotesque worm into something beautiful. Instead, after that very moment, I vowed to become something hideous and enact my dark revenge.

"What was that? A butterfly?" Mahu studied my face and winced at my grotesque appearance. He gave no sign of recognition whatsoever. My muscles relaxed. And if Mahu couldn't see the old Heb in me, no one would.

I strode up to the Chief of Police, pointing at the twisting scar on his leg and his missing toes—very similar to Croc's wounds, similar to my scar, except that I wasn't missing any toes. "Crocodile attack?" I stepped around him, scooped up the fox, and marched to the exit. "Not many people live to tell that tale."

"I will speak with a scribe friend of mine who's been here with us since the early days of el-Amarna as soon as I can," Mahu said. "I'll see if he can help you find decent housing."

I paused. "No. I've only ever met one scribe in this city, Maya, and I wish to deal with him." Maya was the scribe who'd tracked our group's progress those many years ago when we were slaves. He was kind, the man who'd taught me how to read and write when I was young, and he did care for the less fortunate. I'd asked for him as I'd wanted to find out what had become of him and where he stood in the current mix of Akhenaten's followers—so that I could spare him. But if he'd become a servant of the god-king and had risen through these tainted ranks, I'd probably have to dispose of him at some point, as well as Mahu … My heart twinged. I wouldn't let anyone stand in my way now. Shaking my head, my hair waved around my chin and cheeks.

A moment of silence followed.

"Maya is very busy," Mahu replied. "He is the Royal Scribe now."

"Then I look forward to his visit," I whispered.

Chapter 19

Journal Translation

A FEW DAYS LATER, my companions and I marched near the great road, admiring houses along the northern periphery of the city under the heat of a blazing Aten veiled by high clouds. The quiet of the area hovered around us—no playing children, no men selling products from the lower levels of the houses, no one outside.

I'd been wandering the city for days, looking for the beginning thread of a plan. My companions' heads hung, and they muttered and whispered amongst themselves so that I could not hear their words of disappointment or skepticism in what we were doing.

A bleating carried around the house now in front of us, breaking me from a numbing trance that the sweltering heat had forced me into. I paused for a moment and glanced around. Then, veering into the shadows of a narrow passage between the house and an adjacent one, I left my companions behind. I paced on and neared a small plot of land hidden at the back by all of the surrounding structures, a plot with an encircling, low mud-brick wall. Another similar cry rang out—sheep. One of the animals jumped onto a crate with a bang and released a high-pitched bleat that stung my ears. Not unusual, but something else grabbed my attention—all of the animals had large, curled horns. They were all rams. That was … I recalled Mahu asking me something about such animals.

As I crept closer, I spotted a high, open window in the mud-brick wall of the giant house. I leapt up, grabbed the sill, scrambled with my feet against the wall, and slowly pulled myself up. No one was inside the inner room; it was only lit by fading rays of the Aten. I tried to squeeze myself into the opening—I'd used house windows as a means of escape plenty of times in my youth—but my shoulders smacked into the sides, too broad now for the narrow opening. I was about to let go when a statue muted by the shadows inside caught my attention, a statue only as tall as my knee. But the depiction wasn't clear, only the vague shape of a man. I dropped back to the dirt, and the sand crunched as I crouched and glanced around. No one else was outside.

I grabbed the sun-bleached and cracked wood of the gate leading into the mud-brick enclosure for the animals, about to jump over. But I paused. A black beetle—a scarab—rolled a ball of dung across the dirt just inside the animal's pen, near a bucket of water. I dropped to my knees, scooped up the beetle, and held it out in my palm, studying its reflective black surface and pinpoint red eyes. The creature was only about the size of one of the segments of my finger. The jagged protrusions along its front two limbs poked into my palm as it scuttled across my skin, its four other clawed legs latched on to its perfect ball.

"I need your help, my friend," I whispered and ran back for the window. I leapt up and caught the sill with one hand. Heaving with all my might, I kicked off of the wall and rose up enough to drop the beetle inside. A faint ting sounded as it hit the hard floor.

I whispered under my breath, words I'd used a couple of times in the past, words of the arcane, and I traced ancient hieroglyphs into the air.

Everything went black. My mind shuddered in protest. The clatter of tiny insect legs sounded in my ears, and the smell of something foul filled my nose—the ball of dung—but somehow I perceived it as sweet, like honeyed bread … and saliva wetted my mouth. Then the fading light of the Aten opened up around me, revealing the tiled floor and mud-brick walls inside the house. Four windows of images filled my sight, as if I now had four distinct eyes, which only disoriented me and clouded my thoughts.

My clattering legs scuttled about the interior as I searched for something, something I couldn't comprehend … a dark hole? As my scarab form pushed itself along and rolled a ball of dung larger than my body, I crawled over something on the floor—leather with straps, probably a sandal. But it stretched out beneath me like our boat of the Sea People's, as if sailing a river of dirt. My fragmented gaze with the four images settled onto something in the shadows, a towering statue of a man. It appeared as gargantuan as the Colossi of Amenhotep near Karnak, reaching for the heavens while watching over its domain. A man with the head of a—

"Let's get back to our boat," a voice said, tearing my mind away from the vision.

Everything went dark again for a moment before I blinked with my own eyes. I was sprawled against the outer wall of the house, as if I'd passed out.

Sharp fingers dug into my forearm. "Are you okay?" Tia pulled me around. Her gaze wandered across my face. The others were all with her. "I hope that whatever this mask is you're wearing, or all your plotting, isn't negatively affecting you."

I grunted and nodded. "I'm fine."

She pulled on my arm to try to guide me back between the houses. "I don't like this. There's still daylight, and someone may see us sneaking around behind this house and throw us back into slavery for good."

"Do not say such things out loud," Seneb said, his head turning as he searched for people within earshot. His fingers tightened, as if clutching weapons, but his weapons were still on our boat.

I stooped and picked up another perfect ball of dung, one without a scarab, beside the ram's water bucket. "We cannot return to the boat quite yet." We'd never be able to break into this mansion of a house without being caught by someone, perhaps guards or the owner inside.

One of my companions behind me let out a quiet sigh of disapproval.

I turned around. "Is anyone here an artist of any type?"

Seneb's eyebrows rose. "I used to enjoy whittling wood when I lived in Nubia."

"Good." I held out the dung ball. "I need this carved into the shape of a ram's head, one with large, curled horns."

Seneb eyed the dung as he pulled a small knife from the waist of his kilt and extended his fingers. "What is that?"

✳ ✳ ✳

The rank heat of the desert pressed in around me as I stepped back into the police building, leading my companions by the distance a parent would lead a dawdling child. The burning torches inside the expansive interior room were dim but crackled as they burned. Fewer armed men now scattered the area, and only two filthy men swayed and teetered as three policemen forced them to sit on the dirt floor.

Mahu stood near the center of the room, dictating to a slender man in a pristine kilt who scratched notes onto a parchment lying across his writing palette. This scribe paused, reached out for a jug, and threw back a long swallow of what would be nutritious beer—which Egyptians all drank for sustenance more than anything—before wiping at his mouth with the back of his hand.

Striding up to the Chief of Police, I said, "I know of a blasphemer right here amongst the elite of el-Amarna." I extended a closed hand.

Mahu stared at me without any reaction, as if he were pondering the shock of my accusation.

"If I am not mistaken, Mahu, you questioned me about bringing animals of worship into el-Amarna—animals of the false gods," I said, my fingers still hiding what I held.

Mahu cleared his throat. "I did? Yes, I ask everyone this." He glanced down at my hand.

"And if the tales are true, there's no one who has enjoyed disposing of blasphemers more than Suty, with the exception of perhaps Akhenaten himself." I nodded at a scribe beside Mahu. "You may want to record my findings." I turned back to Mahu. "And the people tell me that Ay likes to be kept current on information pertaining to any important happenings in all of Egypt, more so than even the god-king. I request that you summon these men, and I will reveal the location of the traitor in your midst. They will not be disappointed." I uncurled my fingers to reveal the carved head of a ram about the size of a few grapes.

The jug of beer fell from the scribe's hand, cracking on the floor and releasing thick liquid that formed a brown puddle.

Mahu cleared his throat again as he scrutinized the image of the ram's head and rubbed his chin. Veins popped along his forearms. "Where did you find this, or is it yours?"

"Within the house of a man who still worships the ram of A—" I said, pointing northward. "The ram of the unspeakable one. The animals are housed in the back, and religious items will be found within the house."

Mahu's eyes narrowed. "And how do you know all of this? Are you setting this man up ... perhaps to acquire his house?"

"I have never been inside of that house to do so," I replied. "But I saw something. You can use anything you find against me, if at that time you believe me to be false."

Mahu stood silent for a long moment as he studied the object in my hand. "If a man of Egypt, much more so of el-Amarna, indeed still speaks of and worships the forbidden ones, he will be punished accordingly." He cleared his throat and the scribe fumbled around, adjusting his parchment and palette before making a scratching notation. Mahu lowered the volume of his voice. "But if you make such accusations and you are wrong, you will receive a similar penalty for the accused crime."

I forced a smile, but my stomach burned. I'd seen the image of a man with the head of what I thought was a ram inside that house when I'd seen life through the senses of a scarab. But my thoughts quickly shifted ... Was Suty, Akhenaten's bodyguard—a man who happily inflicted horrid punishment on others—really going to arrive if I convinced Mahu? How I longed to destroy that monster of a man. But I could not kill them all now, and I did not want to. First, I wished to tear them apart, to make them paranoid, and to suffer at least a fraction of what I had. But what if they brought the cloaked hunter instead, the Devouring Monster itself? Did the hybrid creature of the underworld still perform Akhenaten's bidding? Could it still remember me and sense magic of any kind?

My grip tightened on my sword hilt. I nodded at Mahu. "I have seen it."

Mahu's chin wrinkled, and he shouted at several of his nearby policemen, pointing at them, "Summon Suty and the royal guard, and relay a message to Ay and Pharaoh."

Within a few moments, a gray horse snorted through flared nostrils as a policeman led it just inside the entryway of the building. The slapping of its hooves and the clatter of the wooden wheels of a chariot followed, the animal hitched to the chariot. Two policemen leapt into the chariot and the driver snapped the reins, spinning the horse around before driving it outside, headed north with the pounding of galloping hooves.

Chapter 20

Journal Translation

My companions and I stood in silence along the northern border of the city, waiting outside the enormous house of the man that I hoped was a true blasphemer.

A chill slid into the air, the late evening around us quiet and still.

Mahu paced around the perimeter of the house in question, away from a contingent of his policemen, his gaze fixated on the ground as if he pondered or feared any outcome of whatever was about to happen.

The rumble of chariots and the thunder of hooves emerged, coming from the great road in the direction of the palace. Dust spewed into the air as if a cloud rose in their wake. The haze obscured the Aten, which settled toward the western horizon, and changed its yellow glow to brown.

A deep voice bellowed, and the steeds' nostrils flared with exertion as they slammed to a halt, jostling their carts. The white foam of sweat dripped from their necks, coating their leather reins like soap. A musty scent rode the air currents.

"Who lives in this house?" An uneducated dialect pierced the swirling dust cloud that wafted over us, which made the air feel thick and gritty as it entered my throat and lungs. I knew this person. A monster of a man stepped from the haze, a scar running over the side of his shaved head and through a deformed ear that pointed up and outward like a pig's—Suty, the man who'd inflicted most of my physical punishment when I'd served Akhenaten.

Fire lit inside my stomach, rising up my chest and into my throat. My face heated with rage, my fingers pulling the sword from my belt.

A strong hand yanked my sword arm behind my back and twisted it, like with the boy who'd tried to steal the glass from the shopkeeper. Pain spiraled through my joints. I reached for my other sword.

"Not now," Harkhuf whispered from behind, his voice sharp. "I do not wish to halt your desires, but this is suicide. For all of us."

Tia flashed a smile at Suty and stepped in front of me, catching my other arm before it pulled my other sword. "My husband, Rem, has promised—"

"I don't give a goat's horn about you or him," Suty said, his disfigured ear twitching as he talked. "I've come to find a traitor."

"A *councilman* lives here," another familiar voice said, stepping from a chariot led by a brown horse. The horse snorted and pawed at the road with a hoof, scratching through the packed dirt. "One who has been with us before the beginnings of this city." This man emerged from the swirling dust cloud, his long hair specked with gray and his skin the pale shade of the elite. He carried a reed pen and a writing palette—Maya, the scribe who'd watched over my companions and me back when we were slaves, a good man. Using his reed pen, he brushed his hair behind his ears—ears like cups.

Suty grabbed a spear and sword from his chariot, kicked through the door of the house with a crack, and tromped inside, past splintered wood. Two soldiers followed at his heels.

Maya scratched notes onto his papyrus.

Screams erupted inside the house—a woman, a man. I bit my lip, my hands trembling.

More screams. Animals bleated and cried. My heart twisted and ached. What had I done?

"There are false idols in here," a soldier inside the house yelled.

A handsome older man wearing a dense wig and stark orange eye paint stepped from the chariots. Two women followed at his side, fanning him with large leaves. Ay—Nefertiti's father, now Akhenaten's vizier—the second-most powerful man in all of Egypt, and the man who blamed me for putting his daughters at risk for a plague.

Suty appeared, dragging an old man out of the front door. Blood dripped from the man's nose and left eye, which was already swollen shut and red like a tomato. The man's hands flailed, trying to grasp the doorframe and stop himself from being dragged away. But Suty lifted the man into the air and dropped him onto the front walk with a thud.

Suty sneered at his victim. "You've been hiding your treachery for years. Right under our noses."

"Did you believe that we'd never think to look so close to the house of the Aten?" Ay asked the man as he stepped closer, his fan-bearing women following his every step. "And I thought we'd wiped your scum from Egypt years ago."

The man trembled, covering his face. "Please, don't let it devour my soul," he shrieked. "I only desired to unite Egypt, the way it was during Amenhotep's time."

"Akhenaten will see you before you die," Ay said, and Suty kicked the man in the ribs. The man grunted and collapsed.

Two soldiers led a ram out of the front door. Its head and curled horns jerked side to side in an attempt to escape. The animal bleated, its tongue hanging from its mouth.

"This is your god?" Suty asked, indicating the ram. "This filthy beast? It shouldn't even be the god of a brainless imbecile."

The man crawled for the animal on his elbows. "No, please, Amun is still with us. He aids the starving and the common man. We need—"

Suty kicked the old man in the mouth. A crunch sounded, and teeth scattered across the walkway.

Suty turned and swung his sword, cutting the ram across the neck. The animal collapsed on its side with the sound of a hollow drumbeat, and blood pooled around its horns.

"If this is your god, why does it die so easily?" Suty laughed. The soldiers behind him chuckled. "People believe such foolish things, people like you—who we all thought was intelligent."

The old man grabbed his face and buried it into the dirt.

"Skin this sheep," Suty said to the guards. "We roast his god in his own kitchen and dine on its flesh tonight. And we make this traitor partake in the feasting."

The guards went to work, cutting and hacking the dead animal like butchers. Shadows crawled across the scene like fingers of the dead as the

Aten sank below the horizon. The rank heat of the desert plummeted with the emerging twilight.

After the guards dragged the carcass into the house, black smoke and the overwhelming smell of scorched flesh carried out, making me gag.

My stomach cramped with such pain that it almost brought me to my knees.

Akhenaten's Egypt thrived on fear, pain, and terror. But at least one old man working in the very midst of Akhenaten's madness had probably tried to work with Pharaoh and the people, although he did not agree with the changes that Akhenaten had made, changes that came well into this man's lifetime. Perhaps this man had striven for reinstating acceptance of others and their beliefs, right here at the heart of Egypt's intolerance. And I would cost this man his life and probably his soul ... A casualty of war, I suppose, but I despised the sacrifice. I'd hoped that my actions would lead to a quick invitation to the palace, but my need for vengeance must've suppressed my intuition—shadowing all other consequences.

Salty blood ran into my mouth from biting my cheek so hard.

A black cloak emerged from the shadows surrounding the farthest of the horses and chariots. The smell of rot and death grew suffocating. I gagged and choked, my blood running cold—the Devouring Monster was here.

The hooded creature lumbered up to the old man, grabbed him by a now crooked arm, and dragged him through the dirt to a black chariot. The man screamed in terror. After tossing the man into the chariot, the cloaked monster leapt up behind him. The black horse at the front reared, its eyes glowing with a tint of green, before wheeling about and racing back for the palace. Skin-prickling shrieks carried in their wake.

Suty's hulking form stepped before me, his enormous shadow covering my entire body. Only the red of twilight surrounded his silhouette.

"I am Ay, vizier of Egypt, the right hand of Akhenaten—Pharaoh himself," Ay said from beside Suty, stroking his chin as if lost in thought. "You and your woman may join us at the palace tonight for our feast so that we may reward you for your discovery." He made a circle in the air with his finger and glanced back to the soldiers, indicated for them all to leave.

Maya leaned against a wall of the house, wiping at his lips. His face carried a green tint, barely visible in the fading light. He made some scratching notations with his reed pen on his palette, his hand trembling. "W-we will leave a chariot for Rem, for his transportation tonight." He faced me. "You may also reside in this house for the time being."

Several guards struck flint and lit lamps before Maya stumbled onto one of the remaining chariots. Then they all raced away, their lamps floating through the growing darkness like ghosts.

Ghosts—like so many people I'd come in contact with. And what about Mahu's tale of my mother? What really happened to her, and who was she? Had she actually survived my birth but then been shunned? If so, then everyone had lied to me, including Father, to hide something …

My hands caressed the sanded wood of Maya's offered chariot and then ran along the spokes of its wheels. The mightiest weapon in the world—the horse and chariot with a shielded driver and an archer inside. My skin tingled. I'd read about this years ago and longed to acquire such a weapon. And Paramessu once claimed that he'd been one of the best chariot drivers in the Egyptian army.

I'd use this very weapon against the enemies who'd left it for me.

Seneb stroked the equine's neck. The animal's eyes were wide, its nostrils flared as it snorted—it was still spooked from the shouting of the victims.

"Can this horse run as fast as our two?" I asked Seneb.

His boyish eyes widened as he stepped back and studied the creature, his hands rubbing at his cheeks. "No."

"Then attach both of our horses to this chariot instead," I said.

No one said a word.

"Do it," I said. "Tonight we have a feast to attend."

Chapter 21

Journal Translation

I SAT INSIDE OUR NEW RESIDENCE on the northern outskirts of el-Amarna. The spirits of Amun surrounded me, the stubble on my arms and legs sticking up as if something watched me from the shadows beneath the lamplight. The stench of fired flesh still hung in the air. My mind exhausted itself with scenarios that could unfold at the coming feast—my heart preparing for the emotion that would ensnare it and again tempt me to take rash action.

Tia, Paramessu, and I loaded into our new chariot led by our two horses. Darkness encompassed the land, broken only by spots of firelight flickering in the distance beyond the dark expanse between the northern houses and the palace.

Paramessu drove the horses north along the great road. The wood of the chariot bounded and rumbled along beneath me as trumpets blared in my head to a triad beat. Only the stars and waxing moon lit the way.

The wind gusted with a sudden burst, as if we rode into a gale, sweeping dirt up from the desert and assaulting my exposed skin. A wall of swirling sand formed in the moonlight in front of us, as if a barrier to Akhenaten's palace. A sinking feeling arose in my stomach. Was this magic from Akhenaten? This would not deter me.

Paramessu tugged on the reins of our steeds.

I shouted over the wind, "We ride through it."

Paramessu glanced over his shoulder. "It's a sandstorm, springing from the earth before our eyes. It will spook the horses and could suffocate us if it grows large enough. We should turn back."

I snatched the reins from his hands and snapped them. The horses jerked the chariot as they raced on. I did not wish to harm the horses, but this was too coincidental, and I would not stop now. The swirling dirt approached quickly, and the nostrils of our horses flared as they snorted in fear and folded their ears back.

We plunged into the flying grit at a full gallop. Paramessu and Tia ducked into the chariot and covered their heads. Dirt rubbed over my skin and into my mouth while scratching at my ears. Our horses pulled us from the other side of the thin wall, and the flying grit vanished in an instant, the night beyond as still as stagnant water.

I glanced back. The dirt stopped swirling and settled back to the ground in a haze that reflected pale moonlight.

"I won't forget that for a while," Paramessu said as he stood up on the rumbling chariot and jerked the reins from my hands, the horses still driving us on.

A cone of firelight sprang up ahead, inside the palace walls, its light reaching out to the el-Amarna valley.

Tugging on the reins, Paramessu slowed the charging equines as we approached the palace. Guards blocked a gated entrance, and lines of stakes ran along the side of the road here, fires burning at the top of each. The music in my head fell silent.

The palace's guards held their spears and shields just below their padded-leather caps and eyes. One angled his spear at us. "State your business."

I smirked. We could use our new chariot to run these two down like—

"Master Rem has arrived for the feast," Paramessu said, his posture rigid as the horses stomped with impatience. His hands tightened on the leather reins. "Ay invited him and his woman."

"Yes," the guard replied. "They are expecting you." He turned and shouted something over his shoulder. A guard standing atop the walls yelled to someone inside the compound, and the gates parted and swung inward with a loud creak.

The guards stepped aside to allow us entry. "Leave the chariot in the courtyard."

After the horses pulled us inside, we unloaded. Armed soldiers surrounded us. I slowly withdrew my swords and left them on the chariot, and Paramessu left his shield.

"Any other weapons?" a soldier asked as he and another circled us, their eyes searching our kilts.

"I usually never travel without my swords," I said, "but I understand that Pharaoh does not know me. If only he knew my devotion … I do not carry other arms."

The soldiers surrounded us and led us through the lamplight of long hallways and extensive chambers. Rattles shook to a beat. I held my hands to my ears, but it didn't block the sound—the music was only inside my head.

Exquisite murals surrounded us: a towering god-king crushing enemies with a club, shooting arrows from a chariot, or stomping on hordes of people. But in other reliefs, Akhenaten appeared as a loving family man, praising the Aten as its rays brought life and ankhs for him, his wife, and his daughters.

Drums joined the rattles in my head—a quiet thumping.

A roaring fire appeared through an open doorway, the heat of its flames washing over my exposed chest and face. Black smoke billowed out of the roofless chamber, sending the reek of seared flesh into the starry sky. Laughter erupted from a few men standing beside the bonfire. Something was on a spit, roasting over the flames—multiple animal carcasses.

The drumming grew louder.

Guards stood along the periphery of the chamber in silence. Men and women sat at tables positioned around the fire, throwing back drink and tearing into meat with oily fingers. They shouted to each other in a deafening racket that competed with the crackling flames. There must've been a hundred people celebrating.

An oddly deep voice echoed over the crackle of the blaze and the ruckus, drawing my attention. "Bring the ram's leg."

My eyes adjusted to the darkness on the far side of the fire. Steps led up to a raised platform. A throne of gold sparkled in the light, but shadows danced across the body and face of a man. Black-painted eyes closed, appearing like sockets of an empty skull. Akhenaten.

A thundering drum rattled my skull. I shook my head, and the internal music I'd been intermittently hearing since my return to this world quieted.

Heat, anger, jealousy, rage—my body trembled in a rush of emotion. My breathing quickened, as if I'd just sprinted a mile. The bane of my very existence was here …

Akhenaten stood from the throne in his hunched posture, his gangly hands and arms motioning from the shadows for a servant to hurry back to him. His elongated face with sunken cheeks and thick lips wrinkled into a scowl. The people at the tables fell silent, leaving only the sound of hissing and crackling flames.

The servant handed the god-king a golden plate with raw meat and bones piled in a heap.

I stepped closer.

"This man," Akhenaten shouted, spinning around. His voice shook the room like the roar of a pack of lions. His wing-like shoulder blades slid under thin muscle.

The wrinkled face of an elderly man appeared beside Pharaoh's knees, the whites of his eyes bulging in the night—the previous owner of the house that we'd just acquired.

"A man we all trusted and treated as friend and family has betrayed everyone here," Akhenaten said, "betrayed the Aten, betrayed *me,* God himself!"

The man cowered, and my heart fluttered. I stumbled to a table near the steps leading up to Pharaoh's throne. Tia and Paramessu joined me, their eyes wide as they took in the scene, their postures rigid with fear. We all sat down on the fire-warmed wood of a bench.

"Do you deny any of the accusations?" Akhenaten said.

The man's head dropped.

Akhenaten waved gangly arms. "Not even an attempt to defend yourself? You could at least lie and tell me that some newcomer who wanted your house planted the images of the false gods. You disgust me, and so does your vilest of souls. Open your lips."

Pharaoh tore a hunk of flesh from his plate with a ripping sound. Blood dripped across his hand and ran down his forearm in a stream.

The victim's jaw trembled as it opened.

Akhenaten shoved his plate in front of the old man. "Tonight you dine on the raw flesh of your false god. Eat."

My eyes closed. If the man ate the ram's meat, would Akhenaten spare his life or soul? My stomach twisted and knotted, causing me to double over in pain.

The victim's hand trembled as he reached for the meat, slowly pulled off a chunk, and brought it to his lips. Tears trickled from his eyes. Red flesh slid into his mouth and his lips closed, his jaw chewing—slowly.

Akhenaten kicked the old man in his side. "You will eat it all." The man crumpled onto the golden plate. Akhenaten bellowed with laughter, tossing his head back, the crowns of Upper and Lower Egypt glistening in the firelight.

Rage burned inside me, my hands searching for my absent swords.

"My pharaoh," a man in a wig said, striding past my table—a handsome face with orange eye paint—Ay, Nefertiti's father. "There's someone at the gate, a messenger. He says he's discovered something strange."

Akhenaten glanced back. "A messenger interrupts my feast and the punishment of this unfaithful bigot? He can wait through the night and morning, until after my chariot ride along the great road."

"My god-king," Ay said, approaching, his volume lowering.

Akhenaten spun around. "Messengers may die under the heat of the Aten if it is to my benefit or choosing. I do not concern myself with such things, only the profits of Pharaoh."

Ay stopped and slowly nodded, as if swallowing a response.

Akhenaten nodded at the old man I'd ousted. "Now get this heathen out of my palace for the last time."

A figure cloaked in black emerged from behind the throne without a sound. The stench of rotting flesh reached my nostrils, making me gag. The Devouring Monster lived right here in the palace, performing Akhenaten's bidding as if Pharaoh were Anubis himself?

A golden hilt slipped out from the long sleeves of the monster's garment—the hilt molded into the image of a crocodile's head. And a blade of bone emerged from these golden jaws, the actual mandibular bone of one of the great beasts, the row of crocodile teeth forming a serrated edge. The hand that held the weapon was deformed, with missing fingers and claws, and a jagged scar, red and hairless, running along one edge. At least Croc had been able to maim this monster, but no one else seemed to be able to harm it.

Another shadowy figure in black wavered behind the Devouring Monster, as if a figment of my imagination, its glowing green eyes muted by white linen.

A Dark One.

Here? Was it only my imagination, or could I see ghosts now that I had died? But legend said that they would again rise up against Egypt and—

The old man screamed as the Devouring Monster dragged him away to a dark exit, the man clawing at the tiled floor of the palace with a high-pitched scratching that made the roots of my teeth ache. He left only trails of blood and broken fingernails.

The Dark One followed after him.

Chapter 22

Journal Translation

I TURNED AWAY, NOT WANTING TO ponder the fate of the old council-man at the hands of the Devouring Monster. There was nothing I'd be able to do at this moment except lose my soul.

The attendees of the feast clapped and returned to their deafening conversations, their voices echoing off the chamber walls all around me.

A contingent of women in silky white dresses sashayed through the scene, looking like princesses amidst drunken sailors. Most were servants who followed after three women. The sweet chorus of harp strings being plucked by a delicate hand arose in my head. A horse-faced woman with red eye paint headed the group: Beketaten, Akhenaten's sister and one of his wives. My heart lurched recalling the night I'd let myself be tricked by her—believing that she was Nefertiti coming for me in the darkness …

Music grew louder—the harp strings being plucked faster and with more determination. The face behind Beketaten's was soft and cute, younger, with blue-eye paint: Mutnedjmet, Nefertiti's younger sister—the one with the rampant curiosity. We'd spent many nights snooping around Memphis together, searching for answers to Pharaoh's fake plague. But tonight her eyes were drawn, her face tight, as if she hadn't smiled in years. She'd never worn eye paint before, either, at least not when I'd known her. She used to be so full of life.

Mutnedjmet and Beketaten parted, making room for another to step forth. Scents of rose and feathery citrus permeated the room. A flowing white dress, a heart-shaped face sculpted as if art for the gods. Green-painted eyes. But even more beautiful than I remembered … My heart pumped three times before stopping for a moment.

Nefertiti.

The harp chords turned to a whisper, all the noise of the world falling still. I only saw her. Love in its purest form? I'd grown to almost despise this woman over the years, for who she'd become and for her choices, but all of that could've been Akhenaten's magical manipulation of her mind. Now that I'd seen her again …

With her nose held high and a flat-topped crown upon her head, she swayed past me up the steps and took a seat beside Pharaoh. The other women surrounded her. She motioned for a servant to fetch her a golden plate of food and smiled—so happy that she appeared intoxicated. I could see it in her eyes.

My stomach squeezed as if someone crushed it in a grip. I heaved but swallowed a rising wave of fluid. Heat rose into my chest, up my neck, and burned my face like fire—jealousy in all its vicious torment and anger with all of its teeth sinking into my heart like the jaws of the Devouring Monster itself. I could feel the festering disease that I carried inside my beating heart send a rush of black blood coursing through my body. Such vengeance. I had no hope in controlling it, even though I'd steeled myself before we'd left. And I'd hoped that time would've dulled my emotions …

But here she was, after all the years since I'd asked her to run away with me and find love and happiness, after all the years toiling in slavery, all the years of traveling to the far reaches of the world—the vast majority of my life having slipped by without being able to spend it with her and find fulfillment and true love. Instead, my vile master, the murderer of my father and the previous crown prince, spent his life indulging himself with her beauty.

Blood ran onto my tongue, the salty taste resulting from biting my lip far too hard. I swallowed, and the rage inside me intensified, as if I thirsted for blood—not only from myself, but also from others. Blood would be spilled soon. My fingers dug into Father's bronze bracelet on my wrist.

A servant delivered a golden plate to my love's delicate hands, which were nearly as pale as milk. She shook her head and said something to the servant woman but patted her arm, as if a caring friend.

Had Akhenaten poisoned her mind with the great magic that he carried or by some other means? Was she completely changed, even now still under his control? He'd gotten to her before I'd finally asked her to run away with me. I'd waited too long building up my courage, waiting for the right moment. This had led to my entire life playing out along the wrong path—a trail weaving up and down mountains but in view of the flat path that I had foreseen for myself.

Multiple young girls, their daughters, paraded behind the women, taking seats at a table behind the throne. Then a boy followed. He walked as if attending a morning breakfast, relaxed, but with a limp. One of his feet was misshapen, stump-like, and he carried a walking stick. But on his head rested a crown of gold. The boy hobbled up the steps and sat in a golden chair behind Pharaoh, beside his mother, Beketaten. His features appeared common, like mine. I stifled a gasp. Could the boy prince, Tut, be my son, or was the night I'd spent with his mother too long ago?

"Now where is this man?" the oddly deep voice of Akhenaten called out, silencing the entire chamber again. "The one who brought the devil-worshipping traitor to justice?"

I swallowed my rising dread as I clung to my bracelet for strength. My former master was looking for me. But he was far too narcissistic to remember much detail about me, including my bracelet.

"There he is," someone shouted. Maya, the Royal Scribe, rose from his seat, brushing his long hair behind cup-like ears before pointing at me. "Rem."

"Stand, my subject," Akhenaten boomed.

I brushed my hair forward, around my cheeks, and stood, slowly turning to face Pharaoh.

Akhenaten grinned, his eyes narrowing as he leaned forward, the black of his painted lids growing like hoods. He studied my face and the magical mask as he sat still for a moment. Could he still sense magic in any form? "The Aten recognizes your accomplishment—achieved because I allowed for it. You are, however, hideous. The Aten wishes you to acquire a mask and to cover half of your face with it." His fingers clutched the heads of two golden sphinxes, one at each armrest.

I slowly exhaled. Did my former master control an actual sphinx—is that how he helped enforce his rule? But no one had controlled the sphinx in a millennium—or so I'd heard. I didn't even know what that meant, controlling statues.

"You are welcome for the blessing of the accomplishment, Rem," Akhenaten said.

Choking back all emotion, as the magician had tried to teach me those many years ago, I nodded. "Thank you, my pharaoh. You are a kind and generous god, the only god. All the people of Egypt must know how lucky they are to have you as their one creator. I will seek a mask."

He stood and stared in my direction. "And who is that beside you?" He stepped to the front of his raised platform and extended a long finger and fingernail.

Did he recognize Paramessu, even with his shaven head?

"Stand and let me see you." He motioned with a wave.

Paramessu cleared his throat, slowly pushing himself from his seat.

"No," Akhenaten's shout echoed around the chamber like thunder.

Paramessu's face paled as he clung to his seat. I glanced around for an escape route, my heart hammering in my ears.

"Not you, her." He pointed at Tia, who sat between us. "A beauty. Is she royalty where you are from?"

I nodded.

"And where is that?" Akhenaten asked. I could feel a hundred pairs of eyes burrowing into my soul, their curiosity searching for answers.

"Hierakonpolis," I said, recalling the city where Father said I was born. I didn't have time to answer with anything else, and only someone from Egypt would be able to answer with a city name other than Thebes, Memphis, or el-Amarna.

Akhenaten shook his head. "No one of any significance is from there." He stared at Tia and tapped on his sunken cheek, which created a hollow thudding. "I will bless this woman of yours by taking her into my bed this night."

I stumbled back and nearly tripped as my lower leg hit my wooden seat.

Paramessu grabbed Tia's arm. "I will die before I let him touch you," he whispered.

"Then you will die, and he will still have her," I whispered and grunted for him to be silent. Then louder, I said, "Surely, my god-king, you do not need to expend yourself with my boorish wife. She is beautiful but is nothing compared to all the women you have—especially the queen.

Our queen is not only stunning, but I've also heard that her heart is pure gold, that she has a razor-sharp wit and undying love for her kingdom and all of its people. One such as her could never be bought with material possessions or power." As I uttered the facetious words, a light burned inside my heart, fighting the fetid disease that I harbored there. I trusted that Nefertiti could not truly see herself for what Akhenaten had transformed her into—and the obvious disparity of my claims. And she would never expect mockery, probably had never experienced it. But I needed to pull her back out of the darkness that had engulfed her soul as soon as I possibly could.

Nefertiti cocked her head, studying me. Her plump, red lips rose into a smirk. Mutnedjmet stood and stared at me with wide eyes, and Nefertiti winked.

Akhenaten stepped down to us. "I take whatever woman I desire."

Nefertiti didn't bat an eye in surprise. Pharaoh had many women, including sisters, daughters, cousins, and a harem.

Something felt like it wrapped around my beating heart and squeezed. I could not kill an immortal god, especially one who'd already arisen from death. And this confrontation was happening too quickly—I'd not yet managed to turn a single soldier or even a slave against him.

"Yes, my pharaoh." I knelt on the hard tile floor and shoved my palms outward in the sign of adoration. In my youth, I'd learned how to placate the anger of Akhenaten. But my soul twisted in defiance, my recently obtained pride and the light in my heart shattering and crumbling into the dust around me. Father would be disappointed. I could feel and almost see the rot of my inner organs crawling along the outer muscles of my beating heart, turning it black.

Pharaoh's walking stick of gold clacked against the tile as he stepped before my bowed head, his golden sandals shimmering in the firelight.

Paramessu stood.

"I have not even had the chance to present the gift that I brought for you," I said quickly, rising up on my knees. "But please take my wife; I'd find nothing more satisfying than to know Pharaoh, God himself, has shared my woman, even if she is not worth his efforts."

Paramessu coughed.

"But before you depart with her, let me bestow jewels upon you—jewels only befitting of the one god."

I would crush the malevolent rapture that Akhenaten would experience when witnessing a man's jealousy by showing eagerness to share a woman with him. He would be less inclined to take a woman if her man did not care or would enjoy the affiliation. That would lessen his desire. As the magician had indicated those years ago, no one knew Akhenaten as well as me. In some sick, twisted way, I was a great weapon of sorts against his all-consuming power.

My gaze rose, meeting Akhenaten's. Light shone within his irises beneath the dark hoods over his eyes. His burning desire for Tia ebbed, and he appeared to lose interest in her.

"Servant, bring the gold from the chariot," I said.

Paramessu glanced at me, and his clenched fists relaxed. He dashed off.

Akhenaten grabbed Tia by the chin and turned her face to the left and right. She lowered her gaze. He stuck a long finger into her mouth and she gagged. Akhenaten grinned. He removed his finger and slapped her across the face—a clap sounding.

Tia cowered. I gritted my teeth and stood. I would not tolerate this—it was how he'd treated Nefertiti all those years ago.

"She is not worth my efforts," Akhenaten said.

Paramessu strode back inside the open-air chamber with what appeared to be a golden man.

Chapter 23

Journal Translation

PARAMESSU MARCHED UP to Pharaoh, carting in a man-sized object of pure gold—the inner layer of a sarcophagus, to encase a royal mummy. But it was faceless. Red and blue stones ran in circles around the margins and across the chest. Firelight danced on the metal. Whispers and gasps ran through the royal family and the councilmen who were packed into the chamber as the bonfire crackled.

"I had this fashioned for you," I said, lying about this incomplete and empty sarcophagus that we'd found in Amenhotep's tomb. It may have been intended for an immediate family member, although we'd pounded out the unfinished name. "Gold from the mines of Nubia. Much of my wealth has gone into its creation. Only the face needs to be chiseled and shaped. I could not watch an artist create a flaw in such a masterpiece—your face, the face of the immortal god-king. I believed that your artists would be superior craftsman and that they could mold it as they studied your divine features, capturing its essence for others, for all of eternity."

Akhenaten ran a hand along the smooth gold of the empty face. A spark lit up between his fingertip and the metal—his magic coursing through his skin.

"You made this and transported it all the way from Nubia?" His eyes didn't blink as he studied it.

"Yes," I said.

"What were you doing in Nubia?" he asked. "You, a lesser man from Hierakonpolis?"

"Trading goods around the world, my god-king," I said. "That is how I made my fortune. Decades of traveling, bargaining, and … other tactics. But it has paid off, and now I share most of it with you. You are the only reason that I returned to Egypt and to el-Amarna after all this time. I wished to look upon the mightiest being that ever walked the earth."

Akhenaten raised a hand over his head and made a come-hither motion.

His hulking ogre of a bodyguard, Suty, lumbered over, his clean-shaven head glistening with sweat.

"Take this to my chambers," Akhenaten whispered. "I would like to compare it to the one my artists have made. If this one exceeds my artists' abilities, cut off their hands and find more talented people to sculpt my face into this gold."

Suty nodded. "With pleasure. Those weaklings need to get roughened up once in a while." He hefted the priceless sarcophagus onto his shoulder and strode out, disappearing into the darkness.

Another man shuffled forward—he had a head like a watermelon and no chin, as if the fat of his belly and chest blended into his face: Pentju, the doctor who'd worked with Akhenaten to devise, falsely diagnose, and spread the fake plague that killed my father. Only Akhenaten and Suty's vile hands had inflicted more suffering. Pentju—the doctor who'd tormented me—one of three men who needed to die, along with the black-cloaked monster from the underworld.

"My god-king," Pentju said, tapping his hidden chin, which sent ripples through the fat of his neck. "If this gift does not exceed the golden sarcophagus that you currently have, I humbly ask for it to be used to cover my body when I pass."

"Hold your tongue, Doctor," Ay said, rushing down the steps. "I am the vizier and serve only Pharaoh. You serve everyone here. Lesser men help lesser people. And you misdiagnosed my niece, a daughter of Pharaoh, who has suffered because of—"

"That is a lie," Pentju said. "I found a lesion of—"

"The stores need gold, my pharaoh," Maya said, stepping forward. "We can use this to purchase grain from the outside world—more than we'd need for years."

"This discussion is over, you bickering men," Nefertiti said, rising from her throne. She paced along the raised platform. "The boy-prince will have a lifetime before he needs such an item. Therefore, this one is mine. So sit down, or Suty will cut off *your* hands."

Ay glanced up at her, his upper lip wrinkling.

Nefertiti folded her arms. "Sit down, Father."

Was this what my Nefertiti had become? Was my entire life, my life chasing after the idea of this perfect woman, all a lie?

Ay spun around and marched off, exiting the chamber. Pentju shuffled away to a table, sat down, and stuffed his face with charred meat.

Akhenaten, in his stiff-legged gait, descended the stairs and then departed, using the same exit as Suty. The royal family rose and left, followed by the councilmen. Only Tia, Paramessu, the soldiers stationed under torches at the periphery of the chamber, and Pentju remained. Beads of sweat dripped from the Royal Doctor's forehead and landed in his beer mug as he grabbed another plate. His lips smacked and his teeth gnashed on moist meat before he tossed his beer back in a long swallow.

Nausea rolled through my stomach ... but something called out—a meow.

Two cats wandered around, crying out for morsels. One was gray, the other stark white. Ribs protruded from their sides, and the bumps of their spines showed along their backs. The white one hopped onto the table near Pentju and grabbed a piece of meat with its teeth.

"Get away, you dirty beasts," Pentju said and backhanded the cat off of the table. The cat hissed as it sailed away and crashed onto the floor with a thud. The doctor laughed. "Even beasts dine on the flesh of the old gods." He turned and winked at me. "Please eat and enjoy yourselves before you depart."

"To someone who only speaks the truth about disease and diagnoses," I said, biting back the cold edge of anger from my false words, "to he who understands true affliction more than any man in the world—I will heed your advice." I held my jug of beer high in a salute.

Pentju grinned, his jiggling cheeks turning red.

Something soft rubbed around my ankles, and a purr sounded as crystal-blue eyes stared into mine. The white cat was back. Its mouth popped open from its sunken face with cloudy eyes as it released another meow—such an old creature. My heart softened. Reaching down, I stroked under its bony cheeks. Dangling skin hung from its lower belly, as if the pet had been obese at one point but was now emaciated.

My eyes closed as I realized this was the son of Hapu's, the magician's cat, left to fend for herself after he'd committed suicide. And no one was caring for it. Could it even be the same cat the magician had had when I'd stolen his pomegranate? No, it would be thirty years old. Unless it was also magical. But perhaps the magician only found similar looking cats for his pets.

I grabbed a hunk of tough meat from a discarded tray and held it out for the animal. The cat snatched the meat from my hand and gobbled it down. Then she sat, waiting for more. Something was attached to her neck, under her chin. Reaching down, I removed it: rolled papyrus, fashioned into a collar. Strange. I'd never seen anything like that before. I examined the roll of papyrus—it appeared blank, but there was an edge to unroll it, like the messages that the magician had used to train me how to read and—

The cat meowed.

I ripped a piece of tender meat from a pile of bones sitting on the tray. But I paused. A carving knife sat beside the bones, covered in blood. Brown juices seeped out of the meat in my hand and rolled across my skin like oil. I took the knife and tucked it into my kilt.

The white feline sat on her protruding haunches, waiting, her blue eyes boring into mine. I held out the meat, and a face appeared in my mind, one with deep wrinkles traced with black paint, and gray eyes stared back at me, as if the old magician stood right here. I jerked upright.

"I hope you have lived in the moment and enjoyed some of your life," the face of the magician in my imagination said as I looked upon his cat. "But not lived only *for* the moment. Such is the way of Akhenaten. You can still work toward your goal and relish in the present without using up everything you'll need tomorrow and beyond."

I nodded, as if the magician really spoke the words to me. Was I only wishing that he'd taught me this, or was this some kind of magic?

"I know I was harsh with you," the face of the magician continued, his pale gray eyes now the icy blue of his cat's, and unblinking. "But if I was not, you wouldn't have been ready to compete with everyone around you. You had to rise from nothing, while all the others had been training since childhood for their given positions in society. I'd never say you were special, or you'd expect your road to be too easy and you'd have accepted a miserable fate and given up many years ago."

"I was not special," I said. "Just an ordinary boy."

The magician's stern face broke into a grin of agreement and faded into the night around me.

His cat snatched the tender meat from my palm and lumbered away, the dangling skin at her belly bouncing side to side.

Papyrus crinkled between my fingers as I played with the rolled-up papyrus collar. I teased it open. A message was written on the inner surface:

> For any man or group that has succeeded and returned to the palace of el-Amarna, heed these words: Darkness has settled into my soul—my ba wingless and the light of my ka dwindling. I cannot hold out much longer. This regime of Egypt is suffocating my resolve. Time draws to a close. But I have left you the start of a small army, one that no one will suspect. My act of hatred was a ploy. Make them powerful.

The parchment drifted from my hands and floated on a breeze into the roaring flames. It sparked green and ignited, turning to ash in an instant and releasing the smell of rotten eggs.

Chapter 24

Journal Translation

I WALKED DOWN THE long corridors of Akhenaten's palace under mounted lamps whose flames sputtered and created wavering shadows.

"I'll meet you at the chariot," I said to Paramessu as I guided Tia away by the soft area at the small of her back.

"Where are you—?" Paramessu tried to say, but I put a finger to my cracked lips. He pointed at the knife hilt protruding from my kilt and stepped back. "Are you delusional? Surely, you do not believe you'll get very far with a knife."

After waving him and Tia off, I veered down a hallway in the opposite direction of the palace's entrance. A guard was stationed ahead, standing against a wall. I turned down another hallway and crept deeper into the unknown of the palace on silent feet. My heart raced, my mind alive. Darkness settled around me with a raw feeling of secrecy and deceit.

I arrived at a junction where hallways and chambers ran off in multiple directions. There was a window overhead and an open doorway to a courtyard … and no one was outside.

I penned a quick message on a papyrus sheet. Then I pulled the carving knife from my waist, cut myself, and screamed loud enough to wake the intoxicated. Sharp pain bit into my upper chest and arm. I yelled again as I tossed the carving knife out the window.

Within seconds, heavy footfalls echoed through the halls all around me. Stomping regiments carrying torches and spears emerged from opposite corridors.

I lay on the floor, clutching a bleeding gash that ran across my chest and upper arm.

Soldiers surrounded me with spears pointed and shields raised.

"He sliced me and ran out into the night." I pointed to the courtyard and grimaced in real pain as warm blood streamed down across my abdominal muscles and dripped onto my kilt.

The soldiers glanced all around.

"You three, into the courtyard," a soldier in a padded cap said, motioning for three others to hurry outside. "What happened?"

"I-I'm not sure," I mumbled, trembling. "I saw someone sneaking around in the shadows. I followed them, but I think it was a trap. Someone else jumped out from around this corner and threw me down. They tried to slice my throat or impale my heart, but I struggled with them and they only got this one slash in before dashing off. I didn't see either one of them well." I groaned and curled up into a ball on the cold tile floor.

"Find them." The soldier motioned for the rest of his men to search the palace, except for one. "You, fetch the doctor."

Voices echoed from outside and deep within the palace.

"You're the man who turned in the traitor, aren't you?" the soldier asked. I nodded. "Rem."

"What's that?" He noticed a piece of papyrus on the floor but grabbed my shoulders and propped me up against the wall. "The doctor will be here soon." He snatched the note—the note I'd just written. The papyrus crinkled as he unfolded it. "Writing. You read?"

"I can, but not now," I said, exaggerating. "The pain is unbearable."

He scoffed. "I've seen worse in training. You'll be fine. You elite men never experience real pain to compare your minor injuries to."

Spears and shields clattered as another row of soldiers arrived, stumbling a bit and appearing as if they'd just awoken. The stench of rank sweat permeated the air as the watermelon-headed doctor pushed through the group.

Pentju knelt and looked at my chest, prodding the edges of the gash. "Superficial."

Stabbing pain shot through my skin, into the deeper muscles of my chest. I winced and groaned.

"I will wash it and stitch it up." He wiped dripping beads of sweat from his bald head. The smeared grease of charred meat still stained his cheeks. "You'll be fine, but it will leave a scar."

"I found this," the soldier said, handing Pentju the papyrus note.

The doctor's eyes ran back and forth over the message. "We have another traitor in our midst, in this very palace." His eyes gaped, his hidden chin wrinkling as his mouth fell open. "They've taken revenge on the man who reported one of their own."

The soldier beside me glanced about. "I thought they'd all been killed off years ago."

Pentju slowly exhaled. "So did I. Akhenaten and Ay must be informed of this." He glanced back over his shoulder at the guards who'd arrived with him and handed one of them the fake letter. "But first, stop everyone from leaving the palace and find out how many people have already departed for the city. You"—he pointed at me—"will stay here tonight." He grunted as he hefted his massive bulk and stood. Two soldiers grabbed me under my arms and pulled me to my feet. They assisted and guided me as we walked down shadowy corridors.

We entered a large chamber filled with tables of various sizes, many covered with bronze or obsidian surgical instruments. Pentju lit another lamp inside before grabbing a bucket of water. He wiped at my cut, and stinging pain ran across my skin. I bit my lip.

He handed me a bottle of wine as he lifted a curved needle with yellow sinew attached to one end. "You might want this."

I threw back a long swig, which was bitter and acidic. My tongue tingled.

"Take another drink, then on three I will start stitching. One …" He jabbed the needle through my skin, which tugged at the inner layers of flesh.

I shouted in surprise. The string passed through my skin with a quiet tearing sound and stabbing pain ran across my chest.

"It's strange, but patients don't jerk as much when they're surprised." He weaved the string and closed the gaping hole in my skin as he continued to run the needle through my flesh.

"I have come to see for myself," a female's voice said as quiet footsteps approached the doorway outside. She entered—Mutnedjmet, Nefertiti's sister with the rampant curiosity, a potential flaw in my plan, someone I did not fully understand. She crossed her arms over her chest and stared at my wound, her light-brown eyes surrounded by deep blue paint. Her gaze slowly rose to meet mine. "You seem familiar to me."

"How so, my lady?" I asked between flinching as the doctor continued stitching my wound.

Her gentle face wrinkled as if in anguish. "But the person you remind me of would never have had a man put to death or had his soul devoured." Then, under her breath, she said, "You've only added to the harshness of the world. I've long been broken, but whenever I see other men such as yourself like this …" She shook her head. "The larger pieces of my heart shatter into smaller and smaller fragments."

I sucked in a sharp breath as my heart twisted with guilt.

"What is this?" Mutnedjmet picked up a jar of clear liquid from a table and held it in front of the doctor.

Pentju barely averted his eyes from my wound. "An astringent agent."

Mutnedjmet stepped closer and dumped the contents of the jar over my shoulder. The acidic liquid rolled down my chest and across my wound. Such burning pain. I groaned and gritted my teeth.

Mutnedjmet spun around and stormed out.

I gasped for breath for several seconds before the burning in my open wound subsided.

"Have you always tried to alleviate pain?" I asked the doctor, knowing that he'd tortured me in the solitary cave while feigning to study his fake plague. The pain of the stitching intensified, and I glanced down at the gaping wound—blood and the jagged margins of my moist flesh. My head spun. I glanced around the room and took slow breaths. I had to keep my focus.

Bloodied scalpels and gripping instruments sat on the tables beside bottles of colored liquids. Body parts floated in glass jars. I shuddered as I pursed my lips, imagining Father and the others who'd suffered because of Pentju's lies.

"Sometimes pain and suffering is needed to obtain knowledge, and to convince the masses," he replied. "Death to the few for the greater good of the group."

"Well said, my good doctor." I clenched my fists. "But each of us will feel great pain at some point. You and me. Even the elite of Egypt. Perhaps it is a kind of retribution."

His eyebrows rose as he looked up from closing my wound. His hands paused. "You mean when we each pass into the next world, alone?"

I nodded, picturing what kind of death would best suit this deceitful manipulator of men ...

Chapter 25

Journal Translation

THE RAPPING OF KNUCKLES on wood sounded—someone knocked at the door of my new room in Akhenaten's palace. Tia, Paramessu, and I lay on thin blankets on the floor, but Paramessu and Tia lay apart, respecting the roles they currently played.

"Hello," Suty, the ogre of a man said as he stepped inside into the dim lighting of a dying lamp. His pig's ear twitched as his eyes narrowed—studying my wound. The air grew heavy, as if drained of its breathable aspect.

Another man entered—Akhenaten, whose dark eyes met mine. The rearing cobra and the vulture protruded from the fused red and white crowns upon his head.

I bolted upright.

"You?" Akhenaten said in his bass voice as he scrutinized me. "The one who brought the traitor to justice? Coincidence? But you did not see the person who attacked you?"

I shook my head. "But there are at least two more of the unfaithful right here in your midst. One lured me into the trap."

Akhenaten's long fingers clenched, his deformed thumbnail still carved into the image of the Aten rising between two peaks. His knuckles popped. "They will lose their souls!" His voice carried to the far reaches of the palace.

Tia scooted far away and huddled into a corner.

My heartbeat quickened. Images of my younger self and the beatings I'd suffered at the hands of Akhenaten filled my head. I gritted my teeth and stood in defiance of his terror, although cold sweat trickled down my back.

Akhenaten tapped his sunken cheek, which created hollow echoes from his mouth. "But why not kill you? Would that not send me a more powerful message of defiance or resistance?"

"I am skilled in combat, my pharaoh," I said, "having traveled the world. I was able to fight off my attacker, as he only wielded a knife, even if he used the advantage of surprise. And who am I, really?" I smiled to myself with my hidden meaning. "No one of significance. The shock of an attack inside the palace while leaving the victim alive to tell the story may inflict as much terror as a murder."

Akhenaten's thick lips pulled up toward his dark eyes.

"And I probably wasn't their primary target," I said. "Yes, I may have discovered a blasphemer and taken up residence in that man's house, but those who are a part of his cult may desire a much more powerful victim for their retaliation."

Shadows and firelight wavered across Pharaoh's face. "Like who?"

"Well, I'd say you, but you are an immortal," I replied. "They cannot kill you. So then I'd ask myself whose death would harm you most? A family member? An advisor?"

Akhenaten scoffed, but his shaded eyes wandered as he mulled over something. A minute of silence followed, as if he'd never thought about who mattered to him before—as was my suspicion. "I almost said Nefertiti—my prized possession, but"—he glanced back at Suty—"it would be my only son, Tut—to destroy my lineage."

I nodded. "My belief as well, my god-king. If I were you, I'd triple the guards around Tut, as well as assign multiple soldiers to any others you'd want to protect. But only use those whom you know you can trust. Whoever these people are, they will have the advantage of surprise."

Akhenaten pondered something for a moment, as if considering for the first time what people he really knew. Maybe the paranoia that ran rampant in his head in his youth would blossom again.

"Why didn't Ay or my mindless soldiers or councilmen advise me to increase the protection for Tut or Nefertiti?" He turned and glared at his monster of a bodyguard. "Perhaps this stranger should be in my council."

Suty backed out of the doorway. "I ... can't think like that. That's Ay's job."

"Send word to Mahu and get him and his police to reside in the palace for the time being." Akhenaten shoved past Suty's bulging shoulder and stepped out into the hall. "The city does not need as much of a disciplined hand as the palace does right now."

Suty snarled at me but followed his master. Their slapping footsteps and the clacking of Akhenaten's golden walking stick faded into the distance.

"I do not know you," Paramessu said after a minute. "What are you plotting?"

Tia rose to her feet. "He's confronting his former master, Pharaoh himself. But how he's planning on achieving his revenge, he's still keeping that a secret."

"I'm doing something that someone should've done years ago," I said. "Now you must find me two men in this palace who can be killed without too much upheaval—people of lesser importance. And not too old, or people won't believe they are the ones who attacked me."

"How will I know if they are deserving?" Paramessu asked. "And are you hoping to find more blasphemers here? I think that would be difficult, especially after the display at the feast tonight."

My forehead wrinkled. I'd forgotten that this former captain of the Egyptian military would have at one time sworn to protect Pharaoh, his family, and his council. He may have a hard time with this. "All the men in this palace gave up their morals and beliefs for power, wealth, women, and other gains. Everyone here is responsible for the suffering of the people of Egypt, which includes the children in the barracks … All but perhaps two people who reside here are deserving."

Paramessu nodded, but the muscles at his jaw tensed.

I lay down to sleep, but my mind drifted for hours. Who close to Akhenaten could I abduct? I wanted to take Nefertiti more than anyone, if not Tut, and I could use gold and riches to draw Nefertiti in, but she'd never be alone and vulnerable. Then whom, and what could I use to lure them in?

Chapter 26

Journal Translation

OVER THE NEXT TWO DAYS, we were not allowed to leave the palace. Tia, Paramessu, and I dined with the royalty, roamed the open areas of the palace and its courtyards, and slept in our provided room.

"You may go as you please," Ay said, stepping into our room as the Aten's light waned into evening. But his eyes were narrowed as he studied me and my magically distorted face, as if he didn't trust me or he hated me for getting into Akhenaten's good graces so quickly. "There's been no sign of the blasphemers, and many people had already left before we'd sealed the exits. No traitor is going to do anything now, at least not until we appear to relax our guard."

"Thank you," I said. "I will have my servants keep watch for suspicious activity in the city and report anything to you at once."

"Yes, and if you return to the palace, ask for me. The guards will find me," Ay said and marched off.

Soon after, we rode away from Akhenaten's palace on our chariot into the night. But Paramessu only trotted the horses, their pacing hooves pounding like the beating of music, complementing the vibrations that the axle and wood of the chariot sent through my body.

Paramessu reined in the animals as we reached the street in front of our new mansion. We unloaded, and I walked up to the flickering torches on either side of the front door.

"Finally decide to come home?" Harkhuf's voice came from the shadows around the side of the building.

"We were detained," I said as I swung open a new, wooden front door and entered the dark mansion.

Harkhuf stepped into the torchlight out front and followed us inside. "I bet you were. Started some kind of ruckus, I presume. Police have been running about the city knocking on doors. They started the night you left."

I faced Seneb. "Purchase me a black cloak and a large sack. And if you can, find a snake and a large scorpion. That would be much appreciated."

The dwarf brothers exchanged wide-eyed glances.

I went straight to bed to avoid any more questions.

⁕ ⁕ ⁕

Another day passed with no more excitement than Akhenaten parading himself and his queen up and down the great road in their divine cycle of birth, death, and rebirth. In the midst of the display, I briefly instructed my companions about their duties for my latest plan. Akhenaten's shiny chariot of gold raced along like a beam of the Aten, the white horses heaving for breath, their plumes of feathers waving. All of Egypt cowered in their thundering wake, but chariots of soldiers now trailed behind them, and they all disappeared back into the palace.

"A jubilee," a thin young man shouted some time later, running down the street in front of our house, "for the common people of Egypt." He threw his hands into the air and ran around in circles before carrying his message to houses down the road.

"There's a dust storm like I haven't seen in a while," Seneb said, pointing out the front door into the morning light. A brown cloud hovered over the great road, up north by the palace. "Foreboding, like the air Harkhuf leaves behind after eating too many beans."

Akhenaten was on his way back to the city again. And he'd sacrifice almost anyone inside the palace if it meant capturing and killing those who defied him—those who still worshipped Amun or another god beside himself. He would raze el-Amarna to the ground to find the blasphemers who did not exist.

A horde of councilmen and the royal family rode closer inside their rumbling chariots, throwing up dust like a windstorm.

"This is our chance." I gathered my weapons and gear and walked to the front door of our house. "We must follow them."

Paramessu shook his head. "But all of the military and the police will be watching closely, hiding or appearing to be off duty. If you do something now, you will certainly be caught."

I pushed past him. "Then we will have to be careful."

I hitched our horses to the chariot as Paramessu, Tia, and the two brothers squeezed into the small cart. I stepped onto the back edge, shoved against their warm bodies, and held on to the sides of the chariot.

Paramessu snapped the reins, and we galloped after the procession. My fingers dug into the wood rails as the chariot tore along, wobbling and bouncing over an occasional rut, the bounding wood beneath me shaking my hands and feet as if I tumbled down the side of a mountain. I stared into the billowing dust created by the royal family's passage, imagining the revenge I'd take—or my own death.

The royal family stopped their chariots under the Window of Appearances—the covered bridge that spanned the great road. They unloaded and disappeared into the towers on either side of the bridge. Paramessu reined in our horses, and we unloaded.

The people of el-Amarna swarmed the streets and gathered below the bridge, as if bees moving between hives.

What were they waiting for while subjecting themselves to the rising heat of the Aten? The blanket of off-white clouds that still veiled the Aten didn't seem to help cool any of this city.

Then faces appeared in the bridge's window far above—the shadowy face of Pharaoh, his skin radiating gold. Nefertiti, Suty, Ay, Tut, Beketaten, and the rest of the royal family emerged.

The people cheered and clapped in a deafening chorus.

Members of the royal family threw bread out the window, and loaves rained down on their starving people. Soldiers emerged from the towers at either side of the road, handing out jugs of wine and beer.

My companions and I walked to the outskirts of the mob. Two rail-thin men bumped into each other and shouted, their hands on the same loaf of bread. One tugged at the bread while the other swung a fist at his adversary's face. The loaf ripped apart, and the men fell over backward.

Other people around them screamed at each other, pointing fingers, their faces red.

Someone grabbed my shoulder. My hands found my swords as I glanced back. I spotted gray hair at the man's temples, running back along the sides of his head—Mahu. A spear rested in his hand.

"Don't eat the offerings," he whispered. "The others associated with the palace all know better, but you're new. The food is only for the poor."

"Of course," I said. "I wouldn't take food from the poor, from the children in the barracks."

He shook his head. "Those children also know not to eat the food." He slipped into the throng and disappeared.

What did he mean by that? Was this bread old, or had it gone moldy?

The day wore on, and shadows lengthened across the street. The heat in the middle of the open road roasted my skin but slowly started to decline, the feeling of the heavy weight of the Aten's rays lifting. Workers shut down their shops and joined the crowd. Jugs of wine or beer were in everyone's hands. Music played, but not only in my head. Men lined the streets, beating drums, shaking rattles, singing, and playing stringed instruments.

Men and women started to dance as they walked up and down the great road, wobbling as they passed. "A jubilee," a man with a stump for a hand said, grinning as he pushed around me. "The palace is finally including us." He jumped up and kicked his heels together. "We have waited for so long, and we deserve this."

Seneb wrapped his arm around his brother's shoulder. "A jubilee, like back in the old days, when we served that vile man you killed—except then, we were the entertainment."

Harkhuf folded his arms across his chest and grunted.

Seneb tossed his head back, kicked his feet out to the music, and took tiny, mincing steps. "Just let the music take you." He patted his brother's broad back. "Like the mating dance of the pink flamingos back home. They always eventually break from the group into pairs."

Twilight settled to darkness, and torches lit up around the street.

Paramessu took Tia in his arms and swayed, smiling.

I slapped the back of his shaven head, which left fragrant oil on my palm. "She's my wife, remember." I glanced around for watching eyes. "*You* told the people of the palace that. This is not our time to celebrate. That is when—"

"When what?" Paramessu's posture stiffened. "You confronted Pharaoh, and you didn't do anything but give him a gift and almost let him take Tia. What do you need to do to him, and how long will this take?"

"Now is not the time for questioning." I leaned closer, an inch from his face, the little air between us thick with tension. "You could have turned away from me at any point, but now it is too late. When I am done, you will know. But this will all take a lot of time."

Paramessu huffed and strode away into the crowd. I glanced back. Tia had already disappeared. Seneb danced away, leading Harkhuf but hardly blending in with the masses until at least twenty more Nubian dancing dwarves lined the streets, back-flipping and tumbling as they paraded north.

I glanced around. No eyes were watching. And only Nefertiti, Tut, Akhenaten, and Suty remained at the window, drinking and talking amongst themselves. They shared a laugh, drowned out by the music and the rising racket of the drunken masses.

Lowering my head, I squeezed between drunken men and women and produced a large bottle of my own from my sack. There must've been tens of thousands of locals laughing, hugging, kissing, and singing. The rank smell of sweat surrounded me.

I approached the tower that the royal family had entered. Guards surrounded councilmen and women in the area as they all drank and danced at the edge of the street. Hiding amongst the commoners, I snatched glances at the elite as I circled them. Hours wore on. The soldiers were still armed but grew wobbly, stumbling around and talking to each other as they too partook in the festivities. But there would be other unseen eyes with more discipline lurking in the shadows.

One old councilman stumbled beyond the line of soldiers, approaching a woman while wearing a big grin that revealed many missing teeth. Other councilmen followed after him, wandering out into the crowds. Their soldiers didn't even follow them, as if they weren't supposed to …

I hunched over and slipped beside two teetering women, one stocky, one thin.

Then I saw her—Mutnedjmet—blue-painted eyelids and a face as cute as I'd ever seen. She was shorter than the other women, standing still, her face stern and her arms folded as if she despised everyone and this entire party. No man stood beside her. *Oh, Mutnedjmet, how you've changed …*

Close by, Beketaten talked to Nefertiti, both having come down from the Window of Appearances. Many daughters and the one son, Tut, even raced about screaming, playing some kind of game with each other. *Akhenaten, would you even sacrifice your own family for an opportunity to kill those who oppose you?* Was I doing the same thing with my companions? I shook my head.

But Mutnedjmet would have the smallest amount of undercover protection or military men watching over her. Akhenaten wouldn't care if she was taken and wouldn't expect it.

"Do you want to become rich?" I asked the two women that I walked behind, tapping one on her shoulder. I hid my face with my long hair and the sack I was carrying.

The stocky one looked up, her dark eyes wide and bloodshot. She stepped away. "I have a man."

I flashed two leaves of gold, the hieroglyphs hammered out of their surfaces so that they would be indistinguishable. "These are yours, if you and your friend can draw that woman out here and get her to talk to me." I pointed at Mutnedjmet and to a dark alley between two buildings.

Their eyes gaped. The thin one gasped, putting a hand over her mouth. "G-gold?" She brushed her dark hair from her face. "I've never seen it other than on Pharaoh, the queen, or his chariot."

"You'll have everything you desire for years to come," I said.

"What do we do?" She stood straighter, although she wobbled side to side.

I shrugged—I didn't understand women. "Think of some enticement or curiosity that would make yourselves leave the security of a group and take a small venture out. Then, when you've come up with that, tell this woman the opposite."

Gold and riches might tempt Nefertiti, but Mutnedjmet was different from her sister. Her curiosity was what always drew her into our past adventurers.

The women stared at me, then looked to Mutnedjmet. "Are you serious?" the stocky one asked, pulling at her dress. "What is that supposed to mean?"

"We'll need the gold in advance," the other said.

"Only if you can accomplish the task," I replied.

"Then how do we know you'll keep your word?" the first asked, stepping closer.

"I guess you don't, but what have you lost?" I asked. "A moment of time away from your jubilee? But if I do, you will never have to wait on the droppings of Pharaoh ever again. Accept the challenge."

They both turned to each other and whispered. Then the stocky woman said, "You'd better not be tricking us."

"You'll find your gold inside this bottle"—I held up my jug of wine—"if you accomplish the task. If not, enjoy the wine."

"Are you some sort of magician?" the thin one asked.

"But if you look inside before you've performed my request, there will be nothing at all." I flashed my best smile and handed the wine over to the stocky woman. "One of you can hold the bottle. The other"—I pointed at the thin one—"must get that woman to look into the alleyway. Then your tasks will be fulfilled. I don't expect you to be able to convince that woman to walk into the alley."

The thin woman swallowed. "I can convince her." She stumbled away, approaching Mutnedjmet. I backed into the alleyway, donning a black cloak supplied by the brothers. Tia, wherever she was now, and if she and Paramessu still trusted me, should also be cloaked and setting up a similar situation, intentionally letting an amulet of Amun slip out from her cloak for a moment as she bribed two random Egyptian men. She'd reward them with gold if they'd start a riot nearby.

"Hello," I whispered into the darkness.

"I am here to help," a female child's voice replied.

Remaining in the shadows, I peered back around the corner, watching the street.

The thin woman spoke with Mutnedjmet, the woman's hands shaking as she motioned in my direction. Mutnedjmet's eyes widened as she glanced over.

Was she telling Mutnedjmet about a creepy man with gold? I'd already rolled up and slipped the gold leaves inside the wine bottle I'd given her friend, so they'd have it no matter what happened.

Mutnedjmet shrugged and took another look around at all of the royal soldiers before walking to the alleyway. One guard near her noticed her leave and nudged another. The first whispered something to the other but waited a moment before slowly following her.

I strode away into the cool blackness, lit a lamp, and scooped up the bony girl who hid in the shadows—the emaciated girl from the barracks.

She hung over my shoulder, weighing less than my sack of supplies. I crept along and almost made it to the end of the alleyway before the girl started screaming and pounded on my upper back with her tiny fists. She would've been watching for Mutnedjmet, and that was the signal.

Mutnedjmet would see a figure cloaked in black apparently abducting a child, like what had happened with the Devouring Monster and the fake plague when we were young. I didn't know how much she'd changed but doubted she'd take the time to run back to the soldiers and tell them, not if she thought she'd lose sight of the abducted child. If she was still the same person I'd known—unlike Nefertiti—she'd follow me immediately.

Yelling from drunken men erupted in the street behind us, carrying over the noise of the celebration. Something shattered, and thuds sounded as if people fought amongst themselves or broke into nearby houses. Then the deeper and more controlled shouting of guards and soldiers answered. The distraction of the riot had begun.

I turned a quick corner without looking back and strode down another dark alleyway. I paused and subtly peeked over the girl on my shoulder. Something moved through the shadows out of the previous alleyway. Mutnedjmet was following me, albeit cautiously. And I could not let her realize that I was waiting for her to keep up.

I led Mutnedjmet deep into the city, between buildings, across roads, through properties, and onto a stairway. Then I stepped down to a small basement. This basement was beneath the run-down barracks where the children slept. A single torch flickered from the darkness below.

Two men waited for me—a soldier from Egypt's military and a younger councilman. I let the emaciated girl go, and she snuck away, through the shadows and out into the night, unseen.

Chapter 27

Journal Translation

I EXAMINED THE EGYPTIAN soldier and the younger councilman, who were both gagged but had their arms and legs free. "Hide these men," I said into the shadows of the basement below the barracks. "She's coming."

The outlines of two short men in black cloaks and another tall man in similar garb grabbed these hostages and pulled them into the darkness behind a mounted torch. I extinguished my lamp, and the torch and darkness engulfed us

I followed after them.

Quiet footsteps carried down the stairway and echoed off the chamber walls all around me. I tightened my grip on my swords. The faint white of a dress floated down through the shadows. I swallowed with apprehension. My skin crawled with fear.

Mutnedjmet screamed. Thrashing and kicking sounded as she struggled against two men in black. I snuck around her and crept back up the stairs to the basement's entrance.

"You are now a hostage of the worshippers of Amun," Paramessu, one of the people playing an abductor, cackled. A faint light sprang to life below, reflecting off of Mutnedjmet's face—but her abductors remained in shadow.

"You took the wrong person," Mutnedjmet shouted. "Help! My bodyguards are right behind me."

"Oh, we know who you are," Paramessu replied in a strained voice, to mask his own. "And that is why you are here. You are of Pharaoh's family."

Mutnedjmet laughed. "You've *really* been misled if you think that my well-being will influence Akhenaten." She heaved for breath as she struggled against the grip of her abductors and the bonds that were being wrapped around her limbs. "And if you desire to punish one of the Aten's most faithful, you've taken the wrong person from the palace. *Anyone* else would've been a better choice. I am more like you than you know."

"You are nothing like us," Paramessu said. "We must take vengeance for Amun. And your guards are already dead, their bodies in an alleyway just outside."

Silence, then more grunting and bumping—sounds of a struggle.

"I welcome death over this life," Mutnedjmet said. "But I guarantee that you will not hurt Akhenaten by bringing pain upon me."

"We will see," Paramessu replied. "When he finds your remains and the mask of the ram, we believe that he will feel plenty."

"That would upset him," Mutnedjmet's voice strained as she tussled about, "but not because I am dead. He will focus only on the fact that there are people here who still worship a god other than himself. Pharaoh sees this as a personal insult, one so ignominious that people will lose their souls. And if he doesn't catch you, others—innocent people—will suffer."

It was time for me to take action. I lit a lamp and set it down beside the entrance, the light of its flames chewing at the darkness down below, its warmth radiating across my side. Drawing my twin swords, I descended with heavy footfalls.

Mutnedjmet screamed as if being attacked.

The abducted Egyptian soldier and the councilman—who were not true blasphemers, as we couldn't find any others—stumbled into the flickering light. Both of their gags were removed, and spears sat in their hands as they turned to face me. Their eyes were wide, as if surprised beyond comprehension—they had no idea what was happening.

I disposed of my cloak and raised my swords.

"Who are you?" the councilman shouted in anger as the guard raised his spear. "You will suffer greatly for this. I will watch and savor your pain as the Devouring Monster carves your chest open and bites into your beating heart."

The guard snarled and lunged, jabbing his spear at me.

I deflected the weapon with one sword, metal ringing against metal. Then I slid in closer and used my other sword to cut a slice across his neck. The soldier collapsed.

"You will die, slowly." The councilman swung his spear at me like a sword.

I bent backward at the waist, and the wooden shaft of the spear whooshed over my head and chest. After righting myself, I leapt forward and caught the councilman around the neck. I covered his mouth as I plunged my blade into the soft portion of his lower back, where his spleen would reside. And I whispered in his ear, "We've come to destroy the abomination you worship as the one god—what you relinquished all of your morals for in return for power. You have assisted in the devouring of innocent men's souls, judging them as if you were Anubis himself. At least those of you that I dispose of will not lose their souls without proper judgment."

The dying councilman lurched in surprise, bumping back against my shoulder. His voice was airy and weak. "You could not do this with a million men."

"That is why I only brought six ... and a cat."

His body went limp, and I let him fall to the ground in a heap.

Spinning to Mutnedjmet, I advanced. Was she one of them now, one of Akhenaten's women? She squirmed and fought against ropes binding her wrists and ankles, her eyes wide, her face pale as she gasped for air.

I cut through her bonds. No, this was Mutnedjmet, one of the only members of the royal family who was different. "It is fortunate that your beauty caught my eye at the jubilee ... and that I followed you and then your guards into the alleyway. But you should be more careful, my lady." I bowed to her. "And I do regret to inform you that these men or their helpers killed your two bodyguards."

Her tone was airy with surprise or burgeoning sadness. "You ... saved me from these murderers." She took a few breaths. "If I wasn't the only outcast in the palace, maybe I'd have more personal guards, or more than two who aren't so eager to imbibe until they pass out."

"There were only two attackers here, but more may be coming." I extended my hand to her as I looked for my cloaked companions in the shadows—the abductors who'd taken Mutnedjmet and the two Egyptians hostage. Only darkness. I released a stale breath.

Mutnedjmet glanced about the room, panic making her eye movements wild.

"We should go," I said.

I sheathed my swords, and she took my callused hand with her smooth palm. Her skin was cold.

We crept back up the stairs. Memories of Mutnedjmet and I sneaking into the temple in Memphis and finding the Mummy Makers preserving Thutmose's body played out in my mind. I grinned, remembering how scared we had been at the time. It all seemed nostalgic and harmless amidst the present situation and its consequences.

The sandaled feet of ten soldiers pounded the road outside, their torches creating a halo of light around them as they banged on house doors, searching for something.

"Over here," I said, waving to grab their attention.

They turned and rushed over. "Lady Mutnedjmet, are you all right?"

"This man saved me." She patted my arm. "And you will find the bodies of my abductors down there." She pointed down the stairs.

"Go inform the others that we've found her," the first soldier barked to several of his men before turning back to Mutnedjmet. "We have small contingents scouring the city. I am so relieved that you are okay. Are there any more men down there?"

"No one still alive," she said.

"You two"—the soldier pointed to more of his men—"accompany them. The rest of you, follow me down there." He stared with gaping eyes into the darkness leading into the earth.

Mutnedjmet, two soldiers, and I paced between buildings and alleyways, back to the great road.

Two bodies lay propped against the side of a building, motionless. Spears and shields lay beside them.

Mutnedjmet gasped, falling to her knees as she raced over and touched one's face. "They did get my guards, my only trustworthy guards." She sniffed. Twinkling droplets of water reflected moonlight as they ran down her cheeks. "I should not be the outlet for their anger."

My eyes closed in remorse as guilt for Mutnedjmet's loss weighed on me. But these men were servants of Pharaoh and thus obstacles in my path. And Wahankh had followed through with his part of my plan and ventured into the city this night to make sure my target was alone. He was still able to overcome his fear, which at one time had driven him to bully the meek. Helping that man with his greatest weakness, even though I'd suffered at his hands during slavery, summoned a tingle of pride within my core.

"We must move back to safety." I tugged her along by the wrist, leading the way. "It is too dangerous for you out here."

Torches lit the expanse ahead—the great road. But it was deathly quiet.

"Do these jubilees typically end so suddenly?" I asked Mutnedjmet as we inched through the last alleyway, the buildings on either side only allowing us to see a sliver of the road ahead.

"No." She shook her head. "They rage on through the night ... at least at the palace. Pharaoh doesn't throw many celebrations in the city, not for the commoners and the poor. I can't even remember the last one we had out here."

There was no movement along the great road, no sound, but an image arose before me, perhaps only in my mind. A tree sat in the center of the great road, its twisting bark appearing to suck in the light with blossomed flowers of sheer blackness—the tamarisk tree. A white, linen-wrapped face peeked out at me from behind the trunk. Eyes of green glowed beneath the Dark One's mask.

I shivered in fear. Drawing my swords, I stepped out of the alleyway and took in the scene. People were everywhere, but—

Bodies were strewn across the great road but clustered beneath the Window of Appearances—Egyptians in ragged kilts with unkempt hair, foreigners, men, women, and even children.

Gasping, I raced out into the street. Had they passed out from too much drink?

I cradled a child's cold head in my arms, shaking her and screaming—not a child from the barracks. Mahu had said something about warning them ...

Her limp body flopped around in my hands.

A gentle hand settled onto my shoulder, followed by sobbing and hugging arms, which came from behind.

"They are dead, all these poor people." Mutnedjmet sniffed as she pressed the side of her face against my back.

Dead? I fell to a knee in utter shock. Who would do something this brazen and rash? Innocent life, taken in such numbers ... Palpitations struck my heart. My head and gaze rose, searching our surroundings. Besides the two guards with us, no other soldiers or royals remained—their chariots were all gone. Something burned hot at my waist—the blue ostrich feather of truth, the one Akhenaten had given me to always remember my shame. Was all this death also my fault, since I had begun the trickery of inciting paranoia and the reemergence of blasphemers here in the city?

I glanced skyward, focusing on the empty window of the bridge overhead.

Darkness lay within.

Chapter 28

Journal Translation

MY CHARIOT BOUNDED NORTH along the great road, heading for Akhenaten's palace. Mutnedjmet, Paramessu, Tia, and the dwarf brothers rode with me, all crammed onto a tiny platform.

The lights of the palace came closer. My stomach burned as if acid were eating a hole through its outer wall. Anger seethed through my bones, the sight of all the innocent dead still running through my mind.

"She was very brave," Paramessu whispered into my ear by turning his head from the front of the chariot. I barely heard his words over the clatter of the chariot and the pounding of hooves on packed dirt. "In such a situation, I've seen men tremble and falter."

"Mutnedjmet is but a piece of my puzzle," I whispered back, picturing her resilience in spite of believing that she had been abducted by people meaning to kill her.

Paramessu slowly faced forward again, but his head made a subtle shake of disappointment in me.

"Stop." A guard outside of the palace's gates held up his spear and a torch.

Paramessu reined our charging horses in.

"Move aside and open the gates," Mutnedjmet said, leaning out to be seen. "I have returned, no thanks to the royal soldiers. Rem is in Pharaoh's favor tonight."

The guard's face fell flat in astonishment. "L-Lady Mutnedjmet." His jaw quivered. "I didn't know that you had not returned."

She glared and folded her arms as the gates opened. Our horses trotted us inside.

A bonfire raged in the distance again, and we strode straight for the open feast hall.

Men and women still held bottles, stumbling around the crackling fire and laughing as they patted each other on the backs and told stories. The royal family lounged upon the raised platform, smirking as they spoke to each other.

I weaved around throngs of drunken councilmen to the steps leading up to the throne. But I paused below Akhenaten, and my companions followed suit.

Suty bellowed with laughter as he sharpened a sword, his feet dangling over the edge of the raised platform. "Never did so much killing in my whole life," the monster of a man said to the watermelon-headed doctor beside him, "and I didn't even have to get dirty. Although I like the fighting part. This seemed like cheating."

"Cheating?" The doctor placed a hand to his chest and leaned back in feigned shock. "It is so much easier when the killing is done for you through disease. Then you don't have to even see your victims until their souls have already fled their bodies." He chuckled and gnawed a hunk of meat off of a large bone with a ripping sound, its juices dripping down his hidden chin. He looked back over his shoulder. "My plotting went well, Pharaoh."

"I designed the plan," Ay said, his upper lip wrinkling as he stared at Pentju. "The credit for the performance goes to the vizier."

I ascended the steps, but Mutnedjmet shoved past me. "My pharaoh," she said, standing before Akhenaten. Pharaoh looked up, a wicked grin hiding beneath the shadows of his crown. "I was taken."

Akhenaten's smirk disappeared.

"This man"—she motioned to me—"saved me. And he killed my two abductors, both of whom still worshipped the false gods and wished to send you a message of defiance."

The black on Pharaoh's eyelids grew as his eyes narrowed. He glanced at me, the tension of his stare piercing the distance between us.

"But you didn't need to kill all those other people in the streets; they were not unfaithful to you." Mutnedjmet hit her knees with her fists.

"I am sure that we killed at least another one or two non-believers." Akhenaten rubbed his chin. "Perhaps they would never admit it to any living thing, but someone there probably still held the old gods in their heart. It is just a matter of odds. When so many die ..."

"How can you be so cold?" Mutnedjmet said, fists clenched and face beet red.

"Mutnedjmet." Pharaoh sighed. "I tolerate you because you are Nefertiti's sister, my cousin, but you cannot comprehend the mind of a god. These were only poor people, people who deserved the life they lived—those disfavored by god. He does not miss them or mourn their passing. They were cursed or diseased or poor because in a past life, I wished it be so. They did not help el-Amarna with building, selling goods, or other services. It is the price the people had to pay for the treachery of the few right here in my city." His dark eyebrows climbed his forehead, elongating the black paint beneath. "The people needed a lesson. And the Devourer will be sent tonight to consume the hearts of those whom I have chosen to die."

Mutnedjmet planted her hands at her hips, glaring at Pharaoh.

"Sit down!" Akhenaten screamed and pointed for her to leave. The chamber fell silent.

Mutnedjmet wrinkled her forehead but shuffled away.

Tense silence continued, broken only by the pop of the flames.

"Are you a tracker of the unfaithful?" Nefertiti asked from beside her pharaoh. She focused on me, her eyes searching my face and body.

My forearms tensed.

"You found that councilman's house, and he'd been here for many years." She grinned, her perfect face and the deep green above her eyes captivating me. But a sparkle was buried in her eyes—growing suspicion of me? "And now you've killed two more, possibly the two men who attacked you right here in the palace?"

"Be wary of this traveling merchant," a male voice rang out from within a crowd of councilmen. "He is false!"

"I seek vengeance against the type of men that I killed, my beautiful queen," I said in truth, my cheeks hot with anger. "Mine is a long road of suffering." I knelt, gently taking her fingers and kissing the supple skin on the back of her hand. Rose and citrus flooded my nostrils. My head swooned. "As a child, my family was deceived by the worshippers of a false god. I lost my mother and father to them. And ever since, I've traveled all of Egypt and the outer world, helping to expose such men and their lies." I stared into her eyes. "But now I have come to—"

Akhenaten stood, his head and shoulders towering over me. Shadows danced across his body. "Then you are one of us." He grabbed me under my chin with bony fingers and pulled me to my feet, away from Nefertiti. "My councilmen are only envious of your accomplishments, like my family was of mine. There was also just a riot in the streets because some female worshipper of the false gods paid a couple of men to start an uprising. Mahu just recently confirmed this after the arrest and interrogation of the initiating parties."

The chamber fell silent again.

Akhenaten's dark eyes bored into me. "You and your servants will have rooms within the palace from tonight forward. And you will join the council. At least three men with the vilest of personalities recently lived inside these very walls without anyone knowing. I could use the aid of someone not so lazy and unfocused, someone with determination, someone who can crawl his way under the mask of the people in this city and even in this palace and determine who they really are without them even knowing it. All of these people"—he waved his hand at the packed chamber—"only tell me what they think I want to hear. But you have been sent here to assist me, perhaps by my future self. I think I remember it, actually ..." He tapped his cheek, which created those hollow echoes in his mouth, and his eyes wandered over some thought.

I nodded and dropped to a knee. "I, too, believe this is so." I hid a grin.

"Take a seat upon the platform this night." Akhenaten motioned down beside Mahu, who stood with his arms folded—the only man of the hundreds inside this chamber who didn't celebrate tonight. No, there was another beside him: Maya, the Royal Scribe. Maya sat and stared off into the night, his face drawn.

"What kind of suffering has a man such as yourself seen, as you previously suggested?" The question came from the handsome man in a wig beside Pharaoh—Ay. He intertwined his fingers, his eyes narrowed and accusing.

"Traveling the world is no easy task," I said. "Horrors await behind every bush, and behind many men. Even in Memphis, I've seen—"

"You said you were from Hierakonpolis." Ay's gaze ran up and down my body.

"I am." I bowed my head so that my long hair fell across my face. I gripped my bracelet. "But I spent time in Memphis."

I turned away, my bones shaking with the fear of being discovered. I marched to a far chair beside Mahu and Maya.

The bellowing and shouting of the celebration returned. I dined on fleshy tubers, both sweet and salty, and the brothers, Tia, and Paramessu joined me, taking seats by my side.

"Like demons devouring spirits of the dead," Seneb whispered in his slight Nubian accent, his smooth face shifting across the masses, many of whom now danced around the roaring bonfire in the center of the open chamber.

"I see your suffering now," Harkhuf grumbled in his thicker Nubian accent between chomping into the red pulp of a juicy watermelon, shaking his head. His biceps bulged. "This is something that I never could've dreamt of."

Paramessu remained silent, his head down, focused on his plate. Was he seeing the hideous truth of Akhenaten now, the folly of his ways for serving this pharaoh in the military?

Tia patted my back, sending vibrations through my chest. "This is why we trust you. We just need to know how far you plan to go." She scrutinized the royal family as if she were putting it all together.

They'd all figure out how far I wanted to take this, if they hadn't already. Then would they stay or flee to save their souls? Perhaps Wahankh was the only wise man among us.

Chapter 29

Journal Translation

A HAND SETTLED ONTO THE back of my head and ran down over my long hair. I turned away from a plate of grains and the sickening celebration and feasting of the councilmen and royal family of Akhenaten.

"Would you join us for a moment?" a quiet voice asked. Mutnedjmet stood there, forcing a smile. She took my hand—hers soft but with underlying strength. She tugged me up to a standing position, and I followed her behind the throne.

A group of women lounged on chairs under a burning torch, drinking from bottles—Nefertiti and Beketaten standing out from other royal wives or family members that I did not recognize. They giggled, their torsos swaying with drunkenness as they whispered into each other's ears. The women looked up as we approached, and they fell silent.

Mutnedjmet motioned for me to sit. As she lowered herself into a chair beside Nefertiti, she said, "I just wanted to thank you for what you did for me—I know that you risked your life. I believe they would have killed me just to retaliate against Pharaoh." Her bright eyes danced with energy, reminding me of the Mutnedjmet I'd once known.

I eased myself down onto the deep cushion of a lounge chair. "Some men are not right in the head. Revenge is all that drives them." I forced a smile.

The blue paint on and around Mutnedjmet's eyelids grew as she closed her eyes and lowered her head.

Nefertiti winked at me. "Any woman would be very lucky to have such a brave hero." She leaned back in her chair and crossed her legs beneath a silky white dress. Glistening oil covered her exposed skin, reflecting the torchlight. Her shaven legs showed just a hint of muscle tone. "You can find all the comforts of the world right here. And living out your days in splendor will bring you much happiness. I truly wish that everyone, even the poor, could have all of this." She spread her arms to emphasize the celebration. "Then we could have paradise on this earth."

She did care for everyone, not just herself and the elite? Perhaps it was only the world that did not have enough to go around, or perhaps Akhenaten had found that weakness in her and exploited it until it had twisted her into something dark, like me with my consuming disease of vengeance. Maybe I could still pull her back out into the light and save her, for good.

"Someday, when I find the right woman—" I bit my tongue. But could the indulgences that tempted Nefertiti into this life also draw me in? I'd never have to work so hard again, nor experience so much suffering. To always be taken care of by others …

Nefertiti's eyebrows rose. "The woman there"—she pointed over my shoulder at Tia—"is that not your wife?"

"It is." My insides twisted. I should be wary—my infatuation with Nefertiti could cause me to make mistakes.

"Typical man." Nefertiti shifted her legs and pulled her dress down. "Always looking for another. Mutnedjmet, maybe you do have a chance with him."

Mutnedjmet's face turned bright red, contrasting against her blue eye paint. She shook her head and shot her sister a menacing glare. "Nefertiti is always trying to set me up with any single man that she deems worthy. And her standards for me are not that high, so this happens often. I apologize."

"But you have Pharaoh himself," I said to Nefertiti. "A woman could not desire anything more."

She shrugged and wobbled as she took a long drink followed by a slow swallow. "I'd thought so at one time. He is who he is. I wish he were different, a kinder, better man, but …"

"Nefertiti has grown accustomed to the power and takes it for granted," Beketaten, Akhenaten's sister, said in a nasal voice, the tip of her nose twitching as she talked. "When the god himself takes hold of your body, you lose control. There is nothing more intoxicating than to be with the most powerful man in the world. He just doesn't come to visit me like he used to." Beketaten uncrossed her legs and remained in that position.

"And you," I asked Mutnedjmet. "No husband?"

Mutnedjmet looked away, her chin furrowing. "No." She swallowed, her eyes vibrating again, as if seeing some memory. "I was in love once and gave it a shot, but that was all. I haven't found another man I've felt that way for, so I could never make it work with the others I've met or when they've tried to arrange my marriage." She glanced down, uncomfortable with everyone's attention on her. "Beketaten has Akhenaten's son."

A smile engulfed Akhenaten's horse-faced sister. "Yes, the crown prince, Tut." Her head fell back, her face beaming.

Nefertiti took a long drink from her bottle. "But you'd slept with someone else as well, one time, a servant and a traitor. You were not pure for Pharaoh, and Tut may not be Pharaoh's."

The smile on Beketaten's face vanished in an instant. "That servant boy couldn't have gotten anyone pregnant. And it'd been too long between that servant boy and Tut's birth. You know that, Nefertiti; you just like to bring it up. Tut is Pharaoh's child."

"Only daughters for Nefertiti." Mutnedjmet nudged me on the calf with her toes. "Six of them, all girls."

Nefertiti took another long drink, her exposed legs flexing as if she felt that she'd failed at accomplishing her greatest expectation in life. I felt the same …

Tense silence descended around the women and me, but soon the bellowing of drunken men carried up from below the platform.

"Tell me about this traitor boy." I placed my chin on my fist. "When did this happen?"

Beketaten pressed a bottle to her lips.

Nefertiti leaned forward, her eyes glowing. "He was a servant of Pharaoh's. Well, before Akhenaten was pharaoh. The boy was kind and brave, but weak. He'd offered me a chance to run away with him once, after many years of fawning over me." She smiled to herself, as if the offer had really meant something to her or that it still did. "Only one of many offers that I'd received as a young woman, but I will always remember his and not only because of what Akhenaten did to him after."

"And you didn't take him up on the offer?" My insides churned with emotion as I focused on keeping a relaxed face. She'd thought I was a good person, just weak, but that was when I was so young. I was much different now. I could still see the personality that had originally drawn me to her. It was still in there, just buried and hidden in the midst of the palace and how it functioned.

Nefertiti's lips curled as if she were fighting off a smile, her hardened façade having faded, her pupils dilated by too much drink. "But Pharaoh was my other option, and he didn't allow me to ponder much of anything or to think for myself."

I leaned back against the wooden slats of the chair. "Well, it wasn't even a comparable decision. A feeble servant or Pharaoh."

Nefertiti nodded, but her eyes wandered as if she regretted something and was still now considering the choices she'd had.

"Unless she wanted a life full of love," Mutnedjmet said. "That boy was enamored with you and would've done anything he could for you, sister."

"Ah, love." I pursed my lips as I stroked my chin. "We all search for it but rarely find the emotion reciprocated by one we feel the same way for." I studied Nefertiti's conflicted expression with a tensing forehead. "But you did not love the boy, my queen?"

"He was a servant boy, so when I pictured the life I'd have with him versus Akhenaten …" Nefertiti took another swig. "I do miss him though, sometimes. That was a memorable time." She sighed. "I wouldn't trade my life as queen, but for some reason, the past ten or so years have blended together like a tapestry with bleeding colors, and I have a hard time recalling much of the details of—"

"Would you have chosen love, Beketaten?" I attempted to casually bring the conversation back to what I wanted to know without making it too obvious. "True love, even if it came in a form you did not expect?"

Beketaten smirked and wrinkled her face before taking a long drink.

Mutnedjmet kicked her lower legs out and dragged her sandals back across the tile at the foot of her chair. The she winked at me, as if she knew something no one else did. "I would've given that boy a chance. He fought for what he believed in with everything he had, even if it wasn't much. And everything was already stacked against him—starting with his mother."

"Heb's mother?" I nearly fell off of my chair as I straightened. "What did she do?"

Beketaten slapped her knee and laughed, high and nasal. "They told him his mother died during his birth. He probably felt guilty his entire short life. But none of us here would've liked her. She was also a blasphemer and organized some kind of uprising years and years ago."

My heart stopped beating for a moment.

"Similar to the resistance that Thebes had in the early days of Akhenaten's reign," Beketaten continued, "before they were crushed. And can you even believe that there were blasphemers still here?" She waved her arm around to indicate the chamber. "What a shock lately with—"

"A-a blasphemer?" I stuttered. "The traitor boy's mother?"

"His mother didn't want to embrace the Aten as the one true god." Beketaten sighed. "It must be hereditary among the disfavored."

"What happened to this woman?" I asked.

Beketaten burped. "I think she was burned along with the other barbarian pagans involved in the uprising."

"Where was that?" I leaned back and rubbed my forehead in an attempt to not appear so interested, though my soul writhed around in my bones. Had I asked too much, pressed too far, and made myself even more suspicious?

Beketaten shrugged as she looked at Nefertiti and said, "That was many years ago and the details are not really a memorable part of Egypt's history."

"What about the boy's father?" My fingernails dug into palms. I couldn't stop now; I needed to know. "Did he also revolt?"

"No." Mutnedjmet's eyes grew misty. "That boy's father gave up his own freedom to serve Amenhotep so his son would have a better life. Unfortunately, Akhenaten didn't allow the boy to benefit from his father's sacrifices."

I bit my lip and clung to the chair, my legs straining to leap up and my mouth wanting to scream out in sheer rage. My father probably left my mother or took up servitude after she died in order to give me a better life, but Akhenaten stole that future from me. And now Father was dead, his soul lost. My fingers reached for Father's bracelet ... But Mutnedjmet's attention focused on my hand and the bronze on my wrist. So instead, I gripped the smooth metal of my sword handles. I'd go on a rampage now and kill as many in this chamber as I—

"Then the boy's father supposedly contracted a plague and his body was burned." Mutnedjmet placed a hand on my arm, as if to soothe me. "But it wasn't a disease."

"Yes, it was," Beketaten said. "People all over Egypt were catching it and dying."

"Only those who questioned Pharaoh," Mutnedjmet replied.

"That is how life works," Beketaten said. "Many diseases only strike the deserving, by the will of the Aten."

I forced a few deep breaths. "And so what happened to the boy?"

"They say that he died in the desert or at sea." Tears trickled down Mutnedjmet's cheeks. "But his *ba* has been seen. Men traveling the desert have claimed that the boy's *ba* has told them that they will be punished if they find love. And women have said that the *ba* threatens them if they do not love him."

I coughed. My *ba* hadn't even been released from my soul—not yet. How had these wild stories come to be?

Nefertiti ran a finger across her plump lower lip. "Why are you so interested in this boy?"

"I study the vile, the treasonous." I stood. "It gives me understanding so that I can better hunt these people and remove them from this world." I pivoted around on my heel and strode away.

Chapter 30

Journal Translation

DREAMS RAGED IN MY HEAD as I slept in my room in the palace. I was a child along with Mutnedjmet and Nefertiti. Father was there … and so was my mother.

Something kneaded on my chest, and sharp claws poked into my skin, waking me with a jolt.

"Croc," I groaned as I shoved him away. He meowed and rubbed his soft fur against my back. The vibrantly white inner walls of the palace glowed in the moonlight streaming through a high window. A thick fog clouded my mind. How old was I? Was I still a child, serving Akhenaten in Memphis? It seemed like too many years had passed, too much suffering, but the haze of sleep remained. I rubbed my eyes and yawned.

Croc nudged into my cheek with his bony face. I scooted away but scratched under his chin. Gray hairs stood out from the orange around his eyes and nose—his face was much more sunken than I remembered. *Croc, how did you age so quickly?*

My eyes wandered as I wondered how long cats lived. I'd read somewhere about fifteen years, possibly up to twenty if they were lucky.

My gaze locked onto the walls surrounding me—there were no vibrant floral paintings like in Memphis, but images of the Aten covered the walls. My stomach sank. I remembered exactly where I was—inside the palace of Pharaoh Akhenaten in el-Amarna.

Tia slept on a bed on the far side of the room, keeping her cover as my wife. Paramessu and the others slept in another room.

Croc's tail curled around my wrist and Father's bronze bracelet. How old was Croc now? It had to have been more than twenty years since I'd rescued him from the river when I was a young boy and he a kitten. How long would he live? He was looking old now, and stiff. Maybe with whatever power he carried, he could live longer than the average feline, but it didn't seem he had many years left.

"You can't ever die." I pulled Croc in close and hugged him.

Croc made a high-pitched cry of contempt and jumped away. He sat on his haunches and licked at the draining wound on his back leg before limping about the room.

"You're the only family I have left."

He rubbed against my leg.

What if he died before I finally faced off with the Devouring Monster? I'd have no hope of winning that confrontation ... How could I speed up the process of getting closer to Akhenaten while disposing of some of those in power, those around him? Would it still take decades, as the magician had suggested to me before I'd fled Egypt?

The moonlight eventually faded as pink rays from the morning Aten streamed through my window.

I scooped Croc up around his thin midsection, jumped up, and placed him on the windowsill before shooing him out. If the people I used to know saw me with an uncommon orange and white feline, it might increase the chances of someone recognizing me.

My head drooped in thought as I wandered through the palace corridors. A footstep scuffed the tile behind me, and I glanced over my shoulder. Only shadows and distant lamplight filled the hallway.

I paused and took a couple of steps back. "Hello?"

The dark silhouette of a man whisked through the light of the distant lamp moving away from me without a sound. The stubble on my arms and legs rose as the tingle of trepidation crawled up my limbs. Was I being watched? And by whom, or by whose orders? The people of this palace had grown suspicious of me, even if some were hiding it.

"The council is meeting," Mahu said, striding from the shadows of the corridor opposite to where the recent figure had disappeared. He walked toward me alongside Maya, whose writing palette rested at his side.

"During the day?" I asked. "I thought we only celebrated at night, with feasts?"

Maya brushed his hair behind his cup-like ears as he strode past me. "Something of importance must be discussed. This is about you."

My muscles tensed as my hands instinctively reached for my swords. Had they discovered me or my friends?

But I couldn't run away now. I slowly turned and followed the echoing footsteps of the Chief of Police and the Royal Scribe through a network of corridors and into the audience hall—the same chamber we'd feasted in. The room was open to the midday Aten, the heat making the still air hard to breathe. Everyone else was already there, taking seats and facing the raised platform. I sat on a cushioned seat on the lower level.

"The Hittites," Akhenaten said from his golden throne, "are advancing on our northern territories." Several servants fanned or shaded him with giant palm leaves. "We have just received word. The messenger from several nights ago did not carry an offering with him as he should have, or I would have granted him an audience more quickly. He died of dehydration, waiting. But this morning another messenger arrived and told us the news. And this is not the first time the Hittites have attempted an attack in the last few years. They are growing braver and more vicious." His fists pressed down on the twin sphinxes on the arms of his throne.

"They still fear you like the world's only god," Ay said, rubbing at the orange around his eyes and wiping sweat from under his wig.

Akhenaten grunted, and his lips retracted into a snarl.

My mind raced with questions. I hadn't seen Pharaoh's most powerful foreign wife, Kiya, since I'd returned—the woman Akhenaten had received from the north and held in his palace in hopes of dissuading her angry father from ever attacking Egypt. Akhenaten seemed to have threatened harming her if outsiders ever attacked Egypt. Such a hostage wouldn't have been needed in Amenhotep's time, as there had been a stable relationship of peace. But once the vile son took control, the relationships with the outside kingdoms turned sour—starting at Amenhotep's last sed-festival. The last I'd seen of Kiya, by way of visions through the desert fox's eyes, she was rising in power amongst all of Akhenaten's wives, rivaling even Nefertiti. Some kind of tension had been growing between those two women, and now Kiya was nowhere to be seen.

Pentju stood. "El-Amarna is the greatest and the most powerful city the world has ever known." Sweat dribbled down his forehead, across his cheeks, and onto his thick neck. "Perhaps we should keep all of the army here and let the Hittites have some of those wastelands beyond the old borders—from your father's reign. We don't need those lands anymore."

If I were to grow closer to Akhenaten, I'd have to drive a wedge between him and some of his most trusted advisors—but never question Pharaoh himself. "The doctor is wise"—I also stood—"in the ways of medicine. But to offer his advice on war, a field where he would display childish incompetence, is folly."

Gasps and murmurs erupted throughout the audience hall. The doctor's face flushed red as he stared at me, his lower lip twitching.

I faced Pharaoh. "The doctor should stay silent on such matters."

"And who are you?" Pentju shouted, pointing at me. "A traveler just recently returned to the land of the faithful. You shouldn't even be here."

Councilmen all around jeered, their voices radiating off the walls.

"That man's right." Suty pointed at me before banging his fist on his shield, which created a boom. "No smart doctor knows anything about war. We should go and crush any enemy of the Aten."

"Silence," Akhenaten said, his deep voice echoing up to the sky. Everyone fell silent and didn't move. Pharaoh smirked as he tapped his cheek and studied me. Nefertiti leaned forward in her throne beside him, her eyes also locked on me.

I bowed and nodded. "Nor should you listen to the advice of a bodyguard with a brain the size of my cat's, especially when it comes to plotting military operations."

Suty huffed and drew his sword. "I could crush you like a beetle. I was in the military before I ever set foot in the royal guard. I was the best, and that is why I am the bodyguard of Pharaoh." He walked down from the platform, staring me down. The pointed pig's ear on his head twitched downward.

I held my head high, my heart pounding as my hands reached for my swords.

Akhenaten waved to Suty without taking his focus off me. "Return to my side."

"I wish to decapitate this outsider," Suty said.

"You may be able to," Akhenaten said. "But not at this moment." He paused for a second. "And what would your suggestion be, then … Rem, is it?"

"I've never led an army," I said, "so I do not propose to have all of the answers. But I have led my few men into battles more vicious than anyone here has seen, against monsters that the people in this room—inside the most protected of all cities—could not even fathom. And I have studied the arts of war and its past successes and failures for decades."

Nefertiti rose and paced along the edge of the raised platform. "What then do you think our position should be? You aren't making any friends here, newcomer." She pursed her lips as she examined me.

"I am not here to make friends," I said with genuine truth, glancing down at the men seated around me. "I am here for Pharaoh and his queen— to perform to the best of my abilities against those who oppose Egypt."

Suty slowly stepped back up the stairs. "Please, let me cut off his arms."

"I would not advise holding so much of the greatest military in all the world right here at el-Amarna," I said. "And even this greatest military has grown soft during the years of the previous pharaoh, even under your mighty rule. No real wars and a lack of fear and training have made them weaker. They may still be the mightiest army in all the world, but they are not in their prime."

Akhenaten leaned back, his face falling into dense shadow.

"They must be sent north," I said. "And put into rigorous training as they travel—to show the enemies of Pharaoh that the Aten is not to be challenged by anyone. Much less by mindless foreigners hiding in the chaos surrounding mighty Egypt."

Silence.

Would Akhenaten take the bait and make el-Amarna more vulnerable for my true objectives?

The clapping of one man's hands sounded—Akhenaten. "I admire your resolve to punish those who defy me, the one true god. And you have already punished others. But my intention is to live for the joys of the moment, here in this paradise."

Ay stepped closer to Pharaoh. "You should be wary of this man. We do not know him."

"If you had not let that last councilman and others worship a false god within my very city, perhaps I would place your advice over this man's," Akhenaten said. "He has punished with vicious judgment all those who oppose me." Pharaoh straightened his golden breastplate of a necklace. "But it is bizarre that he was involved in every instance. I will keep most of you here in the comforts of the palace, as you have been loyal for so long."

"What about him?" Ay pointed at me.

"He will be leading a small army, an expedition north, to confront these Hittite barbarians." Akhenaten smirked. "I will make him a captain of the military. And if he is true, he will be able to train one of our smaller and softer regiments well enough to drive off the Hittites. Then he may return to his rightful place among us. Then, Rem, you may enjoy the remainder of your days as royalty right here in the holy city."

I swallowed. He must've grown suspicious of me. This wasn't how this was supposed to go …

"My decision is final." Akhenaten held the golden scepter that he used as a walking stick before him.

"If you command it, I will go," I said, "but I must bring my men with me, as they are trusted soldiers."

"Do not send this man," Mutnedjmet said as she stood. "He has already established himself as one of the most active men in this palace of indulgers and—"

"Sit down, daughter," Ay said, the hatred burning in his eyes for me easing a bit. "It is not your place to discuss the matter." He turned to Pharaoh. "What regiment will you send with this new captain?"

Mutnedjmet folded her arms and remained standing.

"Some of the police and slaves of el-Amarna," Akhenaten said. "We could live with less construction within the city for a bit. And if Rem loses and the Hittites advance, we will still have the greatest army the world has ever seen to go to war then. And our military is not as weak as Rem believes." Pharaoh smiled and applauded me again.

Chapter 31

Journal Translation

MY COMPANIONS FOLLOWED ME—even the muscular Wahankh, although his head hung, his hair grown out from stubble to nearly jaw-length as it draped over his face. We all trailed Mahu, whose long legs flexed as he strode between the buildings of el-Amarna toward the rising Aten. The marching footsteps of a contingent of about a hundred of Mahu's policemen followed us.

"You can only take a small fraction of the current slave population," Maya said from beside me, his pen scratching against papyrus as he made a notation on his scribe palette.

Harkhuf fondled his bow and the feathers of an arrow, the fronds rippling through his fingers as he marched. "I've missed them. They feel like ... weapons that belong in my hands."

Seneb shook his head at his brother's comparison and whispered to me, "He doesn't get it and really should just stop trying. How hard would it be to say they feel like extensions of my fingers, or limbs that I should've been born with, or—"

"How many of these Hittite enemies are there supposed to be?" Harkhuf asked.

"We don't know," Mahu said, "but estimates from the recent attack put the invading horde at nearly a thousand."

These Hittites wouldn't be trying to take over the kingdom with those numbers, probably only attempting to claim some of Egypt's land as their own. "So Egypt's military could easily crush them if Pharaoh would send only a small fraction of its soldiers north with us?" I asked.

Mahu didn't respond.

"And how many slaves are we able to take with us?" Paramessu used the butt of his spear as a walking stick.

Did this former captain long for battle, or was he worried? Tia strode beside him, her eyes dripping with concern. Paramessu had a woman now and maybe even desired a family more than another battle.

"We can take about five hundred slaves," Maya said. "And kind Pharaoh has allowed you to take the younger and fitter men to wage your war. He is not dumping children or the elderly on us."

My war? My upper lip wrinkled in disgust. How about a few thousand trained soldiers or twice as many slaves? "He has children as slaves?"

"The children of slave families, yes." Maya scratched his ear with his reed pen. "They are taken from their parents and put to work, as god intended, or they wouldn't have been born at all, or at least not born to a slave family."

"Do they ever get to see their families again?" My grip tightened on my sack of supplies. Images of my own enslavement ran through my mind.

Maya frowned.

Fire ignited in my heart. To inflict pain and suffering on men as Akhenaten did was horrid enough, especially the taking of their souls, but to also seek out and punish the children of the poor and of the slaves—to take the only thing in this world that was precious to these people and that could possibly make their miserable lives worth living ... There could be no greater sin.

"Like picking the strongest animals in a diseased herd," Seneb said. "We get untrained slave laborers to help fight a battle and are supposed to be happy that they are not children or old men?"

"How will we ever train them?" Tia asked.

"It'll take months to reach the northeastern region of the kingdom," Paramessu said. "The dwarves and I will train them as best we can."

"We will surely die," Wahankh said, his head still hanging.

"You can leave," I said, "when the time comes and we are far from el-Amarna. You'll be free of your master." The last part I added for our cover since Mahu and Maya were in earshot.

The buildings of el-Amarna opened up to the eastern desert and to the Aten rising between the two peaks, but elongated clouds covered parts of the giant orb like patches of rising smoke. Still, the warmth of Aten's rays blanketed the ground. Rows of disheveled men stood in the expanse, their kilts torn and covered in dirt.

"This is our army," Mahu said. "They will be equipped with spears, shields, and armor—after we board the boats."

The dwarf brothers grunted and sighed in disbelief.

"What will keep them from running away?" Tia's shoulders slumped as she looked upon the jumble of teenage boys and young and middle-aged men.

"They still fear the greatest punishment of all," Paramessu said. "If they die in battle, they will not have to live a life of slavery, and their souls will go on to the next life. If they run, their hearts will be devoured."

Would these men prefer to even die in our coming battle rather than be victorious and return to slavery? That mentality would not favor us.

Mahu stood proudly, veins popping along his arms. "You chosen slaves of el-Amarna, this is your moment, your time for redemption. The enemies of Egypt advance on our borders. Pharaoh has granted you the opportunity to crush them."

The men glanced at each other, disbelief showing in their wide eyes and wrinkled foreheads.

"We sail north upon the Nile." Mahu turned and marched back west through el-Amarna for the river.

The police fanned out and surrounded the slaves, driving them after their chief.

I marched behind the masses.

Sunlight danced upon the rippling waves of the Nile, the water as blue as the patches of cloudless sky. The royal family and the councilmen of the palace stood about a hundred feet away along the shore, watching. A small armada of run-down ships waited for us just beyond the banks.

Reflections of the Aten temporarily blinded me.

"I know you," a male voice said. "I know all of you."

A thin man with shoulder-length dark hair pointed at us. Sharp features on a thin face ... I knew this man ... Chisisi, our former comrade.

My throat and chest constricted with apprehension. This former freeman had fled el-Amarna with us to lead our group of helpless slaves, or so he thought. Then he'd finally abandoned us, on his own accord, when I decided I needed to return to the lake at Crocodilopolis and lead our group without manipulation and lies. We had all wished to be rid of him and to never see him again. Now he was an el-Amarna slave? His limbs were thinner than I remembered, his skin haggard and dirt-stained. But it was him. My heart twinged. What suffering had he seen in these past months?

"Why have you returned?" Chisisi yelled, stopping amidst the marching line of slaves and staring at me. "And what happened to your face?"

Harkhuf drew the arrow on his bowstring and aimed for Chisisi's chest. I stepped into his line of fire and strode up to Chisisi as he continued to bellow, his face as deep red as a rose.

"What are you doing here?" I whispered, grabbing Chisisi around the thin muscles at the base of his neck and pulling his sweaty forehead onto my chest.

"They found me." Chisisi thrashed to get away, but I held him firm. If he told Mahu or the royal family who we were, we'd all have our chests cut open with the serrated crocodile blade of the Devouring Monster so that the Devourer could consume our still beating hearts. "I traveled for a bit after Crocodilopolis but was desperate and starving. I returned here to the capital to find work, but I looked like a slave. The police didn't believe me when I told them who I was, and they threw me in with this miserable lot. You have to get me out of here!"

My heart raced. I glanced back at the royal family. Akhenaten and Suty were not in attendance. Thank the gods. But the others all watched Chisisi and me. How much had they heard? Ay and the doctor would be looking for any reason to undermine me.

"I will make you a freeman again," I whispered to Chisisi, "but you need to act the part of a slave until we are far from here. If you get us killed, do you really think they will reward you, a slave, especially once they realize that you also ran away from el-Amarna all those years ago, and well before your allotted time to leave?"

He stopped struggling. "There's only one way to find out." He shoved away from me. "If I bring you all to justice, then they might grant me my freedom. And I will not wait long for you to release me. If I have to lift another block or do your bidding, it will be over for you. Then I will tell him"—he pointed at Mahu—"and all of the rest of them."

I grunted and stepped close to Chisisi again to keep our voices from being heard. "We will not help you, then. We no longer accept your intimidation and manipulation. We sail north to war, and you will stay here, a slave."

"No." Chisisi knelt and tugged on my kilt with dirty hands. "Please, please, help me. I cannot go on as a slave. I wish to die everyday. There's nothing but pain and anguish, having to watch slave children suffer as they build this city. I cannot bear it any longer." His face fell flat but his eyes wandered over memories. "I am a new man, changed from when you knew me."

Sympathy tugged at my heart like a mud brick—he felt for the suffering of the children.

"There will be plenty of chances for me to release you in the coming days." I glanced back at the curious royal family. Mahu and Maya approached, and Mahu raised his spear.

"I do not want to be released," Chisisi whispered. "It hasn't worked for me. I am no good as a leader. I've chased my dreams only to fail too many times. I wish to travel with you, find a group of friends ... and my place as one of you, even if I am only the dirt on your sandals."

"They will never want you with us again." I motioned to my companions. Mahu was only twenty feet away now, his nostrils flaring and his breathing heavy and raspy.

"I am begging you with my very soul." Tears brimmed in his eyes.

I gritted my teeth. The brothers would never accept this man again. But now that Chisisi had seen what we'd been through as slaves and I knew what he'd experienced, I couldn't leave him to die, not like that. No animal, not even a deceitful man, deserved such a fate, only perhaps Akhenaten and his faithful councilmen.

"I will find a way." I shoved on his chest. "You have my word." Then I kicked lightly at his stomach and yelled, "Get away from me, you miserable locust! I am glad you ended up as a slave after you ran away from my farm and your indentured servitude."

Mahu aimed his spear at Chisisi's face. "Is this slave bothering you?"

"No." I brushed off my kilt. "This former farmhand is right where he should be. He ran from my land, where he was needed, just before harvest season."

"You own a farm as well?" Maya stepped up behind Mahu, his eyes narrowing.

"Of course." I shrugged. "I spent many years traveling but am not stupid. I still invested in our kingdom and in a long-term source of food."

"Where is your farm?" Maya made a note on papyrus. "Surely not in el-Amarna, or I'd have heard about a recent purchase. There is little farmland here."

"Many miles south," I replied. "Much closer to Thebes."

"But you were born in the north?" Maya asked.

"I bought what I could at the time." Heat rose in my face. "Is this some kind of inquisition before we head to war? You may question me again upon our return, but not now, unless you are coming with us."

Maya shook his head and long locks. "I am the Royal Scribe. I will stay in el-Amarna, but Mahu will be joining you on the expedition to oversee his men."

"Mahu is traveling north with us?" I asked. "Pharaoh or Ay wants someone to watch over me, don't they?"

Maya muttered under his breath, "Pharaoh was angry with Mahu and his policemen when they could not find and apprehend the two men who attacked you in the palace. He thought this expedition would be appropriate punishment for them."

I pivoted and strode away for the boats.

Harkhuf paced beside me. "Was that slave really Chisisi?"

I nodded.

"He could be trouble," Harkhuf grumbled. "No one else has seen us in well over a decade, but Chisisi knows us. And these people still remember you and this legend you created for yourself."

I swallowed.

"He cannot come with us," Harkhuf said. "I will toss him overboard during the night."

"We will take pity on him for the time being." I marched faster.

I stepped across a long ramp, its flimsy wood bowing beneath me as I walked, and found a spot at the rear of our creaking boat. My companions followed me, then all of the police and slaves loaded into the remaining vessels.

The people of el-Amarna cheered and shouted from the banks, and we pushed off, leading our armada north. Nefertiti and Beketaten stared but made no acknowledgements. A small boy wearing a crown waved and pointed, and a shorter woman blew a kiss—Mutnedjmet. Chords of the harp rang in my head, that damned music I couldn't rid myself of. Mutnedjmet's eyes shone against her blue eye paint and dark hair. She even bowed, and something slipped out of her white dress at the neckline—a dangling necklace. I gasped, my heart releasing a wave of warmth and opening to possibility. I couldn't see the necklace from this distance—it was probably a meaningless jewel—but at one time, she'd shattered an amulet of Bes and vowed to wear it for me until there was justice in Egypt.

Chapter 32

Present Day

THE AIRPLANE LANDED WITH a sharp bounce, shaking the row of blue seats that I sat in and jostling my hips and spine. I'd arrived at the airport back in Cairo.

Images of the journal's story flashed through my mind, of Heb leaving Mutnedjmet, like I had left Maddie. Then images of Akhenaten and Nefertiti followed, along with the artwork they'd left behind of Akhenaten wanting to appear like a loving family man. But then again, Hitler and Stalin had done the same thing in their own portraits, and Hitler had even used Akhenaten as a reference for his own agenda. Hitler had also refused to relinquish the most famous bust of Nefertiti and return it to Egypt. But it was weird, because the elegant beauty of that bust was only skin deep. Modern CT scans revealed that the ancient sculptor had fashioned the underlying limestone to show many wrinkles and a bump on the queen's nose.

The plane's rapid deceleration stopped abruptly, flinging me forward. I leaned back against the force and arched my hips so I could dig my phone out of my pants pocket and turn the device on early as we taxied into the terminal. There was a message from Maddie.

I held my breath as I put the phone to my ear.

"Gavin," she said on the message, her tone hesitant. "I got your message, although it was hard to hear. All I could make out was something about your bracelet. So … I have good news and bad news."

I swallowed.

Her voice turned chipper. "The good news is that I saw you give your bracelet away to a kid, so I followed him after you left. I knew that thing really meant something to you and you were just upset. I know about your dad and what you two went through … so I paid the kid fifty bucks and he gave it back."

My heart leapt up into my throat in eager tension.

"But the bad news is that I actually had a lab tech who I work with analyze it." She took a deep breath, and an edge arose in her voice as the rate of her words slowed. "When I went back to get it a week later … don't get mad here."

I clenched my teeth.

"He said he'd lost it. He never loses artifacts, but he'd said he'd already examined it and the bronze was more current day, probably a century or two old, definitely not over three millennia old."

My eyes closed in frustration. The bracelet was a fake? It was probably better that my dad never knew, then. But that meant the dream I'd had and the hope of interpreting the markings on the inner surface of the bracelet wouldn't mean a thing.

"Sorry, Gavin," Maddie's message continued. "I asked the tech to keep an eye out for it. His lab's a mess, and it could've just been misplaced. If not, I'll buy you another one like it. Bye." Her message ended with a click.

The passengers around me stood from their seats, opened the overhead bins, and yanked out their luggage.

Maddie hadn't even sounded or acted awkward in the message, like I'd expected her to after our last conversation and parting. What did that mean? Did she not even care that I was gone, or had she not even really noticed?

I groaned in frustration. Maddie had been staying with a friend at an apartment near the university before Kaylin, Aiden, Mr. Scalone, and Jenkins had arrived and rented out the penthouse suite at the Four Seasons.

If her boyfriend was there, I guess I'd have to interrupt them this time.

✳ ✳ ✳

I pounded on the metal outer screen door of an apartment; the front door just beyond was closed. The stifling heat of Cairo, the wind, and the dust swirled around me and assaulted the exposed skin of my face as I stood on the cement walkway.

No answer.

Should I call her?

I turned around to walk back down a long metal stairway.

A pop and a creak sounded behind me as the front door of the apartment opened.

I slowly pivoted around.

"Who are you?" a male's voice asked—his face was veiled behind the screen door, but it was deep red, either really hot or angry. He was tall, his frame large and muscular, although he had a protruding belly—Erik, Maddie's on-again off-again boyfriend since college or high school.

I stepped closer. "Gavin. I recognize you. We've probably seen each other fifty times since we met." *You're an idiot.* "I need to see Maddie."

He didn't open the screen door for me. "She doesn't want to see anyone."

"Well, then you can just tell her I'll be waiting outside until she does." I leaned up against the railing along the walk, the heat burning through my long sleeves and into my skin. I jerked my elbow off of the railing.

He groaned and shut the door.

"Gavin?" Maddie's muffled voice said from inside.

How would she feel about me being here? I'd come back after running away in an attempt to salvage my own kind of life and career back home, but at least it wasn't before I'd rescued her from danger. My hands shook a bit out of nerves and anger. She'd partially forced me away or had at least convinced me I should go and give up the dream of finding the Hall. What was she going to say to me now?

The front door popped back open, but not the screen door.

"Gavin?" Maddie's long dark hair was tucked into a bun on top of her head, her sheer glasses appearing over misty blue eyes. "What are you doing here? I'd thought you'd left Egypt."

"I—I did," I said, then cleared my throat. "But I came back. I need to talk to you."

"Okay, Erik was just leaving anyway." She turned back to the interior of her apartment.

"No, I wasn't," Erik replied.

"Yes, you are," Maddie said and folded her arms. "Get your stuff. I booked you a flight back home, and it's leaving in a few hours."

Erik ranted from behind the partially closed door and banged around inside before yanking the front door all the way open and kicking open the screen door. He stormed out and bumped into me before huffing as he stomped down the metal stairs.

"Douchebag," I said. That was at least a good sign.

Maddie motioned for me to come inside.

The interior was dark, the blinds drawn to keep out of the sun. A struggling AC unit rattled from the lower end of the kitchen window. The apartment was still baking hot, but smelled falsely fresh, as if Maddie often used a fragrant aerosol spray.

I removed my fedora and wiped thick sweat from my forehead with the back of my hand.

Maddie sat on the couch—an off-yellow piece with square armrests that didn't have much in the way of padding.

I slumped down beside her, the cushion sinking deep into worn springs.

"Maddie," I said, studying her down-turned head. "I thought we couldn't find anything else."

She stared absently at the dingy carpet. "You always leave, Gavin."

My chest and chin jerked back in surprise. "*You* wanted me to leave. I wasn't giving up, I was listening to you."

Her eyes closed. "I was angry. Because of what happened to me, what you and Kaylin did when I was abducted, us never finding the Hall, and just everything going on and what I'd been through. I might not have actually wanted you to leave. I needed someone to talk to ..."

"And Erik was there for you?"

She shook her head and her bun wobbled side to side. "Erik didn't even come looking for me when I was abducted. I didn't know he was coming now, nor wanted him to. He just showed up, like you. I wanted someone close to talk to, but not him, not now. I'm furious with him."

"But your voicemail greeting made it sound like you were happy Erik was coming to visit and that you were taking off work to spend time with him."

"I'm sorry," she said as she wrinkled the bridge of her nose and looked at me out of the corner of her eye, "but I didn't want you to think I was hurting and ... maybe I wanted to make you jealous—for you and Kaylin, and for leaving. Looks like it worked."

I bit my lip, pondering the situation. I didn't understand her but overall was mildly happy with her reasoning. Or would she get upset again and ask me to leave as well?

She leaned back against the couch and stretched her legs out. "Gavin, I just want to know that you aren't going to give up on everything when something bad happens."

"I flew all the way back here," I said, frustration rising in my voice. I hadn't given up on my chance to become a doctor completely for Maddie, but the administrators at school still hadn't contacted me. "And you let me know that you don't have my bracelet, so I didn't fly all the way back here for that. Please, tell me what may make you feel better. You can talk to me and tell me anything that happened to you, your suffering, or whatever."

She scoffed. "I can't just spill everything out to you on a simple request. You left for a week and now suddenly you're back and want to be my hero again?"

I buried my face in my palms in frustration and took a deep breath. I had turned into my absent dad with her, although I'd made nearly every decision to try to avoid that. "I'm sorry. I didn't mean it like that. I came all the way back here for you, to help make you feel better."

"Well, maybe if you're here with me for the next week or so and can help take my mind off of everything, I can stop thinking about what I went through. Maybe I'll start feeling more like myself and can face some of the stuff I experienced and share it with you. But I can't guarantee it."

I lowered my hands from my face. "I understand. And I thought I might be able to make you feel better by doing what you love most."

Her left eyebrow climbed her forehead as she studied my face. "Oh? And what is that?"

"Looking at ancient Egyptian sites together, ones not related to the Hall."

"I'm not sure I'm ready for that yet, either." Her lower lip protruded. "But I am glad you came back. Maybe we can just hang here for a few days, but no dinner dates out. And I'm sorry that I lost your bracelet and that it turned out to be a fake."

My eyes wandered as thoughts ran through my mind, thoughts I'd been obsessing over nearly as much as Maddie's well-being, since getting on the plane back to Egypt. "I don't think the bracelet was fake or someone studying ancient Egypt wouldn't have"—I used my fingers as quotes—"'lost' it. If he gave it back, I'd believe it was worthless. Maybe it was real, or even a replica, but how many other antiquities has this guy lost?"

"Everything's not a conspiracy," she said, but her eyes lit up behind her lenses as she pondered my words. "I don't know if he's ever lost anything before. But why would he take this one small bracelet?"

"Are Mr. Scalone and Kaylin still here in Egypt?"

"Yes," she said. "I talked to them the other day. They were going to meet with the Minister of Antiquities, as they're still trying to locate clues and find the Hall. That's Mr. Scalone's only job right now since Kaylin hasn't given up and he technically still works for her and her dad. Aiden's still here, too."

My stomach churned. After a couple of weeks of not finding anything to go on, was I the only one who'd thought it was hopeless? Well, the others were getting paid or were inherently rich already. My future career had been at stake ... "Did they know about the bracelet and that you took it to this lab tech? Could they have taken it from the lab?"

She adjusted her glasses as she thought, then she said, "They did visit after you left, and it came up. But how would they break into some lab and steal it, and why? That was your dad's, I thought, and had nothing of real value. Even if it was a real artifact, how much could that one bronze bracelet be worth?"

I ran my hand along the felt brim of the fedora in my lap. "As much as the entire Hall of Records."

"*What?* No, maybe a few thousand dollars to the right buyer—*if* it was genuine," she said. "It was bronze, not gold. Or did you mean it meant that much to you because of your dad?"

"No," I said and sat straighter. "Because I wrote a letter to the dead, like an ancient Egyptian, like in the story inside the journal translation."

"Right," she said, "I need to make a copy of that entire story before you go again. It might be the most important find from our entire expedition, besides the otherwise-raided lost tomb of Amenhotep."

"Then I had the most vivid dream," I said. I cleared my throat. Had I received answers from my dad in that dream, like Heb with his father? No, that was too unbelievable, but I needed something to help keep me going now. "And someone, possibly Heb, visited me in the dream."

Maddie's head lurched back as she studied my face.

"He showed me the bracelet that he carried ... and it was the same as mine."

Chapter 33

Present Day

MADDIE SIGHED AND THREW HER messenger bag down onto her kitchen table—a folding card table—with a hollow thud. "Gavin, I think you finally lost it and fell into the trap of believing everything in that ancient story. You might be getting desperate to find something, maybe even to help my mood, but a dream with the characters of the journal being something other than a dream?" She shook her head. "If you're reading about them all the time, it isn't too unbelievable that you'd dream about them."

"You were the one who was always trying to convince me that the story could've been real when I was doubting it early on," I said, leaning forward in her sagging couch. But that probably did sound crazy—I should've brought it up more subtly and didn't even know why I'd thought she'd take it seriously.

"But," she paused, "I don't doubt the mind's ability to think in alternate ways when you've been considering something so hard for so long. So bringing it up in a dream is definitely possible. Your subconscious may've kicked in and helped you unlock some memory or thought."

My head fell back against the hard upper frame of the couch. "You're right. In my dream, Mr. Scalone and Kaylin and Aiden were all there too, in Cairo as well as at my med school and my mom's house."

She reached into her messenger bag and tore out her laptop. Cracking it open, she went to work, her fingers tapping and clicking on the trackpad and keys like her life depended on it. "I'm not holding out any hope on this bracelet theory of yours, as I don't believe everything is a conspiracy, but since you've got my interest going again, I need to see those hieroglyphs."

"Do you have pictures of the hieroglyphs on the inner surface of my bracelet?" I asked, lurching out of the deep cushions of the yellow couch.

"Of course," she said, still hitting keys. "I do that with everything I find that could relate to ancient Egypt. I can't believe you never did."

I scoffed in defense. "Well, I looked at them all several times over the years since my dad gave it me, and again after I'd been in Egypt, and they didn't make any sense."

Pictures of my bracelet popped up on her screen—the flat facets of the outer surface, the rounded ends. Then there were pictures on the inner surface: a cluster of small hieroglyphs, shallow and worn.

"They're hard to even see," I whispered, leaning closer, my heart rate elevating as my face hovered over her shoulder. The scent of almond wafted from her skin and hair, filling my nostrils.

Maddie magnified the picture multiple times and adjusted the contrast as she imported the picture into her computer simulator program that allowed her to adjust the angle and proportion of light—her primary research tool for her PhD work studying the effect of shadow and light on ancient Egyptian art.

The hieroglyphs stood out.

A scorpion for sure … and a pharaoh wielding a club, and another of the same pharaoh wielding a hoe? He was about to strike several enemies with the club—enemies half the size of the mighty pharaoh. And scorpions hovered in the sky, and also stars—no, not stars, flowers.

Maddie tapped on the screen with a short fingernail and then rubbed her chin as she studied the images for a few minutes. She adjusted her glasses. "The sounds that the images evoke don't seem to mean anything, and neither does reading them with their potential clustered meaning, like typical hieroglyphs. Maybe it spells out a cryptic message, but it's probably just hieroglyph gibberish to entice tourists."

The images reminded me of something, something recently triggered in my brain because it was mentioned in the journal … Was the journal guiding me? If so, what was its connection to my dad's bracelet? That bracelet probably couldn't have been Heb's.

That was it—the hieroglyphs on Maddie's screen were similar to the images engraved upon the Scorpion Macehead, the legendary weapon of the

Scorpion King, probably King Menes, the first pharaoh of Egypt. He was a caretaker of his people as well, distributing food and prosperity to all, not just pursuing violence and conquests. But how could that help anything?

"There's more." Maddie clicked to another image that showed a close-up of another portion of the curving inner surface of the bracelet.

An image of a single arm and hand held a round structure, an offering; a half square with protrusions, a gateway; a clenched fist ... I vaguely recalled scrutinizing these images many times over the years since Dad had given me the bracelet and more recently in Egypt, but some mighty pharaoh making an offering to the gateway of the river—the translation of the hieroglyphs—still didn't make any kind of real-life sense and could mean any number of things in ancient Egypt.

I gazed upon another image that appeared to be two spheres just split from a perfect overlap. "I think the first set of images are referencing the Scorpion Macehead."

"The Scorpion Macehead?" Maddie's head jerked back. She sat in silence for a minute. "I guess those images do appear familiar, like those on the mace head. So this would be saying to take the mace head to the gateway that is revealed by the river and two suns or spheres."

"Two suns?" I whispered over the rattle of the AC unit. My mind raced with memories of the story in the journal. Or the moon and the sun? "An eclipse?"

Maddie shrugged. "If this really means something, your bracelet could be telling us to bring the holy trinity—the three parts—to a gateway. The eclipse or lack of light, the sun as the father; the river of the earth, the mother; and the Scorpion Macehead or the pharaoh, the child?"

I couldn't recall any more hieroglyphs on the bracelet, but I hadn't put much thought into Dad's trinket before. "Were there any more images?"

Maddie shook her head and adjusted her glasses.

I fell back onto the stiff plastic of a folding chair sitting beside the table and let out a long sigh. "Well, then, this gateway still remains a mystery, and now that you've been rescued, the Minister of Antiquities would never allow us to borrow the Scorpion Macehead—if he ever would've let us."

She glanced over at me out of the corner of her eyes, her lenses partially veiled by the colored reflection of the computer screen. Her eyes flicked back and forth, and she brought up more images on her laptop. "I did some research after you left and located a few older images inside the *serdab*. They were taken over a century ago, so I digitized them."

Black-and-white images popped up on the screen, stacking on top of each other.

My eyes widened as I scooted closer to her, the thin aluminum legs of the folding chair screeching as they rubbed on linoleum. I glanced over her shoulder. The clue that the *serdab* at the step pyramid was supposed to reveal, the hieroglyphs that would've been illuminated by starlight, had recently been scratched away. Would the desecrated markings be clear on these old images?

Maddie imported the black-and-white pictures into her simulator program and magnified them, playing with the origin of the light source. Shadows twisted and stretched across the indentations and protrusions of the *ka* statue trapped inside the granite *serdab*—simply a box to hold the image of Pharaoh.

The hieroglyphs on the statue's chest were visible. Maddie zoomed in as best she could on the old photo.

There were so many tiny hieroglyphs.

She turned the side of her face to me. "Which ones would've been illuminated?"

Squinting, I studied the image. "Right at his false beard and upper chest." A run of hieroglyphs was there—a pool, a crocodile—

She released a quiet grunt as she examined everything in her altering light and shadow display. "I think the starlight would've indicated the oasis with the pool and crocodile. This looks like you were supposed to locate the guardian of the pool in the western desert—Sobek himself."

"I did that." The pitch of my voice rose an octave. "There was nothing but a skeleton of an enormous crocodile—one that appeared to have been killed by the same method as in the ancient story of Heb. I have a bunch of videos on my phone of the skeleton and of us digging out all the sand that filled up his chest cavity over the years."

"But did you look at it during an eclipse and under water?"

My chin jerked back then I shook my head. "How could we create an eclipse? And if the bracelet's message is real, doesn't that refer to the final gateway to the Hall, not the guardian at the oasis?" We'd also dived into water, Lake Nasser, to locate the original site of Abu Simbel, but Abu Simbel wouldn't have been underwater at the time the path to the Hall was laid; that was recent from the damming of the Nile. And the Faiyum oasis was expansive but not deep. It couldn't possibly hide a secret temple.

Maddie pursed her lips. "By the guardian's position then?"

"What?"

She pointed to the next hieroglyph on the *ka* statue, the one below the others that probably would've been illuminated by starlight—a distorted man? "Then it says 'by his position. To know the true guardian of the Hall.'"

"The crocodile skeleton was facing the oasis," I said. "That's it. Nothing the size of an ancient monument could be buried or hidden beneath the oasis, plus they couldn't have built it under a lake."

"People still argue that the ancient Egyptians couldn't have built the pyramids. So I wouldn't put it past those geniuses and architects." She ran her fingers across the trackpad and hit it several times. "I've got all your videos on here from before you left." Multiple videos popped up and the last one played.

The cracked bones of a massive beast appeared so close to the screen that they were difficult to discern from similar-colored sand surrounding it. The picture zoomed back. Aiden was there, using a shovel to fling sand away from the flat bones of the creature's head, which stretched longer than Aiden was tall. His tiny fox panted at his side.

Maddie leaned back and interlaced her fingers on the desk. "I'm surprised by how much Aiden was helping. He even appears excited. Kaylin always said that Aiden had been beyond worthless his entire life, which I took to mean he was lazy, lost, and without any amibition at all. And before I was taken, he didn't do anything with this much heart in it."

"You can't judge him based on the prejudices of his evaluator," I said defensively for Aiden, or maybe even a bit for myself and my past mistakes as images of Kaylin filled my mind. "Especially the judgment of someone like Kaylin. Aiden was the only one of them who really helped me find you."

Maddie sat quietly for a moment as her eyes wandered. "You'd better decide for good if your dreams here are really that important to you, because if by some stroke of genius we actually find the Hall, we can never go back.

You won't ever be a normal person with normal friends who like you just for you—Kaylin is a case in point. Think about how she's come on to you."

We watched every video I'd made. I ran my hand through my short hair and then squeezed the plastic seat of the folding chair I sat on. *Please, let there be something.*

The picture zoomed out and bounced as I walked around the skeleton and took in the oasis, my footsteps crunching through thick sand. Maddie adjusted the lighting, making it darker so the bones of the skeleton stood out much better.

"See," I said, almost leaning into Maddie. "Only the oasis. I guess we could go back and dive down in there, but it's huge and a muddy mess and not as deep as—"

"Shhh." Maddie clicked back through videos and watched as the picture zoomed out. She adjusted the angles of light on still images.

A couple of long hours passed, my fingers growing raw and my hands tired from clenching the seat of my chair.

"I'd searched most of the bones," I said, "before I got word that you were being held nearby. There wasn't anything marked into the skeleton."

She paused from adjusting a picture of the painted cliffs. "What's that?" She pointed to a dark shadow looming over the lower wall, directly beneath the image of the crocodile. The lighting she used was as if the sun were just rising over the horizon, casting long shadows all around the base of the cliff.

My chest tightened in suspense. But I shook my head. "It's just the shadow from the crocodile skeleton. I'm telling you, that thing was massive."

She zoomed in on the shadow. "It looks like a sphinx."

A sphinx beneath a crocodile? But it did look like a sphinx: sitting position, legs extended, head up and gazing outward. Somehow, with the angle, the shadow of the elongated head of the crocodile was distorted—the head appeared round. "What? How could that be a clue?"

She clicked open another video and hit the pause button. "Look how the crocodile's positioned." Her hands shook with excitement.

"He's facing the oasis," I mumbled, "maybe due east. But a lot in ancient Egypt faces the horizon and the sunrise."

"Yes, but look how he's sitting."

"The skeleton is sitting?" I leaned in. The bones of its legs were folded up and stretched out in front of itself. "It doesn't look like how a crocodile would sit, but it's been dead for thousands of years. And a skeleton can't exactly be made to stand, not like how crocodiles typically do in water for hours on end."

"But it could've been laid on the sand as if it were alive, basking in the sun." Maddie's eyes darted around the screen. "And all of its legs look the same, as if on purpose. Its tail is also curled around itself, like it was intentionally positioned to create that shadow."

"Okay …" My jaw dropped in disbelief. Its head was also raised and angled, unlike any living crocodile. The skeleton didn't at all resemble a sphinx, but its abnormal positioning was now obvious.

"Its head is raised like a cobra, like a guardian. And its face is angled out as if watching for—"

"I've never seen a crocodile sphinx," I said.

"Right, so what does this mean?" She tapped the side of her glasses. "There are thousands of sphinxes in ancient Egypt."

"That the Sphinx is the true guardian?" I asked.

"How would it still hide something that people haven't found by now?"

I leaned closer to the laptop and tapped on the screen with my finger. "The placement of this shadow compared to the painted image of the crocodile on the cliff face would seem to indicate that there's something above it. Or below it. The Sphinx sits below the crocodile? Has anyone searched the Sphinx during an eclipse and underwater? And brought the Scorpion Macehead to it at the same time?"

Maddie's head jerked to the side in surprise, and she scoffed. "What are you talking about? How could someone do all that?"

I shrugged. "Didn't you just ask me the same thing?" The Sphinx was supposedly as old as the pyramids, but some researchers suggested that the wear it had received could only have been from massive amounts of rain, not Nile water—and it resided in a desert. Torrential rains fell on Egypt ten thousand plus years ago. Some believed the Sphinx predated the pyramids and the ancient Egyptian civilization. But that was all conspiracy theory, and Maddie would never believe any of it. "Some observers have pointed to a lodged stone just behind the right ear of the Sphinx. They think it might be the doorway to a secret chamber hidden inside the massive statue itself."

"That's ridiculous," Maddie said. "Sonar has not shown any chambers within the Sphinx, only tunnels and columned halls beneath it—likely leading to the Great Pyramid."

I stood up and paced around the cramped kitchen with the suffocating fake fragrance. "Where is the Scorpion Macehead?"

Maddie spun around in her chair. "In Oxford. But there's an exact replica in the Museum of Egyptian Antiquities here in Cairo."

"Okay," I said. "So we've already decided that the Minister of Antiquities is not going to just give us an artifact."

"Discovering the Hall could make a PhD turn into a lifetime career—for both of us," Maddie whispered. "We'd become two of the greatest Egyptologists who ever lived." Her face turned pale. "Are you suggesting that we break into the museum and take the mace head?"

Chapter 34

Journal Translation

WE DOCKED ON THE eastern bank of the Nile a week after leaving el-Amarna to begin training our new army.

The clash of spear on shield rang through the open desert as our makeshift army trained.

"They'll never be able to drive off an army of Hittites." Paramessu spread thick oil along the axle of our chariot—the only chariot in our army of slaves and policemen. And our two horses were the only animals of war. We had donkeys, but they would only pull our supply carts. "Don't strike for the shield," Paramessu said at a sparring pair of disheveled men beside us. "You're only helping your adversary if that is your target."

"Like I've shown you," Harkhuf bellowed, his triceps bulging as he swiped with the butt of his spear at a slave's hand.

Wood collided with bone, issuing a loud crack. The slave, a young man with protruding ribs, howled in pain, dropped his spear, and hopped up and down as he clutched his hand.

"If you defang the snake," Harkhuf said, "you can make your enemy defenseless."

"Wouldn't you rather fight a snake with no fangs?" Seneb shot his brother a sneer while taking the wounded slave's hand and bandaging it. "Rather than trade strikes with something so deadly?"

"If he doesn't learn, it won't only be his hand he loses in a battle," Harkhuf growled, "it will be his head. I might have saved his life."

"Like a daddy lion swatting his cubs and convincing their mother that it's good for their character." Seneb patted the slave on his back.

Wahankh twirled his spear overhead with a whooshing sound and slammed it into Chisisi's shield. At the moment of the cracking impact, Chisisi jabbed with his spear at Wahankh's throat. Wahankh ducked the blow.

"If all of them had been training with us over the past years," Paramessu said, "like Wahankh and Chisisi, we might stand a chance." Veins bulged from his temple as he watched Chisisi, the man who had once tried to woo Tia. His resentment for the man must run deep.

✳ ✳ ✳

We sailed for weeks, as far as the Nile would take us, then set off on foot, traveling east through the desert. More weeks faded. A pain grew in the pit of my stomach, more so with each passing day. I'd finally returned and faced my former master but could not see a route to overthrowing him. Now I wasted more time defending his borders while he lived in the comfort of the palace with his army and the companionship of the woman I loved. My stomach cramped and I doubled over but kept marching beside the plodding hooves of our horses and our rumbling chariot. I didn't ride in the chariot because I'd need the animals fresh for battle. And the sooner we drove these Hittites off, the sooner I could return to el-Amarna.

An Egyptian fortress sat on a hilltop to the north, its walls stretching to and away from us—a former border of the kingdom. The walls had crumbled, and giant openings dotted it like a fence. Abandoned. The building loomed overhead but carried only as much foreboding power as a rock mountain.

"The ancient Fortress of Sneferu." Mahu nodded in its direction. "And the surrounding Walls-of-the-Ruler." These crumbling walls appeared like vertical desert with arrow shafts sticking from the mud brick like reeds.

We marched on for endless miles.

"Halt," Mahu said and grabbed my shoulder, jerking me into awareness. "My scouts tell me the Hittites have overthrown the outer fort." A policeman whispered into his ear. "Our enemies grow more daring, sensing Egypt's increasing weakness. They will spread down the coast and through the peninsula from sea to sea like a disease. Then they will put pressure on old Egypt. And Egypt will not be able to take its lands back, not unless the military at el-Amarna is sent to war."

Paramessu nodded. "That is why we must devastate the invaders. If we can show them that Egypt it still strong, the Hittites will fear Pharaoh's divine wrath and power and will look elsewhere for expanding their empire."

"Even with our hundred policemen from the holy city and five hundred soldiers," Mahu said, "we cannot face them out here in this empty desert. They are roughly a thousand strong."

Harkhuf scoffed, his face still clean-shaven, which exposed his bulging jaw muscles as well as his contempt. "Our soldiers?"

Seneb elbowed him in the ribs.

How had we ended up here? My plotting since our return to el-Amarna had been going so well, but perhaps too well too quickly, as the magician had warned me those years ago. He'd convinced me that infiltrating Akhenaten's council would take decades to accomplish with appropriate diplomacy. Now those who resided in the palace didn't trust me and had sent me away to die in a war they were not concerned with.

How could I have been so blind? Did I think I would race out to the far reaches of Egypt and destroy our enemies with a single blow ... with slaves instead of soldiers? Perhaps Akhenaten had wanted me to fail, to die. Suty, Ay, and Pentju certainly wouldn't mind if that happened. Had they influenced Pharaoh's decision?

Tia leaned over to Paramessu. "Should we flee Egypt forever?"

"I still have not seen or faced my father," Paramessu whispered to her. "And I have vowed to protect Heb—forever—as he saved my life more than once. Also, Heb has not yet accomplished his goal of winning Nefertiti."

My poor friend still didn't understand the haunting depth of my vengeance. And could I ever really still win Nefertiti? Even if by some miracle I could become nearly as powerful as a Pharaoh and make her desire me, would that be for the right reasons?

"We go back," I said and shouted for our entire army to turn around.

Paramessu faced me and raised a newly shaven eyebrow.

"To a more stable fortress." My upper lip wrinkled in defiance as we marched back. "We must defend Egypt's borders if we are to return and help Egypt, its people, Nefertiti, those children ..." Images of all the dead people littering the great road popped into my mind. That Egypt could not continue. And I'd rather die here and now than run away and live out my days knowing that the creator of such horrors still existed and that he could still perform similar deeds at any time.

"But how can we ever defeat these Hittites with this army?" Paramessu asked.

"Because we have to. We need to return to el-Amarna, soon." I recalled some of the magician's words of wisdom. "Their wish is to take portions of Egypt, but it is my will to defeat them."

Paramessu looked skyward, and his pale eyes closed in frustration.

"The Hittites will pursue us," Harkhuf said, the striations of his dark triceps standing out as he marched. "A confident enemy will use its momentum to swallow land in its wake, driving the fearful even farther inward."

"Like a lion stalking a wounded antelope," Seneb said, his boyish face rigid.

"We could use that against them," Chisisi said in a quiet voice as he brushed his hair from his face. "I am not trying to lead, just a suggestion."

I nodded.

"Get away from us." Harkhuf balled up his fists as he turned and bumped into the former freeman. "Your leadership almost cost my brother his life. And I would love to use you as a target to achieve the *only* archery feat I have left to accomplish—the one that would make me a master archer of Kush." Harkhuf had once mentioned this challenge before we'd visited his homeland—having to release three arrows before the first hit its mark, the arrows almost simultaneously puncturing both eyes and the open mouth of an enemy while pinning him against something. But he had to do this in real combat when fear, doubt, and distraction were everywhere. No wonder there hadn't been a master archer in centuries or longer.

"I am sorry." Chisisi lowered his gaze. "I have changed. I will not ever attempt to lead you; I'd just like to march at your side ... or even behind you."

"I'll put an arrow through your brain if you ever put Seneb or Tia in the way of danger—ever," Harkhuf growled.

"I believe that he needs our help," Tia said, her eyes cloudy with concern. "He is a broken slave, like we once were."

Paramessu shot her a scowl.

"I read his character before you ever worked your way into my heart," she said to her lover. "Even if we hadn't ended up together, I'd never have settled for Chisisi." She rubbed Paramessu's long arm. "You don't need to worry about him, but he needs us."

"He will fight bravely," Wahankh said—one of the few times he'd even spoken on this trip. But Wahankh knew what it took to face one's greatest fears. "I would be okay with allowing him one more chance."

Seneb shrugged. "He never actually ended up getting any of us hurt, despite his poor judgment and choices. And I have a soft spot for the broken."

But they didn't know the entire truth—that this man had put them in grave danger for his own potential gain back in Crocodilopolis. "Chisisi"—I placed a stern hand on his shoulder—"you may now play the part of one of my servants, a freeman and one of us. If we do not treat you as a slave, that status may soon be forgotten by all." What would become of this man? Would he, like the others, be able to overcome the demons of his past and incorporate himself into the group without having any authority? I had to believe that he could, that we all could overcome our demons—even myself.

Harkhuf grunted and jabbed a finger into my ribs. "Then if he betrays us, you have to agree that you will be the one to kill him … or I will not tolerate this."

My throat constricted with anxiety as I imagined the horror and pain I'd have to suffer to kill someone who was not my true enemy. But my actions had already led to the death of a councilman who had secretly defied Akhenaten for years by worshipping another god. There would be no redemption for everything I would have to do to pull Egypt out of the blinding, hypnotizing curse of Akhenaten's Aten. I slowly nodded.

Chisisi smiled and clapped Wahankh's back before grabbing my wrist. "Thank you, thank you. But I still don't understand one thing." His stern features narrowed. "Why I am to play one of your servants?"

My thoughts wandered. This man could not learn of my objective in el-Amarna. "Yes, that is all you need to know. And if you break the role at any time, with anyone, before I tell you it's okay, you will be killed. Our lives depend on you playing your part."

He nodded. "That is how you are safely living in el-Amarna, a disguise …"

Giant walls towered from the hilltop ahead, spanning across the countryside—the same fortress we'd recently seen. Outer walls lay in ruin.

"There." I pointed as I turned and marched up the incline. "This is where we'll make our stand."

"It looks like no one has manned this outpost in years." Paramessu shaded his eyes and wiped sweat from his brow. "These walls will not keep them out."

"I recalled something after we passed this way the first time," I said. "An old man atop the watchtower at Elephantine said something to me as a boy. He mentioned the old walls up north and to the east. The pharaohs of old implemented a heinous idea that continued for centuries, something that kept their enemies at bay without sacrificing their men." I jogged ahead, curious.

Heat pounded down on my shoulders and back as I hiked the steep incline. Heaving for breath, I approached the walls of the fortress partially buried with sand and not crumbling like the outer walls. Water still ringed the base—a moat, fetid and dark, fed by trenches and flashfloods from the surrounding mountains. Every animal in the entire region would need to come here to drink. Could that have fed enough creatures over the centuries to keep them alive, creatures lurking down in those depths?

Digging into my sack, I pulled out a papyrus-wrapped packet. I tore through the outer layers. Salt and smoke bombarded my nostrils and my tongue wetted with saliva. Dried meat from a duck—something I'd saved from Akhenaten's jubilee in case I'd ever need it.

Holding out the meat, I crept to the water. Too murky to hope to see into and still, like glass. I held out my hand with my index and little fingers extended, forming the magical ward I'd learned as a boy, the one I'd used several times to repel danger. The water bubbled. I dropped the hunks of flesh and leapt back as they splashed into the water. Black droplets splattered across my lower legs. My offerings slowly sank, disappearing but sending ripples out across the surface, the water appearing as if it were liquefied obsidian rock.

I waited.

Bubbles rolled up to the surface of the moat and popped, a small cluster, but more followed. Then a wave sloshed through the murk and pelted the shore.

They were still here.

Chapter 35

Journal Translation

THE ENTIRE DAY HAD nearly passed, and we'd prepared the fortress as best we could. Originally, only one old bridge had spanned the moat and led into the fortress. This bridge's timbers were dry, gray, and cracking like baked mud. But more bridges in the same condition had been stacked and stored inside the fortress. We'd painted them all with thick lamp oil until they glistened like new. And now there were twelve bridges crossing the wide moat that encircled the fortress, and all of them led to areas on the mud-brick inner wall that we'd painted black with mud from the mountain trenches and around the moat. If the enemy arrived in the dark, they could be fooled, as these painted regions looked like fake entrances into the fortress.

The red and yellow light of the setting Aten fell across my face and interrupted my reading. I cocked my head and tucked my books about war strategy back into the sack the magician had given me. I climbed the stairs to the walk around the walls of the fortress of Sneferu. The surrounding millennia-old Walls-of-the-Ruler, our ancient border, crumbled as they stretched out across the desert. Thankfully, the fortress's walls were in much better shape. How long ago had all of this been abandoned? Since Amenhotep had increased the size of the kingdom and found peace with the outer world?

Everything had been still and quiet, but I thought I'd heard something more than imaginary music.

Something swirled in the distance. A brown haze—a cloud of dust billowing up from the desert as if a windstorm raged across the land.

Faint shouting and hollering carried across the desert. Drums beat in the distance.

The army of the Hittites was here.

Mahu ascended the stairs and clapped me on the shoulder. "They've arrived. And will instill fear."

"Light the torches," I said, standing and pacing along the walk of the ancient fortress. "But don't make it obvious." The Aten sank over the horizon, its long rays of purple and pink scattering across the sky. Shadows stretched across the desert and angled around the fortress.

"So, we want them to know we're inside," Paramessu said, "but we don't want them to know that we want them to know it?"

I shot him a grin and rubbed his smooth head for good luck. "Precisely."

The captain rolled his eyes.

"Did you convince Tia to stay inside?"

"I could not." He grimaced below a shaven eyebrow.

"I'd have preferred it if she wouldn't have come at all."

"After what we'd been through, I could not convince her to stay in el-Amarna while I went to war."

My emotions swirled through the fibers of every one of my muscles: fear, excitement, tension, remorse, and a tinge of anger—the emotion that never completely vanished.

Harkhuf, along with his brother, placed bunches of arrows along the walls.

I patted Harkhuf's meaty shoulder. "We will all hide and *not* fire until I give the order."

"You think all these bridges are going to confuse them?" Paramessu's pale eyes clouded with skepticism. "Don't you think we'll be able to kill more of them if we just start loosing arrows as soon as they're within range?"

"How many archers do we even have?" I asked. "Yes, I believe Harkhuf is a master, and we have Seneb and me, but the three of us cannot kill nearly a thousand Hittites before they pound down the real gates. We need to drive fear into their hearts and make them want to run and never return."

Paramessu's strong jaw tensed beneath his hooked nose.

"If this scares you"—I banged on his shield with the flat of my sword—"you may not want to return with me to el-Amarna. The odds there will be much worse."

His face went pale.

Drums sounded in the distance, followed by hollering. The Hittites must've spotted the flames inside the fortress and wanted to intimidate us. The intangible smell of fear seeped from the hearts all around me and thickened the air like fog.

My blood turned cold. But this enemy had no idea what waited for them.

The pounding footsteps of an army echoed across the mountain cliffs at our back. They ascended the hill to the fortress and would be upon us in minutes.

"I am thankful to die a freeman." Chisisi bowed to my companions.

"And I not to live in constant fear," Wahankh said, although his knuckles were white, his hand shaking on his spear.

"And I am thankful that I can love another man after my father's death and the ordeal with my uncle." Tia kissed Paramessu on the cheek.

"And I no longer fill my days worrying about my and my brother's futures," Seneb added. "I feel more like a mindless insect than I used to, one who cannot ponder a time other than the present, and I am happier."

Harkhuf silently glared at Chisisi. He'd never forgive the man who almost cost his brother his life.

Chisisi and Wahankh both exited the fortress, headed for the back cliffs.

I wished that Croc were here beside me, but I wasn't thankful for anything. Not now. So much turmoil still raged inside me, burning my stomach and rotting my heart. Not until I'd taken Nefertiti from Akhenaten and faced—

Foreign voices shouted. Hundreds of feet stomped on wood, the hollow echoes sounding like the sweetest music. I motioned, and the policemen fanned out, encircling the inside of the fortress walls. I crept to the lip of the walls.

Harkhuf's biceps contracted and veins popped from his skin like snakes as he nocked an arrow.

"Wait." I held a hand out at his face.

The last rays of the Aten faded from the desert, leaving only a wisp of red across the western sky, like foretelling art from the gods.

Harkhuf grumbled. "Until they break in? The gates are as old as the bridges."

"We'll have a minute or so." Paramessu held a spear, its tip wrapped with cloth.

Tension weighed heavy in the air around us. Marching footsteps grew closer.

Something banged against the mud-brick of the fortress, then on the real outer gates.

"Now!" I shouted as Tia ran to us with a lighted torch.

She lit the oil-soaked cloths around my companions' arrows and spears as we stood up over the ramparts.

The Hittite soldiers looked up.

Harkhuf, Seneb, and I released flaming arrows. A Hittite soldier shouted and pointed at the sailing bolts. Others laughed as our arrows missed their men. But the arrows plunged into the old wooden bridges with a thud … and then a crackle.

All of the oil-soaked bridges glistened in the firelight, and flames ignited. Hittite men screamed as the bridges burst into infernos. The night lit up as if the Aten burned in a circle around the fortress, the heat soaking into my skin.

More screams.

Many Hittites flung themselves over the sides of the long bridges into the black water. Others burned.

Those who'd jumped over disappeared beneath the liquid surface of the moat, their ripples carrying like waves. Heads bobbed back up to the surface and arms flailed as they attempted to swim the distance back to the shore.

But the heads of these soldiers were yanked beneath the surface. Cries of sheer terror came from those in the water. Panic set in, soldiers climbing over each other as they pushed their comrades down deeper.

Hungry jaws snapped all around the surface of the moat, and reptilian eyes shone in the firelight. The waters ran red. The sound of bone crunching carried up the walls, tingling the roots of my teeth—the crocodile breeding program of old was still a vicious weapon.

Arrows rained from above, Harkhuf releasing three for every one of mine and Seneb's. Spears flew from the hands of Paramessu and even Tia, as well as from many policemen.

Some of the Hittites that plunged into the moat reached the outer shore and fled into the night, shoving through the remainder of their army as they screamed in horror. Seneb blew into a trumpet, and a brass cry rang off of the surrounding cliffs, shaking the night around us.

War cries erupted from the mountain cliffs at our back.

All of the slave soldiers and more actual soldiers of Egypt charged down the slopes, led by Mahu, their spears advancing as they encompassed the rear half of the fortress walls. Chisisi and Wahankh ran at the forefront side by side, their shields raised and their spears poised for exposed flesh.

The rows of Hittites turned and readied to face them but took several steps back, driving those behind them into the moats. Enemies at the rear of their ranks shoved into their comrades to avoid the red and black waters and dismantled their formation.

Egyptians crashed into the Hittites. Clangs of metal sounded. Men shouted. The bronze of our men's and our enemy's weapons shone red.

The momentum of our army drove the enemy into the moat. Scaled tails whipped across the water and green jaws snapped. Men were dragged down into the murk. Others thrashed around, attempting to spear the crocodiles or fight Egyptians. But the viscous water and the mud along the banks weighed them down. Arrows and spears flew from our men atop the walls. The Hittite numbers plummeted, and soon all of their soldiers along the backside of the fort were either thrashing around in the moat or bobbing motionless. One man, rather than enter the water, scrambled for a bridge burning like a bonfire. As he neared, his clothing ignited. He turned and ran for the front of the fortress. Other soldiers parted for him, and his flaming figure sprinted down the mountain past the rest of his army.

The Hittites at the front of the fortress must've seen the burning man run past or heard the fighting at the rear over the roaring flames and screaming men. They marched, circling around both sides of the walls. But those in the front lines halted immediately when they saw the carnage there as well, and our army.

The flames of the burning bridges leapt for the sky, and islands of bodies littered the water.

I grinned as I recalled the face of the magician and uttered a quick thanks. All of the strategies that I employed had come from modifications of his teachings or from within the books that he'd left for me.

Our army yelled and charged again at the last half of the Hittite soldiers.

The Hittites turned and fled down the hillside, and our warriors pursued them.

Chapter 36

Journal Translation

WE TENDED TO THE WOUNDED until the Egyptian soldiers and slave soldiers returned to the fortress, having chased the remaining Hittites back beyond Egypt's borders.

Our men brought a few Hittite prisoners back with them, the captives' wrists bound as they scuffed their feet through the desert and approached the fortress.

I waited inside the open gates with my companions.

"You ended up scaring all of the surviving Hittite men so badly they probably evacuated their bowels enough for the next month," Harkhuf said. "I wouldn't want to come anywhere near their first camp site after that battle."

"After they departed such a camp site," Seneb added, "I imagine it would look like the aftermath of the slaughter of an entire field of dung beetles—all that would remain would be balls of feces, everywhere."

I shook my head and climbed the stairs to the walk along the walls of the fortress. Yes, the stories that those frightened enemies would tell of their last battle might keep their armies at bay for a while, but now was not the time to jest. Now was the time to return to el-Amarna.

I stood tall upon the walls as the heat of the late morning Aten rained down on me. Paramessu stepped up beside me, his shaven head glistening in the light. Tia stood on his other side, and the dwarf brothers joined us, folding their arms across their chests as they looked down upon our army.

The policemen, soldiers, and slave soldiers rested below.

"Every slave here deserves a choice," I said as I paced along the walk. "You slaves may either come home with us to el-Amarna, or you may stay at the fort and protect our borders."

Men all around whispered and muttered amongst themselves.

"If you return to el-Amarna, I have no doubt you will remain slaves and be put back to work building more of the city," I said. "But out here you will be free soldiers, battling our enemies. And I promise that I will speak to Pharaoh about making you freemen and soldiers for how you fought here on this field of battle. You deserve to be freemen in Egypt."

Silence.

Soon after, we waved our goodbyes as most of the slaves stayed behind to man the fort. But some followed my companions and me, as did the Hittite prisoners and police of el-Amarna.

We traveled on foot before we found our run-down boats still waiting beside the Nile. After loading everyone up, we threw open the sails and headed south.

I only made one quick stop on our return to el-Amarna, venturing out into the countryside around the empty palace at Memphis. I traveled alone, having ordered the others to all rest in their boats for a day at the port.

The rays of the Aten punished me with their brute force, but I located the cave in the desert—the one I'd been imprisoned in as a child when I was blamed for carrying the plague.

The giant door in the hillside was closed. I pulled on the crumbling handle. Nothing. I heaved with all my might, and something cracked before the door shuddered and creaked as it swung outward. The rank odor of human waste streamed out along with the inner shadows and unnerving silence.

I pinched my nostrils shut and crept inside.

Something waited for me. A twisted corpse with scraggly gray hair basked within the shadows and light along the inner margin of where the sunlight reached. A mummy, created by the aridity. But this mummy was not prone; it sat up, clutching at the rock wall even in death and faced the doorway as if waiting to one day be released. My heart bucked and my stomach wrung with pain. This was the old man who'd been in here with me, the one who'd lost his mind long before I'd ever met him—Akhenaten's first servant, who'd overheard something he was not supposed to. But everyone was told that this man had gone mad and had to be confined. That corpse could so easily have been my own … my fate if I'd not received help from the magician and all my other companions.

I knelt in pain and anguish as I brushed a fingertip across the hardened skin of his forehead. And I cursed the Aten as I had that night as a boy in the desert when Akhenaten first took Nefertiti. But at that time, I'd believed that was why my life turned out to be so harsh, because I'd cursed the one god … now I knew better.

A hint of white drifted through the darkness deeper inside the cave, perhaps only in my mind. The linen-wrapped head and face of a Dark One appeared.

"I will avenge you," I whispered into the darkness—to all the souls that Akhenaten had tormented—and marched from the cave, returning to our boats and sailing south.

The eastern desert finally opened into the familiar valley surrounded by mountains and a blanket of cloud cover. Buildings sprawled across the countryside, the farmland scarcer here than anywhere else. El-Amarna.

We unloaded. My muscles and joints ached, weary from travel as I packed up our supplies and Seneb walked the horses and chariot to the great road.

The heavy footfalls of armed men approached.

"Chief?" a man asked as he and others appeared at the edge of the great road—policemen. The spear and shield in the man's hands nearly fell from his grip. "Mahu? You've returned. W-we didn't think we'd ever see you again."

Mahu forced a grin as he waved at the few Hittite prisoners. "Take the captives to the barracks. I need a rest."

Nodding, the policeman jogged up and grabbed two enemies by their bound wrists. Mahu and the remainder of his force who'd just returned wandered off into the city and disappeared.

My companions trailed behind me, headed north along the great road. But the Aten did not take pity on our exhausted bodies as it rained down its scorching punishment through the clouds.

Tia's head hung as she glanced over at Paramessu, who had increased his distance from her since returning to el-Amarna. She'd grown more withdrawn over the course of our prolonged charade with her as my wife. These past months with all of our trials had to have been hard on everyone, but for these two lovers to also have to force themselves to stay apart whenever anyone was around must've been torture. They needed each other's comfort.

I brushed up against Tia and whispered in her ear, "Go to him and tonight do not worry about anything else in this world."

Her head jerked as she glanced up at me, but a grin slowly crept across her lips.

I followed them and stepped inside the house we'd obtained in the northern suburbs. We all found beds and slept, possibly for days.

❋ ❋ ❋

Knocking sounded at the front door a few days later.

I rubbed my groggy head and eyes and yawned.

"Master Rem," a voice called from outside. "You're summoned to Pharaoh's council."

I stumbled to the door and swung it open. The Aten had crested it zenith. The Royal Scribe, Maya himself, waited there. He pushed his hair away from his face with his reed pen and said, "Pharaoh demands your presence at the council."

"We will see him tonight for the jubilee." I folded my arms. "We've been gone for many months and—"

Maya's lips pursed. "No, I've been ordered to bring you now. If this wasn't important, he would've sent someone else." He motioned with a nod, indicating three waiting horses and chariots.

Chapter 37

Journal Translation

I ENTERED PHARAOH'S OPEN-AIR audience hall under the waning afternoon Aten. My companions followed me.

The murmur of conversing councilmen radiated off the walls and carried out of the open roof.

Slapping footfalls and the clanking of Akhenaten's golden scepter echoed across the room as he ascended the stairs to his throne. He turned to me and stared, the rays of the Aten reflecting off his golden body and temporarily blinding me.

"Mighty Rem, slayer of the Hittites," he said, his bass voice deeper than normal, as if he'd just awoken.

Suty, the hulking monster of a bodyguard beside Pharaoh, sneered down at me. Nefertiti's green-painted eyes stared in wonder.

Akhenaten smirked, shadows covering his face but his dark eyelids pulled back. "From what my messengers tell me, you frightened the mightiest enemy of the outside world so much that we would be surprised if they ever consider so much as walking in the direction of northeastern Egypt."

I bowed low and extended my palms out in adoration, a cover, but I spoke words of truth. "Everything I've accomplished in my life is in one way or another because of you, mighty Pharaoh."

Akhenaten's smirk rose into a beaming smile, his thick lips swallowing his cheeks. "I sent you out with a group of mere slaves, and you returned as a creator of soldiers, dispatcher of enemies, wielder of the flame and the crocodile … a champion."

Nefertiti hadn't blinked, still watching me.

My heart fluttered, as if butterflies flew about inside of it and desired to lift it out of my chest. Warmth radiated through my core. And a look of interest, possibly even desire, from Nefertiti, the woman I'd longed for all of my life? Tingling ran down across my skin, the stubble on my arms and legs protruding.

I stood and stared into Akhenaten's dark eyes. "I left some of the slaves as new soldiers for the outer fort, but they will all need to trade shifts with the excess military here if they are to remain vigilant and keep our enemies scared and at bay."

"Whatever happens in my kingdom is known to me." Akhenaten's deep voice echoed through his face as if it were a tube.

My tongue tensed and pulled back into my throat. Was that a subtle threat hinting that he knew my identity? No. He was blind in his ignorance of birthright and status. I knew him better than anyone.

Akhenaten folded his arms against his sagging belly as his thick lips pulled up into a smile. "So now I will name you a commander in the Egyptian military. You will train more slaves as well and expand your army. Kneel and bow."

Suty and three other servants stepped down the stairs and approached us.

"All of you." Akhenaten's gangly finger flicked about my companions.

My lips pursed with suspicion, but my knees slowly settled onto the hard tile of the floor, and my head drooped. Paramessu and the dwarves followed my lead. Had Pharaoh finally given up hope that the Hittites would kill me and decided to have it done himself? The servants and Suty approached, and my shoulders tensed.

They reached out, and I flinched as I glanced up, my hands finding my swords. But necklaces dangled from their fingers, and they placed them over our heads—chains with gilded flies lining their lengths—the golden necklaces of bravery. Warmth rose inside me and fought off the crushing sensation of my inner turmoil.

Akhenaten applauded. "Rise, my new commander ... and his soldiers."

My knees wobbled. Overwhelming emotion tempted me to bask in Pharaoh's offered glory, to remain this type of hero for Egypt. I'd finally achieved something in this life, something almost no other man had done.

Would this change my life here in el-Amarna, make it worth staying and accepting everything as it now was?

Suty's fists clenched so hard that the vessels and tendons in his neck bulged. Ay's face turned red all around his orange eye paint. Anger? Jealousy?

"And since you haven't done so, my queen had our artists create this for you," Akhenaten nodded at another servant, who produced a half-mask of bronze with a jagged edge for the forehead and nose. "Now you can finally cover that hideous side of your face, at least while in my company."

I took the mask and buckled the strap around my forehead, the metal cool against my skin, the vision of my covered eye restricted.

Pharaoh tapped his cheek, issuing a hollow thud. "From this moment on, you will live here and oversee a portion of the military, unless in the future I decide otherwise. You will burn away the softness that our soldiers have come to expect from life and reintroduce them to harsher training, drills, and war. They must be ready for anything."

I nodded. Energy surged through my body and out my limbs like lightning. My heart raced. Power coursed through my bones as I stood straighter and rubbed the smooth outer metal of my new mask. I was now one of the most powerful men in all of Egypt, in all of the world. The feeling was invigorating, and I embraced it. I could issue commands to nearly anyone … Suty, Pentju … and they'd have to submit to my authority?

"Will you accept your new duties?" Pharaoh asked.

I turned to Nefertiti, who still watched me, as did Beketaten. The queen blushed and smiled. Maybe if I bettered myself and took responsibility and gained power, I could be in a better position to entice Nefertiti and find the person I knew growing up, the kind and loving person still buried in her soul.

The tingling I'd experienced a moment ago ignited like the inferno of the bridges at the fortress. My time had come, and I saw an alternate, easier path illuminate in my mind. Drums beat in my head alongside strummed chords of the harp. "I will. And training will begin today."

"You are a mighty man," Akhenaten said, "nothing like Pharaoh, but your bloodline must run close to my own."

"Very close." I recalled Father, Amenhotep's most prized servant.

Akhenaten waved at a far entryway. "There is another reason I have made you a commander and will name you my Seeker of Blasphemers."

A wide man lumbered in, the rank smell of sweat preceding him—Pentju, the doctor. Droplets of sweat ran down his watermelon head as he heaved for breath. He looked heavier than the last time I'd seen him.

"We still have unfaithful people living in this very city," Pentju said, the rolls beneath his chin waving as he talked.

Two soldiers marched in behind him, dragging a rolled-up rug.

"Open it," Pentju said, and the guards unrolled the rug. A body lay inside, mummified and twisted upon itself, as if the victim died in agony. Its mouth gaped in a silent scream.

I shuddered in horror. What was this?

"That is how we know some of the unfaithful still reside here," Pentju said.

Akhenaten spat. "Because the Aten only strikes demon-worshipping pagans with plague. And another disease has struck. We have been dealing with this for a while, but ten people have died recently and several more are sick, quarantined in the barracks."

The plague? No, probably another trick of Akhenaten's to justify committing genocide on those he did not care for. Father's face filled my mind, his broad smile, his loving hugs, the bronze of his bracelet digging into my back as he wrapped his arms around me …

Pharaoh settled back into the blinding light reflecting off of his golden throne. "You must also take on the task of becoming my seeker. The Devouring Monster does not sense any more magic, nor the remaining unfaithful, but you have unveiled blasphemers where it could not."

"Who was this man?" I pointed at the twisted corpse. "I will need more information to find those connected to him."

"He was one of mine," Mahu said, standing up near the raised platform. "A policeman who worked in the barracks, but not one who ever accompanied us north."

My mind muddled with possibilities. Why him?

"I will accept your request and will take vengeance upon *all* of those who wish harm to Egypt and its people," I said to Pharaoh.

Chapter 38

Journal Translation

A COUPLE OF WEEKS LATER, I lay on my reed mattress, which was anchored to a wooden bed frame, in my room inside the palace, but I could not sleep. Tia breathed quietly, her head upon the crescent pillow designed to keep scorpions away from the face.

After spreading a thick blanket down across the tiled floor, I sat with my head between my knees, lost in thought and planning.

Whistling sounded through the window above. The harps in my head grew louder—at least, I assumed they were only in my head.

"Seek out the singer," Tia said as she cracked an eye open.

I froze with suspicion. What did that mean?

She shrugged as if she understood my unspoken question. She was up to something.

"Have you met with the merchant yet and received the shipment?" I asked.

She nodded. "Everything is taken care of, so you do not have to worry tonight. We have the crates of your special wine stored nearby." She pointed to the window. "Go."

I stood up and inched over to the window. Leaping up, I grabbed the sill and peeked out, my shoulders too broad to fit through the opening. Only the flicker of distant torches dotted the darkness beneath a giant moon.

"You must see this," someone whispered from my doorway.

I dropped back down to the floor and spun around.

Paramessu stood at my doorway under shadows cast from the lamp in the hall.

"See what?" I asked.

He folded his arms across his chest. "I won't be able to explain it to you. You need to come with me and see it for yourself."

My muscles tensed as I reached for my swords.

"You won't need those." He shook his head. "Not this time."

His fingers wrapped around my wrist, but he paused and cast Tia a longing stare. His gripped tightened, crushing my skin.

Tugging on me, he pulled me out into the hall. We walked down corridors, not acknowledging the soldiers on duty, and stepped out of the palace. The palace's outer perimeter walls shone with speckles of torchlight. But gray moon- and starlight spread across the desert between the palace and its outer walls, the night air cool as it caressed my body.

I shivered. "What are we doing?"

"I've been awakened by singing every night since we've returned." He led me on. "It's smooth like river water but rubs at my heart like sand."

A hum arose from the darkness, taking over the plucking harp strings in my head.

We tromped through bushes that released the sweet smell of incense, and short trees intermittently obscured the moon. We'd entered the royal gardens.

Pale light glimmered just ahead—stars and the moon reflecting from a pond so still it could be a mirror. It appeared as if I could walk over and pick up my own star ... or drown in the unobtainable attempt.

The humming grew louder, intermixed with a soft voice—silky smooth, like Nefertiti's robes, but sad and haunting at the same time.

My heart twisted with sorrow as I crept closer. A woman sat at the far end of the pond. Reflected moonlight shimmered across her dress like butterflies flapping bright wings. My mouth gaped as I stood in awe, my breathing shallow and quick. Her face lay in shadow. The harps in my head rang with sweet chords.

I turned to Paramessu. "Who is—?" But he was gone. Why had he taken me here?

The woman stopped singing, her shadowed face peering in my direction.

"Did you come to the pond for answers?" she asked in a voice I recognized immediately—Mutnedjmet.

"I—I ..." I stuttered as I stood straighter. "I heard something, something odd."

"Odd?" She rose to her knees and leaned over the pond. Her silhouette blotted out the reflection of the night sky. Reaching out, she touched the surface, and ripples radiated outward, disturbing the entire mirrored world. "Odd because there was sadness and now we only celebrate the moment, indulging beyond reason?"

"Odd because it was ..." I swallowed but the words spilled out, "the most beautiful thing I've ever heard. It made my heart ache, a feeling from so long ago—almost a past life."

Standing on delicate feet, she swayed over and took my hands. Starlight shone across her gentle features. I couldn't do anything to resist. "Who are you?"

I cleared my throat. "I am Rem, a traveler, but one of the faithful—to Egypt."

She smiled, studying my face. "You remind me of someone, someone I knew a long time ago."

"I think that because I rescued you, your judgment is clouded," I said. "I am no one."

"Not so much in stature," she looked me over as she ran a finger down my mask, "but you look a bit like he did, without the protruding veins on the side of your face, and you have the same personality. But it's as if you're hiding it."

"Who is this person you speak of?"

She lowered her gaze as if she were embarrassed. "A boy. One I knew as a little girl. He was a servant of Akhenaten."

"A servant to Pharaoh himself?"

She nodded.

"The same one who ran away and died in the desert?" I asked.

She turned my hands over and traced my palms with her fingers. "Yes, or at sea. I believe his heart still wanders, searching for the true love he felt but did not receive. What happened to you?"

"I cannot be his reincarnate if that is what you are suggesting." A warm tingling sensation from her touch on my palm spread up my forearm. Was she using magic? I'd never felt so enraptured. "I am too old." She might be trying to trick me into revealing something, even if she did not like Akhenaten. Then she might tell someone, which could lead to my death. She had long ago told her father on me about running around the city with her at night when I was supposed to be quarantined for carrying the plague. That had led to severe punishment …

She sighed. "No, you are too old to have been born again as him. But you did save me."

"I didn't really do much."

She took a deep breath. "And there is a plague ravaging el-Amarna again. Any chance you want to go look into this and see if it is real, rather than a cover for something else?"

My chest constricted. Did she suspect that it actually was me, Heb, returned from the dead?

She pressed her lips to mine.

I almost collapsed. So soft and tender. My heart thundered in my chest as my pulse hammered in my ears.

"Thank you." She whisked by me, disappearing into the night.

I stood in shock for a moment. Releasing a long breath, I turned and walked back to the palace, heading for a specific room.

Paramessu lay on his bed, sleeping. Marching straight up to him, I grabbed him by the neck and squeezed. His eyes popped open, fear and surprise escaping from his very soul.

"I've spent all the years of my life planning what I would do in el-Amarna when I returned," I said, my teeth clenched with anger. "Do not meddle in my affairs by forcing me into a situation like the one at the pond."

He jerked out of my grip, almost falling off the bed. "You brought Tia and me together, even in the beginning." He sat up. "You helped show her that she could still feel love and then let us lie in each other's arms, even here. I was trying to return the favor, and I thought it might ease your suffering."

My hands trembled, and my face grew hot, sweat dripping down the inside of my mask. "No love can cure the festering disease that has planted its roots into my heart. Black mold flows through the vessels of my body like the sludge of the crocodile moat. If you put my objectives at risk, the only reason that I've lived for all of these painful years, you will be sorry. Just make sure that you've made the appropriate arrangements with the cooks and that you are in position when the time comes."

Grabbing his neck again, I shook him before spinning around and marching out.

Chapter 39

Journal Translation

I LAY IN BED FOR A couple of days, pondering my encounter with Mutnedjmet, and my hatred. My stomach cramped and burned as badly as it used to when I was young, when I forced myself to serve Akhenaten in order to be around Nefertiti—the submission that had poisoned my soul so deeply I would never discover an antidote.

My hatred was driving me into darkness, into becoming a man similar to Akhenaten—my nemesis, my very affliction. Or was I already him? And if so, how could I ever help Egypt?

I'd already not only put the souls of any person associated with me at risk, but also the people I called my friends and family. No one was safe from me and the plague that I harbored. But how else could I have achieved all that I had and still accomplish all that had to be done? I hadn't followed the righteous path, but I'd followed the only path that led here.

Screams carried down the corridors of the palace.

Jumping up, I donned my half-mask and ran out of the room in the direction of the commotion—the audience hall.

Suty stood on the throne platform and held someone by their foot, dangling them upside down over the edge.

Akhenaten paced in front of the victim—a middle-aged but younger member of Akhenaten's council who wore yellow eye paint. Most of the council and royal family had arrived.

"And the magician planned to do what?" Akhenaten asked, his deep voice carrying outward as if originating from a horn.

The man's kilt dangled over his body, leaving only his head exposed as he wailed. "Please don't take my soul."

"Then speak truthfully and quickly." The black above Akhenaten's eyes appeared like the sockets of a skull and sucked in the sunlight.

The victim squirmed. "I didn't know his full plan. The son of Hapu had been training me since I was a child. Then he committed suicide and left me aimless."

I gasped. Another one of the men that the magician had been training to help overthrow Akhenaten? He'd spoken of such people.

"But you were supposed to use diplomacy to infiltrate my council and work your way to the top?" Akhenaten asked.

Pentju waddled forward from below the throne's platform, holding a scalpel and tongs.

"Yes!" the victim screamed.

"To what end?" Pharaoh paced before him.

"To influence the rule of Egypt."

"And that is all?" Akhenaten motioned to the doctor. "To whisper in my ear, to advise me? Remember, your soul is at stake."

Pentju used the tongs to grab the man's yellow eyelid.

The victim screamed again. "To win over as much of the council, royal family, and military as I could over the years and turn them against you. So that we would not remain a blind nation worshipping one false god while destroying the kingdom."

Akhenaten froze, but his gangly arms dropped to his side. "Is there anyone else in this palace who *stands against me*? If so, speak now and your soul will be saved. If not and the Devouring Monster or I uncover your treachery, you will wish that you had never been born."

Silence.

"Then the sentence is final," Akhenaten said. "Doctor, take this man to your lab and inspect every one of his tissues, anything that could explain how he could be so traitorous. When you are done, I will send the monster to devour his heart." He motioned at the victim, all of his thin muscles bulging with rage. "Anyone else who is ever found to stand against this family will be tortured just as viciously, their families killed, and all of their hearts consumed by the beast."

Yellow liquid flowed from under the victim's kilt, up his neck, and over his face as he squirmed and grimaced. He screamed, and the stench of urine wafted about.

Suty dropped the man on his head with a crack.

The man fell silent in a limp heap.

Soldiers dragged him away by limp arms, and the doctor followed.

My heart raced, my limbs trembling. What could I do? I followed Pentju through the shadows of the corridors.

The soldiers pulled the victim into a chamber littered with tables, where bloodied surgical instruments rested. The man screamed and thrashed about as he regained consciousness, banging tables together and scattering the metal instruments. A rotten smell of death permeated the air. I gagged as I waited outside.

After strapping the victim to a solid table of mud brick, the soldiers shoved a wedge between his teeth, which drove his jaws apart. Then they left, giving me a nod as they passed.

Stepping inside, I asked, "Do you mind if I watch?"

Droplets of sweat ran down Pentju's forehead as he glanced back at me. He snarled and shook his head, the waddle beneath his chin wobbling to and fro. "I am not fond of you." He paused in thought. "But not many appreciate the art that I've developed over my lifetime. If you are interested, you may watch, as long as you respect and consider my opinion when I speak to you or Pharaoh in the future."

I nodded. "Is your art the ability to save lives?"

"More like ... studying disease." A string of drool escaped his mouth. "It fascinates me how the darkness burrows into certain tissues and eats at it until the tissue dies, and then spreads to other areas." He licked his lips and grabbed tongs. "Especially the teeth. Disease is always buried in their roots." He stuck the tongs into the victim's gaping mouth.

The victim thrashed around and mumbled as he tried to form words, the wedge-gag holding his jaws wide open.

I nodded at the victim. "I missed this one. I thought I'd found all of the traitors and wiped them from el-Amarna."

"Don't blame yourself." Pentju picked up and examined several scalpels. "He was trained to appear as the most agreeable councilman of all."

I grabbed a cold scalpel with an obsidian blade from a table beside me. "But I do blame myself." I inched closer. "I always have."

"You could learn a few things here, if you can stomach it." The doctor thumbed through bronze cutting instruments that had serrated teeth.

"Did you dissect the dead of the poor from the last el-Amarna jubilee?" I asked.

His hand froze.

"All those dead people littering the great road?" I said. "The children …"

"No." He shook his head, his tone flat. "I've already studied the poisons that we used on them—from the seeds of the strychnine tree. Odorless, tasteless."

My fingers squeezed the smooth handle of the scalpel in my hand. "How does it kill them?"

"Typically with seizures and convulsions that lead to asphyxia." He shrugged and extended a small saw into the victim's mouth. "Only boring findings upon dissection of its victims. And not worth the effort even in the young, who I typically prefer to study, but only if they house diseased organs." He lifted the victim's lips away from his teeth with the instrument. The victim's yellow-painted eyelids pulled back in utter terror.

How many men, women, and children had suffered similar horrors at the hands of this doctor?

I grabbed Pentju from behind—around the thick of his flabby neck—with the crook of my elbow and drove the scalpel into his chest. The obsidian blade pierced his thin skin and thick layers of fat with ease.

He screamed. I squeezed around his throat, choking him. "You always did like to study children the most," I whispered in his ear as I pressed the metal of my mask into the back of his head.

His jaw gaped, his face white. "Pharaoh will make you suffer," he mumbled as he struggled for breath.

"Then yell."

He screamed again.

"That is exactly what the soldiers of the palace expect to hear from this chamber right now." I kicked the back of his knees.

The doctor crashed down with a thud, toppling wood and bronze tables and spilling instruments. The rolls at the base of his skull jiggled. "Who are you?" He rolled over to face me.

"A boy from your past."

He trembled as if he lay in the cold snow atop the island mountain of Keftiu. His hands reached for the scattered instruments.

"A boy whose father was murdered. And you ordered the burning of his father's body for harboring a fake plague." I stepped on his heaving chest and pressed him down against the hard floor. "A plague you intentionally misdiagnosed to instill fear in the people who opposed Akhenaten. A plague with lesions that were really created by snakes and scorpions carried by the Devouring Monster."

His eyes gaped and then narrowed, his forehead wrinkling in thought.

"You are a slimy traitor to Egypt," I said, heat coursing through my body, rage igniting my cheeks like fire. My stomach burned but let go of its tension. I savored the sensation, as if I were releasing a thousand demons from my soul. "Because of you, Thutmose was murdered and now Akhenaten has driven Egypt into chaos and despair for all but the men who scramble to kiss the dirt that he has walked upon. You are one of the men to blame for the situation here. How does it feel to sell everything you are and betray everyone around you with your lies?"

"*That* boy?" His lips quivered. "But Akhenaten sent him into slavery and he ran away and died. The Devouring Monster was supposed to find and consume his heart, more surely than any man that Akhenaten had ever killed. And Akhenaten put some curse on him ... I think upon his sandals, so that the Devouring Monster could feel his presence whenever he came around, the same kind of magic that Pharaoh fashioned into an amulet he created years ago, one that could detect magic, so that they could hunt the—"

Sucking in a quick breath, I glanced at my sandals. Newer—from the previous owner of the farm I'd purchased. But I'd had my old sandals long before slavery and kept them until just before we sailed back to el-Amarna.

"I've returned from the dead." I smiled. "And I am also one of the magician's students." I untied the bonds that held down the victim's arms and legs and pulled out the gag. It jerked free of his teeth with a pop.

The victim stood on shaky legs, his eyes wide, too shocked to say anything.

The doctor yelled again, but his cry ended abruptly as I stomped on his mushy chest, beside the buried scalpel. Air shot from his lungs with a huff. Then he groaned and rolled onto his side.

"Run as fast and as far away as you can," I said to the would-be victim. "Leave el-Amarna and never return. When I am done with this man, they will think that you broke free and killed him."

The would-be victim's shoulders shook, his eyes bloodshot.

My heart twinged. Those eyes could've been mine. His life could've been mine, if I'd stayed and worked over the decades—ascending the ladder of Akhenaten's council while serving him indefinitely. But was my current path superior? I could still end up where this man had just been ... I shook my head. "Do you understand?"

The would-be victim's head bobbed in an exaggerated nod.

"Go!" I pushed the man away.

He ran out of the doorway and disappeared down the corridor.

The doctor grunted as he swung a scalpel at my Achilles tendon.

Kicking out, I caught his wrist with my foot, which jerked his hand and sent the instrument skittering across the floor. The doctor winced in pain and grabbed his wrist.

I crouched over his face and wiggled the scalpel handle that was still embedded into his chest.

He screamed in pain.

"I can kill you and then feed your heart to the Devouring Monster," I said, knowing that I probably wouldn't go as far as erasing a man's soul. Such judgment should be left up to a higher power, one that understood everything a man had done—one such as Anubis. "Or you can take your own life now and keep your soul." I held out the wooden handle of another scalpel.

The doctor swallowed, his eyes darting around as sweat streamed down his face. He gagged and coughed, the throaty sound echoing around the chamber.

"You will only have this last moment to decide," I said. "Otherwise, I take your heart."

Grabbing the handle, he yanked it from my closed fist and swiped the other end across his throat in a single movement. His eyes bulged as if they would pop from his skull. But no blood ran down his throat. He pulled the scalpel handle away from his neck … there was no obsidian blade attached to the other end.

"No!" he yelled.

"After everything that you've done to Egypt and to my father, did you think that I'd let you go so easily?" I stood over him and drew a sword. "You deserve a lifetime of slavery, starvation, and working until your body breaks at your joints."

He scooted away, his body squeaking against the tile as he held a hand out in defense.

"Luckily for you, I am kinder than your master."

Chapter 40

Present Day

THE MUSEUM, A MASSIVE PINK mansion composed of many outer archways, sprawled across what must have been an entire city block of Cairo. It stood two stories tall with a pink dome on the center of the roof. Crowds of chattering people filled the streets with a racket and poured in or out of the museum's doors. Cars raced by, honking more often than I imagined horns blaring in Los Angeles.

Shadows grew long as the Aten sank toward the western horizon, and the heat pressed down on me more than at any other time of day. I paced along the sidewalk across the street from the museum, chewing on nuts I'd purchased from a street vendor while trying to hide from the sun under the leaves of a lone tree. The crooks of my elbows were sticky, as was my back and the backs of my knees.

"There you are," Maddie said, finally. Her dark brown hair was down, draping around her shoulders.

"I didn't think you'd be able to find me in this mess." I gave her a quick hug, and her body tensed in my arms. Was she still upset with me? "What'd you have to do?"

"Get this." She held up a brass key. "The professor who's the department head at the university out here has his own copy."

"A key to the museum?" I asked, my eyes stinging as they dried out from gaping open. "Did he give it to you?"

Maddie looked away to a passing crowd of tourists and then to the shouting locals trying to grab their attention to sell some item or service. "Let's just say I had to lure him out of his office. If I'd brought you, it would've been more suspicious. You didn't think that you or I could break into the museum and steal anything without getting caught, did you?"

I glanced across the street at the massive museum. No way. I couldn't break into a car with its windows down. "So you think we should wait until it closes and then sneak in?"

"Unless you believe you can break through glass and take the mace head without all the tourists around you noticing."

"Won't there be alarms?" I asked.

She forced a tight grin. "That's why a fellow PhD student is meeting us here and taking us inside to a private study room that he practically lives in for his thesis research on some of the mummies and artifacts in there. My research is primarily at the ancient sites, so the workers at the museum don't know me as well as they know him. I convinced him and our professor that I needed some time studying something new to take my mind off of everything I've been through recently. They felt sorry for me. And I can't slip through security systems like an international art thief. The key is for a way out. But there are also security guards in there overnight, and they monitor the cameras."

I swallowed. How could we steal an artifact and not get caught? "It's going to close soon. We should probably go in now and see exactly where the mace head is kept so we know where we're going. That way we can move as quickly as possible."

She shook her head, her long locks swinging back and forth. "No, the first thing security will do after a robbery is review footage from the day before to see who was really interested in the missing piece. I don't want my face on a camera near the mace head, and I already know where it is. And since it's only a replica, it's not protected by alarms or anything crazy. It's just sitting in an exhibit behind glass."

"Do we have to break the glass?"

She held up a ring in which at least fifty smaller keys filled its curving length like a middle school janitor's. "I'm hoping the department head professor also has a key to that specific exhibit, for research, but I don't know."

I sighed. "Let's hope we have plenty of time. When does this other student arrive?" I tried not to stare at the museum.

Her head bobbed as she thought about something and then typed a text on her phone. "He's not the most punctual, and it was on short notice. But he should be here by now. He's an easily distracted Icelandic man."

Someone said something behind us. I couldn't understand it, but it wasn't Egyptian.

Maddie spun around and smiled. "Hi, Kristjan." She stood and hugged a lanky young man with short, sandy-brown hair and rosy cheeks. Maddie stepped back, revealing the man's suit jacket and tie, and motioned to me, but this Kristjan held on to her waist a bit too long. I guess Maddie had her choice of plenty of guys wherever she went, so I'd need to accomplish something, or I might lose her for good. "This is my friend Gavin. He's the one I told you about." Maddie tore my fedora from my head and removed my sunglasses in an instant.

"What are you—?"

She hid the objects behind her back and smiled at her colleague.

Kristjan nodded, extended a hand, and rambled a few words, although it took me a minute to realize he was speaking English with an incredibly thick Icelandic accent. The only word I picked up was "Maddie." I smiled and shook his slender hand.

Kristjan spun about on a heeled shoe, said something that sounded like "gray tool," although it wasn't, and waved for us to follow him across the crowded street. His thick soles clapped on the pavement as we weaved between throngs of tourists and shouting locals who seemed to press in around us and create more heat, also bringing a wafting stench of body odor. Kristjan must've been on the verge of heatstroke.

Maddie tapped me on the shoulder and stood on her tiptoes to whisper in my ear. "I don't want your fedora disguise on the museum cameras before we get inside, either." She pushed past me and marched on.

What?

We approached the main entryway under the towering cement archway with pillars and statues of gods, although they appeared more Roman in influence than Egyptian, and waited in a long line where the tourists chatted in many different languages as they purchased tickets and continued on through a security line. I studied the workers taking tickets behind the glass partitions, then the armed security guards just inside. Sweat dripped down my forehead as I tried to act casual, but my foot tapped the cement steps with nervousness.

Finally, Kristjan approached the ticket booth and flashed some kind of identification on his jacket. The attendee, a young Egyptian man with a jutting forehead, waved him through and even mentioned his name. Maddie did the same and slipped a few bills into a slot at the lower edge of the window as she motioned to me.

The attendee waved me through.

The temperature didn't drop as we entered the building, no AC, and wound through rope banister lines.

Kristjan said something over his shoulder and Maddie nodded. He lifted the rope of a banister and motioned for Maddie to step under. She ducked and shuffled through. I followed her.

An armed security guard stood in front of us and said something in Arabic. I froze.

Maddie stood straighter and flashed her ID. "Research."

The guard glared down at her, his face rigid with disgust.

Kristjan stepped forward and pulled Maddie back before speaking to the guard in Arabic and showing his badge.

The guard grumbled something and turned away to face the incoming masses.

Kristjan led us around the visitors and main rooms, along a sandstone-colored wall, and up a few steps before stopping at a doorway. Metal jingled as he fished out a ring of keys and flung the door open.

We stepped into a small, lighted room with a table and chairs in the center. The air was thick and heavy, as if it hadn't been ventilated all day. Kristjan scooted stacks of paper and a box of latex gloves to the side of table, clearing an area as Maddie sat on a creaky orange chair and dug through her messenger bag to remove several folders. I sat beside her. A few ancient statuettes sat in a glass box in the middle of the table, staring back at me with crocodile, lion, and hippopotamus eyes.

Kristjan said something again, and I picked up, "Down the hall. Lock up and leave before they close."

"We definitely will," Maddie replied. "We'll only be here for an hour or so. If I need any more artifacts, I'll come find you."

He exited and shut the door with a click.

Maddie leapt up and fanned her face with her folders, droplets of perspiration trickling down her cheeks. "It's as hot and stuffy as hell in this room."

I leaned back in the stiff chair. "We've got a while before they close."

"Are you really here doing this right now?" Maddie asked, staring at me.

I rolled my eyes. "I can't believe it either." Would I get caught and be thrown into an Egyptian prison tonight, losing any hope of finding the Hall *and* of getting back into medical school? "I missed you, though."

She spun away from me.

A couple of tense hours slowly passed before the rumble of the hundreds of tourists outside subsided and the place fell silent. The lights shut off, leaving us in darkness.

I fished my flashlight out of my messenger bag and clicked it on, shining the beam across Maddie, who'd sprawled out across the table, trying to rest and cool off. "Is Kristjan going to come back and check on us?"

"He had to get a couple things but would've left just after helping us—"

A knock sounded at the door.

Maddie jumped up and snagged her bag. "Hide!" She lunged over to a stack of boxes in the far corner and started to push them away from the wall. The rattle of a key slipping into the lock sounded. I turned off my flashlight and followed Maddie, helping her with the boxes before slipping behind them. A moment later the door creaked open. A flashlight beam hunted around the room, and an Arabic voice called out.

I held my breath.

The door creaked again and clicked closed, leaving us in pitch blackness and silence.

Maddie flicked on a flashlight, stood, and pulled a black cloth out of her messenger bag. She handed me my fedora and aviator sunglasses before slipping the black cloth around her head and body.

I donned my hat and glasses, and a minute later she wore a black burka with only a slit for her eyes. "Good thing your aviators are big. But you also better keep your fedora pulled down low. I've at least convinced myself that if I'm caught I won't go to jail forever—not once they realize I'm the woman who was recently abducted by potential terrorists. I hope they let me go if I threaten to tell my past story to the media."

Maddie turned around and shuffled across the room with scuffing feet, her head low. I let out a deep breath and followed.

She grasped the handle, her hands shaking beneath her black burka. Giving a quick twist, she pressed up against the door and flicked off her flashlight. Darkness engulfed us. Something made a quiet click, and the door popped open. Pale light streamed into the room. Maddie glanced out and slowly crept through the doorway. I rushed over and squeezed between the door and the frame. Soft lighting threw shadows all around the inner museum—an open expanse like a warehouse.

My heart raced as I glanced around and listened, holding my breath. No approaching footsteps.

I eased the door shut without creating a sound.

Maddie turned and pointed over my head.

I glanced up—cameras.

Ducking, I jumped away and hid behind a wooden crate near the wall. My fingers clung to the coarse wood. Dust wafted from the slats. My nose tickled and itched. My eyes watered. I sniffed in an attempt dispel the sensation preceding a sneeze.

Stacks of crates, worn artifacts, and furniture towered around us.

Maddie inched over to me and grabbed my hand before whispering, "I've been in here a hundred times or more. Just keep quiet and stay close. There're hundreds of thousands of artifacts on display on the ground and first floor, and even more stored down in the basement."

"What about the security guards?"

"Keep an eye out," she said. "I have no idea where they are, their shifts, or routes. Sorry, I'm not an expert thief. And we didn't really take months planning this thing."

I swallowed with apprehension and followed her as she led the way down a hall I'd never been in. An open doorway emerged on our right.

Maddie paused for a moment. No sounds came out of there. She peeked around the corner and froze.

Slowly lifting her hand, she waved me on.

We crept out into a long hallway, this one lined with statues of ancient men, animals, and sphinxes. The lighting was still dim, like a closed office building with only an occasional muted light overhead.

The clap of soled boots on tiled floor echoed in front of us.

Maddie tripped and nearly fell before she jumped beside a towering statue of Anubis. I leapt the other way and crouched alongside a seated granite pharaoh and his queen.

The footsteps echoed along the tiled hallway at a rapid pace. A male voice called out in Arabic, sounding like a question.

Had this guard heard something?

Footsteps strode closer. I hunkered down into the shadows.

A black boot appeared out in the hallway beyond the edge of the statue, then a leg in green pants, and the guard's uniformed body. My heart raced. He held a flashlight but kept it directed ahead. Cold sweat trickled down my back as he passed by.

My breath slipped out in panic. But once someone saw that the mace head was gone, they'd alert any other guards in here, and they'd ransack—

"C'mon," Maddie said, stepping back out into the hall. "We have to hurry."

The guard's footsteps faded.

I stepped out as Maddie jogged ahead, leading me through doorways and rooms stacked with artifacts the average tourist would never see. Stopping, Maddie cracked open a metal door in the wall. It led into a stairwell.

"It's upstairs," she whispered.

Of course it was.

We slipped through the opening, and I eased the door shut before we hurried up the stairs as quietly as we could. At the door to the upper level, I carefully turned the handle and cracked it open a sliver. No guards or flashlights in sight. I looked back at Maddie and nodded. I pulled the door open and snuck out onto the upper floor—more of a mezzanine overlooking the vast grand main room of the lower museum.

Maddie dashed off, keeping low as she led me along the side of the walls and around a corner.

She pointed to a row of glass cases. "There. It's one of those." She glanced around and crept onward. I followed.

So many artifacts surrounded us: golden masks, jewels, tools, statuettes, a crook and flail. The world of ancient Egypt was so thick I could almost see the desert and its people here. A tingle ran along the skin of my back and the hairs on the back of my neck stood up, as if I were being watched. A scuff sounded. I spun around. A moving face glared down at me, and my heart lurched into my throat—

Akhenaten.

But it was only a statue, deformed, with an elongated face and eyes, and high cheekbones with sunken cheeks and thick lips. I shivered; it must have been my overactive mind making it seem like it moved, that or the shadows wavering on it.

Maddie jolted upright beside me.

I glanced over to where she was looking. The glass case before her was empty, the door open, as if someone had recently taken what was inside.

"It's gone." She held a hand over her mouth. "The Scorpion Macehead is gone."

What? My knees wobbled. "H-how? W-why?" I swallowed as I glanced around, my eyes landing back upon the statue of Akhenaten. The statue seemed to smirk at me. "Do we return to the study room and wait out the night?"

Voices carried around the atrium below.

"If someone took the mace head and the guards notice, they will search every square inch of this place." Maddie grabbed my wrist and pulled me away. "We need to get out of here, now." She ran back the way we'd come.

I raced after her.

Chapter 41

Present Day

MADDIE UNLOCKED DOUBLE wooden doors laced with metal—standing three times as tall as a standard door—with a click of the key she'd taken from her professor. She eased one of the doors open, and only a quiet grating sounded. She glanced around and then bolted out of the museum, racing off into a concrete sprawl between the museum and the next building across the way.

I froze. Cameras sat above the double doors on both sides and pointed downward, a faint yellow light illuminating the area before the entrance. Empty palettes and stacked concrete slabs littered the expanse outside.

Voices carried around the hallways in the museum behind us.

I darted outside and shut the door before sprinting after her. She veered off, taking a darker street that followed along the side of the museum, dashing into the night on pounding feet.

About a quarter mile away, she stopped in an empty street, leaned over, and heaved for breath as she braced herself with her hands on her knees. She tore the black burka off her head and threw it into a bush, doing the same with the dress.

"What the hell?" she said, waving her hand behind her. "What happened?"

I paced around in a circle, holding my hands up behind my head and sucking in air, a rasp in my throat. Warm sweat streamed down from under my fedora onto my forehead and cheeks. I removed my hat and sunglasses and wiped my face with my sleeve.

"Who would've known to take the mace head?" Maddie asked, straightening as she panted. "They remove exhibits sometimes for cleaning and preserving, but this seems far too coincidental."

I stopped pacing and met her gaze. "Whoever took my bracelet."

"But wouldn't they also have to know about the crocodile's shadow representing the Sphinx?" She pushed her glasses up on her nose.

"It's probably not that lab tech you gave my bracelet to for analysis," I replied. "Only one man stands out in my mind: Mr. Scalone."

"But that may be just because you hate him," Maddie said. "And you have a short list of suspects. Mr. Scalone wouldn't have been able to break into the tech's lab and steal your bracelet."

Mr. Scalone deserved to be hated—an arrogant D-bag who never actually helped anyone but himself and tried to hit on Maddie and Kaylin both, and probably every other attractive woman he met. He acted like a typical overconfident male who wanted respect without earning it or to instill fear by appearing dangerous—a bad boy. He may've been a real treasure hunter, but his perilous stories were unbelievable. He was a phony.

"He wouldn't be able to break into a lab like you wouldn't be able steal keys to the Museum of Egyptian Antiquities?" I asked.

She paused for a moment as her arms fell slack at her side. "What about the hired hands from Luxor who trapped us inside the tomb and abducted me? Seems more likely that—"

"Those two are both dead."

"I know." She rolled her eyes. "But two random men wouldn't be working alone. There have to be more of them. And the weirdest thing, which I've never been able to piece together, is that if they know about the path to the Hall and are watching it—because they only show up when we're following the clues—then they'd already have to know the entire path and where it leads. So why in the hell wouldn't they have revealed the Hall and claimed the discovery for themselves?"

My forehead tensed as I thought.

"C'mon, Gavin." She grabbed my arm above my elbow with stiff fingers and tugged me along. "Let's keep moving and get back to my apartment." She glanced around to make sure no one had followed us and strode off down the street on clapping heels.

I pulled out of her vice-like grip but continued pacing at her side. "I've wondered the same thing. Maybe because when locals discover artifacts illegally, they try to sell them for profit. When the government learns of the find, authorities step in and take ownership of everything."

A group of men passed on the other side of the street, laughing and speaking in some foreign language.

"So now you're suggesting that maybe there's an entire organization of Egyptians who've discovered the Hall?" She sighed. "And these people want to keep it a secret so that they can sell off all of the artifacts on the black market piece by piece?"

I forced a closed-lip grin as we walked past a row of parked cars, a streetlight overhead washing everything in pale yellow. "You might not remember right after you'd been stabbed, but your abductor said to never open the Hall because he believed that the fate of all of mankind and our entire world depended on it." Jenkins had also said something just as he was dying, something about knowing where Maddie was being held after she'd been abducted, but I didn't want to worry her with that at the moment.

Maddie's pace slowed a bit. "Okay, say I agree with your conspiracy theories for just a minute—about Mr. Scalone taking your bracelet and another group of people who know about the Hall. What does that mean for us? What would we do now? Call Kaylin and try to talk some sense into her? She probably wants to stake her claim to the discovery as much as Mr. Scalone." She turned left onto the next dim street, and a single car whizzed by us and blared its horn. A group of people on the sidewalks well ahead of us turned and glanced back, their faces shadowed.

What was that about? Maybe just a taxi. I stepped closer to Maddie. "I could call Aiden and see if he's still with them and knows what's going on. We got pretty close while looking for you, and he might trust me over his own sister. He doesn't like her that much."

"Do you think Kaylin would let Aiden in on anything really important?" Maddie shook her head as her eyes rolled side to side, thinking.

"Kaylin and Mr. Scalone would want to find the Hall as quickly as possible," I said and glanced behind us. I didn't see anyone following us. "That probably means we should meet them at the Sphinx."

"You think they discovered the answer to the clues and would be at the Sphinx already?"

I shrugged. "How long ago was it that the lab tech told you he couldn't find my bracelet?"

Maddie's lips pursed. "At least a week, maybe two."

"That's plenty of time to find help interpreting hieroglyphs." My fists clenched. "Kaylin's not the kind to sit around and wait. Mr. Scalone also photographed and videoed every site we went to. They could've figured out the shadow even by visiting the area over the past couple weeks—it involves light, and it's what we've been looking for in clues this entire time. And it's not as difficult as using a *benben* stone or lines of sunrays from Akhenaten's tomb to form an image. If they did see the sphinx shadow below the crocodile, they wouldn't be searching every sphinx between Cairo and Luxor. Kaylin's pretty smart, but not knowing much about Egypt would lead them to *the* Sphinx without questioning if there are other important ones."

Maddie's face went pale. "Damn it! I hope you're wrong, but maybe we should go to the Sphinx, in case they're digging beneath it right now."

"Do you want to get back to your apartment first and think this over?"

"This is yours." She punched her thighs. "Everything. The letter from your dad—he sent you Dr. Shelsher's original notes that led us to the lost tomb. We followed the trail from there."

"And you discovered the answers to so many of the riddles," I said, my stomach cramping with pain, as if my Crohn's disease were protesting or emerging in a flare-up.

"I can't let Kaylin and Mr. Scalone take everything." Her chin fell to her chest. "But I'm the reason they're here. I didn't think we could ever find a lost tomb and exhume it without a lot of funding and experience."

"We couldn't have." I wrapped my arms around her and squeezed in reassurance. She didn't tense up. "It's not your fault. I gave Mr. Scalone the letter and everything I had when you were abducted. I thought he might help me save you."

She pulled away but grabbed my wrist. "We'd better get to the Sphinx right now. Who knows what they've already discovered. And if they're searching for a secret, they'd be doing it during the night, after the laser light show at the pyramids, when there are no tourists or guards roaming around."

Chapter 42

Journal Translation

I STRODE THROUGH THE CORRIDORS of the palace, my sandals slapping on the floor and echoing down the hallways. Torchlight flickered around my head and cast twisting shadows upon the walls as it also crawled inside the eyehole of my half-mask of bronze.

I'd offered the doctor—the man who'd covered up the murders of my father and others—to Anubis. The others who shared responsibility for those crimes would soon follow him.

"Rem." A whisper sounded from a dark hallway beside me.

I pivoted to face the voice.

Nothing but darkness.

My hands found the smooth bronze of my sword hilts as I imagined the watcher in the shadows who'd stalked me before when I'd traveled about the palace—probably waiting for me to slip up and reveal something of my past or my future objectives.

A silky white dress took shape in the darkness. Green painted eyes emerged. Nefertiti. I swallowed and bit my lip.

Her fingers ran up my forearms, and the scent of rose and citrus flowed deep into my nose, making my brain foggy—captivated. "Our Seeker of Blasphemers," she said, her tone sultry and seductive.

She pulled me into the darkness and wrapped her arms around the back of my neck. Her light breath landed on my face, her lips inches from mine. She ran a finger down my chest, her large eyes lighting up in the dark. "The second-most powerful man in Egypt—well, either you or my father. And you have become one of us, part of the royal family."

Tingling ran down my neck and jolted my heart. Emotions burst forth, beyond the cage I'd fashioned for them from years of suffering and questioning what I'd ever do if I were alone again with Nefertiti. My body shook. Warmth rose from my heart, quieting my angry stomach. My heart raced. Could I stay in this position forever—the general of Egypt's military? I'd accomplished nearly everything I'd desired: wealth, power, Nefertiti's curiosity and desire ... nearly everything but destroying Akhenaten. But if I kept going, I risked losing everything I'd finally gained from all my life's work and exhausting devotion. Should I leave Pharaoh and the rest of his council alone and incorporate myself into their ranks, become an elite of Egypt? Was I following them into the dizzying light of the Aten? I shuddered—it was the worst nightmare of my former self.

"M-my queen."

"Have you ever wondered what it would be like?" she cooed as her fingertips ran across my chest.

"What?" My hands trembled.

She pressed her toned thigh up against the inner aspect of mine. "The most beautiful and desired woman in the entire world?"

"I—I ..." I swallowed. "Akhenaten ..."

She pressed her lips against my ear. "Has bored me for years. So many other women ... And I don't think I ever truly loved him. A secret, just once ..."

I reached around her back with both of my arms and pulled her close. She groaned lightly, her racing heart pounding against mine.

But what if someone came and saw us? I glanced around the dark hallway, the torch overhead extinguished—intentionally?

She grabbed my chin and pulled my attention back to her.

I pushed myself away but took her hand. "Perhaps we can speak openly behind a locked door." I led her down the hallway.

She pulled back against me but hesitantly followed.

I snuck through several hallways and around corners, leading Nefertiti into the audience hall. The fading sunlight of twilight floated through the open ceiling.

"What're you doing?" A harsh edge crept into her voice. "Not here, this is the least safe place I could imagine."

I tensed.

Akhenaten still sat on the throne and spotted us, his black eyelids pulling back. Standing, he studied my hand on the queen's. Then his eyes narrowed into blackness.

"My pharaoh," I said. "The queen was terribly frightened from the sounds of the doctor and the blasphemer." I let her oiled palm slip from my fingers. "I thought it best that she come see you."

Nefertiti's lips parted as she studied my face. "I can handle the torture of the unfaithful," she whispered so that only I could hear. "Witnessing torture is not a good excuse to be holding my hand."

My heart leapt into my throat, but Akhenaten made no sound. He remained as still as one of his sphinx statues, pondering the situation. Pivoting around, I quickly strode away by myself for my room. Pharaoh would never expect that a woman could betray his holiness, would he?

My footfalls echoed through the empty halls, but a scuff sounded behind me in the darkness. Someone was still watching me …

Wheels were grinding quickly now, and things might completely unravel if I were discovered. I'd have to move swiftly.

Stopping at Paramessu's room, I cracked the door and peeked inside. Tia was in there with him. They held each other in their arms and kissed. My stomach cramped with apprehension. I encouraged this, but would it destroy our cover? If one of the royal guards found out and informed me of their supposed betrayal, then to keep our act going, I'd have to kill Paramessu—my pretend servant, my friend—and send Tia into slavery … or worse. And the crime would be my fault.

Spinning around, I placed my back against the unyielding wall outside their doorway and took a few deep breaths. The hallway tilted. Love was coming between everything in my life, between all of my plans.

The presence of someone watching me hovered in the darkness halfway down the corridor. I snuck off the other way and stopped at the dwarf brothers' room, knocked, and entered. "Prepare the fire, now."

Seneb nodded, his eyes unblinking in the faint lamplight, as if in disbelief.

I spent another minute discussing the coming matter with the brothers before marching back out into the corridors.

Then I found a specific open doorway in another wing of the palace, tapped on it, and said, "Suty, I am here to inform you of the festivities."

Grumbling sounded from within. Then the hulking form of a monster appeared under lamplight. A woman lay on his bed, and tears dribbled from her eyes.

"What do you want?" Suty's pig ear twitched. "I'm busy."

"I know this was not scheduled," I said, "but I must insist that you join me in the feast hall—for a grand meal in your honor."

His broken teeth shined yellow in the lamplight. "You might be a commander of the military now, but only Pharaoh gives my orders."

"You are correct, mighty Royal Bodyguard," I said. "But this is for us to settle our past grievances, for good."

"You will never have my respect, newcomer." Veins bulged across his massive chest.

I bowed to him. "I am not asking for your respect, only for a few minutes of your life. I understand that every moment is precious, as you never know which will be your last."

His upper lip wrinkled. "I'll be out in a second." He turned back into the room, grabbed a sword from beside the wall, and tucked it into the back of his kilt. He glanced over his shoulder, but before he saw me watching, I spun away and waited out in the hall.

"You're not going to accuse *me* of being a traitor now, are you?" he asked as he stepped out into the hallway. "Not even Akhenaten would believe that."

I laughed. "Everyone knows you'd never betray Pharaoh. We just need to have a small discussion." Pacing away, I led Suty through the twisting corridors of the palace before arriving in the feast hall.

Akhenaten was gone. But a bonfire burned at the center of the open-air chamber. Two dark-skinned dwarves sat around the flames, and a few soldiers stood on guard along the peripheral walls. The flames crackled and snapped, their heat washing over my exposed skin like rays of the Aten, and probably shimmered upon my half-mask.

"Leave us," I said, motioning to the soldiers on duty. "I am your commander and am ordering you. We are preparing a feast for the palace, and I do not need guards at the moment. Do not return, no matter what you hear, not until there are others who come to attend the feast, those who might need your services."

The soldiers glanced at each other but departed through various doorways.

Drums pattered in my head.

"What is this?" Suty asked, his meaty hand on his sword hilt, which was still sheathed in his kilt. "I might not be the Seeker of Blasphemers, but I am a greater warrior than anyone in Egypt. I could kill you, you little man, with one swipe of my sword. And why are the dancing dwarves from Nubia here?"

"They are only for our entertainment. They will not hurt you."

Suty slapped his knee. "They could never hurt me."

The drumming in my head intensified as if it were all around me. "What is the most horrid thing you've ever done?"

Suty straightened, his ear twitching as he scrutinized me. "I have too many to choose from."

I paced in front of the fire with my hands behind my back. "It would be hard for me to pick only one. I stole fruit and ended up an indentured servant, continued to serve a vile master although the very fiber of my being begged me not to, rescued a dead man from the river—who returned to try to destroy a kingdom—gave up my life for someone I thought I loved and who I believed loved me, couldn't recognize true friendship and betrayed that friend, didn't stand up for myself when being bullied, and had to lick the sandals of people with more power in order to gain power myself." My face grew hot, the flames of the bonfire leaping out and reaching for my skin. Wood popped and hissed as it was consumed by the dancing light.

Suty laughed. "You are weak. The things that I've done don't even bother me, and most men would consider them much grislier than anything you've mentioned. You lose sleep over this?"

"Yes," I said. "And that is why you are here. I want to learn from you so that I, too, can live without the suffocating weight of a conscience—even if I murder innocent men, beat or torture them. I desire to enjoy performing the deeds, like you." I grabbed a large jug from a nearby table. "But of all the mistakes I've made in this life, the ones that haunt me the most, the ones that have really taken hold and planted roots in my heart and will not let go, are when I did not stand up for the weak, even when I was one of them—when I allowed them to be hurt by others with more power—kicked and maimed by you. When I watched Pharaoh eat a priest's heart—devouring his very soul. When I watched Nefertiti suffer at the hands of Pharaoh because you stopped me from helping her. When I watched you torch the body of my father." Drums raged like thunder in my head, as if the music of the underworld or whatever it was begged me to continue. I stopped pacing, still staring at the ground before I slowly looked up. One loud clap of the drums rang, and then silence.

Suty took a step backward. His sword was now in his hand, shaking. "Who are you?"

The dwarves stepped behind him, blocking the doorway we'd entered through.

"You don't even remember burning my father?" I asked.

He glanced around but shrugged. "I've burned more than a few men."

"I was Akhenaten's servant, many years ago. The boy you liked to torture." I stepped closer to him, one of my hands on the jug, the other behind my back on one of my sword hilts.

"No." He shook his head, his arm relaxing as if in relief. "That's impossible. He was a weakling, born a weakling, always a weakling. He couldn't have become anyone other than a slave or servant. Life doesn't work that way."

"You're right." I sighed. "It definitely doesn't, not here in Egypt."

He smiled but nervously glanced at the dwarves—his grip on his sword still loose. "The Aten makes it so that everyone is born into the position they are best suited for."

"Yes, I've heard that my entire life." I glanced inside the jug I held. Full of thick oil.

"Who are you really, Seeker of Blasphemers? You must've known that boy, to remember so much. You take pity on the weak, like him, huh?"

"Yes, it is my greatest flaw." I swung the opened end of the jug in his direction. Clear liquid gushed out, flying through the air in a solid wave. It collided with Suty's massive form, parting and splattering. Suty recoiled and blinked as the oil coated his face, chest, and legs. He shimmered in the light. Viscous droplets dripped from his chin and knees and plopped when they hit the floor.

"What is all this?" he yelled, wiping at his chest and studying the liquid on his palm. "Lamp oil? What are you doing?"

I dropped the jug, which clattered on the tile. "Your world is collapsing. The foundation of everything you believe in is a myth. This world is no longer suitable for men like you, those who perform the most hideous of atrocities if simply given the order from an authority—performed without question or remorse. I am *that* boy." I drew both of my swords.

Suty's jaw fell open as he raised his weapon. Firelight danced upon him. "No, it cannot be." His eyes darted about wildly. He rubbed and pounded at the scar on his head, as if completely disoriented. "That boy is dead. He was no one."

"I have returned from the underworld to send you to Anubis." I advanced. "I *am* Heb."

Suty bellowed, lunged forward, and swung wildly.

I deflected his strike with one of my swords and used my other sword to slice into the arm holding his weapon, disarming him—defanging the snake, as the dwarf brothers had taught me long ago.

His weapon sailed through the air and skittered harmlessly away. Tendons popped from his sliced wrist as his hand trembled. Blood gushed. He clutched his wounded arm against his chest and cradled it like a baby, rocking it. His eyes closed, and he muttered to himself as if trying to pretend this wasn't real, that he was somewhere else.

"Now you have a choice," I said. "You can let the meekest of servant boys slay you, the strongest of warriors, and feed your heart to the Devouring Monster, or you can run into those flames and face Anubis yourself." I stepped aside, motioning at his open path to the bonfire.

His eyes cracked open, his irises vibrating as if an earthquake raged inside his brain. He studied the fire, then me and my swords. Turning his chin back over his shoulder, he froze when he saw that Harkhuf had an arrow nocked on his drawn bowstring—aimed at Suty's back. Seneb held a drum between his legs and pounded on the instrument to help drown out any unwanted noise from this confrontation, although we'd already alerted the people of the palace that we shouldn't be disturbed, as we were preparing for something important.

Suty's body trembled, his eyes flitting about wildly. He lunged for me again with his good arm. I sliced his hand with my sword, and he jerked back, his breathing coming in short bursts. He rocked his wounded sword arm, and his countenance twisted, an appearance similar to what I'd seen on his victims as he bullied or tortured them: fear and panic—the look Suty took so much pleasure in evoking.

Something inside him broke.

Suty sprinted at me, screaming. But he continued running, passing by my side. The flames reached out for him and his oil, as if calling him home.

He burst into an inferno, and the bonfire roared.

Chapter 43

Journal Translation

PARAMESSU'S SHAVEN HEAD and eyebrows appeared at a doorway of the feast hall. He stared at me and the crackling bonfire as the dwarves mopped up the mess of oil and blood. Tia's demure features appeared beside his. Shaking his head in disappointment, Paramessu disappeared back into the shadows of the corridor. Tia followed.

I did not care what they thought; I had already waited far too long, and I wasn't going to stop now.

Then the people of the palace arrived, per invitation, but also perhaps because they'd heard the commotion, if the roar of the flames hadn't drowned out Suty's screams. Councilmen entered, along with the royal family—Mutnedjmet, but not Akhenaten …

I lifted a cup of wine as the masses congregated around the fire. "To the brave," I said as the dwarves handed out charred slabs of meat to the councilmen. The smell of scorched flesh hung in a cloud above the chamber, its haze dissipating into the night sky.

I strode over to Mutnedjmet, leaned down, and whispered into her ear, "Don't eat the meat." But I placed the warm cup of wine into her hands. Then, louder, I said, "To this brave woman." I stepped back and let everyone see Mutnedjmet as I addressed her. "This woman defied the very men—the unfaithful, the blasphemers—that we stand against, and we never even acknowledged her actions. Even when she was captured and it was certain that she would lose her life, she did not give in or beg for mercy. When I arrived to help her, she spoke of wishing to die rather than to live a life that was not hers to choose. If only we could all harness such decisions in the face of terror. This feast is on me, in her honor."

Mutnedjmet lowered her gaze and stepped close to me. "I was not brave," she said quietly. "I was hoping that my guard would arrive and save me while I was attempting to talk my abductors out of their need to kill me."

"Bravery is not in the words that we use or in our emotions," I said to everyone, holding another glass high, saluting Mutnedjmet and the fire. "It is in the actions that we take against fear itself … if our resolve can remain strong when everything stands against us. And no one knows or can fully prepare for when that moment, the darkness, comes to crush them. It must be solidified in who we are."

"The meat is tough and overcooked," an older councilman said, pulling a saliva-coated hunk out of his nearly toothless mouth.

I smiled as I walked up to the man. "I apologize. I have tried to be many things, but a cook is not one of them. I only wanted to share my appreciation for you all."

Others laughed or conversed loudly, threw back jugs of wine, or danced around the roaring flames.

I took a sip of earthy wine, the thick fluid tingling my tongue with acidity before it washed down the back of my throat. Mutnedjmet stared at me, and then at my hands as I lowered my cup. I was squeezing the cool bronze of Father's bracelet, the tension inside me seeping out in my habitual actions.

Someone grabbed my wrist and tugged me away—Nefertiti. She sashayed through the flame-lit night, a flat crown atop her head, her back to me as she led me through the shadows of a row of columns. She turned and pressed me up against the dark side of a column—no one would be able to see us.

Nefertiti ran her tongue across her plump upper lip as she stared into my eyes. "Seeker of Blasphemers, you don't need to celebrate my sister in order to get my attention."

"I—I …" I leaned back against the hard mud brick. My heart raced again, warmth searing my cheeks. Her intoxicating scent of rose and citrus wafted through my nose. Nefertiti, my greatest desire for so many years, was now coming after me …

She slowly ran her fingertips down my chest and stomach. "You shouldn't have led me away from the dark corridor the last time. It almost seemed like you wanted him to catch us."

I bit my lip. Did I? Could I have spoiled the opportunity to be with Nefertiti—one of the primary driving forces of my life—on purpose and not have realized my true intent? Or had I brought Nefertiti to the audience hall instead of a private room because I was trying to get the cogs of my plans rolling at a rapid pace after the doctor's death—before everyone in the palace discovered the murder and came up with a list of people who might have helped the would-be victim? After all, I had been standing outside of the doctor's torture room when the guards left. Since no one would be able to find Suty's body, no one would worry for a while or suspect him to be missing.

"Why?" Her hand stopped at my kilt.

I swallowed. Something felt hot at the waist of my kilt—the ostrich feather of Ma'at. I yanked it out.

"There you are," Mutnedjmet said, her silhouette approaching from the area of the fire. "Sister, why are you taking the commander away from his own jubilee?"

Nefertiti released me and stepped back. "We are having a private moment." She folded her arms.

"Master Rem," Mutnedjmet said as she reached out to take my hand, "would you join me for a short walk?"

I glanced at both of the sisters, my eyes gaping in horror and confusion. My pulse drummed in my ears, and the chords of stringed instruments arose in my head. My stomach knotted, and I winced in pain. Was this some kind of trick to confuse and thus expose me, or was Mutnedjmet trying to save me from myself? Nefertiti's heart-shaped face had immersed itself in my mind, making my heart as hot as fire. But Mutnedjmet's sincere smile caught my eye. The tension in my stomach eased, and I stood straighter. No, I hadn't trusted Mutnedjmet in my past life, and it led to my demise. Surely taking Nefertiti while Akhenaten was still alive would be a grievous error.

I reached out for Nefertiti but held something in my fingers—the blue ostrich feather. Her eyes widened as she saw it.

"What is this?" Nefertiti asked.

"A symbol of my love," I said. "Keep it … for when I return."

Taking Mutnedjmet's arm, I strode away with her into the shadows. But I glanced back. Nefertiti stood in absolute shock, her arms shaking and her lower lip trembling. My heart twinged with sympathy as—

Mutnedjmet grabbed my chin and turned my attention back to our walk. The music in my head sounded so sweet, like the river flowing at night.

"Did you know that at one time, Akhenaten was not meant to be pharaoh?" she asked, the light of the bonfire growing more distant.

"Yes," I replied. "His older brother, Thutmose, was the crown prince."

She nodded. "But even after that, at Pharaoh Amenhotep's last jubilee, a magician—the son of Hapu—was appointed to the co-regency."

My tongue tingled and pulled back into my throat as if I sucked on a lemon. I must not give anything away—this woman was smart. The music in my head softened.

"Pharaoh Amenhotep attempted to remove Akhenaten from his lineage—as Amenhotep did not think Akhenaten would be fit to rule," she said.

What she spoke of was true, as I'd witnessed it myself.

"Pharaoh did that because of me," she whispered.

I stopped in my tracks.

"Yes, I was finally able to convince him that the plague ravaging the magicians and priests of Egypt was a weapon of Akhenaten's." She tugged me onward. "I tried every chance I got, but by the time he understood, it was too late. Amenhotep died soon after, and somehow Akhenaten overthrew the magician."

I remembered riding her to convince her family of their wicked son, but she never seemed to try hard enough. "That is quite the story. Is any of it true?"

She stopped and stepped back to face me. "It is as true as the fact that I never turned in the boy who snuck around Memphis with me—the one who attempted to help discover the cause of the plague."

My hands clenched. Not convincing Pharaoh of Akhenaten's vile nature and of his misdeeds, and then telling her father, Ay, that I was running around Memphis with her while I was supposed to be quarantined were the reasons that I did not trust Mutnedjmet. My anger rose.

"Nefertiti told Ay about those nights, not me," she said, searching my face, as if she suspected something all along.

Nefertiti? No, she wouldn't have done that; I'd loved her and she'd loved …

"Think about it." Deep emotion flowed through her misty eyes. "Nefertiti found me with that boy at night in the slums so long ago—when he and

I finally saw the cloaked man, his magic, and the scorpions and serpents that murdered people. It was not me who turned in Heb. I tried to tell him many, many times that we should work together, but he never listened."

I remained silent.

"Nefertiti is also not the person she tries to be around you," she said. "I don't know if you've ever heard of Kiya, who used to be one of Akhenaten's most significant wives? Nefertiti had her murdered because she started to rival the queen's power and her influence over Pharaoh."

My heart collapsed in upon itself like a clay pitcher that hadn't received enough of the Aten's rays. What Mutnedjmet said made sense. And all of this time, I'd blamed Mutnedjmet and not Nefertiti, who'd refused to run away with me, refused to find love together. Unless ... because I was now powerful these sisters were competing against each other for my attention rather than for anything else. Perhaps they'd say anything negative about one another, especially Mutnedjmet about her more beautiful sister.

"I—I do not know why you are telling me all this, talking to me about that servant boy again." Strumming chords returned inside my head, growing louder and making my head ache, my thoughts jumbled. The harp joined in.

"I understand why he believed my sister over me—the young girl with the wild imagination." She reached for something at her neck. "And although I was angry with him for preferring my sister—for years—the frustration and pain inevitably receded. I only wished to see him again in this life ... Then, after I'd heard of his death, my heart broke. But I still wished for nothing more than to see him in the next life—to tell him everything, the truth about what happened and"—she swallowed and looked down—"the truth about how I felt—something I could never speak of when I was young, something I thought I'd never be able to confess to him in this life."

Her regrets were the same as mine, how I felt about not confessing my love to Nefertiti sooner, before Akhenaten poisoned her mind.

"I am not this boy." I turned my side to her. "We've been over this."

She held something out, something dangling at the end of a necklace. But there wasn't much left of whatever it was supposed to have been. Music sang in my head, a burst of a symphony so sweet—

"Have you seen this necklace before?" she asked. "Or does something inside of you, some deep curiosity, long to investigate this new plague?

Because I never said that Heb was the servant boy's name the first time we talked—you did." She held out the shattered amulet of Bes.

My eyes clamped shut, every emotion other than revenge rushing out of my heart as if the cage I'd fashioned for them had cracked and burst open. Mutnedjmet, as a young girl, had said that she'd never remove that necklace, not until there was justice for Egypt as well as justice for me and my father. Someone here cared ... My eyes stung as tears formed. I spun around, blinking to whisk them away. I was still weak—even after everything I'd been through.

Turning me around by the shoulder, Mutnedjmet took my hand and led me farther away—through one of the several unguarded exits of the feast hall. "And you still wear your father's bracelet and squeeze it whenever you are anxious. I knew it was you."

I wiped at my one exposed cheek, the symphony reaching for a crescendo.

After passing by the outer walls of the feast hall on quiet feet, Mutnedjmet turned and pushed me against the hard mud brick. Reaching up, she unbuckled my mask and let it fall and clatter to the floor. Her arms locked around my neck and she pulled my face down to hers. Our lips met—hers so tender, as if all they ever wanted was mine. She tasted like sweet fruit.

My arms wrapped her waist, and I pulled her trembling body close.

Chapter 44

Journal Translation

MY MIND RACED AS I REWRAPPED my kilt tightly around my waist. The racket of the raging jubilee on the other side of the wall in the feast hall echoed around me, but it seemed like miles away.

I kissed Mutnedjmet on the cheek. She smiled and lowered her gaze, the blue paint around her eyes smeared. The shattered necklace of Bes still dangled on her chest. She was amazing. If only I hadn't been so blind in my younger years. Nefertiti still held something inside my heart, but its bite felt less intoxicating, less agonizing. I exhaled and closed my eyes. Paramessu may've been right—perhaps I should be happy with all that I had: a woman, power, friends, wealth …

Mutnedjmet wrapped her tender arms around my waist and smiled. Her eyes sparkled with a warmth that I hadn't seen in her since she was young. "Don't go."

But it was too late already to stop my plotting. Everything was already moving, and soon I would be discovered and devoured. "I have to." I swallowed and looked away.

"We could flee el-Amarna." She laid her head on my chest. "I'd have loved my life if you'd have asked me to run away with you—rather than Nefertiti. All the bitter years of my life would've been full of such different emotions and events."

My heart wrung in on itself with sadness, the disease seeping out and growing stronger. Could we still run away, even now, and forget the madness here? We wouldn't have to devote another ounce of effort or grief in trying to help people who didn't deserve it … "When I have accomplished what I've come to do." I peeled her fingers from my skin and eased myself away. "This isn't as easy as I thought it would be … But the wine has been flowing, and it should've taken effect by now."

"What do you mean?" Her arms dropped to her sides and her shoulders hung.

"Stay here." The drumming in my head escalated and pounded, making my head ache and causing me to feel disoriented. "I don't want you to see any of this. I want you to remember me as the boy I was, when I was a good person."

I strode away through the dark corridor, the orange light of dancing flames guiding me back. The soft patter of tiny feet followed me. My chin jerked to the side as I glanced over my shoulder. A cat trotted up to me—orange and white. "Croc! What are you doing here? Leave this place." I kicked out and attempted to shoo him off, but he just sat on his haunches.

Trumpets joined the drums, blaring only within me. I turned and walked down the long corridor to the light at the end.

Laughter erupted from every corner of the feast hall, drowning out the crackle of the bonfire—twice as large this night as it ever was. Its flames leapt skyward, reaching nearly the height of the surrounding walls. Men stumbled and danced.

The emaciated, white cat of the magician's lay passed out on the floor just ahead. The sagging skin on her lower belly rolled out—a reminder of how overweight she had once been.

I knelt down and pet her matted fur. She didn't move—her blue eyes wide open. Croc meowed. Waving my hand in front of her face got no reaction. But her sides rose and fell with respirations and an overturned cup of wine lay a foot away, red liquid pooling around it like blood.

She must've drunk the newly arrived wine—special wine that I'd instructed to be served after the jubilee was well under way. I picked up the cup and entered the feast hall.

A servant woman walked by offering more food and drink, probably the first passing round of my special wine. An old councilman groped her backside and grabbed a cup as she tried to pass—her only response was to turn her head and lower her gaze, as if ashamed. She walked away.

The councilman threw back a long swallow and followed her, but a few seconds later, he stumbled and fell, landing face-first on the tile floor with a crack. Teeth skittered out of his mouth. He lay still.

I meandered to the edge of the enormous fire.

Two more men collapsed in crumpled heaps. I pretended to drink from my cup, which hid my grin.

Mahu and Maya toppled from their chairs and lay face down on the upper platform. Pharaoh and his queen were both here, seated in their thrones. Drums raged all around the inside of my head.

More men followed suit, dropping as if a disease wiped them all out, and lay limp.

"What is happening?" Mutnedjmet said from behind me. I spun. She held a glass of wine other than the one that I'd originally given to her, her eyes wide as she looked across the scene.

I shook my head. She wasn't supposed to return with me. The brothers were supposed to escort her—

She teetered and dropped to her knees, then fell onto her side as her arms splayed out.

Men toppled over all across the chamber.

Letting my muscles relax, I too collapsed amidst the masses onto the hard tile. My cup banged beside me and bounced away. Music deafened me. I squeezed my eyes shut, trying to block out the sound that disturbed my thoughts and plans. No use. Was this music of the dead really a curse, meant to drive me insane?

Croc pranced in circles around me and meowed.

I waited for about fifteen minutes without moving a muscle. Silence. Not even the music in my head continued. The crackle of the bonfire had quieted and only small flames still burned. None of the council or royal family—anyone who'd drunk my wine—remained standing. But the sober servants were gone, probably having fled in terror.

I turned slowly, my head low as I faced the throne. I could imagine Pharaoh's horror as only he and I remained unaffected—the only two people left, the one who plotted the scheme and the immortal who would not be affected. Deathly silence surrounded me.

Rising to my knees, I lifted my chin. My gaze met Akhenaten's. His dark eyes burned—perhaps with curiosity, rage, or even fear. But even now he remained seated.

"A poison from Nubia," I said and reached out to caress Mutnedjmet's paint-smeared cheek. My voice carried around the silent chamber, up to the raised platform and the thrones, and echoed off of the walls. "One that I discovered on my travels around the world. No one is dead quite yet. It only paralyzes its victims for a time but allows them to continue breathing so that they will not die without aid. I survived being struck by a dart coated in the poison." I stepped away from my former master, back to the shadowed columns, and felt around the base of the closest. My fingers brushed against something hard, a round club of stone—a weapon. I picked up the Scorpion Mace—the ancient mace that I'd taken from the tomb of Amenhotep—from its hiding spot, where Harkhuf had been told to leave it. Holding it behind my back, I stepped forward toward the throne. I shouted, "But death is coming for the vile."

Seneb, Harkhuf, and Wahankh appeared from the shadows of the exits, toting spears. They moved about the chamber, closing the eyes of the councilmen and making clean strikes for quick, painless deaths. But Chisisi was not with them. Neither was Paramessu or Tia ...

I ascended the steps to the throne, but still Akhenaten did not budge. He was either in shock or unconcerned, as he was indeed immortal.

I stepped over Mahu and Maya, whispering, "Sleep well, my friends. Your ability to move will return by morning. And by that time, the shadow of my life and soul may already be gone." Would they still consider me a friend in the morning or a traitorous blasphemer?

Ay lay sprawled out on the floor in front of me. I did not speak to him, but neither did I kill him. He probably deserved to meet Anubis, like every other councilmember here, but he was still Mutnedjmet and Nefertiti's father. Killing him would probably not be the wisest move for a man in love with his daughters.

I stepped around Beketaten, who lay on her face, her son beside her. For some reason, they'd let this young boy drink wine. I rolled the crown prince over and scrutinized his body—his stumpy foot, his face and eyes ...

I froze. Could this boy actually be my son? Or had too many years passed since my last night inside the Gleaming Palace of the Aten in western Thebes? I brushed the boyish sidelock of hair from his face. Probably not my son. Raising a sword, I closed my eyes. There was too much of his father already in him, and that lineage needed to end here, tonight. I squeezed the cold hilt of my sword with all my might, trying to plunge it downward. But my arm didn't respond.

I exhaled, my body shaking with emotion. I couldn't kill a boy—especially one that I wasn't convinced was pure evil.

"If you become pharaoh," I whispered as I leaned down to his ear, "please right the wrongs that Akhenaten has brought upon Egypt. Do not follow in his footsteps." I stood.

Nefertiti lay across the floor of the platform just ahead. My heart pinged with guilt. Poor Nefertiti, choosing so many things in life that would not lead her to find any amount of true happiness.

Clapping sounded.

Akhenaten stood, applauding me. His deep voice rang out, "You create quite the entertainment. A mysterious traveler rising through the ranks of the military with conquests of the Hittites, a new plague, the death of my doctor, my missing bodyguard, and the interest of my queen and her sister—both of whom I have tasted." He bellowed with laughter so loud that even the dead inside the buried tombs of the Valley of the Kings might have heard it.

"Your maniacal leadership will come to an end." I squeezed the wooden handle of the weapon behind my back, sheathed my sword, and revealed the Scorpion Mace of the ancient King Menes. I held it before me.

Akhenaten took a deep breath and let it out slowly, as if he were captivated with—even enjoying or relishing—this moment. The distorted veins and blue-tinged skin along the side of my face was exposed again, and he studied the area.

My muscles tensed. What was he plotting? He had no one here to protect him.

"I wander at night." His eyes grew distant. "I have ever since I was a boy. When I saw your wife in the bed of your servant, I knew that you were not who you pretended to be. No master would allow their servant to have their woman. And no real master would be deceived by their lessers. After that, I was prepared for you to expose your true self."

My blood turned cold, my confidence fading like the dying fire. Tia and Paramessu still weren't here, neither was Chisisi. Had Pharaoh done something to them?

Croc hissed.

A rustling sounded. Something slipped out from the shadows behind the throne—a black cloak—the rank smell of death and rotting flesh. The air around me turned chill, raising a blanket of gooseflesh across my arms and legs.

My chest constricted in terror—the Devouring Monster. It was here! Why had I not prepared for this ... my soul ... like Father's ...

A golden hilt flashed in the firelight, the gold fashioned into the shape of a crocodile's head. Out of the weapon's shining jaws erupted a blade of bone—the actual mandibular bone of a crocodile, with teeth still attached, which created a serrated edge. The thick hair of a lion covered most of the hand holding the weapon, but there was a mangled area of exposed skin with missing digits and claws—a jagged red scar—the wounds inflicted by Croc.

I stepped back and stumbled over Nefertiti.

The Devourer stepped forward with pounding footfalls.

"We have a present for you," Akhenaten said, and the Devouring Monster revealed its other lion's paw with claws as long as fingers. The digits opened one by one. Inside of its massive palm sat a mummified heart.

I gasped in horror. Whose was that?

"The magician's heart," Akhenaten answered, as if he could read my mind. He grinned as he studied the organ in the Devouring Monster's hand. "I actually killed him myself and staged his death as a suicide—for the people. Men who wield as much power as that magician cannot be trusted. He hid his tracks well. With him, even I needed to use a ruse, a young boy—my former servant—to uncover his treachery. In fact, we used that boy and others like him to discover and exterminate a lot of the magicians of Egypt." He paused for a moment and looked up at me. "I sensed a bit of magic within you some time ago, but it appeared to be beneficial against our outside enemies, and you never used it here—so I let you live."

I held the mace out before me, my insides twisting in disbelief and rage as his words sank in. How had he made me give away the magician? Guilt wracked my—

Croc leapt up beside me, the hair on his back sticking up—his tail three times its normal size. At least Akhenaten would never recognize Croc; Pharaoh didn't bother himself with memories of any animal.

The Devouring Monster hissed as its long, dark hood focused on my animal brother. The shadows beneath its cloak wavered. "A sphinx cat," the monster hissed, its mangled hand shaking a bit. "But the one who can no longer become the guardian. He is cursed." It pointed at the jagged, draining scar on Croc's back leg. "He cannot protect you now."

My head jerked back in shock. A sphinx? I glanced down at Croc, his pupils dilated like black pits. He growled. I'd seen him as some kind of beast, several times. My breathing came in shallow gulps.

"W-why would I care about a magician's heart?" I asked, still retreating.

"Because the son of Hapu was the leader for all you unfaithful." Akhenaten advanced behind his summoned demon from the underworld. "You would have respected him, the wisest man of Egypt. You are another one of those men the magician was grooming to assist him with his ambition of usurping the throne of Egypt, aren't you?" He patted his monster on its cloaked back. "Consume his soul."

The dwarf brothers shouted—a sharp bite of fear in their voices—as they ran for the steps leading up to the throne.

The monster's lion hand rose and disappeared into the shadows of its draping hood. The crunching of dry tissue carried out as teeth gnashed together.

My stomach clenched in anger, bringing cramping pain. Overwhelming guilt suffocated me. The room spun. I'd caused the magician to lose his soul, along with so many others … I tripped over a paralyzed body and smacked down onto my back.

Croc hissed and leapt at the monster. But he didn't grow in size or strength. The Devouring Monster swatted his sailing form aside. Croc flew far over the platform and disappeared into the masses of executed councilmen. Croc hissed in pain but still did not grow into a beast.

I scrambled backward, trying to keep a hold of my ancient weapon.

The rumble of hundreds of footsteps sounded in the distance. Soldiers appeared at some of the exits, attempting to seal off the room. My blood turned to ice. I was doomed. Clawing backward, I tumbled down the stairs.

The Devouring Monster advanced, raising its blade of bone to cleave my beating heart from my chest. Harkhuf and Seneb lunged at the monster together but were flung aside like small children.

Cries broke the silence, and the clash of weapons and rumbling wheels. Horses heaved for breath through flaring nostrils.

"Run!" Paramessu yelled, barreling into the far end of the feast hall with a chariot drawn by two horses. Tia and Chisisi followed, driving their own chariots, Wahankh inside Chisisi's.

I jumped up and sprinted for the far side of the room, searching the piles of bodies for Croc. As I neared the chariots, the pointed ears of a cat were just visible on the other side of a councilman's corpse—the cat also lying deathly still. I darted over, scooped up his limp body, and sprinted for our horses, leaping over more of the dead. The dwarves climbed onto the chariot with Tia as all of the drivers wheeled their horses around.

Egyptian soldiers yelled, sprinting through the remainder of the chamber's exits.

I leapt up into the chariot beside Paramessu, and we barreled into the soldiers, splitting their ranks as they dived aside.

Chapter 45

Journal Translation

WE RACED THROUGH THE night aboard our bounding chariots, the deafening rumble of wheels on dirt and pounding hooves filling my ears. The lamplight of the city of el-Amarna approached quickly, growing brighter.

I glanced back to the palace. No armies pursued us. This last attack hadn't gone at all how I'd planned. Pharaoh was supposed to be dead by now—if a god-king could be killed. If not, I should be lying amongst the dead of the royal family and councilmen of the palace. Everything was supposed to have been decided. And if Akhenaten knew that I was a traitorous blasphemer, why had he let my companions and me kill all of his councilmen? Did he not even care? Or was he not sure until I'd arisen from the fallen bodies of the poisoned? One thing I was certain of: Akhenaten didn't not know who I actually was—he wouldn't be able to comprehend it.

"Do not despair," Paramessu said over his shoulder as he drove our two horses on with a flick of the reins. "The soldiers and their commanding officers will be in utter shock of the scene we left behind—so much death inside their own palace. They will not know what to do. But some who know the heinous personality of Pharaoh and understand that such character is not fitting of a leader. Those soldiers will wish to join us."

I shook my head. But how would they find me? If I saw any military man coming, I'd suspect a trap. I'd lost my chance ... and I didn't know if I could go on living with Akhenaten still ruling Egypt and controlling Nefertiti. If I'd died, even lost my soul, at least I wouldn't have to contemplate my nemesis's victory every waking minute of my life. And Mutnedjmet was still there in the palace. If Pharaoh suspected that anything was going on between Mutnedjmet and me, he'd surely use her against me.

"That was my only chance to take Akhenaten down by surprise."

And I hadn't been able to reason with myself, my disease finally consuming all of me and controlling my emotions and actions. I groaned in utter failure.

My fingers stroked the matted fur of the cat in my arms—I looked down. It wasn't Croc in my hands … white fur, blue eyes—the magician's emaciated cat, and she was still limp, paralyzed. I had grabbed the cat in haste, believing she was Croc. My head drooped. That meant Croc was still inside the palace. But was he a sphinx? And what did that even mean—that he could protect me from the Devouring Monster, at least before he'd been wounded and cursed? But why would the Devouring Monster so clearly tell me this, unless it wanted me to know?

I gently shook the limp cat in my hands. Her head and limbs flopped around as if attached to her body only by string. The poison had affected her as much as the people who'd drunk my wine.

Her pale blue eyes shone in the moonlight, but her irises were darker than any night. I found myself fixating on those black holes that appeared like bottomless pits—portals into the unknown. The night around me grew darker, then a flash of white temporarily blinded me.

"The last spell that I can leave to this world," a familiar voice said. "If you see me here in my pet, then my soul is gone—taken by the abyss, from which there is no return. I am nothing." The voice crackled like dry logs in a dying fire—the voice of the son of Hapu.

A shaven head and a face with deep wrinkles traced with black paint appeared—resembling an amorphous spider's web. A backdrop of white surrounded him. Perhaps this was only in my mind. I shivered and clutched Father's bracelet.

"So even if you've listened to nothing else I've said," the image of the magician continued, "pay attention now. I've left you a mighty weapon. Not so much in terms of actual power, but perceived power is nearly as mighty. My last gift before my supposed suicide. But you've ignored my most important lesson for young boys in this world."

I reached out to him in desperation, but it was as if he were miles away. "I don't know what you mean. I've lost, although I'm still alive—a possibility that I didn't foresee."

"Confidence does not equate to competence," the magician snapped.

My chin jerked back in surprise.

"Not in any profession in any part of the world. No matter what anyone tells you." He jabbed a finger into my chest, and stinging pain spread across my skin—as if he really stood directly in front of me amidst a blinding light. "Your growth, training, knowledge, and ability to plan has left you arrogant—even in facing one such as Akhenaten. You shouldn't have convinced yourself that he would never be able to discover you or prepare for your attack. That left you as vulnerable as the child I trained those many years ago."

My eyes closed in repentance, but also in an attempt to block out the magician. But still he was there, inside my head, haunting me like all of my guilt and regrets.

"You've used everything I've given you," the magician said, "but now you must learn for yourself. You've been hearing my words since you were a boy, even if you did not know they were mine. Remember."

His image and the blinding light around him faded. The buildings of el-Amarna surrounded me as I rode inside the chariot on the great road with Paramessu again. My companions rode in chariots alongside us.

"We should flee this city and never return," Paramessu said, glancing over at Tia, his concern appearing as a foggy cloud in his eyes. "I don't need to face my father again. Tia is all that—"

The emaciated girl from the barracks and several of her friends, who knew not to eat the offerings at the jubilee, appeared in the shadows of the street as we raced toward them.

Paramessu reined our horses in and slowed them to a walk.

"Why are you out here?" Harkhuf asked.

"We can no longer sleep inside the barracks," she said with a shrug. "The guards no longer allow us to use it as housing with the Hittite prisoners in there."

"Do you know of anywhere we can stay in this city?" I asked. "A place where no one can find us?

The girl pursed her lips. "I can show you such a place."

Harkhuf nodded and moved aside to make room for her on his chariot.

Chapter 46

Present Day

THE STRAP OF MY MESSENGER BAG bit into my shoulder as I crept into the darkness of the desert outside Cairo. It was probably after midnight now. Cool air caressed my hot cheeks, and sand hung in the air with a musty grit. The wind picked up, shoving against my fedora in bursts while whistling in my ears.

Maddie clicked on a flashlight, its beam scouting about as her footfalls crunched through the sand. I couldn't believe I was back out here in the Egyptian desert with Maddie, searching for a lost wonder of the world.

A cloud of swirling dirt blew up in front of us, forbidding, as if it were a solid barrier. It hovered only feet away and lifted across the desert—like the wall that Heb had passed through when riding his chariot to Akhenaten's palace for the first time to finally confront the demons of his past. And the sand wall, even if magical, had only been a farce, only fear itself, as he'd ridden through it without harm.

Striding forward, I puffed out my chest and ran into the howling wind and blowing sand. I'd emerge on the other side of this wall and be stronger, without the slightest irritation or—

"Gavin," Maddie shouted.

Grit pummeled my eyes, ears, and cheeks, blowing into my mouth and nose. It felt like sandpaper rubbed the back of my throat. I coughed and gagged and pulled my shirt collar over my mouth. Dirt rattled into my ears with a gravelly scratching sound. Hunching down and closing my eyes, I scrambled on. What felt like a minute later, the wind died and the sand stopped assaulting me.

I glanced around and hacked and coughed. The gusts of wind had quieted, and the dirt in the air had settled back onto the ground. Water streamed from my eyes as I wiped at them with my sleeves. My vision was blurry, and I blinked the grit away.

"Gavin?" Maddie approached. Her outline was hazy, but she appeared undeterred. "The wind's coming in spurts. I was trying to tell you to just wait a minute."

I grunted in frustration, coughed, and marched on into the desert. So much for believing everything in the journal. And if the journal's story didn't somehow correspond with my life, it was probably not a good sign … I'd feel less sure of everything. My vision slowly cleared of dust as I watched the beam of Maddie's flashlight dart about.

"They might see us," I whispered. "Either they would've waited until all the laser light shows on the pyramids were over or had them canceled for the night."

"If I can't see where I'm going, we'll end up in the desert out in the middle of nowhere," she said.

A massive shadow loomed against the horizon, blotting out moon and starlight—the Sphinx itself, with the triangular shadows of two pyramids looming over either shoulder. It appeared as if the Sphinx's head were a black sun rising or setting between two shadowy peaks. The air grew still and cold. Goose bumps rose on my arms.

The mightiest terror of ancient Egypt.

Maddie clicked off her flashlight.

We waited in dark silence—no wind, as if someone had turned off a switch. My eyes adjusted, and the moonlight grew brighter. Distant city lights illuminated the horizon behind us. No one was in the immediate area, but there was something … Faint light darted back and forth around the shadows at the base of a structure ahead.

The hairs on the back of my neck stood on end. Maddie squeezed my arm.

Three giant pyramids shot skyward in the distance, making any other monuments, and even mountains, pale in comparison. The god-like powers emanating from these structures brought a chill to my body and a sense of awe. Such precision, elegance, and sheer power stood upon the desert night like volcanoes upon the open sea.

"Is it them?" Maddie asked as her fingernails dug into the flesh around my triceps. "The lights over by the Great Pyramid—is it more of those men?"

Memories of us having been entombed and of her abduction by those mysterious men probably raced through her mind. Those images flashed through my head. She must be terrified.

"It's probably just Mr. Scalone and company," I said and led her by the hand out across the dark desert, although my knees trembled. I dug into my messenger bag and searched for a pair of binoculars. "A strange group of locals shouldn't actually be searching for the Hall if they want to keep it a secret."

Maddie released a long breath and withdrew her fingernails from my arm as she followed me. "They must be looking for an entrance to the supposed passages beneath the Sphinx. Maybe they decided that the tunnels lead to the pyramids and hoped an entrance could be found there, or they've already searched around the Sphinx and didn't find anything."

We moved cautiously as we neared the Great Pyramid—our feet quietly crunching on sand as we approached several muffled voices.

Beams of white light from flashlights wavered around in the distance before us. These people were just visible in the moonlight but became distinct when a flashlight beam passed over or momentarily focused on them. I looked through my binoculars for a better view. Mr. Scalone, Kaylin, Aiden—holding his tiny fox—and several other men searched about the base of the towering behemoth of the Great Pyramid, the tallest structure built by man for nearly four thousand years. One of the men stepped back, pointed, and shouted orders. He had wavy gray hair and pressed pants … the Minister of Antiquities, but he wasn't wearing his typical white suit.

Wait, what was the minister doing here, and why was he with Mr. Scalone? If the minister was authorizing any type of legal search, it seemed unlikely that they would be doing it so secretively without other government officials around. Unless they just didn't want the public to know about their attempts until something was discovered?

Five or so other men who appeared to be the minister's bodyguards or workers used tools to prod around the stone base of the pyramid. One clicked on a lantern and placed it on the ground, lighting up a small area in a sphere of white.

"It's the Minister of Antiquities," I whispered as I knelt in the gritty dirt and grabbed Maddie by the wrist to pull her down next to me. My stomach spasmed again, releasing increasing pain. Nausea rose inside me.

"I recognize him," Maddie replied, her tone sharp as she looked through binoculars of her own, "as well as our friends. I'd like to have thought they would've called me and asked me to come along with them. They knew I was still in Egypt."

I didn't know what to say to comfort her. Mr. Scalone and Kaylin being here trying to locate the Hall without Maddie made their intentions for the find obvious.

"But they'll never find out how to use the two suns—or eclipse, the mace head, and the river to locate the Hall," Maddie said, her arms tensing as she lowered her binoculars. "At least not without construction machinery and serious digging through stone foundations and walls. If the Hall has been beneath the Great Pyramid for all these eons and not one archaeologist in modern history has discovered its entrance, then these guys won't be able to either."

"But someone did," I whispered. "I think Dr. Shelsher and his student saw the inside of the Hall. I believe that is the only place the story in the journal could've come from. There are no other known sources."

Some of the men prodded around the southern face of the pyramid with shovels, while others climbed up the towering blocks of the outer wall. A few trucks carrying large yellow tanks were parked nearby.

What were those tankers for? Oil, gas, or water?

Maddie rose to her feet and crept closer to the pyramid.

"We better be careful," I said. "If these people are trying to secretly excavate something, they might have a couple men out here in the desert acting as lookouts. And I think there are those who know that the Hall exists and want to keep it a secret."

My warning didn't stop her from continuing to sneak away. I inched after her.

Bits and pieces of our former colleagues' conversation echoed off of the pyramid and carried out across the desert floor and through the now quiet night. "That historical map maker … and another entrance … south face …" The words carried a thick Italian accent, Mr. Scalone's. I froze and planted my hiking boots into the dirt, watching with my binoculars.

The minister replied in well-spoken English with only a slight Egyptian accent, his flashlight shining on a stack of documents or maps in his hand. He thumbed through the papers. "Strabo the … mapmaker …" They must've been discussing the world-renowned Roman mapmaker, Strabo, who had compiled many works. But his *Geographica,* written around the beginning of the modern era, was the only one I'd heard about, as at least portions of the work pertained to ancient Egypt. His writings mentioned finding another entrance on the south face of the Great Pyramid. And for such an esteemed explorer to mistake the known north entrance as south would be almost impossible.

Kaylin's voice carried out to us this time, her flashlight darting about the massive stones of the pyramid. "And … a void … Great Pyramid … recently detected …"

"New void with … King's Chamber," the minister said.

Something else popped into my head, headlines from newspaper articles in the recent years. Researchers had also used sonar to detect a void in the upper reaches of the Great Pyramid, but there were no known passages to it. Someone would have to destroy the inner stone blocks and tunnel through them to reach the void, but that might permanently damage the pyramid or compromise its integrity.

Maddie crept closer to the pyramid in a low crouch, and I followed at her heels. She lowered herself into a small depression in the desert.

"This would … next logical place to look," the minister continued, his words still broken but easier to hear as we got closer. "Unless you want to search around the Sphinx for another week … No entrances into or below that monument."

"Already searching there several nights … and here …" Mr. Scalone said and kicked dust into the air, which hovered in the lantern's light. "Reminds me of the time I worked … former president … searching ocean where he'd thought a sunken galleon would be. Dove for a month before I was able to convince him to look … I suspected the wreckage and we found the galleon soon after."

"All right," the minister said. He dropped his stack of documents. "We can go to the north entrance … look inside, but people have been doing that for hundreds of …"

"Eventually, we'll have to dig through rock," Mr. Scalone said as he lowered his flashlight, hefted a backpack, and marched away.

"The government will never allow it," the minister replied. "No excavations … Great Pyramid or Sphinx, even after discovering chambers."

"Do some dudes know something?" Aiden asked as he pet the fox in his arms, following Mr. Scalone. "Like have powerful officials seen … then kept those places sealed up?"

My muscles tensed. Aiden's thoughts mimicked mine but were probably more conspiracy theory stuff. However, those strange men who had trapped us inside the tomb and who abducted Maddie knew more about the path and the Hall than any historian who had ever published on its possible existence.

The others in their group gathered their equipment and circled around the Great Pyramid. We followed them at a decreasing distance to the entrance at the ground level on the north face—one that in ancient times had been forcefully battered and mined through, although the true entrance sat just above it—another mystery as to why some ancient Caliph would spend so much time burrowing through stone to reach the inner chambers when an easier entrance was already available. Was he hoping to avoid traps? Surely, the sealed doors above would've been easier to break through—doors that may've rested on hinges and swung outward, if you could somehow grasp them from the outside of—

A point of light flashed to our right, and a sharp whistle rang out, echoing off of the towering face of the Pyramid.

One bodyguard who was entering the lower passageway screamed and fell over.

What just happened? I froze.

The minister shouted.

Mr. Scalone kept his head low, dropped his flashlight, and darted off. Kaylin screamed but quickly followed him.

Aiden dropped to the ground, huddling over his fox.

More flashes of light popped up in the darkness, followed by whistling.

Two more of the workers toppled over—a flashlight slipping from one's hand and falling to the desert.

Someone was shooting them … with silencers? I ducked, dropped down on all fours, pulled Maddie down against my side, and covered our heads. Maddie stifled a cry of surprise with an open hand. My mouth went dry as my heart raced.

The minister clicked off his flashlight, covered his head, and ran from the light of the lantern—followed by one of his larger bodyguards.

The remaining workers or bodyguards drew handguns but only one fired into the darkness before more muted gunshots sounded, whistling across the desert like eerie bursts of wind. Unseen men in the darkness yelled, as if others had also been hit, but all of the workers with guns collapsed.

Shouting filled the night in front of us. Within another minute, Mr. Scalone, Kaylin, the minister, and his bodyguard all appeared in the lantern light near the entrance to the Great Pyramid. They all walked backward with their hands raised until they squished against Aiden—just outside the entrance.

Three men holding assault rifles with silencers and wearing *thawbs* with long draping hoods appeared at the rim of light, pressing in on the trapped group. Two of these new assailants stood straight and advanced. The other limped and held a hand over the tan cloth around his abdomen, which was soaked in blood. All of their *thawbs* had a large image of a red ankh upon their chests.

The three armed assailants yelled in Arabic, shaking their weapons and pointing at the group.

I struggled for breath, fear racking my body.

Maddie pressed into me as we remained crouched on the desert floor. "What do we do?"

I forced a deep breath. "I don't want to see them shoot our old friends, but what can we do? If they see us, they'll kill us as well. Maybe we should just report whatever happens to the authorities."

Maddie's body trembled against mine.

The minister replied to the assailants in Arabic and held out his hand and a bag.

One assailant lunged forward and snatched the bag from the minister. He rifled through it and tossed items out into the desert: a book, a journal, a water bottle, a phone, and an object that reflected light. Metal—bronze ... It landed in the sand behind the group.

My bracelet? My chest tightened—Dad's final gift to me ... Either Mr. Scalone or the minister had to have stolen it.

The assailant stopped flinging objects aside and slowly withdrew his hand from the minister's bag. He held a spherical stone of brown and white—the Scorpion Macehead. They'd taken that as well.

The assailant threw the mace head and the bag at the minister's stomach and yelled again. The minister doubled over as the stone buried into his midsection.

Kaylin screamed and hugged her brother, her body shuddering with consuming sobs. Aiden pulled his flat-billed cap down and hugged her back, as well as his fox, whose small eyes darted about. The animal's tongue lolled out in a fearful pant.

Mr. Scalone shuffled behind them all, probably hoping that he could bolt into the pyramid and hide.

"Where are our guards on lookout?" Kaylin said, glancing out into the desert with wide eyes clinging to hope, her words carrying out to our closer position.

"They dead," the assailant replied with a thick accent.

Kaylin's head drooped.

The wounded assailant dropped over into the dirt with a thud, his body lying still. His two accomplices glanced over and prodded him with the muzzles of their guns. No response.

The vocal assailant turned and jabbed his gun barrel at the minister, shouting to the group again in Arabic.

The minister threw his hands up, holding the mace head, as his face turned white. "They don't understand you."

"Open secret chambers!" the assailant said.

"We can't figure out how to open them," the minister replied. "We would if we could."

The assailant pivoted and shot the minister's bodyguard in the chest—the man still rigid with a tall posture as he toppled over backward onto the ground.

Maddie lurched beneath me and Kaylin screamed again.

"Not answer," the assailant said. "Open."

I lowered my chin, placing my cheek against the side of Maddie's head, and whispered, "Maybe these extremists, whatever group these men and those who abducted you belong to, haven't discovered the Hall and aren't already selling artifacts on the black market if—"

"No one's been able to open it since it was sealed!" the minister bellowed. "Unless perhaps Dr. Shelsher did and some kind of colleague of yours, from a century ago, killed him."

"Yes," the assailant said, "tales say he go missing. Curse of mummy." The flash of white teeth from a smile appeared beneath the man's long hood, and he twisted to point his gun at Aiden and the others in turn.

I whispered, "I should help Aiden."

Maddie's voice was an airy whisper. "You'll get shot."

I sucked in a long, deep breath and stood on shaky limbs. "I'll just have to find the entrance."

Maddie's fingers wrapped around my ankle just above my hiking boot, fear giving her grip incredible strength. "Gavin. You don't even know what those final clues mean."

I reached out and slid her messenger bag off of her shoulder. "I'll use your laptop's light simulator program to buy time and hopefully figure something out."

But she wouldn't let me go. "You can still go home, Gavin. I won't judge you." Her grip relaxed.

Should I give this up for good ... again? I tried to ignore the painful cramping arising in my guts. "I'll take your laptop to the pyramid, but you're going back."

The muzzle of the assailant's gun settled on Aiden, and Aiden shouted—high-pitched in terror—as he held up his one hand without the fox and scooted back.

I tried to run. But my feet seemed trapped in the desert sand, and I couldn't force my trembling legs to step toward the Great Pyramid. I leaned forward and groaned, slumping back down into the dirt as my eyes closed in defeat.

Chapter 47

Present Day

MADDIE LAY ON HER STOMACH in the desert under the faint moonlight, looking back and forth from me to the Great Pyramid. An assailant shoved the barrel of his gun against Aiden's neck and forced him down into the dirt.

Aiden screamed, then said, "Don't shoot. I'll do whatever you want."

"We'll find the treasure," Kaylin said, holding up her hands.

Something crunched behind us, and metal clicked.

I whirled around.

A man in *thawb* stood there, eyeing us with what looked like binoculars protruding from beneath his draping hood—night vision goggles? A red ankh image lay upon his chest. He raised a large gun and aimed it at Maddie. "Go to pyramid," he said.

I stood and stepped in front of her, holding my hands to the sky.

The assailant removed his night vision goggles, grunted, and ushered Maddie and me to the Great Pyramid with the muzzle of his assault rifle.

Aiden, Mr. Scalone, Kaylin, and the Minister of Antiquities were huddled against the entrance to the pyramid, the other two assault-rifle-wielding assailants watching over them.

The vocal assailant shouted in Arabic as we approached, our forced steps scuffing through dirt. The man turned his open hood to face us, said something else, and jabbed the muzzle of his gun at me. "You no understand?"

I shook my head.

"Then you die too," the assailant replied. "Unless you open secret."

My heart thundered inside my chest, beating on my ribs like fists on prison bars. "W-we can do it with the help of the woman behind me and her computer."

"Woman no help to man," the assailant replied.

My voice cracked with fear. "Sh-she's figured out more than anyone so far, and she's our best bet to find any secrets here."

The assailant lunged at me and buried the muzzle of his rifle into my stomach, the metal still warm from having been fired. The heat seeped through my shirt.

I lurched and jerked away from the muzzle. The assailant grabbed my shoulder and shoved me onto the ground against the others.

Maddie joined us and sank down onto the stone before the entrance to the Great Pyramid. "I can find this treasure for all of you."

Maddie's trembling hands dived into her messenger bag before yanking out her laptop and flinging it open. The minister, Aiden, and Kaylin—with tears streaming down her cheeks—all scooted closer to Maddie. Mr. Scalone stayed farther back near the pyramid's entrance.

Maddie quickly rehashed everything that we'd discovered—my bracelet, the mace head, and the clues, but the others remained silent.

Kaylin wailed and hugged Maddie from behind in their sitting positions. "I'm so sorry, Maddie. We just, like, thought you wouldn't be interested in continuing, not with all the danger involved and after what happened to you."

Aiden patted my back. "But you came to help us, like real bros? I just followed Kaylin for the excitement. I didn't know anything about none of this stuff and thought you'd left Egypt for good. Did you bring any of my weed?"

I gripped his knee—he was sitting cross-legged—and squeezed it in reassurance. "If we can find the Hall, these men will probably take any hidden treasure, but they just might let us all go. If we can't locate it, it seems like they'll kill us."

Aiden nodded slowly, as if he didn't believe what I'd said or was disappointed that I hadn't answered his last question.

I turned back to Maddie's screen.

"No need computer for this," the assailant said. "Get inside and open passageway hidden from current peoples." He shoved the gun against the back of the laptop screen, closing it, and then stuck the muzzle onto my cheek.

I nearly fell over backward as I winced in pain, the pressure rising as my cheek dug into my teeth and salty blood ran into my mouth. My stomach cramped more vigorously, and I groaned.

"Go!" the assailant screamed and jerked away before pulling the trigger. The muted gunshot exploded right beside my ear, the bullet whizzing beside my head and into the ground.

My ears rang and my head spun as I fell over, but then I scrambled to all fours. Flinging dirt as I moved, I pushed Maddie in front of me and crawled past the opened, modern-day, steel-bar door to the pyramid. The others had already retreated inside.

Darkness waited, broken only by the wandering beams of flashlights.

"Where do we go?" Kaylin shouted from the front.

Maddie glanced at me as I climbed to my feet and looked back at the assailant whose gun was pointed at my face. I turned back to the others. "Follow the passage and then the upward sloping tunnel."

Kaylin led us on down cramped passages that had been bored into the stone blocks centuries ago. The nearly six million tons of stone on top of us seemed to press in around me and created a claustrophobic sensation—my breaths coming in quick gulps as I imagined slabs tumbling down and pinning my arms or legs or crushing us.

The thickness of the air hovered about me, heavy and cool. I'd seen so many pictures of this place, but I'd never thought that I'd break into the Great Pyramid at night. And now this mysterious group of assailants seemed to actually want us to open the Hall when before they'd used violence and abduction to prevent us from ever reaching this point. Had we crossed a point of no return … if the pyramid was the end of the path to the Hall and we'd discovered this, could they then not let us go on living? Did these men actually know that we wouldn't need a computer program manipulating light and shadow to reveal the clues inside, and were they trying to speed up whatever process they were now forcing us to accomplish?

"Go," the assailant shouted from behind. The sandals of the other two assailants also slapped the stone walk as all three followed us inside.

I followed our single-file line, directly behind Maddie. A branch in the tunnels appeared as Kaylin's flashlight beam darted back and forth between them and their consuming darkness. One led down into the earth below the base of the pyramid. The other led up—which Kaylin followed, her heeled shoes pounding on stone and echoing around us.

We ascended a metal stairway with handrails—fashioned into the pyramid in modern times. Then a soaring passage opened up, the walls stepping inward as they rose to the ceiling of the chamber, creating the same actual image as the hieroglyph for ascension. This chamber, the Grand Gallery, was probably only used in ancient times to store blocks that would seal the pyramid from would-be tomb robbers.

A horizontal passage led away from the Grand Gallery to the Queen's Chamber.

"Continue up," Maddie said, glancing back at me again, uncertainty showing in her tense expression.

No one said a word as they examined our surroundings, searching for lost secrets that the greatest explorers of recent times would've missed.

The ascending tunnel we followed eventually leveled off and led us through a straight hallway before ending in a blind chamber.

Aiden, Kaylin, Mr. Scalone, and the minister entered and stopped against the far wall, pressing tightly together. The red granite surrounding us appeared like blood-covered walls.

The assailants paused and waited just outside the room, their guns resting in their arms.

Aiden took off his cap and brushed his dreadlocks straight back above the buzzed sides of his head. "Now what, bro?" His face held a red tinge in the pale light of our flashlight beams as he glanced about, cradling his tiny fox in his arm. "Looks like a dead end, and they have us trapped in here."

I motioned to an open and empty sarcophagus against the wall. "This is what they call the King's Chamber. That granite box is really the only thing that anyone's found inside this pyramid."

Kaylin shined her flashlight around. "No treasure was ever in here?"

"Not in recent history," Maddie said. "It was probably all taken in antiquity. They never even found mummies or other bodies in here. No one or nothing."

"So what are we looking for then?" Aiden asked, glancing between Maddie and me.

Mr. Scalone shined his light onto the walls and ran his other hand along their smooth surface. Pulling out a large knife, he prodded the junctions between the stones. He'd never get a blade between them—a half a millimeter gap at most, superior to what any modern mason could do. And over two million of those blocks had been fitted with unmatched precision.

My mind raced as I paced around the room and spewed anything that I could recall about the Great Pyramid, hoping to trigger some realization with our recently discovered clues. "The pyramid shape was seen as the *benben* stone, the primordial origin of the earth that arose from the chaos and water all around us. It was where the phoenix—the supposed sun itself—first landed, cried out, and initiated the beginning of time. Others have believed that the pyramids were a staircase to the sky or symbolized rays of sun raining down upon the earth—facets of shadow and light as the day wore on, or even a type of sundial. Other believe the pyramid symbolized death and rebirth—the most important aspect of all of ancient Egyptian culture. There are four perfect sides but eight facets, two on each face, which can only be distinguished from above if perfectly timed at dawn or dusk on the spring and autumn equinox—first noted by a pilot in the early nineteen hundreds. Concave lines precisely dissect the four sides to make these facets, which are also in an exact proportion to the base and related to pi—the mathematical number of the relationship of the diameter of a circle to its circumference. And pi was not supposed to have been understood for another couple of thousand years."

I paced the room, feeling along the cool stone of the walls and studying the empty granite of the sarcophagus. What or who would've rested in there?

"This pyramid is more precisely aligned with true north than any other structure built before or after," I said, "including the Greenwich Observatory in London. And this pyramid is also at the exact geographical center of the earth. To have built this gargantuan structure, about twelve blocks—weighing many tons each—would have to have been placed every hour of the day and night for twenty years."

Aiden's head fell back as he took in the spectacle around him before pointing at two shafts in the ceiling. "What're those holes for?"

Mr. Scalone looked up and grunted as droplets of sweat rolled down his brow. "Air vents."

"That's what they used to think," Maddie said, "but they are correctly aligned with certain imperishable stars, including Sirius, the brightest star in the sky. Stars were what the early pharaohs wanted to link themselves to, something eternal. That was another way for Pharaoh to reach immortality … and the heavens."

"So does *this* pyramid have a capstone?" Aiden asked. "Like when we used this"—he held up the pyramid prism souvenir that dangled from the collar of his fox—"to find the hieroglyph at those colossi statues?"

Maddie's flashlight beam settled on the dangling pyramid. "It had one in antiquity," she said, "one created of the finest gold, celebrating the rays of the sun like a beacon. But it's been missing for millennia, along with the outer limestone casing."

No one else spoke for a couple of minutes.

We wandered around the chamber for what felt like an hour. The only thing that emerged was Mr. Scalone's ripe body odor, like milk turning sour.

"You find Hall tonight if you want to go," an assailant standing outside the entrance to the King's Chamber said.

"Let's search another area," the minister said. Sweat trickled down his cheeks, although the temperature inside the Great Pyramid always remained steady—near the room temperature of sixty-eight degrees, no matter how hot it was outside.

I slumped down against the side of the sarcophagus and let my forehead fall into my palm. My stomach writhed about in an emerging flare of Crohn's disease, releasing painful spasms.

What were the chances that we'd ever be able to—

"That newly discovered void inside this pyramid, is it even with this chamber?" Kaylin asked as she tapped on the walls with a small shovel.

"Yes," Maddie said. "But they've already searched for connecting passages, and most local Egyptian Egyptologists dismissed the find as absolutely nothing." Maddie turned to me. "What are you doing?"

I shook my head. "I don't know."

Maddie placed her fists on her hip. "You're not giving up, not now."

I leaned my head back. "No. Maybe I just need to stop trying so hard …
and think about it another way."

She raised an eyebrow as she bent over and felt along the inside of the
sarcophagus. "Daydreaming, like you tend to do?"

Maybe … something popped into my head, a dream? Like the Dream
Stela between the front paws of the Sphinx—the proclamation of a man
who'd supposedly fallen asleep when the sun was at its zenith. His god had
spoken to him at that moment and enlightened him. "Like the Dream Stela."

Maddie scoffed. "That's the prophecy of a conman to help him claim
the throne, solidify his position as pharaoh—like modern day cult leaders."

I shrugged, leaned back against the hard granite sarcophagus, and
imagined myself digging through desert sand at the base of the protruding head of the Sphinx as it would've appeared centuries ago, before it was
fully unearthed.

Chapter 48

Journal Translation

A FEW NIGHTS LATER, I still sat with my head down inside a crumbling house in the slums of el-Amarna. The people of this neighborhood had been decimated by the plague, and no one else in the city would venture here as this new plague struck anyone, no matter their personal beliefs or social ranking.

But in the surrounding city, there would be eyes everywhere—eyes searching for us.

I had no idea what to do or where to go from here. My head hung as I sat on the hard ground in a dark corner of the hovel, like I used to do during my slavery. My stomach gurgled and spasmed at random, creating burning acid and cramping pain. The blackness in my heart had spread and consumed all of me.

"We can still leave this place forever and find a good life," Tia said as her tender hand ran across the sticky skin of my back. "We still all have each other. I think it is folly to expect that every one of us could overcome our past demons, especially when yours were so immense."

Pain twisted inside me. Everything I'd lived all the horrid years of my life for, I was now supposed to just forget and give it all up? How had it come to this? I'd done everything I could: trained and educated myself for decades, gathered strength and companions, toiled for years serving Akhenaten as a servant and then again as a military man working my way up through the ranks of the elite of Egypt, achieved great wealth, discovered some magic within me, and formulated plans that the magician might even have been proud of … But it had all collapsed in the blink of an eye.

I climbed to my feet without facing any of my companions and strode out into the chill night. The cloud-veiled moonlight barely lit the leaning mud-brick houses and streets around me, most everything appearing only as jagged black silhouettes clawing against the pale sky. It seemed as if I walked through the *Duat* once again, searching for a path to the Hall of Judgment.

I strolled with my head down as two staggering men wandered by on the other side of the street. One yelled, "You have any wine?" and then he coughed violently, his body jerking as he placed a hand over his mouth. A scream rang out in the distance, followed by the shouts of men and the clatter of a fight.

I hurried away to my destination and eventually arrived at the entrance of a dark building. I struck flint to light a lamp. A soft flame flickered and hissed as I stepped inside. Firelight wavered across blankets that were placed in rows upon the ground, and each blanket covered something— something that was heaped beneath them. The air smelled stale, as if no one had breathed it in weeks.

Children, still in here? But the emaciated girl had told us otherwise. And I'd heard that the Hittite prisoners had been taken to these barracks after they'd arrived.

Holding my breath, I reached my foot out and touched a motionless blanket with the tip of my sandal.

It didn't move. I tapped at it. Still nothing. I kicked at the stiff blanket and jumped back.

Something underneath flopped over, and the blanket slipped aside—a face as white and as gaunt as a mummy stared back at me. Its mouth hung open as if it had died in excruciating pain, moaning. And its arms were wrapped around its chest, attempting to comfort itself even in death.

I stifled a gasp as my heart raced and my blood thickened.

I should not have come here. The bronze tip of the sword in my other hand caught the firelight, and my feet scuffed as I backed away to the entrance.

I glanced around the shadowy chamber. So many heaped blankets ... But the grotesque corpse regained my attention—nearly identical to the one that the doctor had brought to the palace to show the councilmen and Pharaoh. Was the plague real this time? It didn't appear anything like Thutmose or Father's bodies had, with Akhenaten's false plague that left black and yellow spots all over their bodies. And the man at my feet was different, foreign. Judging by his thin moustache and clothing, he was Hittite—one we'd apprehended and taken prisoner in the field of battle. Had the prisoner carried a disease—one that we'd unintentionally brought back to el-Amarna?

I turned and raced out, extinguishing the lamp and careening down dark alleyways. After several minutes, I fell against the side of a building, heaving for breath as I slunk down into dirt.

Was there anything I could do to Pharaoh now, or should I just leave Egypt forever? And Akhenaten had been so calm during our last encounter. It was if he was prepared for everything, even with all the stealth and cunning I'd used …

Did he know about my grand plan and the massacre of his tainted men? He was a god-king, but he could not read minds, or I'd have known that in my younger years. Then had someone told him? But who? Only my companions and I knew about—

Rage ignited inside me like the flames of a bonfire in the feast hall as images of my companions popped into my mind, each surrounded by darkness. It seemed likely that one of them betrayed me. Chisisi's face appeared first—the discarded companion who'd betrayed us before. And I'd never even told the others about the plotting he'd been involved in when we had been trying to capture that monster of a crocodile at Crocodilopolis. My stomach cramped in guilty pain. If I told them now, they'd lose all their trust in me as well—and I needed them. Taking pity on others was one of my weaknesses. I'd believed Chisisi when he'd said he'd wanted nothing other than to join us again and that he would be happy in his own place—not as a leader. That was not Chisisi. Perhaps that was why Akhenaten was so formidable and why I would never be able to overthrow him. Pharaoh was ruthless. If someone showed weakness or questioned him, they were disposed of or killed. Such characteristics probably made for a much more powerful and terrifying leader. I would never be able to defeat him, much less lead a kingdom.

Could the traitor be anyone else? Not Paramessu or Tia, although they did want me to forget the past and avoid danger—to settle down ... Paramessu would have multiple reasons to betray me. It may have seemed as if I'd almost let Akhenaten take Tia into his bed at the first jubilee we'd attended; I'd pretended to be Tia's husband, which kept them apart for so long; then he'd tried to guide me into finding love and I'd briefly attacked him; he had once been part of the military and he often questioned my orders and rash decisions; and, above all, I'd shared my plans of an all-out attack against Akhenaten, one that he probably believed would completely fail. Perhaps he'd lost all faith in me and decided that his best course of action for himself and to protect Tia was to turn against me and to side with Pharaoh. But Tia was the main one who was always trying to get me to give this all up, to get us to leave. And there was Wahankh, the bully who'd once feared anyone with power but seemed to have overcome his weakness during our previous journeys. Still, he could have lost all faith in me and turned to whom he saw as the stronger leader. Harkhuf and Seneb had already conquered their demons, but lately both of them seemed to always question my commands.

Images swirled in my mind like *ba*—those that had pursued me in the underworld and had torn at my avian body, making me suffer for flying the world at night. The betrayal could have even gone back to before the time of the expeditions north, explaining Akhenaten's sudden change of wanting me to join the council but then sending me off to war. Or was that just typical capricious behavior from him?

I screamed into the darkness, shaking my fists.

A few minutes later, I took a deep breath. No, I was becoming too paranoid, exactly what I was trying to do to Akhenaten without affecting myself. The dwarf brothers would not betray me, and Tia probably wouldn't; I'd helped save all of them, and they were not only grateful but great friends. But either one or more of the other three—Chisisi, Wahankh, or Paramessu—were probably a traitor. And of those, Chisisi seemed to be the far most likely.

I stood and marched straight through the night for the cursed neighborhood in the slums.

As I approached the leaning house that my companions and I had recently resided in, a flame sprang to life as someone stepped out into the quiet street.

I froze. Anyone in the area would be able to see this and then see the face of the person who was holding the torch. Was it the traitor, sending a signal for Akhenaten's soldiers? I drew my swords and crept closer.

Another man wobbled along on the far side of the street, across from the person holding the torch. This man intermittently muttered to himself, as if he were having a conversation with someone who wasn't there.

Was this a drunk from the slums, or was it the act of one of Akhenaten's agents?

The wobbling man shouted and pointed at the light.

Paramessu's voice replied in the shadows behind the torch, answering some question from the man.

The man tripped and fell before scurrying off.

I snuck closer. "Why are you out here, Paramessu, my friend? With a beacon for our enemy?"

The light in Paramessu's hand jolted as he pulled it closer to his head and face, still completely shaven. "I—I thought you may need help."

I lunged forward, the blade of my sword slicing through the air and halting only after it contacted the muscle over his left chest.

Paramessu gasped and stepped back, dropping the torch. The firelight flickered as it hit the ground in a sputter and created moments of darkness and dim, orange light.

"You gave us up to Pharaoh," I said with clenched teeth. "Now you wish to bring his men here."

His eyes were wide in the wavering light. "I—I have not."

"Take up your spear and strike me." I drew a thin line of blood across his chest.

He impaled his skin a little more as he stepped closer to me. "No."

"You have already betrayed all of us," I replied. "Strike at me so I can kill you."

He grabbed my sword hand and forced its blade deeper into his flesh as he stared into my eyes. "I will not fight you."

Seething anger tore through my insides, my black blood feeling as if it were boiling. I tore my hand from his and pulled away. "Do not come after me, you or anyone." I shoved him away. "From now on, I will be acting alone."

I darted into the hovel, grabbed the magical sack that the magician had given me long ago, and strode off into the night.

Chapter 49

Journal Translation

PACING ALONG THE STREETS of el-Amarna, I kept to the shadows and the unlit alleyways, unaware of where I was or where I was going. Anger seethed through my body like blood as my finger squeezed the handle of my sword. I should just rush into the feast hall of the palace by myself and make a desperate last attack, lunging straight for Akhenaten's heart. That would be the only way to end my misery, one way or the other.

I took a deep breath and closed my eyes. Attempting such an attack by myself would only guarantee my death and the loss of my soul. I'd need to make some kind of new plan to attempt to obtain soldiers, horses, and weapons.

Footsteps scuffed the dirt behind me, maybe a building or two away.

I stopped. So did the feet.

Gripping my sword hilts, I walked slowly for the edge of the next building and took a casual left turn. But I plastered myself against the mud-brick wall and quietly drew my swords, waiting.

A cloaked figure emerged in the darkness.

I grabbed and spun the person around, catching them around the neck—my blade's edge just touching the vulnerable skin of their throat.

A woman screamed in surprise.

Shoving her away, I asked, "Mutnedjmet?"

She nodded, turned to face me, and dropped her hood.

I tucked my swords away as I glanced around—although I would never be able to see someone in the night around us. Her presence brought warmth to my heart, but the hairs on the back of my neck stood on end, as if someone else were watching. "What are you doing out here?"

"Looking for you," she whispered. "I am alone."

I lunged forward and kissed her. She melted against me, turning limp like when I'd accidentally poisoned her. An almond aroma floated from her skin.

Her forehead fell onto my chest. "I thought I'd lost you."

I squeezed her tighter. "How *did* you find me?" What if Akhenaten had her followed, or could she be helping him locate me? No. I clenched my jaw until pain rose up my cheeks. I would trust Mutnedjmet this time—until she led me to my death.

"I had someone watching the barracks." Her warm breath spread across my skin. "And I was in the city searching for you. I knew that if you were still here, you'd only venture out at night. Then I found you by your scream, not the wisest thing to do, and followed you."

I exhaled as my eyes darted around. Then she'd have seen my confrontation with Paramessu, but did she know what it was about? "If you can find me, then so can he."

"Akhenaten has predicted that you will seek him out again before long," she replied. "And so he waits with most of the military and police of el-Amarna—who now reside within the palace. He believes that you won't be able to overcome your hate, and that will lead you to your death."

My lips tightened as I held in a deep breath. "I will not be able to defeat him, then. I have failed to put together any kind of formidable army."

"There are those who remain loyal to their commander." She pushed away from me to look me in the eye under faint moonlight. "Soldiers even inside the palace. But by my best estimate, you are outnumbered five to one, more likely ten to one."

I glanced north. Could I find and utilize these soldiers?

"Do not expect them to come find you," she said. "Akhenaten has forbidden it. They'd be forfeiting their lives and souls."

"What can I ever hope to do, then?" I asked. "Sneak into a palace that is guarded by tens of thousands of soldiers? Even if I raised an army that could kill them all, I would not want that. Egypt needs its military to defend it from outside invaders until peace is restored, which won't happen with our current leadership. Right now, we need cleansing from the inside out." I swallowed. "How could I ever even hope to accomplish this?"

Mutnedjmet's chin fell into her hand as she paced around in the shadows in front of me. "Someone you are close to must've informed Akhenaten of your previous plan." She glanced behind herself.

"I have come to the same conclusion," I said.

"Otherwise Pharaoh wouldn't have had the Devouring Monster waiting at his back," she said. "I heard everything that occurred, although I couldn't move, having fallen victim to your tainted wine. I wish you would've told me, but now I'm happy that you didn't. Otherwise you'd probably think I betrayed you." She folded her arms and looked up at me. "I can run away right now with you. We can forget all of this and live our own simple lives far away from here. We'll never have to think about Akhenaten, Nefertiti, or Egypt *ever* again."

I took a deep breath and stared into her moonlit eyes, the blue paint around them appearing as a mask, almost deceitful. "You might not believe me if I say I would like that, but I'd never be able to forget. They would haunt my soul throughout this life and into the next. My insides are more horrid than the outsides of the plague victims. I've been trying to control my emotions for years, but only revenge can satiate whatever festering disease I harbor."

Rage rose anew inside me, my heart pumping and spreading fetid disease throughout my body. Everyone was against me, even my true friends. All of them kept trying to tempt me into giving up. I'd have to attempt to sneak into the palace and slay my former master, or die trying.

I spun away from her.

A meow sounded, and I leapt to the side in surprise. An orange and white cat trotted up to me, holding up one of its hind legs. His entire gait was stiff, and clumps of his hair were missing. Croc!

My heart melted with sympathy, and my rage vanished. I scooped him up and kissed his cheek, his soft fur tickling my lips but also bringing the taste and grit of dust. He meowed and pushed away from my face. "You made it out of the palace." I did still have one friend.

"He must've followed me," Mutnedjmet said.

Croc struggled, and his scarred rear foot with the missing toes dug into my forearm. Yellow goo oozed from a hole in the center of the scar.

A memory popped into my head—the magician's cat, limp in my arms as I carried her from the feast hall. She'd been paralyzed, unable to fight me off...

I hefted the magician's sack but paused and scouted around, although the darkness didn't allow me to see far. Nothing. Petting Croc along his knobby back, I strode off down the street before finding another abandoned house in the slums. Mutnedjmet followed me as I ducked inside and lit a lamp to reveal a single room with an old table. The collapsing outer walls of the structure and compressed window both let in moonlight.

My hands rummaged around in my sack of supplies. My fingers wrapped around a sealed jug—the poison that I'd taken from the deranged Nubian family who'd worshipped the Dark Ones. They'd dipped their darts in this poison and had used it to paralyze their victims, just as I had used it to paralyze the councilmen of el-Amarna.

I yanked the stopper out of the bottle, which popped as it released its hold. Then, taking a knife, I dipped it into the poison and watched dark liquid drip off of the shiny bronze blade, plopping back into the bottle. When only one drop remained, I squeezed Croc into the crook of my elbow and slipped the tip of the knife between his clamped teeth, wiping the liquid onto his tongue. "I am sorry."

Croc hissed and rolled around in my grip like a fish flopping around on the bank of the Nile. He swatted my arm, leapt away, and scrambled up to the open windowsill as he repeatedly licked the roof of his mouth in disgust. But there he sat, staring at me as if plotting his revenge. A minute passed, and his front feet, which braced himself in his sitting position, bent. He wobbled and meowed. His back feet shoved off of the sill in an attempt to leap away, but his uncoordinated, flailing body only plummeted over the edge. I reached out but missed him, and he crashed onto the floor with a hollow thud, landing on his side and going limp. I gasped but lunged over and scooped him up, his body having as much tone as a passed-out drunk.

Turning, I swept my arm across the wobbly table, knocking broken jugs onto the floor with a clatter. I set Croc down on the thin wood, wiped the knife blade clean with a cloth, and stuck the tip of the blade into the draining hole on his back leg.

"What are you doing?" Mutnedjmet asked, stepping up to the table. The whites of her eyes bulged against her blue mask. "Is this because he didn't help you that last time with the monster?"

I could almost hear Seneb in my mind, saying, "Like a pharaoh turning on an unwilling servant." Seneb …

I shook my head. No, I had to do this myself.

Prying at the draining hole in his leg with the tip of the knife, I tried to cut into the scar tissue, but it was tight and binding. I shoved harder, and the twisting, blackened scar tissue released, ripping open with the sound of tearing skin. Blood streamed out and ran down over Croc's mangled foot.

I winced. Poor Croc. But my best friend lay still. I felt along the area and found the swelling that I'd noticed when I'd first seen the wound. I extended the knife tip upward, and more scar tissue tugged and broke free. Hopefully he couldn't feel the pain, but he needed this—he just didn't understand why.

The knife tip contacted something hard, just beneath the skin above the draining wound.

Cutting over the area, I teased apart the thick, hairless skin and dug my fingers in through seeping blood, grabbing for whatever it was—something firm like a rock. But it was stuck, adhered to his tendons or bones.

Holding the knife close to the tip, I used it as a scalpel and cut deeper into the surrounding tissues. Dark blood oozed out and rolled onto the table.

"I will make this up to you, Croc." Guilt rose inside my heart. This had better help him.

I pried at the lump with the tip of the knife, my teeth gritting as I strained, the pressure in my head rising. Something popped, and an object flew out, tumbling across the table.

Mutnedjmet shouted in surprise and jumped back.

I used clean water from a water skin to wash out Croc's open wound, sewed the edges of his skin back together with thin sinew, and wrapped it all in honey—as I'd read in the magician's books about medicine and the treatments for human wounds.

After kissing Croc on the head, I turned to Mutnedjmet, who'd somewhat cleaned and was now studying the bloody object that I'd removed from Croc's leg—it was curving and sharp like a blade but made of some natural substance. The tip of a claw? But it was much too large to be Croc's.

She held the object to the lamplight. "I think the Devouring Monster lost one of its claws in your friend."

Probably when Croc took his lion fingers and he took Croc's toes, when we'd sailed the Nile and Paramessu had almost lost his life to the monster.

She handed the object over, and it stuck to my skin as I tried to roll it around between my fingers.

I fell back onto the floor with a thump and exhaled long and loud.

Croc's chest rose and fell. I'd stay at my brother's side through the night—by then he should regain control of his body.

"You are healed, my brother," I whispered as I ran a hand along the deep stripes of his coat. "Soon, I will be as well, or I will be dead."

Chapter 50

Journal Translation

MY EYES SNAPPED BACK OPEN after having closed for moment. I'd thought I'd heard something.

I lay on the floor in this abandoned hovel, and Croc lay on the table, his chest still rising and falling with respirations. Mutnedjmet was now curled up beside me, her warm skin pressing against mine as her eyelids hung. The flame of the lamp on the table burned low.

Something rattled in the street. Then silence.

I held my breath as I slowly slid away from Mutnedjmet, turning—

Pounding feet thudded behind me, and armed men raced inside the hovel. The sharp edge of cold metal sliced into my back, making me jump in surprise and pain. Something else punctured my shoulder.

"Bring him to Pharaoh alive," a male voice shouted.

Mutnedjmet screamed.

I snatched my swords and twisted around to face whomever this was as warm blood drained down my back.

Soldiers filled the room, encircling me with spears. One of them dragged Mutnedjmet across the floor by her ankles. Another kicked over the table that Croc was on, not even noticing him, or not caring.

"Pharaoh would also be interested to know that Lady Mutnedjmet was here," a soldier with almost no chin said, eyeing her.

My heart raced. I'd be captured and my soul consumed, and with this act of defying Akhenaten, Mutnedjmet would meet the same fate.

Shouting, I leapt to my feet and swung my swords, knocking aside spears as I slashed at lethal targets. I cut into one man's bicep and into another's neck, but at least three spears pierced the flesh of my thighs.

I screamed in pain but cut down two more soldiers before spears buried into my arms and shoulders, releasing more blood. I collapsed, and the soldiers withdrew their impaled weapons with a sickening tearing of flesh before hoisting me up by my arms and legs. My vision blurred like a dream, and my head felt light. This would be the beginning of my end.

The soldiers carried Mutnedjmet and me out into the dark street into the midst of at least twenty men. Several of them held lamps aloft as they started up the street, although my vision flickered with curtains of rising and falling blackness.

A sharp whistling pierced the still night and ended in a thud. The soldier with almost no chin fell, the shaft of an arrow protruding from his temple. Arrows then rained upon the other soldiers as if ten archers were attacking, dropping men all around me. The soldiers shouted and ducked behind their rawhide shields, dropping Mutnedjmet and me onto the hard ground.

Metal smacked into rawhide, and another soldier shouted before a spear tip sank into his chest. He dropped, and Paramessu's face appeared at the other end of the spear, glancing down at me as I struggled to sit, pain wracking my body as I covered my exposed head with one arm.

Paramessu sidestepped a soldier's jabbing spear, grabbed the shaft after the tip whizzed by, and wrenched on it, using it as leverage to pry the soldier's shield away from his body, which created an opening. Tia lunged in and impaled the man.

The whistling of more arrows turned into screams and thuds as more soldiers fell. Soon the whistling stopped, leaving only the sound of Mutnedjmet's and my heaving breathing.

I stood up, but my head felt as heavy as gold, jerking me back and toppling me over.

Strong hands gripped me under my arms and pulled me to my feet. My head dangled as if I could not control it, blackness creeping around the margins of my vision. But the faces of Paramessu, Tia, Seneb, and Harkhuf hovered around me. Biting remorse for my distrust of them followed, my diseased heart barely able to pump against the sludging of my blood.

"I am so sorry, my friend," I said as my bobbing head barely turned to Paramessu. How had I ever thought that he had betrayed me?

Paramessu's hand clapped down onto my shoulder. "For you, Tia, and Egypt, I am with you until the end, whatever that may be."

＊　＊　＊

Light from the morning Aten crept through the high window of another collapsing building, one I did not recognize. Pain wracked my body, and I grimaced as I forced myself to a sitting position. Bandages covered my arms and legs, pulling at tender skin. Mutnedjmet lay on a blanket beside me, her eyes closed in sleep. The others were not here.

Croc sat upon a table beside me, and his ears twitched—then his tail. I watched him for several minutes. His head eventually rose as he looked up at me and crawled on all fours like a drunken baby. He reached the edge of the table and tried to leap off but fell straight down.

But this time, I caught him and cradled him in my arms, stroking the wiry fur of the deep stripes running along his back and sides.

Mutnedjmet sat up and looked me over. "You must rest."

"I can't," I said, glancing to the open doorway. "I must tell my friends not to share any more information, even our whereabouts, with Chisisi or Wahankh. We cannot know which one is the traitor for sure, even though I believe it to be Chisisi. And so we must keep a close eye on both of them and not turn our backs."

"I've already spoken with the four friends who saved us." She ran her fingertips along the uninjured skin of my chest. "That is why we are in another house in the slums and why we have Croc. They said that Chisisi or Wahankh could not have turned us in this time, as they've all been together the entire time. The soldiers who found us probably followed me as I looked for you." Her gaze dropped to the ground in shame. "But now Chisisi and Wahankh do not know where we are, the traitor probably believing we've been arrested and taken to the palace. But the others are watching them while pretending not to suspect anything. And if your true friends give them any information, it will be false."

After I lay back down, my eyes closed on their own as I drifted in and out of sleep.

I was back in the *Duat,* in the Chamber of Judgment. Anubis stood before the scales, and sickeningly sweet incense filled the air. The gold and red carpet ended at my feet.

My heart once again sat in my hands, its squishy flesh beating against my palms and carrying up my arms into my chest. Sticky blood pooled around the organ, caking my fingers.

The scales wavered, and the heart in my hands pounded faster and more forcefully.

"You did not heed the magician's training," the humanoid with the head of a falcon yelled through a parting beak, its voice screeching and ringing my ears. As it stood, its purple robe waved. "And you let his heart be devoured. You also put the souls of your friends at risk for your own gains and caused the loss of souls of the innocent, the councilman who still wanted to help Egypt, and the children in the street, Pharaoh's retaliation for your attacks. And you fight with your friends when they try to help you, even when they try to heal you and show you love."

I tried to scream with all of my might and deny the accusations or explain, but I couldn't say a word. My soul was still frozen, and although I wracked my brain, I couldn't recall a single spell from the Book of the Dead.

The scales wavered but maintained an even weight. I almost sighed in relief, but a ghostly form appeared in the darkness behind the scales—Akhenaten's face emerged. He reached out with cupped hands and spread his fingers. The ashes of my father's body trickled out and landed upon the scale with my beating heart. The side with my heart descended.

The gangly creatures and the baboon scuttled about the area, shrieking and pointing at my descending heart.

I tried to scream again and to point so that Anubis would see Akhenaten, but I still could not move. The taste of salt filled my mouth.

A deep voice echoed through the chamber as Anubis finally spoke. "You've failed mostly in your life by making the wrong decisions and by not acting at the moment given to you." His jackal lips curled up into a snarl as he talked, and stringing drool dripped from between sharp teeth. "Not coming for Nefertiti sooner and saving her soul and mind, stealing the pomegranate, and not killing Akhenaten when you had or will have the chance."

Something unseen tugged on the beating heart that was also still in my hands, as if Anubis summoned the organ to him. I tried to hang on to it, to wrap my fingers around its slippery flesh, but it beat so fast that I thought it would explode between my fingers. The heart slipped away, and its beating slowed and then stopped completely.

Anubis's fingers squeezed the organ, and pain ripped through my chest. He shook his head and threw my heart into the darkness of the Devouring Monster's platform. Crocodile jaws sprang from the shadows and gaped open, their serrated teeth reaching for a succulent meal.

And the face of Akhenaten emerged again, this time beside the monster. He smiled as he watched me ...

Chapter 51

Journal Translation

I AWOKE TO DARKNESS AND A small flickering candle, still lying inside the hovel I was recovering in. The table where Croc had lain was empty, save for empty plates and jugs of spent water.

"How do you feel?" Mutnedjmet asked, standing in a corner of the room, watching me. She was probably trapped here as well, afraid to leave or do anything in her own city because someone might have followed her or the guards who ambushed us, someone still alive who might have seen her with me.

Pain still wracked my body, and my limbs felt stiffer than they had days ago. I grimaced. Red circles had soaked through my bandages. I wasn't getting any better.

"I need to show you something." She rubbed at her eyes, which were red-tinged with sadness. "The body cannot heal with a broken soul. Can you walk?" She stepped over and took my hand in a firm grip, helped me to my feet, and guided me outside. The comfort of darkness surrounded us, the moon again veiled behind a layer of clouds. Cool air wafted across my sticky skin as she led me down dark alleyways and across the great road. Silence hovered throughout the city, the only sound the crunching of our footsteps on sand.

We approached our ship of the Sea People's. The wind howled as it came off the river, bringing a biting chill to my exposed face and chest.

"We can't take that," I said, grabbing Mutnedjmet around her waist and stopping her from approaching our boat. She struggled against my arms. "They will be watching it."

She nodded. "That's why I arranged to have a small skiff waiting, stocked with supplies."

"Where are you planning to take me?" I asked.

"Over the past few days, I was trying to understand why all your scheming is so ingrained in you." She guided me onward. My feet sank into the squishy mud of the banks with a sucking sound. "And I will not try to stop you any longer. Somehow we need to help my sister break free of Akhenaten. Father can still find the light in his heart, like he did when we were children. He'd make a much better pharaoh than the current one. And you need to see something before you die."

"Another god?" I asked. "More treasure? Thebes, Memphis?"

She shook her head as she walked to the docks and quickly boarded a reed skiff away from our boat.

I stopped in my sunken tracks. "How long is this going to take? I need to end all of this, one way or another—very soon."

"I've already informed the dwarf brothers that we will be gone for a couple of weeks." She turned and reached for me. "The brothers, Paramessu, and Tia will be making any preparations they can to help with your and my plans to confront Akhenaten." Her voice turned distant. "I remembered those brothers from Amenhotep's sed-festival—such amazing acrobatics ... Plus time will be on your side. Akhenaten will grow impatient, waiting for your return and retaliation. And the longer he has to wait, the more likely it will be that he slips up. The companions you trust will make sure that neither of the other two have any opportunity to slip away and inform the palace or Akhenaten of any of our plans."

I swung a leg over the skiff. "If Akhenaten doesn't locate our new house in the meantime and kill off all of my companions."

Taking up an oar, Mutnedjmet shoved us away from the bank. Moonlight reflected in the ripples forming around us. "I believe that knowing he has an informant in your group will be enough to keep him satisfied—thinking that he knows something you do not and that he has another way to undermine you. Killing a few other men while you live would do nothing for his ego or anger. He will wait for you."

Mutnedjmet and I stroked through the water with our oars and angled south—against the current—and let the white sail billow open. Wind tore at the fabric like invisible claws, pulling us along with its power.

* * *

Mutnedjmet and I lay side by side along the length of the skiff, shaded by the billowing sail that whipped and snapped over our heads as we skimmed southward. White clouds raced across the blue sky, playing with the sunlight and making it sparkle.

"I'd like a small farm, with goats, sheep, and a few cats," Mutnedjmet said, her gentle hand in mine. "I don't even want any servants waiting on me … but I would like to have those two Nubian friends of yours with us so that we can watch them dance around a fire at night."

I chuckled, which sent stinging pain through my body, as I pictured Harkhuf performing tumbling and back flips as I'd only seen him do once many years ago. "He despised his old master for making him perform against his will."

"Well, we wouldn't make him perform," she replied, "just encourage him. And he seemed pretty eager to help in any way he could, both he and Seneb."

I recalled the tale of Harkhuf's wife and daughter and of the Egyptian slavers that he'd unknowingly led back to his tribe. "Harkhuf has a need to help women. It's his form of retribution."

"Whatever gets him to dance." She squeezed my hand and curled up against me.

Her breath tickled my neck, her supple skin rubbing on mine. I inhaled her almond scent and closed my eyes, treasuring this moment as much as any moment I'd lived.

A light sparkled through my eyelids … I looked up. A soaring cloud appeared, covering half of the eastern sky. Its shape tumbled as it rolled along in the high wind, like raging water, its center opening and rays of sun streaming downward. A lone tree stood on the far bank of the river, bathed in a cone of light—a tamarisk tree. Buds covered its limbs, ready to bloom, but no petals were yet visible. I'd seen this image too many times. When the flowers emerged, they would be black like death. Shaking my head, I rolled over to face Mutnedjmet, and she pressed her back up against me. I placed an arm around her side, leaned into her light scent, and closed my eyes.

"Can't we stay like this forever?" she whispered.

"Right now, I feel that if I died today or tomorrow, all of my pain and anger would dissipate, vanishing into the wind and the water—scattering like dust," I replied. "And no one would care, not even me. My stomach does not burn with pain—the festering disease in my heart held at bay, for the moment."

She was quiet.

I kissed the lobe of her ear. "But like everything, this cannot last forever."

She sat up, pushed away from me, and scouted around the banks. "That is true. We are already here."

A week or more had already passed with Mutnedjmet at my side? It seemed like only a day. And the happiness—one that I'd never experienced before. How fast would my life have flown by if I'd known such love long ago, instead of anguish, and yet still the years disappeared faster than I could ever explain. I scratched a wound on my arm, the edges red and inflamed, but finally contracting and reaching out for each other.

Brush and stubby trees lined the banks. I steered us to the western shore, where we unloaded, grabbed supplies, and hiked out across the desert through the far hills. Hours dragged by under the blistering Aten.

"Where are you taking me?" I asked. I'd considered that she might've only wanted to spend time with me before Pharaoh sacrificed my mortal body and devoured my soul, but she must have an objective way out here.

She hiked away even faster. "You will not understand the description."

Hours later, we came upon a mountainside. She stopped and pointed at something at its base. No hieroglyphs or images dotted the mound of dirt that she indicated, and if she hadn't shown me, I'd have walked right over it.

"The burial mound." She wiped sweat from her brow before tucking her dark locks behind her ears.

"Who's buried here?" I asked.

She took a deep breath, straightening as she took my hand.

My bones tingled, my breaths coming faint and shallow. What was this place?

"Your mother and many other Egyptians once made a stand," she said.

My heart dropped into my churning stomach.

"Against the rise of the one god." Her gaze dropped to the ground. "Amenhotep was okay with such opinions. While he pushed the Aten as the only true deity, he allowed everyone to worship whom they pleased. But a regiment of the military confronted this group on the eve of their protest, many years ago. We would've only been babies at the time."

I braced my hands on my knees. How did she know this? But I'd heard about my mother several times now. The heat of the Aten felt unbearable, pounding down upon my back and shoulders and threatening to push me into the dirt.

"The group of protesters was slaughtered." She winced. "Amenhotep always claimed that he had no hand in the matter and openly allowed others to worship their own gods. And he punished those responsible for the vicious act and their lack of acceptance."

I breathed as if I'd just sprinted over an entire mountain. "But Akhenaten never allowed for such dissidence. I grew up with him as my teacher and he *only* taught me of the Aten. I'd *never* even heard of any of the other gods—I never had a choice."

"They told you that your mother died during your birth?" she asked.

I nodded as guilt and pain twisted my stomach into knots. I gagged and dry heaved.

"That wasn't true," Mutnedjmet said. "I've spent years gleaning this information from the elders. Your mother even took up weapons with some of the others and fought the soldiers—after they'd skewed some of the innocent protesters with spears. She and the others took a stand. But after their deaths, no one else resisted with such open contempt."

My eyes clamped shut, a turmoil of emotions raging inside my heart, threatening to expel my disease out into the world. Deep within, I knew what she spoke was the truth. My own mother stood against the beliefs that an authority had been forcing upon her, her people, and her son. She'd probably done it for me—risked everything so that her infant son would not have to grow up in a world of oppression, one that stifled freewill and thinking.

That was love. But what if she'd given in and accepted the new truth? What if she had been there to make my life better for all of my years? I swallowed in remorse. Father had tried the opposite approach after she was gone, but I'd failed him when I'd stolen that damn pomegranate for Akhenaten and become his indentured servant. My eyes burned with tears, but the moisture wicked away from my cheeks as the droplets fell into the arid heat.

"The son of Hapu," Mutnedjmet placed a cool hand on my shoulder, "worked hard to make sure that they would be together in the next life."

"The magician?" I choked on my tears. "With my mother?"

She rubbed my arm and shook her head. "No, the magician brought the scorched bones of your father here. Your father is also buried in this mound, along with many others."

"H-how was my mother killed?" I asked.

She was silent for a moment. "Her heart was not consumed, if that is what you are worried about. This was before the time the Devouring Monster walked the earth."

"How?"

"Burned, like your father." Her gaze and hand fell from my arm.

My throat spasmed as I gasped again and again between sobs. I couldn't breathe. *Father, you were here? With Mother? You were both burned—unable to achieve the afterlife as you did not have a heart for Anubis to weigh on his scales?* My only family wiped from existence—a woman I'd never known, but now respected as much as anyone I'd ever met. My heart melted into mush, and my disease seeped into my bones. My teeth ground together, building in pressure until a grating rattled through my skull.

"You don't have to go back," Mutnedjmet whispered. "Your life can end differently, many years from now. You don't have to become your mother."

"I am her, and my father," I managed to say in spite of the war raging inside of me, both of my parents tugging my soul and my fate in opposite directions. Images of all the dead souls in the mound before me filled my mind, figures cloaked in black with linen-wrapped heads. Their glowing green eyes shone through their masks and stared into my soul. I was not alone, never had been alone. "The people of Egypt have sacrificed everything for others long before I came, long before I chose to do so. Other souls of the past are linked to me. I cannot give up now, not until I join them."

But how could I possibly challenge the god-king ever again? I'd failed when I'd planned everything, even when I'd had the advantage of surprise. My mind wandered. I recalled the magician's latest words, but they didn't make sense or help me. The papyrus of his last note of advice, the one on his cat's collar, crinkled in my hands, although I didn't remember taking it with me: *For any man or group that has succeeded and returned to the palace of el-Amarna, heed these words: Darkness has settled into my soul—my* ba *wingless and the light of my* ka *dwindling. I cannot hold out much longer. This regime of Egypt is suffocating my resolve. Time draws to a close. But I have left you the start of a small army, one that no one will suspect. My act of hatred was a ploy. Make them powerful.*

What was his army? The girl-priest of Sobek told me that the magician had committed suicide, too overwhelmed with Akhenaten's wicked ways. But she'd hinted that she believed he'd ended his life because of guilt over his last order, the only one of his requests that Akhenaten had ever accepted and enforced—banishing the lepers and driving them out of el-Amarna.

But how could a group of the hideously diseased, their disease not very contagious, ever be made powerful?

Pivoting around, I marched back for the skiff. It was time to finish everything—everything that I'd returned to Egypt to do.

Chapter 52

Journal Translation

I MARCHED OVER A DESERT HILL with Mutnedjmet at my side, the Aten's unobstructed heat beating down on me as if it were Akhenaten himself attempting to curtail my resolve. Wind whipped in my ears and lashed my dry skin and scabbed-over wounds.

Mutnedjmet had brought us to a location in the desert not far from el-Amarna. The clanging of bronze on rock rang in the distance and echoed off a mountain cliff.

"This is where they were exiled to," she said, her feet crunching in the sand.

We crested the hill and gazed down into a sunken pit nearly as wide as the hill itself. Piles of gravel and rock dotted the area, and men and women in tattered kilts swung bronze tools into the stone of the mountain's base, creating a deafening ensemble. Many of these thousand or so people were disfigured. Some had crusty, bulging arms or legs while others had lumps ravaging their backs.

"Hello," I said.

No one turned, put down a tool, or even noticed us.

Then I yelled, the acoustics of the cliff giving even me the volume of a leader—nearly matching the volume of Akhenaten's voice. "Empty promises ... You've probably all heard them, as have I."

Every swinging axe and pick in the pit halted. Faces turned up to me, lumpy and grotesque, a little like the magical mask I wore. The wind died, and silence reigned over the land.

"I have come to bring you lepers back into the city." I pointed at individuals. "Instead of toiling out here until you die or cannot carry on, as those of el-Amarna do not visit often enough or do not provide enough grain for your work. And I know you have awaited this day like the dead await the coming of their family into the underworld. The son of Hapu was also a friend and guardian to me, and he foretold you of my coming and of a battle that must be waged if you wish to be carried out of the darkness. If you trusted him, please put your faith in me now." I took a deep breath. "People of Egypt. That is what you all are—although you were banished for something you could not control. Such disrespect will not be in my world. People will be free to choose what or whom they wish to worship, and what kind of life they wish to pursue. I will never hold you to your birth status, as I have not heeded my own. Each and every one of you has an equal inside even the palace of el-Amarna." I pointed northwest, indicating the far-off lair of Akhenaten as I paced along the crest of the hillside, the Aten at my back. "Every man is born equal—but it is only what you accept for yourself and force upon others that divides us. Today is the day that we seek justice for Egypt, our kingdom!"

I raised my sword overhead. Its bronze and the bronze bracelet on my wrist caught the sunlight and glowed. I bellowed again. "Walk by my side as equals—as all men and women should be—and you will be fed and armed. Today we march for redemption!"

The men and women in the pit glanced at each other. Some hollered with elation; others shook their heads and wandered off.

But a mass dropped their tools and lumbered up the hill to join me.

Mutnedjmet and I timed our arrival back at el-Amarna appropriately. The Aten had set a few hours before we docked at the eastern bank. The lepers were traveling here on foot.

Darkness surrounded us, and there was no sound except for the howling wind. I leapt from the skiff and strode for the southern end of the city—to the slums. Mutnedjmet followed me, silent. We hadn't spoken much on the return voyage as the need for vengeance tore at my insides like scorpions ripping apart insect prey with their claws.

I'd been a terrible leader, putting my desires above anything else, and I'd assisted in harboring a traitor. But this was no longer only about me. I was going to lead my companions one last time.

After knocking outside the open doorway of our hovel, I inched inside—not wanting one of Harkhuf's arrows through my heart.

"Took you a while," Harkhuf grumbled, his triceps bulging as he paced up to me, a small lamp in his hand. "I didn't know if you were coming back."

"And at times, we all hoped that you wouldn't," Paramessu said, sitting up beside Tia. "We hoped that Mutnedjmet would talk some sense into you. We want you to find peace."

"There will be only one kind of peace for me." I paced around in a circle, my stomach cramping with anxiety—I'd waited too long to face Akhenaten again, and anxiety ate at me. "I will face him one last time. And whatever happens, that is it ... even if we both survive. But I swear that will not be the case. Follow me only if you must, only if you cannot force yourselves to turn and leave my side."

"The odds are massively stacked against us," Seneb said, "like a single grandfather amongst a tribe of children."

Chisisi and Wahankh sat up from under blankets, yawning and rubbing at their eyes.

I paused, my rage focused on Chisisi, whom I'd freed from slavery not that long ago.

Chisisi forced a smile. "We have a surprise for you."

My chest constricted against my lungs, the expelling air burning my throat. "I already know—"

Another man sat up—short, vaguely familiar, but I could not place him. My hands found my swords. It was not Mahu or Maya ...

"If I wore the yellow eye paint, would you recognize me?" The man rubbed a newly shaven head. "I've come to fulfill my vow to the son of Hapu—his last request. But then I flee this place, forever. I know nothing of war, only how to hide my true self and grow close to my enemies through diplomacy."

My forehead furrowed. The man whom I'd saved from Pentju's autopsy, one of the other men whom the magician had groomed to attempt to usurp the throne from Akhenaten?

Mutnedjmet took my hand in hers. "And the time for diplomacy is over." The others studied us.

"What is it you're offering?" I asked the stranger as I stepped away from Mutnedjmet.

"I've had my few trustworthy contacts here in the city use the wealth that the son of Hapu left us," the man replied. "We've purchased a hundred horses and chariots from all over the city and discreetly gathered them, moving only at night. They have all been waiting for you out in the eastern desert by the mountain range." He stood and grabbed a sack bulging with contents. "I have done everything I can for the son of Hapu and for Egypt. If you succeed, I may one day return. But I do not know how you can ever accomplish this." He pushed past me. "Godspeed ... my classmate." He disappeared out into the night.

I watched him go, my mind racing with scenarios of my future. That man and I were bound to the son of Hapu by our promises. But now he was running away, as everyone had suggested I should do.

"And we've purchased many spears, shields, and bows," Paramessu said. "But we've emptied the gold stores that we had in this city."

I stumbled into the corner and collapsed onto the dirt floor alone in a heap. The voices of my companions filled the room, but I rolled over to face the wall and blocked them out. Images of me leading a diseased nation into battle filled my head as I forced my eyes shut. I saw only death and destruction before me ... But, as the magician had once taught me, I listened to my heart as it lay as still as it ever would during these days. I traced hieroglyphs into the hard-packed dirt with my fingertip. *Father, please hear my cry for help.*

Hours later, my eyes closed, and I drifted off into a restless sleep.

A falcon flew through a deep blue sky in my dream—as if night and midday fused overhead. Pink clouds floated by. The falcon cried out, so shrill that my skin crawled. Then it dived for me. I leapt aside.

The head of a man sat atop the falcon, a *ba*. No, the head of a woman— one I did not recognize. But she smiled, and love filled her eyes. My heart ached with a bitter sting. Mother? And another *ba* trailed behind her—Father?

"We are dead, son," the woman's head said as her wings flapped in the silent wind above me. The gale whipped at my long hair and streamed across my cracking skin. "People fear the dead, as they cannot be harmed by the living."

Visions of men tearing across the land in chariots suddenly raged in my mind. I gasped and buried my face in my hands, shaking my head.

My eyes fluttered, and I awoke. My skin was damp with perspiration, my heart racing with fear, longing, and confusion.

I'd always believed that the burning of my mother and father's bodies meant their souls would be erased, as if their hearts had been devoured, but was that not true? Had they actually visited me, or was the vision of them in my dream only a dream?

The bright rays of the Aten streaming into the hovel indicated that I'd slept through the day. I rolled over to face the rest of the room. Mutnedjmet still hadn't given up on me—she lay on a blanket on the floor beside me, sleeping. The others sat on the far side of the room, crunching on raw grains.

"If you are still with me," I said, "prepare all of the horses and chariots. The lepers should have arrived, and they will be our army."

Chapter 53

Present Day

I PRESSED MY HEAD BACK AGAINST the sarcophagus within the otherwise empty King's Chamber inside the Great Pyramid. The journal translation and story that I carried was finished. A few untranslated hieroglyphs remained but not enough to even complete another full thought or modern sentence. There was no hope in using that tale as a guide, not this time.

My imagination took over, and I closed my eyes to block out the hunting beams of flashlights.

The Father of Terror, as the Sphinx was known by the locals, would again be covered in many feet of sand—like when commencing the undertaking of its restoration. It would be exactly midnight, just like this night … Maddie would be there by my side, helping dig and uncover lost clues and secrets that no one else could. But it'd be only the two of us. I'd unearth the ancient stela—the Dream Stela—resting between its front paws and translate its meaning, discovering a new take on the wording that hadn't been thought of in the past few centuries. The new translation would drive me to the Great Pyramid as its meaning sank in and an idea took shape in my mind. I'd burst through the metal gates leading inside the pyramid, and all the tourists and guards would've mysteriously disappeared, just like this night.

Maddie would race after me, shouting, "What is it you think you've found?"

But I'd race on. Ascending from the lowest subterranean chamber beneath the Great Pyramid, I'd rise like the soul of Pharaoh, climbing into the Queen's Chamber, then into the King's Chamber. The light of the stars would guide my soul outward through the open shafts overhead, and I'd exit the pyramid like a winged *ba*. But I'd stop on the outer surface and scale the towering walls to the pyramidion—the capstone. I'd stand upon pure gold, which would reflect the rays of moon and starlight. My soul would shudder as realization lost to the ages dawned on me, and Maddie would join me. We'd raise a pyramidion of our own to the sky ... The fiery phoenix would land and cry out, and we'd understand all of the greatest secrets of mankind, of the world and universe ...

I snapped back to the present, leapt up, and shouted, "Give me the pyramidion." I reached out for the fox's collar, the pyramidion that I'd used before—the one that Mr. Scalone had once taken from me at gunpoint before forcing me to help him uncover the lost secret of the Colossi of Amenhotep.

Aiden unbuckled the fox's collar and handed it and the dangling tag of a pyramid to me.

I studied the pyramid's outer glass surfaces and rubbed my fingers across it—smooth and clear. Not the true *benben* stone of translucent yellow like in the journal ... but this would have to work. But how could this fit with the river, the eclipse, and the Scorpion Macehead?

I pulled out my phone and opened the compass, aligning the sides of the prism with the cardinal directions.

"No calls," an assailant shouted, "or you die before any help come."

I held the prism into the air. "Turn off all your flashlights." The eclipse? Or what happened with a total eclipse—essentially the darkness of night or at least twilight.

Slowly, each person clicked off their flashlights.

Pure darkness engulfed us, with the exception of the beams from the assailants' lights just outside the chamber.

"Please turn off all the lights," Maddie said to them.

After a moment, they did as she'd ordered.

A full minute of darkness and silence followed. No one moved, everyone barely breathing.

Then faint light emerged, streaming through the shafts overhead. Starlight. I moved to position the pyramid in my hand. The rays hit the prism and arced onto the walls. A faint spectrum of colored light emerged, but nothing else.

"Look," Maddie said.

I couldn't see where she was pointing, but something on the floor caught my attention. Something glowed green—a hieroglyph—the reverse sign of ascension, stairs leading downward.

"Descend," Maddie said but then fell silent for a moment. "Down to the Queen's Chamber, which should be directly below the entrance to this room. Maybe if we find the Hall there'll be another way out, and we can escape from these men."

After clicking on her flashlight, she raced out of the chamber and side-stepped the three assailants—who cast her barely visible snarls of irritation or surprise. I ran after her, and the others followed.

Metal clanged beneath our feet as we ran back down the stairs of the Grand Gallery and into the other tunnel we'd skipped. This one was tight and dark. But I squeezed into the passage and followed it until it ended in a small room of black rock. A niche of carved stone stood out in the far wall—portraying the inward stepping appearance identical to the Grand Gallery's walls.

Aiden pointed at the niche. Graffiti was carved into the stone around it. "What was supposed to go there? The queen's sarcophagus?"

"No." I shook my head. "They named this the Queen's Chamber a long time ago, but it was probably only a stepping stone for the pharaoh's ascension to the heavens. A statue of the pharaoh probably resided there."

Kaylin shined her flashlight down a small shaft that burrowed into the wall, but it ended in stone not too far in. "But no one found a statue there?"

"They didn't find anything remaining in this pyramid," Maddie said, reminding her.

Aiden eyed the shaft leading into the wall. "Do we have to climb into that?"

"Reminds me of the time I had to escape solitary in Colombia," Mr. Scalone said, folding his arms across his protruding chest and rubbing at the thick stubble on his chin. He tossed his head back, flinging his long locks behind his shoulders.

"I hope not," I whispered in response to Aiden's question. It didn't look like we'd even fit into that shaft, and there was no opening farther in.

Aiden tapped the wall. "Someone carved horns into the wall here, like the devil's. Maybe that could be a clue."

Maddie shined her light about the room, searching while spewing random facts that she probably hoped would trigger some key bit of information in her memory. "The ram and its horns represented the ancient Egyptian god Amun, but ancient Christians morphed him into their devil. Deities in ancient Egypt, Greece, and Rome had horns, but people in newer religions used the horns to convince their fellow believers that if they saw someone worshipping a horned being, it was the devil, Satan, and thus the offender could be put to death. This spurred fear and hate and helped with the eradication of the pagans, one of the largest witch-hunts and holocausts in history."

Aiden stumbled back, as if startled. He pulled the fox in his arm closer to his chest and pet its head. "Kinda like how some people and even fairy tales demonize animals like wolves, foxes, and snakes, saying they kill and eat people, things that aren't really true? Those animals are competing for the same resources people want for themselves, like outsiders and religion, I guess, which is, like, probably the real reason some people want others to fear and hate those animals."

My eyebrows tightened over my forehead and Maddie studied Aiden, the teen suddenly appearing to have changed a bit, to have grown more complex, deeper.

Maddie stepped closer to Aiden and scrutinized the wall with her beam of light. "I guess I'd never really thought of it that way, Aiden." She was silent for a moment. "But the following religions borrowed many symbols from ancient Egypt and incorporated much of the Egyptian underworld into their version of Hell. They also used some ancient Egyptian symbols on their saints. The solar discs over the Egyptian gods' heads became the halo. We Americans have an obelisk in D.C. to worship our gods in office there, or at least the original god, George Washington. And the ankh became the major symbol of Coptic Christians." Maddie shook her head and cleared her throat as she dismissed the image that Aiden was so interested in. "Those horns of the ram are ancient graffiti, not an original part of the pyramid."

A haze filled my mind. Even different types of peoples had so much in common, but they still found ways to use certain similarities to drive themselves apart ... like with Akhenaten's Egypt, like with the assailants outside and us, like with the minister, Mr. Scalone, and Kaylin against me,

Maddie, and Aiden. Were these assailants from some ancient cult or religion, one like Akhenaten's and who'd want to hide the story in the journal, a story wherein Akhenaten's monotheism led to wars and the downward spiral of his country and the surrounding world? But still, why drive us deeper into—

An assailant outside the room shouted and clapped. "You no find by sunrise, you all die in here. Hurry, not much time."

My shoulders tensed and pulled back as I glanced around. How long until the sun rose? Would we ever be able to locate the Hall, even if we had weeks?

The hieroglyphs for ascension were everywhere in this chamber as well. "Turn out the lights again," I said.

Flashlights clicked off.

Within a minute, faint light was again apparent, streaming through two shafts in the walls. I positioned myself directly between the two rays of light and held the glass pyramid into their bisecting paths.

"But in ancient times, these shafts never exited the outer limestone surface," Maddie said from the darkness. "This doesn't make sense."

Starlight fell onto the prism and refracted against the walls and floor. The same hieroglyph for descending lit up on the floor in green light, although there had been no trace of a marking prior. This hieroglyph had a secret purpose.

"What's below here?" Aiden asked, his voice tense.

"The subterranean chamber," Maddie said. "A room carved into the bedrock of Egypt, just below the Great Pyramid. There's nothing down there, though. It's only an empty room and a hallway, and there're no air vents."

"We better look," Mr. Scalone said, and he clicked his flashlight back on. "I've a feeling I'm about to uncover something big, like that time in the Mayan Riviera." He winked at Kaylin as he thrust his chin out.

Kaylin sucked in a deep breath and clasped her hands together, seeming unafraid of or completely distracted from the men with the guns.

My fingers squeezed around the edges of the glass pyramid. "There're two ways down. Back to the tunnel near the entrance, or there's a tight shaft leading straight down with declining slopes along its route. The shaft has a small chamber called a grotto that is supposedly empty as well ... But without climbing gear, I don't think we could go that way."

"Back to the tunnels," Maddie said, again jogging out of the chamber and past the assailants almost as if she no longer feared them—or wanted to find the secret so that she could get out of here as quickly as possible.

The assailants shouted something, the bite of anger rising in their voices. Either they thought we were taking too long or maybe they didn't like that we were finding clues meant to be hidden from everyone for eternity.

We jogged back to the original passageway near the entrance and located the descending corridor, which tunneled into the earth. Darkness seemed to boil out from within, as well as heat and a musty—

"This gate's locked," Mr. Scalone said as he grabbed on to the metal bars blocking the corridor and shook them, rattling metal against stone.

"Move aside," the minister said as he squeezed around Mr. Scalone. The minister dug out keys and unlocked the door with a high-pitched screech—one that seemed to signal that we should not enter, at the risk of our own lives. I shuddered.

"Have you ever been down there?" I whispered to Maddie.

She shook her head and her lips grew taut. "I've only read about it." But she shoved past Mr. Scalone and stepped into the darkness, the beam of her light swallowed by the depths beyond.

She stepped forward, and I followed her.

We traveled downward for many minutes amidst the sounds of harsh breathing and quietly placed footsteps.

The hairs on the back of my neck stood on end, as if something were watching us—awaiting our arrival. My skin prickled, and I shivered.

The tunnel leveled out and opened into a small chamber—unfinished and empty.

"The formless underworld surrounds us," Maddie whispered, her voice airy as she shined her light around and motioned at the room. Two colors of stone made up the chamber: a lighter top and ceiling and a dark lower half. "The world as we know it," she shined her light on the lighter stone, "and the underworld." She lowered her beam to the black rock. "This is where they meet, right here at this level of the earth."

My breath felt cold, and my skin crawled, like insects writhed in my muscles.

Maddie stepped into a narrow tunnel leading horizontally into the bedrock. "Search anything and everything."

Mr. Scalone, Kaylin, Aiden, and the minister examined the room.

I tailed Maddie. A short way ahead was a dead end—the bedrock of Egypt all around us. There were no distinguishable stone blocks here.

We searched the hallway and chamber for another hour. The only thing we found was a small hole about as big around as my head in the floor of the chamber. I shined my light inside but couldn't see a bottom.

Slumping back against the wall, I stared into the darkness of the far tunnel. The eclipse we'd already used, but ... "Will the Scorpion Macehead fit in that hole?"

The minister turned and studied me for a moment. Then he reached into his bag and pulled forth the mace head—the one that Maddie and I had been searching for in the museum.

"Give it a try," he said and set it onto my open palm.

The stone weighed my arm down, heavy, dense, cold, and large enough to smash in the heads of any human enemies.

I leaned over the shaft and held out the mace head.

Complete silence.

"What else have we got to go on?" I asked. Then I dropped it in. The stone rattled around against the tight walls as it plummeted into the darkness.

Someone behind us laughed—one of the armed assailants.

What was he laughing for? Was dropping the mace head a mistake?

Nothing happened. After a few minutes, I stepped away from the opening.

Maddie adjusted her sheer glasses. "The other clue was the river. But the river never should've come up to the Great Pyramid, maybe to the Sphinx but not this far."

"That's why we brought the trucks," the minister said. "Water."

My eyes widened. Were we supposed to flush water down here and bring the Nile to the underworld?

I imagined us spewing water down into that hole. Would that damage the foundations of the Great Pyramid itself? Would it cause the priceless structure above our heads to collapse and crush us like an unstable mine inside a mountain of rock? Or would only one area collapse and trap us down here where we'd starve to death for our crimes? But we really didn't have much of a choice at this point, because if nothing worked, we were going to be executed by these strange assailants. "Attach every hose you bought together and see if they'll reach down here."

We ran back up the tunnel as the assailants watched over us—always close behind. Two of the assailants joined Mr. Scalone and the minister in the cabs of the two tanker trucks as they started them up, the engines both sputtering before revving to life. They drove the trucks right up to the pyramid's entrance, parked, and connected all of the hoses, which resembled fire hoses. About a half hour later, we finally arrived back down in the subterranean chamber, but Aiden and one assailant waited back up with the trucks to turn on the water.

"Give it a tug," Maddie said. "We're ready."

I heaved on the thick, braided hose that wound through hundreds of feet of tunnels and seemed to pull back against me.

A minute later, hissing and whooshing filled the chamber—air being expelled through the line.

I shoved the metal end of the hose into the hole. More sputtering followed, then the hose kicked back as liquid burst out of its buried end. Water spewed out with such force that the hose lifted me from the ground and threw me back. The nozzle shot out of the hole and water sprayed around the chamber like a fire hydrant had burst. The others grabbed the hose and anchored it as I held on to the flopping tip and forced it back inside the hole.

The roar of gushing water quieted, muted by the bedrock.

A minute passed, and then another. I couldn't hear where the water was going.

The stone beneath my feet rumbled and vibrated. I yelled and jumped off of it. The stone rose above the rest, less than an inch at first, but it slowly continued to elevate—a stone that had been flush with the floor, probably with such precise junctions that we never would've even been able to see it in the lighting down here.

Maddie shouted in excitement.

I attempted to grip the slick edges of the rising stone, which were perfectly square. My fingers slipped off of it. "Grab hold."

But the stone rose higher, and handholds appeared, carved into the sides that had been hidden only a moment ago.

We all tugged and heaved at the block as the rising water aided us by lifting it from below. After another few minutes, the stone, tiny in comparison to the other blocks of the upper pyramid, slid free. I shoved on its wet surface, planting the soles of my boots onto the rock floor as we all pushed. The block tumbled over onto the bedrock with a resounding bang, shaking the walls around us. A dark shaft appeared in the place where the stone had been.

We tugged on the hose again, and the water soon stopped.

Shining my light downward revealed only a pool of reflective water about a foot below the floor of the chamber. Now what? I wasn't jumping down into that.

My stomach heaved, vomit rising in my throat. Soon, I'd be in an intensely painful bout of intestinal cramping from my disease, and once it hit, I couldn't do anything but lay down and roll around in pain, vomiting, until I went to the ER.

Bubbles sprang up from within the water in the gaping hole in the floor, and the water level slowly receded.

"What happened?" Aiden shouted as he entered the chamber. He ran over and peered down into the void and the diminishing pool as he clutched his fox close to his chest.

Finally, the water was nearly gone, draining into some other shaft farther down. The hole now visible below us was a sloping tunnel so steep that if we tried to descend, we'd probably slide, like a waterslide leading into the darkness.

Kaylin leapt forward, clung to the taut hose, and lowered herself into the shaft, walking backward down the wall like a rock climber. She shined a small flashlight held in her mouth farther down, beyond the edge where I could see. "There's an opening." She let go of the hose and slipped, landing in a heap with a cry of surprise and a crack before sliding down the slick shaft and disappearing into the dark abyss spewing out from the side of the rock wall below.

Chapter 54

Present Day

I CLUNG TO THE TAUT HOSE and inched down the sloping tunnel into the unknown, beyond the bedrock of Egypt—beneath the Great Pyramid—into the fabled passageways. Was I daydreaming again? My feet seemed to float in the darkness, and I thought I saw green mist swirling down below. A musty odor of buried earth hovered around me. Probably only two men—Dr. Shelsher and his student—had breathed the air down here after it had been sealed off millennia ago. How had *I* led us here?

Clicking on my flashlight from my messenger bag, I cast the light around. Walls of desert-colored stone rose all around me, guiding me to a tunnel that led into a side wall. I let go of the hose and stepped through the narrow passage, which was flat but turned sharp corners. Maddie followed close behind, then the rest of the group, their shoes scuffing as they dragged loose grains of sand across ancient rock. The three armed assailants followed after us. Kaylin, with her avarice for treasure, was already down here somewhere by herself. Hopefully she'd found where the mace head had landed and picked it up, since I hadn't seen it.

Corridors branched off to the sides. But I continued southeast ... which would lead us into the earth and bedrock beneath the Sphinx—where sonar and radar had detected buried chambers. Some people already knew that a secret was hidden there ... hidden for how many hundreds or thousands of years?

After many long minutes, I stumbled into a dead end covered in cobwebs and dust, and I flashed my light around. The stone making up the left side of the wall was a light beige. On the right, the stone was black.

"Day and night," Maddie whispered from just behind me, her voice airy and hoarse with awe. "This is the entrance to something, the underworld …"

Darkness pressed in around me as if the massive weight of the Sphinx overhead would come crashing down upon us. My toes curled, and the hairs on the back of my neck stood up—the haunting presence that I'd felt several times now inside ancient tombs or temples had returned at full force. I shivered and leaned over as my stomach heaved, and I vomited a small amount of bile, the pain in my stomach intensifying.

Maddie bumped into me.

"Wait," I said, holding up my hand and trying to catch my breath. Hopefully she hadn't noticed my rising sickness. I could put us all in even more danger by becoming worthless and a burden myself, like the night I'd ridden along in the ambulance with my friend Sam. "This doesn't go anywhere. Try one of the other corridors we passed."

Maddie and Mr. Scalone studied the dead ends of contrasting stone but gave up after a few minutes.

I followed at the back of our shuffling group now, just behind Maddie.

The lead assailant took the passage branching off to our right. We followed his wavering flashlight beam.

After another couple hundred feet, the corridor ended again in a stone wall.

The lead assailant shouted in Arabic, and we turned back around to follow the third passage—which again was a dead end. But Kaylin was there, shaking as our flashlight beams ran across her.

I sucked in a deep breath. The tunnels beneath the Sphinx could've just been used in its construction and were now empty, but if the Hall wasn't down here, then why hide all this so purposefully and remarkably with a sunken stone-block entrance?

"We clean up outside and watch main tunnel and entrance to pyramid so no one leaves," an assailant said, pointing to himself and the other assailant beside him. "They go and find secret. You go with them." He motioned to the more vocal assailant.

The vocal assailant bellowed, "You, you." He pointed at Mr. Scalone and Kaylin. "Stay in this passage." Then he pointed at the minister and Aiden.

"Go back to last passage." Then he nodded to me and Maddie. "Go to first dead end. One of you find secret."

Maddie and I jogged off down the long corridor in the direction of the Sphinx and arrived at the dead end. Running my palm along the precisely fitted stones of light tan and black, I pushed and knocked. Nothing. Maddie tapped the end of her metal flashlight all around the stone walls, creating a clinking that carried through the compressed space around us.

We walked back along the tunnel, scrutinizing the walls as we went.

Shouting echoed from the darkness.

"I found a fit for the mace head!" It was Kaylin's voice.

"But nothing's happening," the minister replied, his deeper echoes carrying down the tunnels like an approaching subway train.

The walls around us groaned and then rattled with shuddering vibrations, as if an earthquake had started. Maddie clung to me, and I to her. Dirt spilled onto our heads in streams as stone grated on stone in a bass timbre that sounded as ancient as the earth. Was the entire passageway collapsing in upon us because we'd damaged the foundation of the pyramid, or was it the wrath of whoever'd built this place and desired for it to remain hidden?

The rumbling carried on for a full minute, then abruptly ceased.

Everything was still again, only our unmoving flashlight beams piercing the darkness. My fingers peeled off of Maddie's arm as if they'd been frozen in a death grip.

Spinning around, I swung my light past Maddie in the direction of the entrance.

Blocks of stone had slid out of the wall and closed off the tunnel and the passageway back to the others. I sprinted for this new wall.

"We're trapped!" Maddie screamed at the stone blocks in the middle of the passageway and slapped at them with the heel of her palm.

A hollow thud sounded and momentarily shook the walls as stone somewhere else in these tunnels collided and stopped moving.

I glanced down at Maddie, biting my lip to hold back fear that rose like a surging river.

Maddie continued slapping the wall as her eyebrows narrowed with anxiety. Her breathing came in quick gasps. "Not again." Her voice was tense.

Were we trapped inside a tomb again? I flashed my beam of light around. "At least those men won't be able to shoot us here."

Our friends' voices barely carried through the sealed wall.

My light fell onto a void of blackness. The tan and black wall that had marked the dead end was gone. Now there was an opening.

"Maddie," I said. "Maddie!"

She pivoted around. "What?"

"The dead end opened up when the passage behind us shut," I whispered as my skin tingled and goose bumps arose along my forearms.

Maddie glanced back at the wall that had trapped us. "When they used the mace head, it sealed this end off but revealed another exit?"

I shrugged. "I guess."

"Maybe they can pull the mace head back out or turn it back the way it was, and we can get out of here."

"Don't you want to see what's down there first?" I pointed into the darkness as I shined my flashlight beam onto my hand and arm so she could see what I meant.

Maddie swallowed and adjusted her glasses. Then, standing straighter, she strode for the new opening. Her flashlight led the way.

Jogging up beside her, I exhaled a stale breath. The air before us felt as thick as ocean water, but more stagnant. The Nile would lie somewhere just to the east, hopefully through several layers of bedrock.

Could the Hall of Records really be waiting ahead?

I took Maddie's hand, and we stepped into the darkness side by side. Stairs led downward. The darkness was so thick it appeared to swallow the beam of our flashlights about five feet from the source.

Taking a step downward, I shivered as the heel of my boot clunked and released hollow echoes.

Another step, and another.

The stones below my feet were green—deep green like jade.

I swung my light about as we descended. The tunnel around us opened up into a larger chamber, the walls the same color as the steps, which continued to lead downward, as if this were an auditorium without a stage.

The beams of our flashlights carried farther in this chamber, the confines lighting up in dark green. The ceiling stretched high, and the pressure in the suffocating air relaxed.

Narrow steps forced me to concentrate on foot placement, and my limbs trembled with anticipation. My mouth went dry. But these steps were pristine, not just in cut and shape, but without dust or dirt.

Maddie still held my hand but didn't say a word as she picked her way down the green castle of a chamber. Her eyes were wide, and she didn't even appear to blink, her jaw hanging open.

I smiled and squeezed—

Something caught my eye. I swung my light around to a square pillar supporting the ceiling and froze.

There was a painting upon the broad face of the pillar, a canvas of stone, and a towering statue stood beside the pillar. But this was not like any other ancient Egyptian painting in side profile. This appeared lifelike, as did the matching adjacent statue of pure green, more Renaissance in style, similar to Michelangelo's David. The figures in the painting and the statue rose three times as tall as me. All depicted a green-skinned man standing against a massive bull. The man's head was bowed into the crook of his elbow as he leaned against the animal, his face concealed by his arm. But a portion of the man's lips were visible, and they were kissing the bull's head. The bull was as tall as the man and as wide as an SUV. In the painting, the beast's coat was black, but white areas appeared like small wings over its shoulders, and a white diamond of hair lay upon its forehead.

My body was limp with utter fascination. The most beautiful work of art I'd ever seen ... The Apis Bull, like in the journal? But with a green-skinned man? Was it supposed to be Osiris or some man who commanded magic, all of it created in the shade that was given to the occult and to the underworld in ancient Egypt?

I motioned for Maddie to look, but she was already taking pictures with her phone, her hands shaking as if she were in the arctic tundra.

The flat of my hand reached out and rested against the calf of the green statue, the stone as polished and sleek as Greek marble.

"This will reshape perceptions of ancient Egypt," Maddie whispered.

I nodded but waved her on as adrenaline coursed through every one of my muscles. This was it: the moment I'd lived my entire life for.

Our feet landed upon a flat chamber. Narrow hallways stretched off into the distance, painted with vibrant hieroglyphs undisturbed by time. But no stacks of gold artifacts awaited us.

Ignoring the mounting pain in my guts, I jogged and then ran, shining my light upon it all as I went. Maddie raced after me.

The images upon the tunnel walls spoke of a man—no, a boy—who was Akhenaten's servant: Heb. This *was* the tale in the journal ... I could feel his very soul down here in these hallways, right around me. My heart raced and a shiver ran up my spine—a connection to history and to the ages.

Running down long corridors, I skimmed the tale upon the walls for many minutes before I located the place where I thought the journal's story had ended. I pulled out the journal and located the end of the translation. My finger ran over the coarse paper with a quiet scratching sound.

I yanked out my phone and recorded a video of everything as I walked down the tight tunnels. After having read so much of the story and the associated hieroglyphs, the hieroglyphs upon the walls immediately formed images and thoughts in my mind. I could see the story emerge in my head. An encompassing smile arose on my lips. I'd found the end of the story. Exhilaration carried like blood through my body.

Twenty-four tunnels in all made up these corridors, one for each hour of the day and night, which the ancient Egyptians had understood as well as modern man. I breathed in deep. Had the ancient Egyptians shaped our current understanding of the world as much as the Greeks, and did we just not remember their part in the passing down of knowledge, as it was too far in the past?

I stumbled into a dark, dead end. A sarcophagus lay there upon the ground, still, eternal. The lid was twisted across its length, halfway open, the inside empty save for a few small hieroglyphs near the inner base, which were also adjacent to the dead end wall of the tunnel. These hieroglyphs read: The Illusion of Power.

My eyes closed on their own accord. I tried to open them, but my mind could not control my body.

Chapter 55

Journal Translation

MY COMPANIONS AND I STOOD before the foot of the mountains that created the eastern border of el-Amarna. My hair was cut short, as I'd always worn it in my past life—my body newly shaven and smelling of musky oil. The bulging venous distortion along my face was gone, the magic dismissed, exposing my real face to the world. Twilight sunlight shimmered across my toned body, but the Aten hadn't yet descended. The air lay still, creating a heavy silence.

A thousand newly armed lepers stood before us—my warriors who'd marched over the southern hills into the valley—hunched and ragged, with lumpy skin, thick limbs, and gnarled joints. They didn't make a whisper. A hundred chariots, each driven by twin horses, waited before them.

These were the only men I'd get. I shook my head—it wouldn't be enough to ever defeat the soldiers of the palace. We'd be outnumbered about forty to one, even though I'd sent more and more of the military to the borders since I'd become a commander and the Seeker of Blasphemers—for more reasons than one. But this decrepit army was the best I could do. And now was the time, the only time the world would give me.

A strong hand grabbed my wrist. Harkhuf pulled me down to his face, against the coarse hair of his regrowing beard. "You have everything already," he whispered into my ear. "Look around you. I am not one to encourage anyone to run or to deter them from dreams of redemption, but even I must save you from this madness. Give up your hate."

I shook his hand off of me.

"Take your woman and your friends," his teeth ground together with a high-pitched grating sound, "and let us leave this place forever—to find happiness—before it is too late ... before we are all dead."

"Hear me," I yelled, my quiet voice echoing off the cliffs in the distance as I stepped away from the muscular Nubian dwarf—the last of my companions that I'd ever expected to try to dissuade me. My voice sounded loud, powerful. Croc lay in my arms, his eyes just barely peeking open and his ears perking up as the echoes rang around us. "It is time. Don the linens, paint the horses, and mount your chariots."

"Do not do this because you think that she will finally see what you've become," Mutnedjmet said, stepping before me and reaching out. Her tender hand rested against my chest. "My sister should hold no power over you ... not any longer. She didn't see what I saw in you, and she may never. Let it go. Let her go—for good. She should no longer matter, whether you amaze her when you reveal your true self or not."

My heart twisted with painful realization. I paused. Why did I still think about Nefertiti so often, her smiles as she stared at me in the palace and when she spoke of wanting every person to find happiness and comfort? But she also turned down my love for Akhenaten's power and probably ordered the assassination of a rival wife. I'd pursued many things my entire life to become the man she desired ... Was she still driving me—driving me to my death? Would I take everyone I loved with me? I grunted in frustration. Perhaps she'd been my end goal my entire life and had kept me going through all of the horrendous trials I'd encountered. So, no, I couldn't give up on her, on trying to pull her out of the darkness. Not now, that would mean giving up on everything—Father, Mother, my own life—failing completely. I couldn't do that now, not after everything I, and the others before me, had been through. "I do this for Father as well," I stepped around Mutnedjmet, "and for Mother, *and* for the magician."

"We haven't had more than a couple of hours to train these lepers in combat," Paramessu said from his position in his chariot, his pale eyes contrasting with the regrowing stubble of his brows and hair, which was red like flame. "We had months with the slaves we brought north, and still they lacked in ability."

I leapt into the chariot behind Paramessu as the lepers carried buckets to only their horses and poured dark liquid onto the animals' necks and backs, which painted their coats. Others used large or small brushes to add detail.

"The situation is much different." I patted my friend's back. "This army does not need to crush our enemy. We do not actually want to kill the soldiers of Egypt's military, even if they follow Pharaoh. We just need to terrify them."

We waited for the lepers to finish arming themselves and dressing for war.

Paramessu waved to Tia, and they both spun their chariots around and faced northwest. Mutnedjmet jumped into the chariot behind me, our horses still of natural color, but the lepers' animals had all been painted black and covered with jagged green stripes. Drums started to pound in my head—the same music I'd been hearing since I'd died then returned to the world of the living.

Harkhuf and Seneb rode with Tia as their driver. Chisisi rode with Wahankh—the men inside wielding bows, the drivers covering their archers with their shields. We'd all be keeping our eyes on Chisisi and Wahankh, although now there shouldn't be much that Chisisi could do other than attack us, and, with tens of thousands of Egyptian military men doing the same thing, that betrayal shouldn't make a bit of difference. And I wanted to know without a doubt who had actually turned on us, or if it was both of them.

Our army marched—a thousand feet crunching through the desert and a hundred pairs of wheels rattling.

We ate up the ground between us and the palace at a rapid pace, although we were still many miles away. The soldiers of the palace wouldn't see us for some time. Trumpets blared alongside the drums in my head. My fate was approaching more swiftly now than I wanted—although, for the vast majority of my life, this was all I'd yearned for. But now time would not slow down.

The thundering drums and trumpets fell silent. We crested a hill. The palace waited in the distance. This was it—the moment of calm before all chaos broke loose, before all of my planning and plotting played out and was decided in real life. The last moment of calm before I found out if my fate had been decided long before I was born or if I had altered it.

The palace would not even know we were attacking before it was too late; they'd never expect us to have chariots.

I forced a deep, cleansing breath. My eyes closed as I tapped Paramessu's shoulder.

He shouted and snapped the reins. Our horses reared onto their back legs. All around us chariot wheels spun, and men charged and screamed cries of war.

As a single unit, we barreled down the hillside, straight for the palace.

The drums in my head returned and grew deafening, like thunder that clapped over and over again. Our chariot rumbled beneath my feet, but the clatter of its wheels tearing through the dirt, the pounding footfalls of men, and the heaving of the horses were all drowned out.

Music rang.

Our horses charged, their legs extending as if each stride would cover a mile. Their nostrils flared, their eyes wild. Hooves pounded desert.

The desert blurred by as I set Croc down beside me. Nocking an arrow, I drew the taut string to my cheek. The sinew dug into my fingers.

Then it happened.

The horses to my right stumbled. One collapsed, tripping the other—both skidding across the desert with their tumbling chariot in a clatter of shattering of wood. The leper soldiers who'd been inside the chariot sailed out and rolled across rock and dirt. Stripes of green paint on the falling horses blurred against the black of their bodies. A horse far to my left did the same, dragging the other with it.

I gasped as I glanced back, watching steeds, chariots, and the people inside tumble out of control all around me.

More horses collapsed, decimating our army. The music in my head faded.

The arrow fell from my bow as the string slowly relaxed. I stared with wide eyes and a dangling jaw as I glanced all around. What kind of black magic was this?

The dust cloud from our infantry trailing behind us came closer as Paramessu slowed down our horses. Dirt also billowed from the skidding bodies of collapsing horses, carrying up into the sky as if to signal our defeat. The infantry stopped in their tracks, their jerking postures of surprise showing through the rising dust.

Chariots and horses lay twisted all around, and the cloud of gritty dust washed over us.

Our horses stopped under Paramessu's command of the reins, but they still pranced in place, their eyes and breathing wild.

The remaining chariots that hadn't toppled over—only my companions' and thirty others—halted.

Shocked silence hovered over the desert and intertwined with the dust.

We were still probably too far away for the soldiers in the palace to see us, but a massive swirling dust cloud would soon raise suspicion.

I stepped from my chariot, my hands searching for my swords.

My attention settled on Chisisi. What had this man done, and how? Rage boiled up from my stomach, my insides twisting like vines. Striding directly for him, I drew my swords.

Seneb's face was ashen as I moved past his and Harkhuf's chariot.

"I never should've trusted you again." I pointed at Chisisi with the tip of my sword. "Back in Crocodilopolis, when I overheard you talking to the smuggler, I should've known not to give you a second chance. When you offered risking the lives of my comrades for your rise in power, I should've known."

The companions all stared at me. Everyone stared. I'd never told them about Chisisi's treachery that almost cost Seneb his life—a sacrifice for trapping that giant beast of a crocodile. Now they all eyed me with judgment. Distrust hovered in the air thicker than the dust. I'd never be a powerful leader that people would fear. I was too weak. And by not telling them all the truth, even if it was because Chisisi had convinced me that they wouldn't believe it, they'd lose hope in me and give up like the dying horses around us.

I advanced. "I should've banished you or killed you then. I will not make that mistake again."

Chisisi held up his hands, letting the reins fall as his sharp features narrowed. "I regret my actions from our previous times together. But I have paid for them, and I am not responsible for this."

I didn't pause in my approach.

"Do what you must." Chisisi held out his arms—palms up in surrender. "I understand why you believe what you do. But this catastrophe is not my doing."

My eyes narrowed, and I glanced around. He acted just like Paramessu had and wouldn't even fight me. Everyone else focused on me. My insides still burned with rage. What would I do? Kill the man I believed responsible, to instill fear, like Akhenaten would? I could feel the power of my former master's dark character rising within me, threatening to swallow my soul. I would hold so much power over men. And I could rule them. My brain turned numb, my hands moving of their own accord. My swords rose. But my head turned.

My eyes locked on Wahankh, just in front of him.

He made a subtle cringe, but it was there.

I scrutinized him.

Shaking, Wahankh kicked Chisisi in the back, launching him from the chariot. Wahankh turned and snapped the reins. His horses barreled away for the palace.

"Fear is so thick on that one I could almost smell his leaking urine, like with a laughing woman who has had too many babies," Seneb said.

I turned back to Chisisi, who sat up from the dirt and shook his head, which released a puff of dust. He clutched his midsection, and his eyes bulged as he watched our companion flee to Akhenaten in fear of me. What had Wahankh done? The former bully who had confronted his demons … Had he realized that we were doomed and sided with the stronger, as he used to do? And he'd poisoned the horses—like I'd done with Akhenaten's men, slipping the poison into their water without anyone noticing. When he'd seen all the horses that we'd gathered, he must've known we'd use them to attack Akhenaten. He'd still betrayed us even though the others had never let him sneak away to inform anyone of our plans. My knees wobbled.

A hand settled onto my shoulder. Shrugging it off, I spun about, so disoriented that the horizon tilted. I stumbled and nearly fell. Mutnedjmet's soft face was lined with concern, her hand attempting reassurance.

The world around me was crumbling. Croc leapt from the chariot; his orange and white fur blurred as he raced away into the desert.

"In the real world, good doesn't always triumph over evil," Mutnedjmet said, closing her eyes.

"I've heard those words before." I swallowed. Images of me being dragged off to slavery by the vile Suty filled my mind—as if it were happening again, replaying all around me. I trembled with fear, the mind of my childhood self returning—unbroken, supple, still full of hope. Mutnedjmet's gentle face had been covered with tears. I was there—in the past—and also here in this same spot hearing her voice … "Those words were uttered by my own lips. I said: 'In the real world good doesn't always triumph over evil' when I was cast into slavery those long years ago. Do you remember what you told me then?"

She shook her head.

"'Only when you believe that does it become true,'" I replied.

Silence. Her eyes closed, and a single tear streaked down her cheek.

"'Otherwise you keep fighting,'" she said, recalling her final words of encouragement from the past. She opened her eyes and smiled—her smile and misty eyes like a beacon shining in the darkness of the turmoil all around me.

Perhaps I should turn and run … I'd never been so tempted—not with any episode of overwhelming fear that I'd experienced throughout my life. "We should run."

"No." Tears brimmed in her eyes, along with a burning fire. "Not even I should hope to dissuade you now—not even for my own desires in this life. You need to do this, for all of us, for all of Egypt."

Chapter 56

Journal Translation

"FOLLOW BEHIND ME," I shouted to the leper army as I nudged Paramessu. He released the horses' reins, and our chariot rolled for the palace, its wood vibrating under my feet as we crossed the bumpy desert.

I glanced back. The eastern mountains, the cradle between the two peaks that we'd once fled over, the peaks that had drawn Akhenaten to this very place—the birthplace of the rising Aten—turned to dark silhouettes. Now the Aten's sphere sank into the western hills, searching for the underworld.

A few of the lepers stepped forward—the remainder not moving. But they'd all heeded my commands and wrapped their bodies in white linen.

"Do not stop," I said to Paramessu. "They will follow. The most important battles are fought daily, with ourselves—inside ourselves—those which no one else can observe. And at the time of a great war, perhaps the outcome has already been decided ... based on each side's preparations."

Paramessu nodded. Our companions' horses trotted beside us, towing their rumbling chariots—including Chisisi's, with a leper driver.

We'd now appear as the feeblest of attacking armies—delusional or mad.

Horns from the palace blared in the distance. They must've seen our dust cloud and now prepared for our arrival.

I glanced back. Only a few more of the leper mummies had joined the advancing ranks.

Paramessu wheeled the horses about, the tight turn throwing me against the railing of the chariot.

"Do not turn around," I said.

"I will not abandon you." He drove the horses at a gallop back to our army. "Not only for your souls," he yelled, his voice booming as he pointed at the lepers, "but for the souls of all those who came before us, our fathers and mothers—and for all those we leave this world to. Follow Heb, now, or live forever fearing the judgment of Anubis and his real monster—the one we will all face either this day with Akhenaten or the next with Anubis."

"We will surely die today if we march on that palace," a man in the front lines shouted, his arm thick and lumpy beneath its linen wrappings as he pointed at his people. "Do not create an illusion of hope for us. We are but poor lepers who have come to accept our world. Do not be deceitful."

My insides cramped, my stomach churning and boiling over with acid and emotion. Everything I'd felt and held back all the years of my life poured out like water over a fall. "Acceptance of your world is what all of this is about." The echoes of my voice carried around me like trumpets. Drums started to pound in my head again. "What if this was your chance to change your fate? What if you had but one moment in your life to stand and face the powers of evil—those who told you that you were nothing? Those who truly believe they are better than you because of who their father or mother was, or because of what the head of their god is, or because of a disease that you are unlucky enough to contract?"

Paramessu snapped the reins and trotted the horses before the ranks of our mentally defeated army.

"Would you pass your miserable lives on down to your children? Years from now, they will speak of your offspring as the sons and daughters of the lepers who were outcasts from society for the entirety of their lives." I studied the masses. Trumpets blared with the drums in my head. "They will remember your actions. Then, would you wish to return here to this moment and choose again so that you could look your children in the eye—the very beings that make life worth living and fighting for—and tell them to be proud of who they are, be proud of where they came from?" I pointed across the ranks of the lepers as the horses broke into a gallop, their hooves thundering as we raced before their lines, the wind blowing across my face and through my short hair. The drums amplified in my head. "To be proud of you, their parents … because that one day long ago, their mothers and fathers stood side by side as equals to *any* man in Egypt. And those mothers and fathers fought alongside one former slave and overthrew the tyranny suffocating all but one man."

Complete and utter silence reigned. Paramessu wheeled the horses around and drove us back across the forefront of their ranks.

"Today is that day." I nocked an arrow on my bow. "In this moment! To live now is to live forever. Do not let yourselves and your children grow old and die having been forced to worship at the shrine of deceit—created only to ensure Pharaoh's power."

I raised my bow overhead and loosed the arrow. It flew straight up into the final rays of the setting Aten. The metal tip sparkled before it faded into the blinding cap of the sphere.

"Some of you may have wished for this choice to have fallen upon another. But you were put here to decide what is right and what is wrong. What will you choose? What will you tolerate? This is your one chance—the last chance for you and your children to take Egypt back."

Drums raged inside my head, shaking my entire body as the chariot bounced beneath my feet. Twilight settled over the land. Spears beat against shields by the hundreds—a roaring applause as the army of lepers stood straighter. Men and women screamed, as if they had just been born into this world at the same time of day that I had been. My skin throbbed with a power and warmth I had not known a mortal man could experience. The power of the gods coursed through my blood, fighting against the consuming disease that made its home there.

The air above our army wavered, as if every *ba* of Egypt—every one of the dead—flew around and disrupted the heavy weight attempting to suffocate our hope. My breaths came easier, the air cleaner and crisp. The cheering of the lepers grew louder and created a roar that echoed off the cliffs before carrying across the entire valley of el-Amarna.

"I can see why you are a leader of men." Paramessu spun the chariot around and galloped our horses toward the palace on pounding hooves.

The leper mummies shouted and marched after us.

"Lead the mass of them away," I said to Chisisi, "until we are ready. We will approach the front gates ourselves."

Dust again billowed into the air but this time lifted much higher—to signal the heavens of its need to prepare for the coming dead. The desert floor whisked by beneath us as soldiers funneled out of the palace like bees whose hive had been struck. Their spears and shields formed ranks outside of the walls but in disarray. Torches sprang to life in their midst and along the palace's walls. There must've been tens of thousands of them. We had no chance of winning this war.

A hundred yards from the front line of Egypt's police and military, Paramessu pulled the horses to a sliding stop. Only fifty armed lepers followed us as darkness spread over the land. Chisisi had led the rest away, and Tia had driven the dwarves out of sight.

A rumble of laughter erupted from the massive force of soldiers who witnessed the numbers of our pitiful army.

"The army of the dead is here to claim Pharaoh." My voice carried over their masses and echoed off the palace walls as I lit a torch and held it over my head. "Akhenaten's evil reign will release its hold on the world with the setting of today's Aten. But I offer each of you the chance to join me now in victory or to throw down your arms and leave the palace. If you do so, you will not be punished."

Hearty laughter filled the thick ranks of military and policemen.

"I have walked the land of the *Duat,* breathed the same air as Anubis and Osiris while they weighed my heart and, yes, I am not afraid to utter their names," I shouted as the fading twilight turned to darkness. "They are as real as the Aten, as real as you were taught when you were young, and their wrath is coming."

Nothing happened. It was Chisisi's turn to help fulfill his end of plan … would he also betray me? Were both he and Wahankh working together?

The rumble of chariot wheels surrounded us as my eyes adjusted to torch- and veiled moonlight. I tensed. Black steeds with green stripes and eyes pranced in from our left and right, appearing as beasts from the underworld. They snorted through flared nostrils—a sound like bass trumpets—and circled my companions and me. Could the horses sense the coming battle, the death? They stomped their hooves with impatience.

The lepers in the chariots lit torches of their own and rode in disarray through the desert around us, hefting mighty spears. Other figures slowly rose from the desert floor as if clawing their way through the earth, lumpy and twisted bodies wrapped in tattered linens and holding spears or swords. They staggered about as others shambled in from the periphery, hundreds of them.

A murmur arose from the Egyptian army as they stumbled back, their fear wafting across the desert and reeking like decaying flesh. Eyes peered over their shields as they glanced around and at each other, but no one moved. My fingers squeezed the shaft of my bow. We'd still never be able to crush their ranks.

"Hold your lines," an elderly but fit man bellowed, stepping forward with his spear and shield in an attack position, as if he would stop us all. "These dead men cannot consume your souls like Pharaoh's pet—the Devouring Monster—will if you do not fight!"

"Father?" Paramessu said, his strong jaw clenching.

The elderly man's chin jutted back as he stood straight and studied us. Paramessu drove our chariot through the staggering lepers, approaching this man.

The old man shook his wrinkled face and gray-stubbled head. "No, my son, the former captain of the military, fled his company when they were attacked by pirates on the east to west road many years ago."

Paramessu's breathing turned deep and raspy.

"He was always a coward," Paramessu's father said, "and he was never to be seen or heard from again. I was not surprised, only disappointed. He never would've changed, not that boy." His arm tensed on his spear. "And it was better for me to discover his true self when he was young rather than have him hide it all the years of my life and take my place after I was gone."

Paramessu's shoulders sagged. "I had actually found the fleeing slaves. They abducted me and my ship. The military pursued us, but we were lost at sea."

The old man's face only hardened. "Abducted by slaves? You can be no son of mine. I should've known when you were born, born with the red hair—so unlike the rest of the family. I should've understood the sign of weakness that the Aten had already placed upon you."

"I've seen the world." Paramessu's hands shook the reins in sheer anger—something I'd never seen from my friend. "And I've found a woman that I love more than life itself. I've discovered that the slaves who took me were greater men and women than those leading our country. I discovered that I should not blindly follow the orders of a madman in the desecrated name of honor and duty. I have grown."

"My son is dead." The man's face was red, and blood vessels bulged from his temples as if they would burst and spew the first human blood of the battle.

I placed a hand on Paramessu's rigid back. "I am sorry, my friend," I whispered. Then I addressed Paramessu's father. "This man's hair is not a warning; it is reminiscent of the Aten—not Akhenaten—given to him to proclaim his insight and loyalty to those he loves. He cannot be turned by blood or fear. He has lived and determined for himself what is right and what is wrong, and there is no man I'd rather die beside—no man I'd rather call my friend."

His father's hate-filled sneer turned to me. "And you are what? A would-be usurper of Egypt? A barbarian? You are nothing. And soon you will be dead, your soul devoured. We are all only an amalgam of the people that we surround ourselves with. Perhaps, then, it is not all my son's fault that he is the way he is, but also yours—him being only a mirror of your weaknesses."

"Your son's bravery, honor, trustworthiness, ability to love, and valor have rubbed off on me, not the other way around," I said. "I am a better man for knowing him. And now that I look upon his father, I realize that his traits must've been learned elsewhere—especially his ability to love, as that could not have come from you."

Paramessu's father shouted over his shoulder, "This man is well known for using trickery to win battles. Everything that you see around you is nothing more than that."

A single leper shambled toward Paramessu's father. This was the leper with the lumpy arm—three times its normal thickness—and in a mechanical movement, as if he were mesmerized, he raised his affected limb over his head.

The high-pitched whistling of an arrow carried through the night, quickly followed by more. Almost instantaneously, four arrows buried with dull thuds into the linen-wrapped forearm of the leper. The arrows appeared to come from the Egyptian army but would've been the work of Harkhuf and Seneb.

Nothing else happened. The scene lay quiet and still, all eyes watching.

The leper bellowed with laughter, his deep rumbling voice carrying out and echoing as if he were still at the bottom of the pit I'd found him in.

Then another man appeared under the surrounding torchlight, a man with green skin—Chisisi, painted like one of the horses, like the skin of Osiris himself. He boldly marched up to the lead leper in the middle ground between both armies.

Chisisi pulled a sword from his belt, screamed, and with one swift cut, severed the leper's arm above the elbow. The limb fell to the desert floor with a thud. No blood. The leper simply held out his shortened arm and laughed louder, sounding like the most maniacal madman I could imagine.

"The people of my world have arrived," Chisisi yelled.

Paramessu's father's jaw dropped in horror.

The shields of the Egyptian army crashed together as they all stumbled back in fear.

"The diseased tissues of a leper carry no blood or pain," I whispered to Paramessu, his hands still shaking on the reins.

Paramessu trotted our horses up to our dismembered soldier. Chisisi, the man I'd given a second chance to, nodded in my direction. And he hadn't let me down after all. My heart quivered, and my stomach felt hollow. I'd almost killed him because I'd assumed that he'd betrayed us—the man who'd tempted me to believe that my mercy would be all of our undoing ...

Paramessu stopped our chariot beside Chisisi and the leper and said to me, "Perhaps your trust in people, and hope in spite of everything, will be the only reason you could lead these people to victory over the ruthless."

I choked back emotion, and the warmth that battled with the disease inside of me carried into my limbs. Akhenaten could have his Wahankhs of the world—those who only followed out of fear or for their own well-being. And we would use that against them all. We'd instill more fear in the coming battle than even their master would. My mind grew light, and it felt as if it lifted from my body in wonder—as if I were floating amongst the world of the living, like a *ba,* as if I were still dead and had never truly returned from the underworld but was only visiting this world for this very moment.

Tia rode her chariot with the brothers inside up to us.

"Unlike you," I shouted, pointing the bronze tip of my sword at their army, "my soldiers feel no pain. They feel no fear. The curse of the dead, the curse of the mummy, has descended upon you for your master's treachery. The dead cannot be killed again. The Aten has set and is no longer here to protect you. And tonight, the dead have come to reclaim Egypt." I prayed that Wahankh, being true to his character, had raced back into the safety of the palace as fast as he could and hadn't stopped to tell any of these soldiers about our deceitful army.

We advanced, the lepers stepping forward and surrounding our chariots in a wedge formation.

Thousands of the military men turned and fled into the night. Others pounded on and then forced open the gates of the palace and ran inside. The fear wafting from their army now smelled sweeter, like the fragrance of blooming lotuses—and I savored it.

Paramessu's father snarled and lunged forward, charging at the lead lepers by himself, his spear and shield swinging and waving like the arms of a furious beast.

But the lepers surrounded him and grabbed his flailing limbs, dragging him down into their midst. Linen-wrapped bodies covered the area, not creating a single sound. Paramessu's father's shouts of sheer rage turned muffled and then faded to silence.

More soldiers fled, and the remaining Egyptian military recoiled. Akhenaten was a fool not to be here now, driving greater fear into his soldiers' hearts.

Paramessu sniffed, his hooked nose wrinkling, his strong jaw tensing. I patted his shoulder, but he looked to Tia, who drove her horses up beside us and reached out for his hand.

Tia nodded at her lover. "You are my hero."

My heart softened. These were the people I'd chosen to be part of, because they were not like his father, not like Suty, not like Pentju, not like Akhenaten, not like the person Nefertiti had become.

The lepers continued their advance, and Paramessu drove us onward, but still thousands of soldiers blocked the open gates.

I'd driven off those who followed Akhenaten out of fear, mostly fear of having their souls devoured, turning that against those susceptible. Now it was time to turn those who followed Pharaoh's lies and manipulation.

Several of the remaining faces in the front lines appeared familiar—men I'd led into battle against the Hittites. Some were good men who despised Akhenaten's character and his rule. They'd want nothing more than to have a just and kind leader who cared for the kingdom and its people, but they followed Akhenaten because they believed he was the rightful pharaoh, the immortal god-king, and they couldn't even consider opposing him. And others were even loyal to me.

"Those whose souls are loyal to Egypt, even if they are not loyal to this pharaoh, will be spared if you move aside," I shouted.

Another face stood out, a man in the front lines holding a spear—Mahu. His eyes narrowed as he studied my newly exposed, maskless face. He pointed at me. "You should not have returned."

"Mahu," I said as we approached, "my friend. I know the soul that lives within you. And you know what Akhenaten has done to our kingdom, the downward spiral we've seen since the death of Amenhotep. I know you care for the people. Think of the children in the barracks, those you helped feed over the decades. And remember the innocent bodies of all of those lying in the streets after Pharaoh poisoned them to retaliate against the actions of others. Akhenaten does not have the character of a leader you'd like to protect. You knew that when you helped his young servant boy many years ago—the boy whom you saw sneak through a window to get back into his room after he'd been out investigating but was supposed to be quarantined for a fake plague." Then I yelled, "Akhenaten is not a pharaoh any of you would willingly throw down your lives for."

Mahu's chin and head lurched back in surprise. But he quickly recovered and hefted his spear, angling it at me as if he would throw the weapon.

My heart twinged. "I will not fight you, Mahu," I said as we advanced, like Paramessu and Chisisi had done when I'd wanted to fight them. I already harbored far too much guilt, and the lives lost in obtaining my revenge weighed heavy on my conscience, although I ignored it as much as I could until this was all over. "I am the boy I just mentioned. And now I am returning the favor—giving you an opportunity. You know that Akhenaten must be stopped. Call your men away. They will listen to you."

Mahu's eyes closed, and his spear hand fell to his side.

We continued our approach.

The remaining soldiers pressed their backs against the walls of the palace but raised their spears and shields like cornered snakes ready to strike.

"Let them through." Mahu stepped out of the path of our chariot and faced his men.

Gaping eyes from policemen and soldiers all across the outer walls focused on him.

"Policemen of el-Amarna," Mahu yelled. "Return to the city and defend its children. The fight here is beyond us. Only the gods of Egypt should remain."

Soldiers parted in our wake, revealing the open gates of the palace.

Paramessu snapped the reins, and the horses lunged forward, the chariots of my companions following at our heels. The lepers closed in behind us, and some followed, but most stayed to guard the gates.

The banished and the dead of Egypt: the lepers; my companions, the former slaves; and even myself, Akhenaten's former servant, had all coerced our way into Pharaoh's private palace.

Chapter 57

Journal Translation

W E LEAPT OUT OF THE CHARIOTS, our weapons ready as we raced through the lamplit halls of the palace, our pounding footsteps echoing along the corridors, sounding like our entire army followed us.

Mutnedjmet sprinted at my side, a spear and shield in her hands, as determined as anyone to face Akhenaten. The pattering drums and blaring trumpets returned and filled my head.

Harkhuf let three consecutive arrows fly in a flash, and Seneb released another. Royal guards collapsed in the hallway ahead as arrow shafts thudded into them and protruded from their chests.

Adrenaline flowed through my veins and muscles, making my limbs feel numb but inexhaustible. And my mind was still keen, questioning every turn, every decision on where to go. How many royal guards and soldiers would still be inside the palace? There were tens of thousands outside, but hundreds could still be inside.

My companions and the small army of lepers trailing us threw spears, released arrows, and shouted. More bodies of dead soldiers piled up in the shadowy halls as we raced on.

Yelling erupted behind us, along with the clash of metal and wood—the royal guards confronting and fighting with the lepers. I couldn't see back through the narrow hallways, but we'd never make it if we turned around to help.

The doorway I'd been waiting for emerged. The audience hall and Akhenaten's favorite throne would be waiting on the other side. I slowed and signaled for the others to follow behind me. The drumming music in my head silenced.

My hands and limbs, even my very soul, shook with dread—the confrontation I'd been waiting for my entire life drew near. But all of the previous confrontations I'd ever had with this god-king had ended in misery. I was a man now, grown and tempered as if a weapon composed of both mind and body, but could that match Akhenaten's malevolence, immortal power, and magic?

Visions of my recent failure ran through my mind. This was my last chance, Egypt's last chance.

The hum of a hushed voice entered my mind, as if it wanted to sing out, but the music had stopped. An arrow fell from my hand and clattered onto the tile at my feet, my breathing rapid and shallow.

"Do not fear this moment," Mutnedjmet said, clinging to my back with fingers as steady as the rock foundations of the tombs of old. "The fate of your soul is not decided by one crowning moment but rather by a series of choices at many points in time—throughout your life. You've already made your decisions, your preparations, your training on everything up to the present—to these breaths that we take together. The moment is here, and there's no need to question or doubt yourself now."

Images of the past floated around me—memories of my life flashing before my eyes. I'd had so many choices: stealing the pomegranate for Akhenaten, which had led to my indentured servitude; serving Akhenaten better than anyone else so that he only desired my services more; turning back for Akhenaten's drowned body before he was pharaoh and wrongly believing that I'd return to Amenhotep a hero; not running away when the magician offered me the chance to flee Egypt without Nefertiti; choosing to stay with Nefertiti even though it meant I'd serve the murderer of my own father, which poisoned my soul so deeply I would never recover—the rot still festering in my heart; asking Nefertiti to run away with me for love but being turned down for wealth and power; finding friends and traveling to the corners of the known world in search of answers while revisiting each of their homes as well as the demons buried in their pasts; stepping up and choosing to become their leader when they needed one, when their other option was luring them into danger; then forgiving that man and reaccepting him into our group; dying in order become stronger; returning to Egypt and el-Amarna to infiltrate the military and royalty at the risk of our very souls; and finally now to face Akhenaten and Nefertiti.

I forced a deep breath, turned, and hugged Mutnedjmet, breathing in her essence. How beautiful this world could be, and yet how savage had we the people made it.

"Of all my trusted friends and advisors," I said to her, "you are my greatest. I only wish I'd had the wisdom to listen long ago."

She pulled me close, planted a tender kiss on my lips, then shoved me away. Drums beat in unison, deep and echoing, but to a slow rhythm.

I stepped through the last bit of darkness of the corridor, and the light of a raging bonfire erupted around me, the ceiling opening to the night sky above the audience hall.

Guards … everywhere, at least a couple hundred. And somewhere in here was Wahankh, who would let everyone know our mummies were fake.

I nocked an arrow but stepped back, bumping into Harkhuf, who grunted.

I shoved my companions back. "There are too many. Run the other way!"

My companions turned and fled, and I followed, my sandals slapping against the hard tile.

"Finish them." Akhenaten's booming voice rang out, carrying after us. "All of you, go. And if you cannot bring him back to me alive, bring me his head and his heart!"

Soldiers bellowed and pursued us. The rhythm of the drums escalated. The soldiers would trap us inside the tight corridors …

"Turn left," I shouted to Chisisi, who was now at the forefront of my companions, the group of maybe fifty lepers letting us pass.

Pounding footfalls echoed through the hallways, the entire palace booming with cries.

Harkhuf loosed three more arrows in rapid succession, dropping three soldiers in our path. Seneb, Paramessu, Tia, and Chisisi skewered more.

We turned and weaved through the maze of the palace. My comrades would have no idea where I was leading them—our only real escape.

We ran on and eventually passed by the wall where Mutnedjmet and I had kissed. The gentle humming voice in my head returned, this time complementing stringing chords of music.

Bright firelight and crackling emerged again as we reentered the audience hall, our only escape. But most of the lepers stayed behind to guard the corridors.

The hundred-odd soldiers remaining inside the chamber spun around and lurched back in surprise.

Akhenaten lounged on his throne, his face and body in shadow. But he laughed, an echoing bellow that reverberated around the expansive chamber, sounding like our leper who'd pulled off the stunt of laughing while having his own arm cut off. "Kill them, now."

The soldiers readied their weapons and shields and advanced.

"I will release so many arrows that it will appear as if the sky is raining, but raining destruction, like locusts in a pestilence," Harkhuf said as his first arrow sailed from his bow. Seneb turned to his brother, his mouth agape, appearing more unable to believe the comparison that he'd just uttered rather than our approaching deaths. Harkhuf's hands blurred as he released lines of arrows.

Seneb jerked, faced the guards, and loosed arrows of his own, albeit not even at a third of the rate of his brother.

Many soldiers fell—single shafts buried into lethal areas of their bodies that I did not even know had been exposed: the trachea, the carotid artery, through the nose … And then still more toppled over, their ranks being decimated by the arrows of the greatest archer Egypt had ever seen.

But still they advanced.

Ten, then twenty, and even thirty bodies piled up.

A soldier lunged, jabbing his spear at my chest.

I parried his strike out wide with one of my swords, the impact jarring my arm. And I swung for his lead hand with my other sword, but his hand was too far away. Instead, I severed the shaft of his spear with a crack, and the end with the point skittered away. The soldier grunted but swung the wooden handle at me to keep me at bay as he stepped back.

My companions and the few lepers in our midst stabbed at the soldiers as they encircled us—metal ringing on metal or burying into rawhide shields.

But the dwarf brother's arrows continued to execute them, sneaking past any opening in their defenses as the soldiers moved, blocked, or attacked.

I parried a spear strike from another soldier, and that man fell, the fletching of an arrow's shaft protruding from his forehead—just beneath his padded helmet.

The soldiers around us toppled over into piles along with all of our lepers but one. A spear tore into the still-green skin of Chisisi's upper chest. He hollered in pain and dropped to his knees but did not fall. Tia hovered beside Paramessu, striking but unable to drop many of the trained soldiers. Mutnedjmet stood behind me, swinging and jabbing with her spear, which kept some of the approaching soldiers away. But there were still too many. Five soldiers came at me at once, led by one man, his draping shoulders familiar—the traitor, the bully who in the end could not overcome his fear nor side with his friends. He'd chosen the powerful, his weakness ingrained in his soul. Wahankh. The spear in his hands shook as much as it had when he'd stood up to the Devouring Monster for a second in order for us to escape Thebes.

Rage burned inside of me, but I lowered my swords. "You made an unwise choice with us and our horses."

But he and the soldiers around him lunged and struck together. I ducked and parried like a flailing beast, and only the tip of one spear sank into my calf. The other four pulled their deflected weapons back to strike again. But I felt no pain. Wahankh struck—

Three arrows lodged into his face, one in each eye and another through his gaping mouth, pinning him to the rawhide shield of the soldier beside him—the work of Harkhuf, the impossible feat that when accomplished in battle would make him a master archer of Kush, the first in centuries.

Blood drained from Wahankh's eyes and mouth as his body hung motionless.

I stood still for a full second in sheer awe.

The fifty remaining soldiers froze in fear at the sight before glancing around at each other. A dozen fled in terror.

Arrows still rained, sinking into the remaining soldiers' flesh.

"Retreat," Maya called out. He sat on the raised platform and pointed at the far exits, though he should have no real command over these men.

Half of the soldiers turned and fled the hall on pounding feet. The other half advanced but were massacred by arrows. Only a few soldiers remained alongside the piles of the dead, and Paramessu and Tia skewered them.

I pivoted away, sprinted, and leapt up the stairs to the throne.

Chapter 58

Journal Translation

MAYA, THE ROYAL SCRIBE who'd watched over my companions and me when we were slaves, backed away from me as I landed upon the raised platform housing the throne of Egypt. I pulled the Scorpion Macehead of King Menes from a strap running across my back. The ancient weapon of the conqueror felt light in my hands, as if anticipating devouring the soul of Akhenaten.

Drums pounded in my head, ringing my skull.

Nefertiti stood on shaking legs, slunk away from Pharaoh, and cowered in the shadows behind the thrones—the Devouring Monster couldn't also be hiding back there; there wasn't enough shadow to hide a creature that size. Still, I wished I could've carried Croc into the palace with me, but he'd run off around the time I'd witnessed the devastating shock of all our dead horses. And no other royal family member was present ... not Ay, not Beketaten, not Tut. Were they hiding in their rooms—waiting for the attack on the palace to end?

But Akhenaten still sat on his throne, in shadow, apparently alone again as he twirled something in his hand—his eyes focused only on it. Deep blue ... a feather ... the Feather of Truth. The music in my head quieted. I'd given it to Nefertiti during our last encounter, to remember me. But now, did Akhenaten finally know the truth?

I stepped toward Pharaoh, but he was still seated, so calm and relaxed, as if he'd anticipated everything playing out to this very moment—as if he knew exactly what would happen next.

He glanced up at me, the black above his eyes growing as he squinted into the firelight shining at my back. He'd see my newly cut hair and shaven body, but would he recognize the face of his servant boy from so long ago?

"Do you know what this is?" His deep voice was steady as it reverberated inside his throat, as if he had all the time in the world. He raised the deep blue feather and twirled it in the margin between firelight and shadow, its barbs reflecting the light like metal.

I paused then said, "The Feather of Truth. From the goddess Ma'at, the keeper of time—whom every god must answer to, including every male god, as well as every man."

He dismissed me with a flick of his wrist. "One of your own had a bit of wisdom, although I did not fully believe him." He examined the reflected light on the feather as he nodded at the dead bodies below—probably indicating Wahankh. "Your comrade informed me that you wished to usurp the throne, but that coward for some reason seemed to believe that you are the grown man of a servant boy that I used to own. It is ludicrous, I know." He laughed. "But you will not deceive me. The boy he spoke of could not read or write, could not even lift the weapon that you now carry—much less defeat anyone in battle."

I inched forward, hoping to catch him off guard. He still seemed so unconcerned.

"And I do not care what lies you feed your people," Akhenaten tapped his sunken cheek, which created a hollow echo in his mouth, "but you will not trick me into false anger. You are a traitor to Egypt. Your rise to power gave you a taste for it, and now you desire the full meal. But you are nothing more than that—not *that* boy. And you will remain nothing from this moment on, forever."

I scrutinized his golden regalia, his body, and the seat of the throne beside him. What weapon did he have hidden—a magic spell?

"The mind can only comprehend what it understands," I said.

Akhenaten's eyelids grew like empty sockets, his towering double crown shading his face. His lips pulled back into a sneer.

"You still cannot comprehend such a change in a person, because you believe it is impossible," I said and tapped the hard stone of the mace head into my open palm. "That is your weakness."

"I have no weaknesses!" His voice echoed around the open chamber and rang my ears. "And I still would not have even believed your comrade had I not seen this feather and now your arrogance." He held the ostrich feather aloft like a torch. "I do not know what magic you possess to have escaped and survived for all of those years, but I sense very little within you. Aided by others, perhaps, but no threat yourself—especially if you are that scrawny boy. That is why I am unconcerned." His dark eyes snapped up and stared into mine, freezing my body in an instant. Would he crush my chest with his magic and not allow me to breathe—like when we were—

Pressure surrounded me, clamping down on my chest and throat like some kind of giant snake constricted around me. Was this magic or only suffocating fear? I strained for shallow, hoarse breaths, feeling as if I were drowning in the lake again—being pulled down against my will.

He grinned as he studied me. "But do you know why you were special? Why I liked you so much despite your many shortcomings? Why I decided to keep you as my servant?"

I could not speak. Rage ignited in my heart, and my stomach twisted and knotted. His magic and his words could not stop me now.

But footsteps pounded and echoed out of the doorway we'd used to enter the audience hall: the arrival of the other hundred royal guards who'd chased us out of the hall the first time and who must've killed the other lepers.

Harkhuf spun around and raced back to cover the entrance, firing the last of his arrows into the darkness of the corridor. Tia rushed over with bundles of arrows that had been strapped to her back and placed them on Harkhuf's body. Harkhuf entered the narrow opening, where only one man could face him at a time. Seneb sprinted to the entrance and shot arrows over his brother's shoulder. But there would surely be so many of the enemy that even after wading through the bodies of their comrades, they would eventually overcome my friends.

"You were the first," Akhenaten said, and my eyes twitched back over to focus on him.

I strained to move, my muscles burning but unyielding as I fought against whatever invisible power he held over me.

"You were an experiment of sorts." He smiled. "You see, you were the very first person to hear and to believe that the Aten was the *only* god. My father was headed toward that path, but I took it much further. I hated the gods for how they shaped me and for where they placed me in this world—so close to becoming the god-king, and yet I would never have been able to obtain such greatness. But I single-handedly bent and twisted fate."

I dug deep, summoning all the magic I felt coursing through my blood and bones, and recited spells from the Book of the Dead. Sensation returned to my tongue and mouth so that my soul could breathe and eat—the same spell I'd needed to face the trials of the underworld.

"But I wanted to observe you." He stared off into the dead bodies littering the hall below. "You who worshipped only the Aten, you who were completely ignorant of the other gods—especially Amun. I wondered if you would be struck down by lightning or a plague … or find some other horrible end. But I found that time and time again, the only thing that seemed to keep you in your place was *me*. And you, too, kept trying to alter fate for yourself." He paused as he took a long, deep breath. "I have garnered so much power over the years, and yours is minute, of no consequence, but I should never have had to be envious of you, not even for a moment, *ever!*" He snarled. "A pitiful servant boy." His voice rang out and carried up to the heavens.

An ember sparked within me. I paused from my recollection and casting of spells that would help me regain control of my body. Stringed instruments played in my head. I'd struck my greatest enemy in my own subtle way—hardly enough to appease me for his actions against Father, Nefertiti, or myself, but it was something I had not realized. My voice strained just to whisper. "Why? If you saw the afterlife and the Aten, why do all this?"

Storm clouds formed in his dark eyes. "It is true; I have already been there once. I have seen it. We were all part of the same universe—all connected in a web of space and time. There were no gods to reward kindness or dignity. That is why the corrupt and the greedy obtain power over the meek like you, only to be rewarded. Do you understand now? Our world is the world of the gods, with the Aten and Pharaoh. The underworld is for the mortals—everyone being equal there. Here, Pharaoh's law dictates the way everything shall be. I never wanted to become a small, equal part of the universe, a fragment. I need more. And if not in the next world, then I must sculpt this one—the world of the living—into my greatest work of art. Here, I will be remembered forever."

"Anubis will punish you." The volume of my voice increased. The harp and the beat of a percussive drum sounded in my head, joining the orchestra along with the humming voice.

"Ah, yes." He sighed. "The other gods. It will not be all about the Aten before I go to the underworld. Claiming the Aten for myself was ingenious, but still even I desire an Osirian death—to live amongst the greatest of Egypt's men ... for eternity. I will return to the old ways, ask for the favor of the other gods, and make the appropriate offerings before I die. Yes, a traditional religion for myself—in the moments just before my time is up."

I stood dumbfounded and paralyzed, the ancient mace head that hopefully housed some magnificent power now dangling from within my numb fingers. Was madness really just a façade on his quest for ultimate power?

"And what of all the other people, those you forbade to worship the other gods? What would happen to them in the next life?"

He waved off my question with another flick of his wrist. "But I am actually ecstatic that you survived and have returned, although I cannot even remember your name." He used a gangly finger to trace the outline of the mane of one of the sphinxes on his throne.

"Heb," I said, and then I whispered more words from the ancient spells of the Book of the Dead. Tingling started in my hands and feet and spread up my limbs. The humming voice grew louder.

"I care not," he said. "But I had lost sleep at night thinking that you may have died of thirst in the desert or drowned at sea decades ago and that no one would ever recover your body. You see, you insulted me, propositioning my greatest prize—Nefertiti. I had to accept that you may have achieved the afterlife and there was nothing I could do about it. And I also despised the legend of the boy who'd loved so deeply and was so heartbroken that he still haunted the wastelands of Egypt. But now," his lips pulled back into a devious smirk, "I can end all of my suffering. Your soul will be devoured, and your legend will finally die with it, here and now."

A woman screamed.

My head jerked to the side, my muscles still feeling thick, as if they were thawing out.

Mutnedjmet ... A figure in black, with a draping hood, had grabbed her from behind. Seneb and Harkhuf were still occupied, defending the entrance—or many royal guards would come rushing in. Paramessu and Tia approached the Devouring Monster, their weapons angled to attack. Chisisi still remained on his knees, clutching his hemorrhaging chest, which streamed red across his green skin from the buried spear. But he collapsed in a pool of blood, as if fear of the Devourer had sent his anemic body over the edge.

The crocodile-bone blade rose into the air, in the Devouring Monster's mangled lion hand, its hilt of gold flashing in the firelight. The reek of death and decay wafted by.

"No!" I finished another spell and control of my body returned. I could almost see Anubis and the scales beside him, as if we all stood in the Chamber of Judgment now.

Akhenaten rose and approached the edge of the raised platform. "I have decided that consuming your heart first would be too easy." He pointed at me and laughed, a diabolical chuckle. "You will have to suffer first."

"I will run," I said as I fell to my knees. I'd gone way too far without heeding any of my companions' words of wisdom. My need for vengeance would cost everyone I loved their very souls, and now it was too late. I was as vile as Akhenaten for giving their souls up as readily as he'd take them. As the magician had said, revenge was seeping from my heart and through my bones and tissues, rotting my insides like I'd have it do to my enemies. But instead, I'd suffered much more than my enemies ever would.

The Devouring Monster swung its blade of bone but rested its serrated edge of teeth against Mutnedjmet's light dress and heaving chest.

"Kill him, Heb," Mutnedjmet yelled. "This is the last chance—for Egypt."

"Stop," I said. "Akhenaten, I will take her and my comrades and leave Egypt forever. I will never look upon you or Nefertiti again. You can have the final and complete victory. I will relinquish everything if you stop that monster from harming Mut—"

Pharaoh's head fell back as he roared with laughter. "I will have the final victory, but it is too late to change your desires now." He motioned to the Devouring Monster.

Serrated teeth tore into Mutnedjmet's silky dress. Red ran down her chest.

A deafening roar echoed off of the walls as a beast galloped around the bodies of the dead—a giant cat, orange and white. Its joints flexed, its muscles contracting and bulging as it crouched. It pounced and flew through the air.

Sailing over twenty feet, the beast barreled into the cloaked figure with a thud and a crash. They were both sent sprawling. Mutnedjmet collapsed.

The cloaked figure rose, spun around to face Croc, and leapt over to Mutnedjmet's body. "The sphinx has been healed," the Devouring Monster hissed as it crouched and positioned its blade in a defensive stance.

My mind went blank. A sphinx? *He who controls the sphinx rules Egypt ...* I'd heard it many times since I was a child: a fisherman on the banks of the Nile when I'd rescued Croc as a kitten, a familiar old man atop the watchtower at Elephantine, then at Memphis, Thebes, el-Amarna, the palaces, lands far beyond Egypt, Crocodilopolis, the *ba* in the underworld—each time spoken by an old man with wrinkles like trenches and spider veins engulfing his face ... each time the magician calling out to me, cultivating my mind and abilities. But all along, I'd thought that the sphinxes were stone cats guarding temples and palaces ...

Croc rose up on his hind feet, his long tail flicking through the air as he stalked the Devouring Monster.

The Devourer's weapon arm coiled up to strike like a snake, but its other hand reached out and squeezed Mutnedjmet's throat. "Leap at me, sphinx," it hissed. "You cannot kill me in one strike, and even if you harm me, I'll decapitate you, and you'll then be nothing more than a monument for this palace, cast into stone and the head of Pharaoh placed upon your neck—like all the others of your kind over the past millennia. Then I will devour the woman."

Croc crouched and pounded the floor with his hind feet. His tail swished.

I glanced back to Akhenaten, whom I'd yearned to take revenge on my entire life. And this might be my only chance, the only moment he'd be distracted, the moment Anubis spoke of in my dream. But Croc and Mutnedjmet needed me ...

I leapt from the platform, landing amidst the dead and slipping on a slick coat of blood on the tile floor. I fell onto my side with a splat.

But the Devouring Monster itself had mentioned the sphinx in our last encounter—as if it wanted us to know something, something that it was hiding or too afraid to fully reveal.

"No!" I reached out for my pet—my brother—and for Mutnedjmet. "Devouring Monster, hear me." I rose from amongst the dead and stood under the blazing light of the bonfire. "Your master is calling you home."

The Devouring Monster's hood flashed over in my direction.

"I've seen him myself." I spread my arms to the sky, my chest basking in the moonlight. "I have died. And I know that not every being fears and despises you. You are not evil. What you do has a profound purpose, no matter what your current master—who summoned you to this world—has told you. You are not vile or deceitful; you only consume the hearts of the wicked, no one else—not like Akhenaten forces you to do here. Piles of hearts of the deserving await you on your platform, and Anubis himself longs for your return—to enforce his judgment upon the heinous. You are a beloved pet in only the way that a man and animal could understand—something deep, intangible, drowning in innocence and forgiveness—where each of you does not request or demand anything from the other. Your true master adores you. You *are* loved."

Croc sprang into the air.

The Devouring Monster tensed and raised its blade to strike, to decapitate Croc as Croc's open mouth sailed for its neck. But the monster never swung. Rather, it paused for a moment and let its weapon fall from its hand.

Croc crashed into the Devouring Monster and knocked it from its feet, Croc's sword-like teeth tearing into the soft flesh of its crocodile neck. A quiet hiss sounded from the monster—not a threat nor a sound of anger, but a sound of relief. Croc clamped down and chewed, the crunching of flesh following.

The Devouring Monster went limp as it died, its soul fleeing its earthly body so that it could return to the west.

Like a lion with a dead antelope, Croc hefted the cloaked body of the Devouring Monster from the ground and dragged it away into a dark corridor.

Chapter 59

Journal Translation

CHANTING SOUNDED BEHIND ME, coming from inside the audience hall, from the raised platform of the throne.

A spear whistled over my head. Paramessu stood with his arm across his body, having released the weapon in a mighty toss.

Paramessu's spear ricocheted off of Pharaoh's golden skin and giant breastplate as if he were made of impenetrable armor. Akhenaten shouted in surprise, though, which interrupted his chanting and casting of some horrendous spell, but he also swung his golden scepter down at me. It landed with a crack on the side of my face. White flashed across my vision, and the taste of metal filled my mouth as I collapsed onto my back.

Blackness crept around my vision as if I were in a tunnel, and time slowed to a crawl as if the Time Bender had cast his magic over the room, over the entire world. Akhenaten leaned over the edge of the raised platform and pointed at me as his lips slowly moved, chanting and grinning in victory.

In the end, as through everything, I'd failed everyone—but mostly myself—even though I'd never given up. But I'd again missed the moment, the one chance I'd had at victory, as I'd decided to attack the Devouring Monster and to save Croc and Mutnedjmet over killing Akhenaten. If only it would've meant that they'd survive ...

My darkening gaze found Chisisi's dead body, his green skin meant to convince men that he was a god. Then my gaze wandered to Seneb, who still released arrows into the corridor. Harkhuf's cries of resilience echoing out of the corridor would soon turn to pain and soldiers would flood the chamber, crushing Paramessu and Tia. My gaze stopped at Mutnedjmet, who rose to a knee. Her hand gripped her chest, putting pressure on the bloodstained fabric of her torn dress. But she'd have already been dead if I hadn't chosen what I had. Would I choose taking Akhenaten's life again over saving hers if I could do it over again? No. I'd chosen love over hate and would forever continue to do so. My heart burned as if a torch had set it ablaze. My inner pain escaped with a sensation of burning flesh, as if I gave birth to the festering disease that I'd harbored and unleashed it out into the world. I grimaced in excruciating pain and shouted. But in the next moment my heart beat light—free of consuming rot—healed without even the death of Akhenaten but rather from realization, accomplishment, and the love of my friends and Mutnedjmet.

I jerked my head back to Akhenaten, who still chanted as he hovered above me. Reaching out, I extended my index and little fingers in the crocodile ward. Akhenaten was shoved back and fell onto the platform. I jumped to my feet and leapt into the air, hitting the side of the raised platform with a smack. But I also reached over the top and clung to Akhenaten's ankle. And I yanked, attempting to pull him over the edge.

His gangly frame flew over my head as he screamed and crashed down into a pile of dead bodies.

Rolling over, Akhenaten held up his hands, fear still not showing in his dark eyes. But he couldn't have been prepared for any of this … He sneered as I towered over him. "Get away from me, servant. You still do not understand … you *cannot* kill me." His black-painted eyelids closed, the dark paint growing and spreading outward like the wings along the side of a cobra's head. "In this world, one born into your position will never be able to harm me, not—"

I swung the Scorpion Macehead. "For my father, mother, and Egypt!"

The weapon of the ancient King Menes crunched through the thin bones of his arms and smashed into his chest with a thud, the shock of the impact vibrating up my arms and into my core. Ribs splintered and cracked, his sunken chest caving inward. But the firelight around us swirled and flickered, as if his power sucked in our surroundings. Air expelled from his lips.

I ducked in fear, covering my head with my hands and arms—expecting his death to release a blast of magic that would kill me along with him.

Nothing happened, no magic, no fire, no explosion, and no gods screaming, yelling, or crying. Nothing.

I peeked over my shoulder. Was he not immortal? Could he possibly have only been a man—Pharaoh, the god-king, himself?

Akhenaten's body lay still, lifeless. The mace head of the ancient ruler was embedded into his chest. Then his body started to shrivel before my eyes, as if the water drained from his tissues. His skin wrinkled and sucked back against his bones, and his bones twisted as if he were mummifying before my eyes. But only a quiet sound followed—a hoarse whisper as he expelled his final breath.

I gasped in horror. I'd only seen this one other time—when Akhenaten had used the Devouring Monster's blade to cut the heart from the high priest of Thebes, when he'd wielded the power of the Devouring Monster and consumed the poor man's soul himself ...

I studied the mace head of the ancient ruler, the first pharaoh, the pharaoh who received the throne of Egypt from Horus himself. Had it devoured Akhenaten's wicked soul? Was Akhenaten—the primary cause of all my suffering and pain—really gone? I'd thought that love would never even be able to quench the fury of hate I felt for him, and I never thought that I'd live to see this moment ... My heart floated and soared, feeling as if my *ba* were again free to wander the Earth, even in this life.

Paramessu yanked me back by my shoulder. "We need to get out of here," he said.

I fell against him, my strength waning. But he propped me up. "You saved my life," I said between shallow gasps for air. Cries from Harkhuf and of dying soldiers carried from the far corridor—my brave companion continuing to hold the royal guards out of the audience hall—although by now some of the guards would be traveling through other corridors to find another entryway.

"You've saved my life more than once." Paramessu's pale eyes appeared like ice against the fiery red of his stubbly eyebrows. "And that is the reason why I followed you to the bloody end. You are the only reason that I still walk this earth—so in essence you saved yourself. I was just an obstacle in your way."

I looked up at his grin, but the room was still spinning.

Metal rang on metal inside the far corridor.

"Get out of there," Seneb shouted to his brother as he peered into the darkness and loosed an arrow from his bow.

"Heb," said a voice—tender and delicate.

I turned back to the platform.

Eyes surrounded by green paint gazed down at me—the most beautiful face the world had ever seen. My jolting heart stilled. Nefertiti.

She reached out for me from the platform. The humming voice returned to my head and grew to an emotional crescendo. "As of now, you are the most powerful man in Egypt," she said. "Come with me." She leaned over, her dress dangling from her upper chest. "I am still the Queen of Egypt. If you wed me, you will become its king—the new god-king of the world. You can lead us into the splendor that Akhenaten had taken from his people— the splendor that I know you wish to bring." She smiled and sat down at the edge of the platform, her legs dangling near my face. "Only with such power can you hope to lead the kingdom into prosperity. And I desire you."

I couldn't move, could barely think. For her to be mine, as I'd dreamt of my entire life ... Nefertiti had finally uttered the words—part of the outcome I'd hoped for every waking and even every sleeping minute since I was a boy. This was it, the two moments of crowning glory—overthrowing Akhenaten and winning Nefertiti—that I'd longed for more than life itself, more than power, more than friendship, more than helping the people of Egypt ...

"Once I am in your arms, the royal guards will be under your command." She pointed to the echoing sounds of battle coming from the far corridor. "You could do far worse than me. And forget Mutnedjmet; she will not be able to offer you anything close to what I can. She is a naïve child, untrustworthy, and an outcast of the royal family."

I gazed upon her stunning beauty. "Nefertiti, I cannot judge her based on the prejudices of her evaluator. People do not see their own flaws clearly and cannot tell that something is worse in another than it is in themselves."

"Catch me—your queen—the most desired woman in all of Egypt, in all the world," she replied as if she hadn't comprehended what I'd just said.

But my gaze lingered on her face and then over her curves. She was intoxicating ... And perhaps that and her power would be all I'd ever—

"Your most prized possession." She scooted to the edge of the platform.

I held my arms out for her, the warmth of overwhelming emotion spilling from my heart and consuming my body and soul. But I struggled to breathe as a haze infiltrated my mind, making me feel faint. I did not know myself, but this was all I'd ever wanted. The humming inside my head climaxed and made my heart rise. It was time to take up the crown, to join the royal family, and bring Egypt back from turmoil and despair, back from only the Aten.

But someone whispered in my ear, a soft voice, reassuring but strong, as if from my own conscience, "Your friends and Egypt are waiting for you to lead them." Mutnedjmet ran a tender hand across my back as she passed by—headed in the direction of an open corridor. Red ran down her chest and stained her dress, but the slice in her skin was superficial.

Thank all the gods that she was still alive and able—

"But not leading in the same manner that Akhenaten did." Mutnedjmet smiled—the most beautiful sight I'd ever seen. But then she stopped, bent over, and picked up a blade of bone with serrated—

Nefertiti crashed down onto the tile—crying out in surprise and pain, expecting that I would have caught her as she jumped. She lay at my feet, her eyes wide in shock as a pool of congealing blood, the blood of her soldiers, enveloped her hands. Her expression contracted, wrinkling with pain, shock, and betrayal.

I exhaled, long and loud. I had to stop deceiving myself as I'd been doing since I was a boy. Nefertiti's mind had not single-handedly been mutilated by Akhenaten—it was hers and hers alone, although she may have hidden it when we were young, or she'd changed … like me, but in the opposite direction. She was already lost to the darkness, and there was nothing I could do to truly save her. She could only do that herself, if she'd ever been the person I'd thought she was all along. And any real feelings I'd had for her had long ago been consumed by the festering disease I carried. The music in my head vanished, never to return.

"You? You?" she mumbled over and over again.

I did not reach out to help her up.

"Heb," Paramessu said. "We must go. The royal guards will still slaughter us when they see what we've done."

"Seneb," I said. "Get your brother out of there."

"No," the deep voice of Harkhuf shouted back from within the corridor. "If I leave, they will overtake and kill us all."

Seneb glanced back at me. "There're too many."

"Go!" Harkhuf roared from the darkness, but then he grunted in pain. A soldier's scream radiated out of the corridor.

Seneb lunged to the entrance and said, "You redeemed yourself from your past the second you vowed to live for your wife and daughter. At that moment you were a different man. The best man I've ever known."

A split second of silence followed—Harkhuf pausing his end of the battle. Then he grunted in pain again.

Seneb ran for a far entrance, and my remaining companions and I followed into the dark corridors.

The cries of the royal guards rang throughout the audience hall as they burst through several of the corridors behind us.

Harkhuf ...

Chapter 60

Present Day

MY EYES SPRANG OPEN.

I stood beside Maddie amidst the narrow hallways of green stone, hallways lined with so many hieroglyphs that they appeared like a library for the ancients, the tunnels the bookshelves. This *was* the Hall of Records.

But something wasn't right. The eyes I looked through were different, the deep green stone around me a slightly darker shade than when I'd first seen it, like how color is slightly different on different TVs at a store—as if I were seeing it through someone else's eyes. Or perhaps someone else was inside my body with me …

My breathing was slow and calm, not typical. I glanced again at the sarcophagus at the dead end of the final hall—just a granite box with those few hieroglyphs inside and as green as the previous room and tunnels.

A ghostly apparition appeared alongside the sarcophagus in the darkness just beyond my flashlight beam. Cold sweat dripped down my back, and a warm breath blew onto my neck. Something else was down here, painting the walls—a ghost of the young boy from ancient Egypt who'd traveled the world and returned to confront Akhenaten and his insanity. Heb's presence was here, if only a figment of my imagination in this dark place while my mind was filled with terror … But there was also another shadowy form—old and hunched—another man, this one wearing a suit. My flashlight beam focused on this apparition or mirage or whatever it was and shone through it, but when I angled the light to the side so that the figure was at the margin of darkness and light, I could see it best. The old man sat beside the other end of the sarcophagus.

But this image was real.

A *body* was hunched over, dressed in an old-fashioned suit. Tufts of thinning, jaw-length gray hair dangled over its face.

I took a deep breath, stepped closer, crouched, and inspected the corpse.

His small glasses had lenses appearing as the bottom half of circles, and a red bowtie stood out against leathery skin that was mummified by the arid environment. His fingers were clenched as if he'd tried to hold on to something in death—something the thickness of the journal—but both of his hands were empty.

I leaned in closer. A dark stain ran across his slouched head below a single hole between his eyes. Churning bile filled the inside of my stomach again, followed by painful cramping, nausea, and—

"That's Dr. Shelsher," Maddie said.

I nearly screamed as my body jolted, and I leapt away from the corpse in surprise.

After my heart rate settled from the shock of Maddie's interruption, I inched closer and studied the body again. Yes, it would make sense that this body was from the early 1900s. And it was down *here*. It had to be the professor we'd been looking for this entire time. He'd never made it out of the Hall, having been executed by a gunshot to the forehead.

My vision turned foggy, and wandering spirits appeared in the darkness again, floating about like ghosts. I could see him, the professor, as if in a dream—playing out in my head in this altered mental state of exhilaration and fear—my overactive mind piecing together what had happened in here a century ago.

"There's no treasure left down here," the apparition of Dr. Shelsher said, holding a thick journal and a pen in his hands. "The secret they've been hiding for all these years must be buried in this tale. We must finish the translation, for the benefit of mankind."

Another form stepped over, translucent but taking the shape of a man with large, rounded glasses and a suit but no bowtie—Dr. Shelsher's student, whose corpse we'd found inside the lost tomb of Amenhotep. He held an open leather journal with bonds that could tie it closed—the journal I now possessed.

The student slammed his journal closed. "But those men have finally found the entrance to the Hall. We have to get out of here, now."

Dr. Shelsher pushed his sagging glasses farther up onto his nose and shook his head. His gray locks waved in the dim light. "Take your journal and run. You must flee the country, or they will find you. But please, make sure that my trusted colleague receives this letter." He handed his student the folded parchment that my dad had probably received from my great-great-grandfather, who'd received it from that strange drunken man, Dr. Shelsher's colleague, in the Egyptian hotel a century ago, just before the colleague was also murdered. Then my dad had mailed the letter to me on my birthday. "Leave my timepiece inside the lost tomb before you return to England. May another find it if I do not make it out of here alive. They've already been destroying the clues, and we must offer aid to the people of the future if we do not make it."

A hollow bang sounded in the distance.

Dr. Shelsher's pen fell from his shaking fingers. "Those men are wandering the tunnels of the Hall. You can escape. Go, now."

His student turned and fled, his footsteps echoing but growing faint.

Two more apparitions appeared, wearing draping hoods that shadowed their faces. An image of a red ankh lay across the chest of their cloaks, identical to the cloaks of the men who were holding us hostage.

"No," Dr. Shelsher yelled as he held up his hands and his own journal as if it were a crucifix to ward off their evil. "These are the secrets of all the ages of Egypt. People deserve to know the truth."

"They will destroy us all," one of the hooded figures said and raised an old-fashioned handgun.

Dr. Shelsher dropped to his knees.

The professor's journal fell to the stone floor with a clap, and the apparitions faded.

I blinked in surprise as I returned to the present, the apparitions now gone. Cold sweat trickled down my forehead. Another one of my daydreams?

Maddie?

She was there, studying the walls and tunnels as if she hadn't seen a thing.

"Maddie!" I said. She jerked as she looked over at me. "We need to get out of here. They'll trap us down here, and they'll kill us all. It doesn't matter that we did what they wanted."

Her eyes narrowed. "You wanted to help Aiden, remember?"

I grabbed her around the waist and turned her away. "But now I know what happened to Dr. Shelsher."

"Yeah, they shot him in the head," she said. "There's a bullet hole."

"The same people as the ones who're holding us hostage," I said.

"Gavin, they'd be over a hundred years old."

"Well, not the same people," I said, tugging on her and forcing her to walk on, "but the same type of people, the same cult or group. They believe that whatever secret is contained in this story, it should never see the light of day."

"Why would they follow us and see if we could find this place just to kill us?" she asked.

I shook my head. "Maybe they only knew the path outside of here and wanted to see if people could still actually discover the Hall, if it was still possible to do so with all the clues they've destroyed. If we can't find it, maybe they wouldn't feel the need to guard it. Or if they've sworn to protect this place with their lives but have heard of some mysterious wonders, maybe they wanted to see it and feel its power for themselves, like those murderers in the time of Dr. Shelsher. If you'd heard that there is one great abode of evil in this world, and you'd given your life to keep it hidden but then a chance came to witness its horror without affecting anyone, wouldn't you be a bit curious and want to see it, and then seal the bodies up inside, similar to Dr. Shelsher's, so that they may never be found? Maybe they'd only kill us if we found it … or maybe they were going to kill us either way."

"But how can we escape now?" she asked. "We're already trapped."

Voices carried down the tunnels behind us. Wait … how did they … ?

The others must've taken turns opening and closing whatever lever the Scorpion Macehead unlocked to give them access to these passageways. And they'd only have to leave one person behind in the upper secret chamber. So at least one man with an assault rifle would be down here with us.

"Where are you?" Kaylin shouted, her voice echoing through the tunnels of the Hall of Records, which were stacked side by side against each other.

"Here," Maddie shouted back. "You need—"

I clamped a hand over Maddie's mouth to silence her. "They will have an armed man with them and he will kill us."

She tensed.

I tugged her along by the arm and marched back through the final passage of these perfectly straight tunnels.

Maddie tore out of my grip. "Even if we sneak around them and make it back to the moving wall, we'd have to bang and knock so that whoever was left behind could hear us and let us out. And I doubt these men left one of our old friends back there to guard whatever kind of keyhole the mace head unlocked."

"Hey, dudes," Aiden shouted as he appeared under a beam of light near the start of the final corridor. He jogged toward us. "What is this place? And where's all the gold?"

Mr. Scalone, Kaylin, and the minister then appeared farther down the long tunnel, their flashlight beams searching about. Another man brought up the rear, holding the final flashlight—probably the vocal assailant, but he was hidden by darkness.

How could we ever escape these tight confines when the assailant started to execute us?

I nudged Maddie with my elbow. "Go back."

"There's nowhere to run," she said, but she allowed me to guide her to the dead end.

"Get inside the sarcophagus," I said, "and turn off your light."

"What?"

"Just do it," I said. "He's going to kill us all in a minute."

Maddie clicked off her flashlight and swung her leg over the side of the ancient granite sarcophagus, stepping into its inner confines.

I waved for her to hurry up. "Get down, before that man sees us."

She squeezed her small frame between the angular opening created by the off-kilter cover and the sides of the sarcophagus.

I stepped into an opening at the opposite corner of the sarcophagus and slunk down inside.

Chapter 61

Present Day

SLAPPING FOOTSTEPS APPROACHED as Maddie and I hunkered down inside the partially opened sarcophagus at the end of the last tunnel of the Hall of Records. Only wisps of arcing light from flashlights carried through the off-kilter lid.

Maddie's breathing was tense and strained, rasping around the tight, granite confines.

Holding my breath in fear, I attempted to slide the granite covering of the sarcophagus back into a fully closed position—to seal us inside. I heaved, but the stone cover didn't budge. It must've weighed at least five hundred pounds.

"Maddie," I whispered. "Help me close us in."

"He'll hear the rumbling of the stone and will know where we are," she replied.

I stared in frustration at the area where the hieroglyphs had been carved into the inner sarcophagus adjacent to the base and dead end of the tunnel, although now I couldn't fully see them: The Illusion of Power. Any wording, but especially that, was unheard of for the inside of an ancient Egyptian sarcophagus.

"I wish my dad were here," I whispered in fear, although I had no idea what he'd ever be able to do. My stomach twisted and squeezed, which sent excruciating pain across my insides and fluid rising up my throat. I gagged as I nearly vomited into the sarcophagus. I would have to give up soon, as I wouldn't be able to continue through the episode of rising pain, which always led to me writhing around on the floor until I got to a hospital and received IV pain meds.

"No one—especially not the dead—can help us now," Maddie said.

Quiet footfalls drew closer. "Where'd you guys go?" Aiden's voice called out from just down the hall.

Then the slapping footfalls grew louder, echoing down the narrow tunnels, and the assailant shouted in Arabic.

The minister shouted back, his tone desperate. Aiden and Kaylin's voices floated to my ears in whispers.

A gunshot boomed, and the walls of the tunnel shook. My ears rang.

My heart lurched in surprise and fear, and my stomach squeezed again, almost making me black out with pain. But I had to do something for Maddie and Aiden, even Kaylin, and possibly Mr. Scalone—they didn't deserve this. The executions had begun, and they'd removed the silencers …

Kaylin screamed and a thud sounded, followed by what I imagined was a dying groan. More shouting followed.

A chill slid into my soul and jolted my bones. Something else was inside this sarcophagus with us … I felt it crawl inside me. *Dad?*

Music played, but it was not from any source around me. Drums beat lightly in my head, along with the gentle shake of a rattle. The cramping in my stomach receded. Was this the sound my brain created with sheer terror or when my life should be flashing before my eyes?

"The dead can still be some of the most important people," I said to Maddie, repeating words that I'd heard somewhere before … No, I hadn't—I only remembered reading them. I'd never heard those words with my own ears, but my mind now convinced me otherwise. The drumming in my head amplified, and the rhythm escalated. "And they live on inside us. That is why the underworld and death are so important for life and rebirth."

"What?" Maddie gasped.

I gritted my teeth and kicked at the area of the "illusion" hieroglyph with my heeled boot, and stone cracked and fell away, the noise masked by Kaylin's shouts. *The illusion.* I kicked again and broke out chunks of stone only as thick as an old bathroom tile. Pivoting around inside the sarcophagus, I clicked on my flashlight and shone its light into a new opening about the width of a man that led through the sarcophagus and immediately into the supposed dead-end wall of the tunnel.

"We can escape." Maddie's voice was a hoarse whisper as she grabbed my arm and looked over my shoulder. "For real this time."

I should've at least gotten Aiden to come inside the sarcophagus with us before the assailant showed up, but I hadn't known about a real escape. Leaving him out there was my fault, just like my mistake with the elderly diabetic woman in school. "If that man shoots Aiden in cold blood while I run away, it'll haunt me the rest of my life—like my other mistakes. Like with medical school, and with *you*."

Maddie's fingernails dug into my flesh. "How could you possibly help him? They'll shoot you too. And then me."

"You're right." I shook my head, and my eyes shut. "We will leave, and we will live." I squeezed my shoulders into the tight confines of the secret passageway and crawled on my hands and knees, dirt and rock jabbing into my palms, legs, and back.

Maddie wiggled about and moved to follow me.

But images of the elderly woman's face and her foot filled my mind, then Aiden's face, his goofy grin twisting into a look of sheer terror. I saw Dad's face and smile, partially masked by a thick moustache, then Nefertiti, Akhenaten, and Heb. I froze. Maddie's face appeared in my imagination, and then my own … running, leaving … again, when my situation stepped beyond difficult, when I then convinced myself it would be impossible to face …

I crawled backward and bumped into Maddie as I slipped out of the opening.

"I'd rather die than dwell on another mistake for the rest of my life." The muscles in my arms and legs contracted.

Footsteps echoed from outside the sarcophagus.

"I feel like I'm always convincing you to do the easy thing and run," she said. "I admire this, but I really don't want you to throw your life away."

I slid my feet under me, my entire body quaking with fear. I pulled my pocketknife from my messenger bag, but what could I possibly do to a man with an assault rifle? "I always stayed, or left, for you."

Maddie's shoes dragged along stone as she too sat up. "If you go, I go." She rolled her hair up and put it back into a bun on top of her head, as if that would help somehow. "Take this." She reached into her messenger bag and withdrew a piece of metal—bronze—my bracelet. "I grabbed it when we joined our hostage friends."

I snatched the cold bronze and slipped it over my left hand onto my wrist. But I shook my head. "I can't let you come with me. Go through that tunnel and find a great life ... and spread the tale to the world."

"You don't have a choice." She shoved me away and rose to her knees. "I'm following your lead."

Drums thundered in my ears and trumpets blared alongside them as if an orchestra were introducing my next intended move, echoing like a rock corridor was inside my head. Heb, or just my crazy daydreams?

But my legs again wouldn't yield to my commands, telling me to run, live, and reveal the ancient discovery. But I couldn't live that way, not now.

I felt something ... a tingling. Dr. Shelsher, Dad, and Heb were all here with me now ... I could feel them like I could feel the cold granite of the sarcophagus against my legs. I could feel Akhenaten, Mutnedjmet, and Nefertiti. History and time ran through my veins like blood. Both Heb and Dr. Shelsher may've lost in their own time frames—Heb if he conceded and gave up the palace to Akhenaten's men and allowed Nefertiti or her father to rule, which I still suspected since there were no historical references to Heb. Had he and the professor both lost to the chaos and power stacked against them? But now they were here, as if magic still flowed through this modern world—and they wanted to make something right.

The trembling in my limbs ebbed, although my constant doubt and nervousness remained. I would have to act in spite of overwhelming emotion, the type of heroism that Heb had once spoken of when saluting Mutnedjmet's bravery at the feast. I sucked in a deep breath. This was it.

I stood, rising out of the sarcophagus in deathly silence. The others were about ten feet down the hall. Kaylin and Aiden clung to each other, the tiny fox still huddled in Aiden's arms. Mr. Scalone backed away from the minister, who lay on the ground clutching his hemorrhaging upper chest, his face pale. Blood seeped across his white shirt and flowed over his hand like a river.

The assailant shouted as he motioned for the others to face the wall of the tunnel and kneel. They placed their hands behind their heads.

My choices appeared clearer now, my decisions simpler … My limbs felt more powerful, my body more hardened. The pain in my stomach and my nausea nearly vanished.

Hunching over, I dropped my fedora and hung my head. I moaned.

A beam of light flashed over, landing upon me.

Maddie screamed as a distraction as she leapt out of the sarcophagus and out of the assailant's beam of light.

The assailant yelled in surprise and stumbled backward but tripped and fell to the ground, acting as if he'd seen a dead man come to life. His flashlight clattered and rolled across the stone floor as his hood came off to reveal a Middle-Eastern man with a beard.

In a moment, the assailant would realize that it was only Maddie and me, and he'd shoot us. He scrambled back on all fours as he flailed around with his gun. But his hands found the grip and trigger, and he raised the assault rifle.

I stepped past my huddled friends and my hand lashed out, my index and little fingers extending at the assailant—Heb's crocodile ward …

The assailant's arm froze in the middle of trying to point the gun's barrel at me. His face twisted into a grimace as if he struggled against something, as if he couldn't raise his weapon. His skin turned pale and his jaw dropped, his eyes bulging from his face.

I took another step closer.

"What're you doing?" Maddie shouted from behind me.

But the assailant fought against whatever was restraining him and swung the muzzle of his gun around in a circle before pointing it at my chest and—

His gun fired, but another gunshot clapped right beside me, ringing my ears. Metal clinked in front of me, and something whizzed across the skin of my shoulder with a tearing sensation.

Kaylin screamed.

The assailant rolled over and attempted to crawl away for a moment before collapsing into a cloaked heap. Blood pooled beneath him.

Aiden stood beside me, holding a handgun—its muzzle smoking. His hand shook as he dropped the gun onto the stone floor, issuing a sharp clatter of metal.

"I-it's Mr. Scalone's," Aiden said, his voice barely registering over the ringing in my ears as he stepped back and held a hand up to the side of his face. He examined me, as if I were something he couldn't comprehend. "How the hell did you do that?"

I glanced down at my fingers forming the crocodile ward. The bullet that the assailant fired had indented the mid surface of my bracelet, but the metal somehow deflected the bullet just enough so that it only tore through the skin of my shoulder as it flew past me. I didn't even feel the pain, although a little bit of red showed through a tear in my shirt.

Kaylin and Mr. Scalone still knelt and faced the wall, but the bottom of Mr. Scalone's shirt was folded up, revealing the top edge at the back of his jeans—where he always kept his gun. But there was no gun, Aiden having used the weapon as Mr. Scalone should have. All of their flashlights lay on the floor, still on.

Kaylin glanced over her shoulder at me and covered her ears with her palms. She fell onto her side, sobbing.

Chapter 62

Present Day

MADDIE STEPPED FROM BESIDE the sarcophagus, the bun on her head bouncing as she picked up the handgun that Aiden had dropped and placed it into her messenger bag, which issued a rustling of leather. She clicked her flashlight on and shined it around.

Mr. Scalone stood and brushed off his pants, grinning to himself. Lunging over to the dead assailant's body, he grabbed the assault rifle, clicked something near its handle, and then knelt over the minister.

My blood turned cold. What would this treasure hunter do now, and what was that weird grin for?

One of Mr. Scalone's tattoo-encrusted arms extended, and his fingers clamped over the minister's hand—the hand he was using to stem the loss of blood from the gunshot wound in his chest.

The minister's face and lips were white, his eyes foggy.

The ringing in my ears from the gunshots had mostly faded, and I heard Mr. Scalone whisper to the minister, "I will still find the treasure. And I'm sorry that you won't be around to share all the wealth we'll receive for selling it." Mr. Scalone pulled the minister's hand away from his wound, and his blood flowed faster.

"I see it clearly," the minister said between faint breaths. "The treasures should stay in Egypt and be kept in the museum. We should not use them for our own personal ..." he gasped for air and his chest heaved, "gain." His head rolled to the side, and his eyes turned vacant.

"How'd you ever get this far in life?" I asked Mr. Scalone. "If your outsides resembled your insides, you'd be much scrawnier and more diseased then me."

"That's why he needs all those tats and muscle and long hair," Aiden said, although his lip still trembled after having shot and killed a man. "If he didn't have all that, no one would be tricked into believing he deserved any kind of respect, like some of my rich friends who dress like they grew up in the hood."

Mr. Scalone snarled as he stood and faced us, the metal of the assault rifle in his arms reflecting the beams of the flashlights. "It's okay, Kaylin. Get up. We'll get out of here alive, and the minister will have another underling who'll be willing to allow all the artifacts to slip through security and out of the country. And it'll probably cost us less than sixty percent."

I gritted my teeth as heat washed up my face. That was what Kaylin and Mr. Scalone had been planning all along—to stake their claim on the Hall through Mr. Scalone's connection to the Minister of Antiquities and get filthy rich? Would they have even let Maddie and me claim any of it and allow us to use the discovery as the foundation for our careers as Egyptologists, the entire point of this expedition? I hoped there was no real treasure these two could benefit from.

I folded my tense arms. "Mr. Scalone, you better fire off a few more rounds, one at a time but in slow repetition."

His eyebrow arched onto his forehead in confusion.

I pointed behind him into the darkness. "Preferably away from us, down the hall. That dead assailant must've removed his silencer for a reason. If the other armed men outside the secret tunnel don't hear execution style shooting real soon, they may call in reinforcements and come down here with even more men. And I don't doubt that they could hear the shots of an assault rifle, even from where we left them. It will buy us a little more time, at least."

Mr. Scalone's eyes wandered before he slowly nodded in agreement. Pivoting around, he raised the gun and fired. A deafening bang shook the walls.

I covered my ears.

Kaylin screamed again.

Another shot ... then another followed, until he counted one for each of the rest of us.

My ears rang, and my head pounded. But the shots would pacify the other assailants. Those men would probably reverse the motion of the mace head inside whatever kind of lever opened the walls, thinking that only their comrade would come back out.

But what would the assailants do if there was no one waiting when the wall opened again? They'd come looking for us soon after.

Aiden patted me on the back and then fell against me in a big hug. "What now?"

I hugged him back and slapped his shoulder blades. "Thanks for shooting that man. I was just lucky that I'd scared him so much he couldn't even lift his gun. But I doubt he'd have been scared for much longer." Or had *I* used some kind of magic against him—magic from ancient Egypt? No, that was impossible, I'd just utilized the environment, utilized fear to its greatest extent. My mind had overreacted again with the entire situation and the find of the Hall, but my imagination must've helped my act—making my intimidating advance on the assailant appear genuine, making him believe that I was going to harm him.

Maddie hugged me from behind, her body trembling.

The music in my head vanished, and the power coursing through my limbs dissipated.

Kaylin finally stood on shaky legs. "Wh-who are these men?"

"People who believe that others in this world should never read what's inside this Hall," I said. "Extremists who are wary of the religious implications of the story, or the illusion of their power. Heb was a servant boy born with nothing, and he had to rise to challenge the most powerful men in ancient Egyptian society. Coptic Christians did some things in the later years of ancient Egypt, trying to stamp out the pagans, that remind me of these men."

"Is that what all this is about?" Kaylin asked, glancing at the walls of the tunnel as they seemed to press in around us.

Another apparition appeared in the darkness at the margin of our light. I stared. It was a man, an ancient Egyptian from my dream back home, but with a glowing green form. I shook my head and blinked. This man appeared similar to how I imagined Heb, so it must only be my imagination again. The ghostly form of a petite woman rose beside him, and then another man with red hair, another woman, and two dwarves with dark skin. Another daydream. They all faced away from us as they traced images upon the walls—as if they were all painting the hieroglyphs.

"We can't go back the way we came," Maddie said, tugging on my shoulder as if she didn't notice the apparitions—confirming they were only in my imagination, "or the other armed men will shoot us."

Mr. Scalone flashed the assault rifle in front of his chest. "When the wall reopens, I'll just shoot them first."

"Your stories are all bogus," Aiden said and planted his hands on his hips as he shook his head. "You'll probably end up running from them or shooting one of us on accident. You should give me the gun; at least I've done something."

"I agree," I said. "Give Aiden the gun."

Mr. Scalone furrowed his chin and puffed out his chest. "I'm still in charge. You are all ignorant kids." He pointed the rifle's muzzle at each of us in turn, lastly at me. "Don't forget that. I've seen more in any one year than all of you have in your lifetimes."

"Paul," Kaylin said. "Don't threaten them; they're still my friends, and my brother."

"Your friends are testing me," Mr. Scalone replied, the myriad of tattoos on his skin wobbling as he flexed his arms. He didn't redirect the gun's muzzle away from my face. "We just need to find the real treasure down here. Then I'll let everyone go."

"There's nothing else down here," Maddie lied before shining her light along the walls. "We've been through the tunnels. It's just an ancient story."

Mr. Scalone laughed. "You don't expect me to believe that, do you? After all the obscure clues and carefully hidden secrets that we've chased? There's something of real value down here."

"C'mon, Gavin," Kaylin said as she stepped up to me and caressed my arm and shoulder. She pushed the barrel of Mr. Scalone's gun away. "I believe in you, and only you will be able to locate the hidden treasure."

"Gavin," Maddie said, folding her arms. "I hope you know by now that I've always liked you; I just couldn't find someone attractive or love someone who gave up on their dreams. Kaylin still believes she can manipulate you. But before, she never thought that you'd accomplish anything, *ever*—going all the way back to college."

Kaylin gasped and leaned back as she placed her hand over her heart. "I find Gavin attractive and empowered … lately, at least. He's done a lot more than Mr. Scalone."

Maddie's eyes narrowed.

"Maddie." I sighed. "I've always liked you, even though you never really reciprocated the feeling, and I don't get much attention from women … but I'm not a complete moron. Kaylin's a manipulative bitch and I'm not at all attracted to her. I've seen who she really is."

Kaylin gasped again and backed away, bracing against the wall of the tunnel as if she might fall.

Maddie grinned.

Aiden laughed and slapped his knee. His tiny fox trotted up to his side and sat on her haunches.

"But we need to get out of here quickly, no matter what Mr. Scalone and Kaylin are going to do," I said, "so that we can avoid a shoot-out with the other assailants and reveal the true ending of the tale that's been trapped down here for eons. We can shout it out to the world." I turned, clicked on my flashlight, and focused its beam upon the sarcophagus.

Chapter 63

Present Day

I WAVED MADDIE AND AIDEN over to the sarcophagus and climbed into the narrow opening of the off-kilter lid.

Stooping on my hands and knees, I crawled along the smooth granite base, peeking into the blackness of the passageway that I'd kicked open. I released a long breath. The air that flowed out was stagnant, as if no one had seen the inside of this tunnel since the original builders, and no green stone lay within, only dirt and irregularly mined bedrock, like a cave. It led into the dead end of the tunnel.

"I'll see where it goes," I said over my shoulder. Squeezing through the opening, I exhaled and crawled into a low, dark tunnel. Ancient air swept into my lungs with a burning sting as the eons of time crawled into my soul and jolted my bones. Something was in here.

The light of my flashlight barely pierced the eerie darkness in front of me. Cold cobwebs clung to my face and hands. I shuddered in disgust as I flashed my light around, revealing only rock and dirt. I crawled on through the gritty tunnel that pressed in against my head and back.

"I'm coming with you," Maddie said, crawling after me.

"We can't let them take any of the treasure," Mr. Scalone said, his voice echoing from behind and above us, probably talking to Kaylin. Then, louder, "I'll be taking up the rear, so don't get any ideas. I still have the rifle."

His gun ... his only means to power.

Stone grated together behind me, sounding like the lid of the sarcophagus rumbling against the sides. Something crashed with a thunderous bang, its impact crunching and vibrating through the dirt roof just above my head.

I jerked in surprise as dirt dribbled down from the ceiling into my hair, and I scrambled on, worried the tunnel might collapse. Scuffing from Maddie and Aiden crawling through dirt sounded behind me. Had Mr. Scalone removed the lid of the sarcophagus to make more room for himself to get down in here? I shook my head. *What an idiot.* Now the assailants might've heard something they shouldn't have and might wonder what was going on.

The tight tunnel beneath my knees and feet slowly started to ascend. Could this be the metaphorical rise of the Aten from the underworld, leading us to the surface?

Then the tunnel grew taller. I stood, stooped over, as I shuffled along, scanning all of the walls with my flashlight. The side walls jutted out ahead and created a much wider passage.

Then I saw it—the sparkle of metal. Gold.

I flashed my light around as my skin tingled with wonder. My breathing grew quick and shallow, my heart fluttering with exhilaration. Ancient treasure.

Behind me, Maddie screamed, and her fingernails dug into the flesh of my neck.

Golden artifacts lay about the periphery of the widening tunnel, facing inward as if to congratulate or intimidate any intruders.

"This is treasure, original treasure," Maddie shouted. "From the lost tomb of Amenhotep."

My head jerked back in surprise as I studied the artifacts that stretched as far as the beam of my light. From the tomb that we discovered at the very beginning of our expedition, the one that had been raided in antiquity? "Why would you say that?"

Maddie pointed at the encircled hieroglyphs on a golden funerary mask, a mask that made the funerary mask of King Tut appear like a child's trinket. This mask was made of polished gold as thick as granite, lined with red and blue stones in intricate designs. "It's his name in that cartouche."

Maddie pushed past me and ran on, laughing and screaming as if she'd gone mad.

There was actual treasure inside the Hall … I ran after her, my footsteps growing lighter and seeming to float atop the shadows swarming my feet.

This discovery would captivate the world much more than any tale I'd found, and Maddie's and my careers as Egyptologists would be solidified.

"It's all ours," Kaylin yelled from behind.

Aiden ran past her as he tore his cap off and flung it into the air. "We're rich!"

Mr. Scalone slowly brought up the rear, the beam of his flashlight leading the way, the shadows sheathing him in darkness. "We need to sort out the rights and percentages on this find. Right now."

"I'd say that since you were hired by Kaylin's dad, you have no ownership," I said. "You're just a hired hand, like those men we found for the Valley of the Kings." I shined my light on him.

His muscular arms tensed beneath his sleeves of tattoos, and he shook his head, his oily locks waving. "This is *all* mine and Kaylin's." He aimed the assault rifle at my chest.

My throat clamped shut, fear gripping my insides as if it used long fingers and claws. This man was only a bully, but seeing all this might change him. He might actually hurt or even kill us.

Maddie's footsteps crunched into the dirt as she stepped closer. "There's more than enough here for everyone to stake a claim."

"But very little of it will actually be ours," Mr. Scalone said. "The Egyptian government will take ownership of the artifacts and give us a small portion as a reward. And I'm not splitting that portion with anyone."

"You can't do this," I said. "This was my *dad's* find."

Mr. Scalone grabbed my shirt and buried the muzzle of the assault rifle into my stomach. "You will all stay down here."

"No," Maddie said. "You're a sleazeball!"

Mr. Scalone motioned for Kaylin to join us and for Maddie and Aiden to step over by me. "You two, over there. Kaylin, I don't want you talking to your dad before I get this figured out. I have to find a new government official and set that all up again, quickly."

Kaylin pounded her thighs with clenched fists. "Paul, my dad will not tolerate this. He will find you."

"But by then I'll already own this entire place." Mr. Scalone grinned before turning and continuing up the incline.

"You will die," I shouted, although I had no idea why I said it. My skin tingled. All of the flashlights flickered at once, and shadows crawled and slithered all around us, seeming to reach out with claws and teeth before the beams became steady again.

Mr. Scalone glanced back and smirked. "Don't worry, I won't let you die. I'll have someone bring you food and water and get rid of those assailants outside if this ends up taking me a while." He waved over his shoulder and disappeared up the incline into the blackness.

I wished that he'd get what a just world—

A cold breath landed on the back of my neck. My toes curled, and goose bumps arose on my arms. I squeezed the dented bronze of my bracelet.

Everyone was silent, our breaths rapid. What would we—

A scream erupted, a man's, in sheer terror. Mr. Scalone. More shouting and rapid gunfire followed. Then silence.

Maddie, Aiden, Kaylin, and I exchanged wide-eyed glances.

Kaylin bolted and ran back the way we'd come. I gripped my flashlight tighter and raced in the other direction, up the incline of the tunnel, my beam bobbing around. Maddie and Aiden's pounding feet followed me.

Golden artifacts lined the tunnel for hundreds of feet.

Something lay still just ahead, before a dead end.

I froze in fear, casting my light about the area. Nothing moved. Creeping forward, I focused on a body. Blood caked its mangled neck—Mr. Scalone, dead. His shirt was torn open, and a row of four gashes ran across his muscular chest, as if some animal had scratched him while it crushed his throat with its teeth and jaws.

The hairs on the back of my neck stood straight up, and my skin crawled.

I whirled around, flashing my light in all directions. What could possibly have happened to him, and would it happen to the rest of us?

A hieroglyph was engraved into a block that loomed above Mr. Scalone's body, a marking indicating a passageway. I inched over and examined it. The sides of this block were tapered into the wall so that it could only be opened from one side—this side. It wouldn't ever have been able to be shoved inward because the angle of the sides of the block and those surrounding it would only get tighter if forced in that direction.

I glanced back for the others.

But something else lay beside Mr. Scalone's body, something gold.

Aiden stumbled up beside me, his entire face hanging in shock. "He's, like, dead."

I reached down. The statuette of an animal lay beside him, perched on all fours with legs extended ... like a sphinx. But its head was also a cat's, not human, so it was not a real sphinx ... unless what the journal's story mentioned about Croc was truer than our current understanding of history. Stripes flowed along the gold of its body with lighter areas under its chin and belly. Croc?

He who could command the sphinx ruled Egypt ...

My fingers brushed against the polished gold of the statue, and I gasped in surprise. The metal was warm.

"Careful," Maddie said. "A booby trap must've killed Mr. Scalone."

"Maybe," I said. "But if it did, he's already set it off. Help me shove this stone out."

We both heaved, but the stone marked as the passageway wouldn't move. A hieroglyph just below it represented descending ... again. What could be below us? I glanced down. I stood on a panel of darker rock, barely recessed into the floor. A hieroglyph on this rock, partially covered by my hiking boots, depicted a man. I flashed my light around. Just to the side was another tile of stone in the floor, this one depicting a woman.

"Maddie," I said, "stand on that."

Maddie inched over onto the rock, and it sank a hair into the ground. She jerked upright, her eyes widening.

Still the passageway didn't open. I continued to hunt around with my light until I found a third rock tile about twenty feet away.

"Aiden," I said, "stand over there."

Aiden jogged over and stood on the rock, but it didn't budge, and nothing else happened. What now?

Aiden shifted the fox in his arms. "What do I do?"

I flashed my beam around, looking for more tiles of rock, but I couldn't find one. "What's the image on your rock?"

He looked down as he scratched the back of his head. "A cat?"

A man, a woman, and a cat ... were these supposed to represent Heb, Mutnedjmet, and Croc? The stones sank into the ground as well, so they had to be some kind of scale ... *Heb, if you built this hoping a cat would sit still wherever you wished it to, you must've thought that no one would ever be able to accomplish this last feat.* "Step off of it and put only your fox on it."

Aiden's eyebrows rose up under his hat, but he slowly stepped off and put his fox onto the square tile of a rock. The animal sat on its haunches, panting under the beam of my light.

A click sounded, and the tile sank into the earth a bit.

The tapered stone in the wall ahead of me grated and rumbled for a few inches before spilling out into the chamber beyond with a crash and an echoing boom.

The tunnels beneath the Great Pyramid lay beyond, the tunnel where Kaylin had used the mace head to let people in and out of the sliding wall. The other assailants would be in there somewhere, and they'd have heard the crashing rock.

Aiden scooped up his fox, raced over, and grabbed the assault rifle from Mr. Scalone's body. We waited in tense silence, and my fingers nervously traced the margins of my bracelet. Couldn't whatever had gotten to Mr. Scalone also rid us of the assail—

Our flashlights flickered, and a rush of wind carried past me in the shadows, as if something raced by and through the exit.

Another fifteen minutes passed, but still no men appeared in the inner chamber.

I grabbed the sleek neck of the golden cat statue, shoved it into my messenger bag, squeezed through the tapering opening of the false block, and stepped into the tunnel leading back to the Great Pyramid.

Two assault rifles lay on the ground just ahead, along with some kind of tracks. I followed the tracks with my flashlight beam. Streaks of blood ran across the floor, as if something had been killed and dragged away. But there were no other assailants ... and no bodies.

"C'mon, guys," I said, my skin crawling with fear again. Had I somehow made this happen? If not, what could've possibly attacked those men? "Let's get out of here."

Maddie and Aiden climbed through the tapered hole of the false block and joined me. But I paused for a moment and glanced back through the opening, shining my light around, looking for Kaylin. "Kaylin, this—"

Several green apparitions stood inside the inner chamber. Heb, Mutnedjmet, Paramessu, Tia, Harkhuf, and Seneb, they were all there … and a ghostly orange and white cat, and a fox, who paced around their ankles.

Heb lifted a hand as if to wave but held his palms out in adoration. Mutnedjmet grinned, and Harkhuf folded his arms across his chest.

The flashlight in my hand made a popping sound, and the light flickered and vanished. I jerked in surprise. More visions courtesy of my overactive imagination?

The pain in my stomach and my nausea disappeared completely—like magic.

Maddie and Aiden, with their flashlight beams, were already far ahead, shouting for Kaylin to follow us as they jogged back to the pyramid. I hurried after them as my mind wandered amidst the images of the apparitions.

I'd often used Heb's words and knowledge for guidance in my own life, but Heb had used the exact words that I'd spoken to Maddie, those about judging people based on the prejudices of their evaluator. Heb said those words to Nefertiti … And that was when he definitively decided that Nefertiti would never again hold power over him. But I'd uttered the phrase before I'd read that part of the ancient story in the hieroglyphs upon the walls of the Hall of Records.

Could time possibly work in reverse? Could Heb have helped me and yet I have also helped him in his moment of greatest need? Was it only my translation of the newfound words and hieroglyphs that I made them say exactly what I wanted them to, or could Heb have been reading a journal about me, or somehow have been watching my life and used my words as his own? With all that'd happened in the Hall and with this journal, especially the crocodile ward and Mr. Scalone's and the assailants' deaths, could I continue to dismiss everything with some logical explanation? Or had the world actually lost some kind of magic long, long ago?

Chapter 64

Journal Translation

E L-AMARNA HAD FALLEN into disarray for at least a month, but today Queen Nefertiti summoned me, her sister, and my companions back to the palace. She probably hoped to restore order—as at least half of the remaining military now sided with their former commander, not a pharaoh-less queen.

"This could still be a trap," Paramessu said, his hand on Tia's lower back as we passed through familiar lamplit corridors, our footsteps slow but determined as they echoed off of the surrounding mud brick.

Seneb marched beside us with Croc in his arms. Was Seneb still nervous, worried that the Devouring Monster might return?

And Mutnedjmet walked at my side, carrying a sack.

"No," I said as I stepped out into the daylight and returned to the audience hall. "Not even Nefertiti would order the royal guards to kill her sister and me, at least not while ten thousand soldiers wait outside the palace for our return."

The sky opened up overhead, and cloud-muted sunlight streamed through the open-air court. But the rays felt cooler, not so rank with heat.

Mahu and Maya stepped up to face us. "My pen is yours," Maya said as he used a reed pen to tuck his hair behind cup-like ears. "And I will use it in any way that I can to help remedy Egypt."

Mahu reached out and grasped my shoulder in a crushing grip. "Heb, the servant boy, my friend."

"Welcome," a voice said, arising from someone on the throne and drowning out all the clatter and murmurs from the mass of royal guards who filled the chamber. Nefertiti sat there, wearing the fused crowns of

Upper and Lower Egypt. She stood and folded her hands as Mutnedjmet and I approached, our arms intertwined. "Sister," Nefertiti said, smiling.

Mutnedjmet nodded in acknowledgement. "Father," she said to a man standing in the shadows behind Nefertiti—Ay.

"I will not waste anyone's time." Nefertiti stepped to the edge of the platform where she'd fallen and I hadn't caught her. "Egypt is in a state of disrepair, and much work must be done to restore it to glory. Already, the hordes of Hittites sense our weakness and advance in the north. We must work together and not fight for the throne, or the kingdom will be overtaken."

"I will not kill any who are undeserving," I said and nodded to Ay, whose favor I would still like to earn, as he would be my future father-in-law, just not by way of the sister that I'd always imagined.

"Then you accept me as your queen?" Nefertiti asked.

I glanced to Mutnedjmet and then to Paramessu.

"Unless we are to divide Egypt further," Mutnedjmet whispered, her breath warming the lobe of my ear, "we should not wage war inside the kingdom. The Hittites are strong and ambitious. And if you desire to take the throne, my sister will surely wage war against you, utilizing everyone who still believes in Pharaoh's conventional successors."

"I accept you as the Queen of Egypt," I said, unable to say that Nefertiti was *my* queen.

"Excellent." A smile broadened across her face as she soaked in her new, uncontested power. She was now the most powerful person in the world—which she'd probably longed for her entire life. She closed her eyes for a moment, the green paint around them glistening in the sun. "But there is one more obstacle." Her eyes popped back open as she turned and motioned for someone to stand.

Beketaten stood from a chair and ushered the boy at her side, placing him in front of her. Prince Tut. The boy hobbled on his deformed foot, and his walking stick clacked at his side. He appeared feeble, but so had Akhenaten, who was probably his father. I scrutinized Beketaten. Her son being the spawn Akhenaten would have granted her so much power ... but now she'd probably want people to believe that he was mine. I couldn't trust her. And too many years had passed since I'd spent that one night with her, and the boy was deformed, like Akhenaten.

"The prince will assume the throne when I am gone," Nefertiti said. "Will you and your military accept that?"

Something tugged at my stomach—worry and anxiety. Would the same monster that had lurked within Akhenaten have been passed down to his offspring, or could the boy be different, could he be raised in another manner?

I studied Prince Tut. "I will not harm an innocent boy. And as long as the boy holds Egypt's interests first when he is pharaoh, and not his own, I will not unite others against him."

The boy's dark eyes sparkled, his pupils deep, like tunnels to his soul. He smiled and held his palms out at me in adoration.

Warmth rose inside me, but I said, "You may feel differently when you are grown and understand everything I did." Or had he also suffered greatly at the hands of his father?

The boy nodded without a word.

"Then you shall be Commander-in-Chief of the military and lead our forces against our outside enemies," Nefertiti said. "You will restore Egypt's army to its previous splendor, one that has not been seen since the peace of Amenhotep swept over the known world."

"I accept."

"Good," Nefertiti replied. "Then let us come and claim the bodies of each other's dead so that they may find the afterlife and live in peace."

Egypt's new queen marched down the steps and led us away through the winding corridors.

After walking through the long hallways of the palace, a chamber opened up, its many torches crackling upon the walls and warming the air. Bodies lay on mud-brick slabs inside, some in piles, others alone. The reek of embalming agents hung thick.

"You will find your comrades in there." She stepped to the far side of the entryway, holding her hand out as an invitation for us to enter the room. "I have other pressing matters to attend to. Once you are done here and have buried your dead, you may live in the palace and rest for a spell before assembling an army and traveling north."

"Thank you," Seneb said, his eyes wide as he looked in through the entryway upon the body of his brother. "But we will never reside here." He stumbled into the chamber with scuffing feet.

We all followed him.

The dark-skinned body of Harkhuf lay on a slab, his eyes and mouth closed. Wounds covered his body, as if he had refused to give up and die after being struck over and over again. But there was no tension in his face. He must have been completely relaxed when he died—more relaxed then I'd ever seen him in life. Chisisi's green body lay beside him, a hint of a smile on his lips—the man that I'd put trust in beyond reasoning, the one who in the end hadn't let me down. Hopefully the skin tone would help appease Osiris.

Mutnedjmet hugged Seneb from behind. "I am so sorry about your brother."

"I am not." Seneb wiped away his tears before stroking Croc's fur. "He never found peace in life. May he discover it in death. I am happy for him. He will finally find his wife and daughter and again be their guardian."

I patted Seneb's shoulder, which quivered as he released quiet sobs. "I'm sure that his family is his first priority," I said and grinned. "Much more so than pleasing Anubis."

Seneb set Croc down and helped me place the rigid bodies of our two companions on cots. We hoisted Harkhuf while Paramessu and Tia took Chisisi.

We turned to exit, but I froze. Another body sat alone in the shadows at the far end of the room, twisted and sunken as if already mummified.

I was drawn to it—pulled by some intangible force.

Akhenaten's mummy lay twisted and gnarled, clutching at itself, his mouth gaping open in a silent scream. Chills ran up my spine, and I shivered.

Mutnedjmet dropped the sack that she carried onto the tile floor, and its contents clanged together. She reached inside and pulled out the Scorpion Macehead of King Menes and then the devouring blade of crocodile bone and teeth.

"We don't need to take any more souls," I said. "If the mace head didn't devour him when I crushed his heart, then perhaps we should leave it up to Anubis. I believe that Akhenaten will suffer appropriate consequences for everything that he did."

Mutnedjmet didn't respond. She lay the serrated blade of bone at Akhenaten's side and hoisted the mace—bringing it up over her head, as if she meant to slay a giant.

She swung downward. The stone mace crunched into the crocodile bone and the golden hilt. A clap rang out and shook the walls, and a gust of wind howled, lifting me and throwing me and the others, including the bodies we carried, down. The very foundations of the palace quaked. My ears buzzed, and my eyes gaped in shock as I looked to Mutnedjmet, lying on her back beside me. She pointed as she held her other hand over her ear.

The mace head had smashed the crocodile-bone blade to pieces, its serrated teeth scattered in all directions. The air above the weapon wavered, as if *ba* flew free from the weapon and hovered overhead, swirling in a massive flock ... I saw an image, if only in my head, of linen-wrapped faces with green eyes glowing through a mist, their bodies cloaked in black. The Dark Ones—the inappropriately lost souls, the unjudged of Anubis ... they were released, hoping to confront the challenges of the underworld and find eternal life.

A trance of deep thought and emotion took over my brain, all of the recent events and their possible meanings replaying over and over.

"I would've liked to live without emotion," I said as my fists fell open in sorrow. "Damn my life and all that hurts me. And I wish to have found you sooner, lived our lives, avoided Akhenaten. I should've just asked you to run away with me instead of ..."

"Horemheb," Mutnedjmet wiped at her eyes, which smeared her blue paint. She remembered my birth name and not the nickname I was always referred to by everyone. "Without emotion, we'd only have life, death, eating, and sleeping. Thought and problem-solving may give you interest, but emotion is what celebrates life—what makes us human. It is the strongest of all bonds. It brings pain but also so much joy. The perfect innocence of life cannot be completely extinguished by evil. To watch your daughter"—she patted her lower abdomen—"run about and play with others, without a care in the world, her only thought how much fun is she going to find ... Now that is a spectacle worth living for, for the joy of others, your loved ones."

I fell into her warm chest, blinking rapidly, fighting off tears. "You are the wisest person I've ever met, and I've met some very wise people."

"I will be with you the rest of my days," she whispered into my ear as she cradled my head and kissed my cheek. "All that we can do now is choose how to spend the time we have."

I smiled as warmth spread through my entire body. Love. "But part of me is still afraid that you only love me because you think that I saved you from those abductors below the barracks." My head drooped farther. "That was only a ploy to infiltrate the royal family."

Mutnedjmet shook her head. "I've loved you since you were a boy, and the actions that you've taken here have not made it more or less real. I knew that it was you the very first night you came to the palace and attended the feast … You were holding your bracelet for reassurance, and then did it again later with me—the same as you'd done all those years before with the same bracelet that you'd taken from your father. And I suspected what you were up to and that things might not be as they appeared."

We retrieved the bodies of our comrades, and Mutnedjmet guided us out of the palace. A blue sky awaited, the Aten shining brighter than I'd seen it in some time. A billowing white cloud sailed overhead. As it raced by in an unfelt wind, it parted in the center and sunlight streamed through in distinct rays, like steady bolts of lightning. I could almost see the ankhs being offered to those waiting below. But no people stood there, only a tree in the distance. A lone tree. Straight and proud—a tamarisk with full blossoms of pink that bloomed before my eyes. The petals floated into the wind but hovered about the tree like bees.

I stopped right in the middle of the great road and lay down in the dust with Mutnedjmet and Harkhuf's body. Croc meowed and sat on his haunches, and the magician's white cat and the desert fox joined us. Paramessu, Tia, and Seneb lay down as well. I pointed to the sky and let my mind wander, watching how the soaring clouds danced and played with the sunlight, making it sparkle—watching it all just as Father and I often had when I was a boy.

My hand found the bronze bracelet on my wrist. Warmth from the metal carried up my limb and into my heart. Birds dived from the sky through the part in the clouds. I could see them all around me, circling. And all of these birds had human or animal heads upon their feathered bodies—men, women, children, and animals of the world.

An elderly man's head sat atop an albatross, his wrinkles entrenched so deeply into his face that they appeared as lines of a spider's web—the magician. Then came the face of Harkhuf, Father—he was one of the *ba*, as distinct as Mutnedjmet's face beside me—and Mother. They smiled, even Harkhuf's rough face. Father's and Mother's wingtips brushed against each other as they dived down at me, paused, and then soared up into the air together like they were holding hands and disappeared into the sunlight streaming through the part in the clouds.

I shuddered with joy as I felt the *ba* of all of the souls flying around me. Happiness, exhilaration, nostalgia, and a hint of sadness welled up within me. The dead—all the people and animals of the past, the present, and the future. They were all still here, part of this world, only in a different way—memories and fleeting bonds.

I felt the connection not only to humanity, but to all living things, the earth and the universe, like we were all different strands of some intricate web—a brilliant gleaming architectural wonder that no man could yet comprehend. Any pain or suffering that we brought to others not only tore the fabric of our own lives, but also our connection to the universe and to all of time. Love seemed to work in the opposite way, healing.

Epilogue

Present Day

MADDIE AND I HAD informed the Egyptian government of our discovery of the Hall and the mounds of golden artifacts. All of the paperwork and rights were being debated, as well as what to do about the mysterious assailants and the death of Mr. Scalone and the Minister of Antiquities.

But Maddie's and my careers as Egyptologists were solidified, and a small portion of the riches would be ours. I'd publish the tale so that others in the present could learn and understand what Heb had struggled for—Horemheb, actually. My mind wandered in rising awareness, as if floating free. I'd read much about Pharaoh Horemheb in my past, and now that I finally realized who the ancient story was about, I felt shocked, like the tale had sucked me in too much and I hadn't foreseen the outcome. But now my thoughts were clear, as if a curtain of fog had permanently fled my mind.

Maddie took my hand in hers as we sat overlooking the expanse of the Nile from the balcony of our penthouse suite at the Four Seasons. The sun was setting, and the temperature dropped as orange light danced across the water. The hum of the flowing river drowned out the city noise. "Do you believe that the tale in the journal was real, at all?"

"Do you?" I asked as I turned to her and studied her smiling face. Aiden sat in a chair on her far side. This was now our room. Kaylin was staying with her dad somewhere else in Cairo.

"Well, there's a lot that's known to be true," Maddie said as her gaze wandered over my face. "The rise of King Tut and Nefertiti taking the throne, although using men's names, and not for very long, as she died of a bone infection or tumor in her hip." Her lips pursed as her eyes wandered, and she adjusted her glasses.

My forehead furrowed as my mind wandered over the tale. The same magic I thought I'd witnessed was the same magic in the tale. Perhaps the entire story of the journal was fact … Throughout my adventures in Egypt, I'd believed more and more but still had always thought it was just a legend, a myth. Were other myths of the world similar in that they were real or at least based in truth? Were tales of magic really about some unexplainable power that had been lost to the ages?

A gentle breeze rustled my short hair and caressed my cheek. The colors of the fading orange sunlight around me seemed deeper, fuller, as if life itself had turned deeper. Should I tell Maddie about the magic? Would she believe any of it? Maybe someday, but she knew better than anyone I had an overactive imagination.

Aiden yanked his earbuds from his ears and scooted closer. "What happened to this Heb?" The tiny fox was curled into his lap, her eyes closed.

"Horemheb was his real name," I said. "He ruled Egypt for some time following the time of the tale, after the debated succession of pharaohs following Akhenaten, who all only ruled for a short time. Horemheb then ruled for a decade or two, cleansing the kingdom of Akhenaten's madness. Then, as Heb never had a son, he transferred the throne to his friend Paramessu. Paramessu was very old when he became pharaoh, finishing Horemheb's saga and taking up the name of Rameses for a couple of years until he died. His wife, Tia, became Queen Sitre. Those names and their changes are fact."

Maddie leaned back and gazed out over the timeless river. "All of the ancient documents that have been discovered about Horemheb only claimed that he was a mortal man who rose to the position reserved for god-kings and immortals. Others may've later exaggerated him and his accomplishments to hide the fact that he was only human, but he never claimed to be more."

Aiden scratched his head by tugging on the flat bill of his cap. "That would've, like, crumbled the perception of a pharaoh."

"I think that was why the Hall was hidden so well," I said. "Horemheb didn't want anyone to find and condemn it. He wanted to leave the truth so that others in the future would know Pharaoh was only a man or woman, if future rulers stepped beyond reason. Maybe in later years, the ancient scribes told only a redacted story of Horemheb—a common or even noble birth, a man who became a general, Commander-in-Chief of the military, and who was an advisor to King Tut. Maybe they thought the people still needed to believe in the immortal pharaoh."

Maddie rolled her eyes. "And it didn't take long for that concept to rise again."

"What happened?" Aiden asked.

I took a long drink of sweet lemonade, condensation running down the sides of the glass like rain. The cool liquid washed over my tongue, its hint of sour creating a tingling sensation as I swallowed. "Paramessu's grandson, Rameses the Second, claimed to be an immortal god-king and usurped and built more monuments than any other pharaoh in Egypt's history. He crushed all of Horemheb's work in trying to educate the common man about the illusion of power, birthrights, hierarchy, and fate. Rameses the Great, he called himself."

The mysteries of the world and of man ... How beautiful this world could be, and yet how savage had we the people chosen to make it?

"So then why is Tut now the most famous pharaoh of Egypt?" Aiden asked.

I slid out of my chair and crouched down over my bag. "Because they tried to erase him from history. It wasn't until Horemheb's rule that it really became okay to be an Egyptian pagan again. A king's list was found in Paramessu's son's—Sety the First's—tomb, with no mention of pharaohs in between Amenhotep the Third and Horemheb."

Aiden rubbed the buzzed side of his head. "So no one knew where to find Tut's loot because the maps, memories, and his tomb's whereabouts had all been destroyed?"

Maddie nodded. "And Tut's tomb was hidden by tons of silt from flash floods. So an insignificant pharaoh is now the most famous of all, because Howard Carter found his tomb with all of those precious artifacts still inside."

Aiden removed his hat. His dreadlocks were gone, his head shaved down to red stubble, just like Heb's sidelock that'd been removed when he became a man. "So what happened to Akhenaten's mummy?"

I shrugged as I sank back into the soft slats of my chair.

"In the tunnels, there was an open sarcophagus for Akhenaten," Maddie said. "His name was on it. The inside of the sarcophagus was empty, but there were impressions in the stone, as if something had lain in there for millennia but the body just got up and walked out."

I scoffed. But my mind wandered. I mostly believed in Croc now, so maybe I shouldn't discount everything ...

I dug around inside my bag for something. My phone brushed my fingers.

A couple of days ago, I'd seen that I'd finally received a call from the medical school. They'd left a message near the time that we would've been running around inside the Great Pyramid, and I hadn't listened to it. My finger hovered over the play button for a moment, but I deleted the message instead.

Reaching into my pocket, I dug out my wallet and found the black-and-white photograph of my dad and myself—as a child before the backdrop of the Sphinx. I finally studied my dad's smile, no longer concerned about that stern look on the boy's face. I reached for the bronze bracelet on my arm, and my fingers found the comfort of its warm metal. Dad's bracelet, Heb's bracelet, the bracelet that saved me by bringing me to Egypt, away from my previous life, and then saved me again by deflecting a bullet meant to kill me. Its bronze was now deformed, but it was not destroyed.

You really brought me here, Dad. This was all because of you, everything that I was able to accomplish.

I felt around inside my bag again, searching for my one intact treasure that I'd kept, for my dad, Horemheb, Mutnedjmet, and Croc. The gold was now cold and still, but my skin tingled as my fingertips pressed against it. I pulled out the golden cat-sphinx and held it up into the slats of twilight sunrays streaming through the pergola overhead.

The statuette sparkled and momentarily blinded me. A voice as clear as Maddie's sounded, but only in my head, along with the patter of drums, an aged voice. *"You are only a man; take the treasure you have, prepare for the future, but don't forget to live in the moment. See the clue."*

I jumped up, my heart racing. The twilight, or some kind of magic, glowed green upon the golden cat in my arms. Were Croc, Horemheb, and the magician trying to tell me something about one last secret or treasure?

I flipped the statuette over, studying the light and shadow that ran across its surface at different angles. Maddie pressed against me, her eyes wide with curiosity. The drums faded, no more voices ...

"What is it?" Maddie asked, her voice airy. "Is there another clue?"

Maybe I was only supposed to live an ordinary life and should continue behaving like a common man, as Heb had done most of his life, even if I'd achieved something grand. And that was what I'd always longed for, to accomplish something great by just following dreams that inspired me, my dreams to be myself and not let power and the world change me ...

And then I saw what the voice had meant: Maddie's eyes. They sparkled brighter than the gold in my hands. I momentarily went blind again. To be her hero, I had to be there for her even when this new high wore off, not just rescue her once and believe I could live off that accomplishment the rest of my life.

I set the statuette aside, laced my fingers through Maddie's hair, and cupped her head behind her ears before I pressed my lips against hers.

She melted in my arms.

About the Author

R.M. SCHULTZ has been enthralled with ancient Egypt and its lost secrets for decades. He lives with his wife, daughter, and many pets in the Pacific Northwest.

Note from the Author:

First off, thank you for choosing to spend your time
reading this book. There are so many stories to choose
from, and I am thankful that you decided on this one.

If you enjoyed the story, please consider rating
and reviewing it on Amazon and Goodreads.

Made in the USA
Columbia, SC
20 April 2019